Tumbledown

Other Books by Robert Boswell

Novels
Century's Son
American Owned Love
Virtual Death (as Shale Aaron)
Mystery Ride
The Geography of Desire
Crooked Hearts

Short Stories
The Heyday of the Insensitive Bastards
Living to Be 100
Dancing in the Movies

Nonfiction
The Half-Known World
What Men Call Treasure

TUMBLEDOWN
A Novel

Robert Boswell

GRAYWOLF PRESS

This publication is made possible, in part, by the voters of Minnesota through a Minnesota State Arts Board Operating Support grant, thanks to a legislative appropriation from the arts and cultural heritage fund, and through a grant from the National Endowment for the Arts. Significant support has also been provided by Target, the McKnight Foundation, Amazon.com, and other generous contributions from foundations, corporations, and individuals. To these organizations and individuals we offer our heartfelt thanks.

Published by Graywolf Press
250 Third Avenue North, Suite 600
Minneapolis, Minnesota 55401

www.graywolfpress.org

Published in the United States of America

ISBN 978-1-55597-649-1

2 4 6 8 9 7 5 3 1
First Graywolf Printing, 2013

Library of Congress Control Number: 2013931489

Cover design: Kyle G. Hunter

Cover photo: Sarah Palmer

This book is dedicated to all the clients
who survived my tenure as a counselor
and to the one who didn't.

We all have two lives:
The true one we dream in childhood
And continue to dream as adults in a misty substrate;
The false one we live among others,
The practical life, the useful life—
It ends up sticking us in a coffin.

—FERNANDO PESSOA
(WRITING AS ÁLVARO DE CAMPOS)

Tumbledown

PART ONE Opening Day

. . . time, like money, is measured by our needs . . .
—GEORGE ELIOT

1

There are yet states of being that have no name, anonymous human conditions that thrive at the periphery of powerful emotion the way bedroom communities manacle a city. James Candler and Elizabeth Ray reside in such a place. Separately. They are new arrivals. Candler showed up the last week of January, purchasing a big stucco house snouted by a two-car garage. A few weeks later, Elizabeth Ray paused in her pale subcompact to eye his residence. Neither the ugliness of it nor its enormity could dissuade her. She circled the block several times to look it over. Around the corner, she parked at an apartment complex. Her studio-with-balcony rented by the week.

The subtle pleasures of suburban life would prove difficult for Candler to seize. Shoving the mower around his front lawn left him without the humblest sense of accomplishment: what could he *do* in that yard? The elementary school down the street spawned a daily parade of idling station wagons and SUVs, a surprisingly civil motorcade that left gaps to protect the right-of-way at every household drive, but the polite convoy struck Candler as a funeral procession for the ozone layer. He managed to locate a decent local restaurant, a steakhouse that also served Mexican food, but it played CNN day and night on an elevated screen the size of a motel mattress. "I don't suppose you could turn that off," he asked. The waiter, a Sinaloa transplant who walked past Candler's house every weekday morning, holding hands with his fourth-grade daughter and practicing English according to her strict instructions, smiled and shook his head, saying, "People like." Even the spitting applause of sprinklers oppressed Candler, reminding him of waking as a child to a snow-covered television screen and the disturbing sense that he was sleeping through his life, and it would soon be time to die.

For Elizabeth Ray, it was an entirely different place. She looked for Candler—or evidence of him—when she visited the coffee shop, either of the bars, the grocery, the hardware store. Any aisle she turned down could reveal him, any booth might hold him. Every niche and corner resonated with the possibility of him. If the man in line ahead of her at the bank did not turn his head, he could be him. Every day she imagined the smallest details of his life.

Meanwhile, he did not know her—or thought he didn't.

People encounter life in vastly dissimilar ways. Some insist their days are orderly and unchanging, vessels on a slow-moving assembly belt, each identically filled by invisible hands. For others, the days are relentlessly complicated and unpredictable, as different, one from another, as patients waiting to see a therapist. But for everyone there comes a day when the filling no longer fits the vessel, when the therapist finds himself pouring out his heart to the patient, when air is indistinguishable from water and *out* is the rough equivalent of *in*, a day when even the voice of god carries a dubious tremor.

Such days are worthy of our attention.

Informally, the place was known as Liberty Corners. It consisted of a few housing developments, some old farms and roadside businesses, and a handful of fashionable new concerns—wine shop, bistro, gym with machines and mirrors. Elizabeth Ray's apartment was on the third floor and faced the two-lane blacktop known as Liberty Highway. James Candler's house was on a street distinguished by sidewalks of red paving stones. He worked at a residential treatment center in Onyx Springs, an easy commute south on the two-lane and east on the interstate. The drive she made to La Jolla was longer and laden with traffic. Her move to the Corners had nothing to do with convenience.

On this particular day—the day James Candler would come unhinged—he was up earlier than usual, his morning beginning with the smell of brownies in the oven, a dripping spatula in his mouth, and an uncertain feeling in his gut that he was about to do something devastatingly stupid. He had woken to this feeling for several days now. Elizabeth Ray (she called herself *Lise* these days, pronouncing it like a rental agreement) remained asleep. The clothing boutique where she worked did not open until noon, and she slept best in daylight. She was dreaming that her neck had sprouted an extra head, identical to the original except for its sneer and the authority evident in its skeptical eyes. The heads vied for control of her body. A recurring, unpleasant dream. In a short while her mind would insert itself as a disembodied voice, reminding her that it was not possible to have two literal heads, and all she needed to do was change her position in bed to end the dream. This all-knowing voice was new, a manifestation of her waking self in the world of her sleeping self.

Oven time required: twenty minutes. Candler washed the mixing bowl and sponged off the counter before heading for the shower. The year was 2008, the month April. James Candler was thirty-three years old. He was a little paunchy, but he didn't even own a scale. Women were attracted to him. He was liked at his job and had friends dating back to high school. If the rumors flying around the Onyx Springs Rehabilitation and Therapeutic Center were true, he would soon become the youngest director in its history. This fact pleased him and worried him and would contribute to his undoing.

Lise Ray had just turned twenty-seven. She was an only child. After some years of estrangement, she was close to her parents. By means of an online social network she had reconnected with friends from high school, all of whom were married, still in Missouri, saddled with demanding children and husbands bent on disappointing them. They openly envied her freedom and referred to California as if it were a supernatural realm. Lise had constructed this life out of the tundra of her previous life. Every day she let herself feel astounded to be free of that old life.

Down the hall of Candler's oversized house, a friend whose marriage had failed slept fitfully, having sought out Candler in his time of need. One of his clients—a schizophrenic boy as fragile as a whisper—had revealed that he was in love with another of Candler's clients, a beautiful and damaged girl who, Candler suspected, was living with a man. *What to do? What to do?* He was facing a controversial promotion, could not afford his combined house and car payments, hardly knew the woman he was engaged to marry, could barely keep up with his clients' complicated lives, and had just signed on for his fourth credit card. *Tick tock, his head was rocking.* He wiped down the shower stall and sprayed it with cleanser. He squeegeed the shower door. The more uncertain his mental state, the cleaner his bathroom.

Candler was the only man in his office who didn't just stop at the Donut Hole and grab a box of the glazed when it was his turn to supply the goodies. The women in the office baked their own: berry-stuffed muffins, pastries with patterns of icing that changed color and design according to the season, and on one occasion, Kat—a technician on the evaluation floor and Candler's sometime lover—brought homemade baklava, the crust as delicate as the eyelids of exotic birds. Candler made a point of matching their efforts. Or at least approximating them. After one wretched attempt at baking from scratch—a doomed and debasing carrot cake—he resorted to boxed products. (The miserable cake had never solidified, a brown mush that sloshed in the Pyrex bowl like an aquarium model of a sewer.)

How Elizabeth Ray first met James Candler was a story she had told a thousand times, but only to herself. Candler did not know the story. It was only a story from her point of view. *There once was a girl with two heads,* she might begin, plagiarizing her nightmare, *and the stupid head had taken charge.* Usually she was in bed, the room dark, and she could not sleep. She never began with the same sentence. *There once was a girl who aided the gruesome monsters in her own abduction and then volunteered her body for their grotesque experiments.* She had grown up reading science fiction, which colored her narratives, but the essential plot was always the same: the blind girl in the forced labor camp is not only freed but made to see, the bump-n-grind slave girl in a society that has discovered how to turn sex into electrical power is whisked away in a forbidden non-sex-fueled vehicle whose fearless driver detours to let her see the darkened windows of her former master's house. And so on. Bad movie plots for the kinds of bad movies that had never cast her, in all those years, not even as an extra.

Candler dressed himself in a gray suit and blue tie. No one else in his office wore a suit to work. *One of the perks of living in Southern California,* Clay Hao had told him, *no costume required.* Hao was the senior counselor in their office—their *pod,* according to the Center's guidebook. Candler's pod had four counselors, three techs, and a secretary. The Center had a total of eight pods. Of the thirty-two counselors and eight psychologists eligible to apply for the position of director, twenty-seven had more seniority than Candler. Yet he had accelerated past all of them.

The administrative board had chosen Candler to be the Center's new chief. The official interviews were still weeks away, but the real search had already taken place. It had not been pleasant. The board members had taken a meddlesome, prying, semierotic interest in his private life. They were a gray-faced bunch with concretized features, and their attitudes matched their outward appearance—*gargoyles* intent on finding another of their species. Three of them had come to Candler's house bearing a Boston fern. A housewarming gift, they claimed, meandering through his rooms, fondling his knickknacks, even swinging open the refrigerator door. Except for its size and a few upscale pretensions, the house was a conventional tract home. Candler had gotten a deal on it—what had seemed like a deal—and the board members liked that he had not moved to San Diego to live the bachelor life. They even appreciated the size of his residence, believing the extra rooms were meant for a family. They were perhaps the only people who approved of his car. *Debt,* noted one gargoyle, *is a stabilizing influence.*

Sometimes Lise told the story in the first person: *I found myself on an alien planet* (by which she meant Los Angeles) *and longed to become one of the native creatures* (she'd moved there to become an actress) *even as they tortured me* (a thousand auditions and never a part). She was three years distant from that alien world, having escaped to a neighborhood in San Diego known as North City. She had rented a garage apartment not far from the boutique where she worked—close enough to walk. Now her commute was an honest forty minutes; yet she believed the move to Liberty Corners was every bit as necessary as her flight from L.A. It had even changed the way she told the story. She strove now for realism: *There once was a girl who mistook the roar of hell's ovens for the noise of a freeway.*

Well, something like realism.

Candler buttoned his shirt—the odor of baking brownies filling the house—and lashed his tie to his neck. He had risen early to stake out the damaged girl's house. He needed to know whether she had a lover. She might be putting herself at risk. She might be putting the boy who loved her at risk. Even as he was unraveling, he was trying to do right by the people who depended on him.

He returned to the kitchen and what he saw baffled him: two eggs on the countertop, perfect in their white ovalness, like thought bubbles from another dimension. Was it possible—it couldn't be possible—but was it at least *conceivable* that he had forgotten to put the eggs in the brownies? He could see himself expertly cracking the eggs on the rim of the bowl and dropping in the yolks and whites, but where then were the emptied shells? And since when was he an expert at cracking eggs? He stuck his hand inside the maw of the garbage disposal, but the kitchen timer—shaped like a tomato for some reason—rattled and he freed his hand to stop it. The oven's hinges creaked. The brownies in their transparent pan were the appropriate color and, unlike the carrot cake, looked quite solid, but they were as flat as a paperback novel.

It was a shabby office in a shabby building on the same shabby L.A. block as the bar where she worked. But the man himself, the counselor she was required to see, was young and in a suit, and his part of the office—not even a room, just partitioned space—was clean and had that *spotless* smell. He did not hide behind his desk but sat directly across from her. He was not handsome, exactly, but he was unexpected. There was something about the way he paid attention, how he moved his limbs. She wished she had gotten herself up a little.

At that time in her life, she called herself Beth Wray. By adding a simple consonant, the homely *Ray* became the exotic *Wray*, like the actress in the palm of the giant beast. She had chosen the name when she was seventeen. Beth Wray sounded like *Death Ray*, and that was the effect she intended to have on audiences: a fatal device from the conceivable future.

This was the stuff she planned to tell the counselor—how preposterously young she had been when she moved to California, how juvenile her fantasies. Her indulgent parents had let her skip the boredom of sixth grade for the boredom of seventh grade, which meant she was always the youngest and most susceptible in any classroom, and wouldn't it be ironic if that were the reason she had fallen into this life? That intelligence was the root cause? Such was the sort of commerce counselors expected, but this one wouldn't let her talk about any of that.

"What brings you here?" he began.

"Probation requirement," she said flatly.

"That's like telling me a taxi brought you here."

She actually *had* taken a taxi from her apartment, and for a moment she indulged the idea that he was psychic. (She was all of twenty-three when she entered that immaculate office, not far removed from *Death Ray*.)

"The legal system has taken you by the shoulders and seated you across from me," he continued. "We both understand that. But what's going on in your life that people can force you to do things you quite obviously don't want to do—such as show up at nine in the a.m. to talk with the likes of me?"

The nameplate on his desk read *James Candler*. He looked right at her and did not look away. His eyes were the green of spring leaves. His eyes were the green of a forest pond. His eyes were the green of a traffic light instructing her to go, get on with it, *move*.

Over his car's leather seat—Candler drove an absurd car—he placed a folded towel, setting the warm pan of brownies on top of it. Eggs or no eggs, they would have to do. The garage door climbed in clanking segments, revealing an indecisive spring sky the romantic color of candle smoke. He could not say why he owned this car. John Egri, the outgoing director, drove a sleek black Corvette, a vehicle he treated with such care that Candler had actually seen it only once, but he heard about it frequently. Candler had not envied the Vette until fate stuck its wet nose in his crotch. The parent of a bipolar teenager, strapped by the expense of enrolling his daughter in the Center, decided to ditch his car payment, and Candler unaccountably bought the metallic red Porsche Boxster. Something about Egri's Corvette and the opportunity for a bargain led him to purchase it, trading his pickup as part of the transaction.

A bargain, but he had to reallocate monthly expenses from his checking account to his credit card or he couldn't pay for the thing. He economized, quitting the gym, dropping cable television, forgoing the newspaper, shifting the thermostat out of the comfort range. All of which might have been worth it if he had liked the car, but he quickly discovered that he had no affinity for the beast. It seated two, unless someone was willing to crawl into the tiny space behind the seats, and came with a Tyvek cover, a giant windbreaker to be daily stretched over its glistening body, a chore roughly as difficult as dressing a dead man. Egri advised him that he was adding needless miles by driving the car to work. To which Candler responded, "How am I supposed to get there?"

Beth Wray didn't have a satisfactory answer for his question. He wasn't interested in her family, her youth, her past, her present job, how she was feeling, or the immediate circumstances that forced her to see him. He wanted to know what really brought her to his office. He was so insistent, she thought about the boy who had taken her virginity in the back of his VW van, that adamant little prick of his no larger than a wine cork.

A painting hung on the wall behind Candler's desk, a crude depiction of a man with a transparent body. *What do you see when you see through a man?* Merely the wall behind him, evidently, bits of paper tacked to it. A weird piece of art, probably by some mental patient, but she understood why he liked it. At the same time she knew he would not let her talk about it. *What has brought you here?* She felt unbalanced, as if she were running on uneven ground, as if the earth were shuddering— all this while she was nestled in a chair. She actually looked up to the hanging lamp to be certain there wasn't a literal earthquake.

His eyes were bloodshot. She thought he might be hungover. She liked that about him. It made him human. She had been arrested in the raid of a party. The cops had found her partially dressed and ridiculously stoked on cocaine. He would possess a folder with the details, and this embarrassed her. She wasn't that kind of person. She had taken a job dancing to get by until she was cast in a movie, a play, a televised drama. Years inexplicably passed. She wound up turning a few tricks, but only with men she was attracted to. At least initially. Once she had done it a few times, the offer of good money became impossible to refuse. She had serviced two men the night she was arrested and might have done another. It didn't mean anything.

She had told the lawyers from the district attorney's office that she was a farm girl from Missouri, which was almost true, and that the guy who brought her to the party had disappeared, which was the gospel. People at the party had given her cocaine, she explained, and helped her off with her clothing. No one particularly believed her, but they dropped the prostitution charge and gave her probation for the drugs. She had to get a legitimate job, and she found one at Amoeba Music in Hollywood. Her shift ended at six, meaning she could still strip in the evenings. She was required to take a weekly drug test, and she gave up everything but booze. She had to see a counselor once a week for twelve weeks, which put her in James Candler's office, just down the street from Bare Barracudas. The counseling center was in an old building, brick covered with countless layers of paint, and the patients in the lobby were just the same, lacquered in their troubles: poor and drug addicted and alcoholic and out of their minds. Neither she nor he belonged there. She had been mistaken for a real prostitute and drug user, and he? Something for his résumé, she guessed, as he had the unmistakable appearance of an up-and-comer—smart, well dressed, vaguely handsome, and unreservedly compelling. He filled a room merely by entering it. (This, she knew, was precisely the attribute she lacked as an actress.) And yet he had a hangover and a soft belly, and the light in his eyes wasn't merely intelligence.

Candler felt obliged by the size of his monthly car payment to whip through county intersections and fly up the freeway ramp. The car filled with the smell of brownies. *Exit interstate in point five miles.* The Boxster's navigation system seemed to have no *off* button. When he entered an address, it provided perfectly omniscient directions, but if he entered nothing it still wished to guide him, advising him to turn around, head in the opposite direction, seek a new destination. It had the peeved voice of a disgruntled librarian.

Zigging and zagging past a family in a hatchback, he caught sight of a primer-gray Plymouth Road Runner executing a comparable maneuver two lanes over. (To certain men, the red Porsche changing lanes was like the waving of a flag.) The Road Runner was flawlessly restored, missing only the final layer of paint, that frowning chrome grill and masculine automotive posture a product of the 1970s. (An emissary from the past trying to make its way in this brave new world in the only manner it knew how.) Candler ignored the car, accelerating ahead of a Pathfinder and a Civic. When he switched lanes, he found it impossible not to glance in the rearview. The Road Runner was passing the same Pathfinder, the same Civic.

This is ridiculous, Candler thought and self-consciously slowed down. The Road Runner pulled even, and Candler felt an absurd urge to hide the brownies. The driver—another young, well-dressed man riding alone—offered a smug nod before zooming by.

That *fucking* nod. That arrogant fucking nod.

Candler cut in behind him and narrowed the gap. They flew in tandem, like migrating birds, down the freeway. Congestion at an exit slowed their pace until a seam materialized in the traffic, a diagonal gap from one side of the highway to the other. Candler slid the Porsche into the seam, angling effortlessly across the lanes, passing the Road Runner as if it were parked. (Despite the ultimate outcome of this action, Candler could never disown the glee he felt at this moment, the witless pride in recognizing opportunity and seizing it.)

Recalculating, announced the omniscient librarian.

The Road Runner emerged in the side mirror several cars back, vanishing and reappearing in the rearview. Horns sounded, followed by an exclamation of brakes, as the car veered brazenly from lane to lane. That other well-dressed, solitary male driver did not know when to quit.

"I hear you," he was saying, "and I have no reason not to believe you. You're telling me that the circumstances that have led you to my office do not genuinely represent your character. I hear you and yet *here you are.* Why? What has brought you here?"

The hour ended on the same question with which it had begun. Beth Wray spent the next week working on it, jotting down ideas while she peddled T-shirts and compact discs, keeping the notebook in her locker at Bare Barracudas, hustling in to make amendments, trying to prepare an honest response instead of the usual bull. When Monday morning came around, she put on a simple black skirt that her mother had given her and an unrevealing white blouse. She spent an hour on her hair and makeup. It had rained during the night, and in the cleansed air the sunlight shone mercilessly, the scruffy street and moldering buildings ruthlessly exposed. The only open chair in the waiting room had a rusty stain. She stood with her back to the wall, her flopping heart like a fish that had outgrown its bowl.

She was given a different counselor. James Candler was out of town, a job interview, but he should be back for her next appointment. The new man had an utterly conventional approach, and she was reluctant to tell him all she had spent the week working to discover. He hadn't earned it and he wasn't particularly interested in it. Yet she told him more than she intended, and it had nothing to do with him. It was what James Candler would have wanted. She couldn't spend the week trying desperately to be frank with herself and then drop it because he was out of town. That would be disrespectful of him. It would diminish the transformation she had begun—the raw ingredients of her soul finally beginning to simmer.

Some things in this life seemed like magic.

As Candler watched in his rearview, that stupid, speeding, swerving car lifted off the ground. The Road Runner took flight. Its chrome grill filled the rearview as the car spiraled through the air like a tossed football. The last Candler saw as he rounded a curve was the airborne car colliding with a light pole—a flyaway pole—which bounced high into the morning sunlight and down the freeway's shoulder.

It was almost three miles to the next exit. Candler's hands on the steering wheel trembled and his gut was gripped by an immense fist. He was incapable of thinking in words. *Exit interstate in point five miles,* the librarian commanded. He obeyed and circled back, retracing the drive. When words resumed their occupancy in his mind, they appeared singly: *fire, carnage, death, responsibility.*

Beth Wray filled the notebook with thoughts and reasons and explanations. She put in her Amoeba hours and came to a decision: she would do whatever James Candler advised. She spent her day off repainting the kitchen in the apartment she shared with another actress. She bought a modest floral dress to wear to her next counseling session. On the Friday before her Monday session, she drove directly from Amoeba to Barracudas and changed into one of her outfits. She was fourth in the rotation, which gave her time to get a few happy-hour joes to buy her drinks or splurge for a private dance. When she saw James Candler at a table near the stage, she thought he might be a mirage. She slipped across the room before he spotted her. His going-away party was taking place at the bar. There were four men and three women in the group, dressed in their professional clothing, some of them enjoying themselves and some conspicuously uncomfortable. On their table a brightly decorated cake read SAN DIEGO OR BUST and showed a busty woman made entirely of icing. One of the dancers baked such cakes and embellished them elaborately, package deals for office celebrations. Unlike the other dancers, the cake girl was an ambitious woman. "One day I'll own this place," she had told Beth. "One day you'll work for me."

James Candler watched the naked women but he didn't have the ugly hunger, the vapid glaze, or the macho anger of the usual customers, and yet he wasn't feigning distaste like others in his group. He was better looking than she recalled, or was made attractive by sitting among his colleagues, surrounded by the Barracudas' regulars. He hadn't chosen to come there, yet he obviously appreciated women. She was reminded of the cottage belonging to bears, the porridge that tasted just right.

When it was her time to dance, Candler's party had cut the cake but had not served the slices, the professionals tipsy now. *His eyes will be spiked with blood in the morning,* she thought. Her cue came and went. The first song of her selection—Madonna's "Vogue"—bounced out over the speakers. If he had left the bar before her spot in the rotation, who knows? Maybe she would still live in Los Angeles. Maybe she would be a full-time whore by now, or perhaps she would have sweet-talked some millionaire into setting her up with a house. Instead, she kept the job at Amoeba and took a second job at a diner, waiting tables. She had the breast implants removed, quit bleaching her hair, and dropped the W from her name. After completing the requirements of her probation, she relocated what remained of herself to San Diego. She did not move there to pursue James Candler, though she entertained daydreams of running into him. She moved there to escape Beth Wray, that spectacular and hopeless teenage invention, that deadly beam of wonder.

There was no fire. The first evidence of Candler's imbecilic actions was a liberated strip of tire in the passing lane, a knobby artifact, like a black egg carton. Not far beyond that dark shred of rubber, the Road Runner itself appeared, its ruined body resting on the shoulder of the interstate, hunched over its rims, the roof pancaked. From beneath the flattened car, liquid wings spread across the asphalt. Candler held his breath and lifted his foot from the accelerator. Two men stood just beyond the heap. The first was a highway patrolman, taking notes, and the second was the driver, his suit rumpled and torn but his body intact and erect. The driver recognized the Porsche. He offered an uncomfortable smile, a half shrug. When the highway patrolman turned to look, the driver mouthed something, motioning for Candler to keep going.

What could Candler do but obey? *No one was hurt,* he told himself repeatedly, while his gut worked to make him consider all that could have happened.

Recalculating, the librarian reminded him.

Every month or two Lise searched online for James Candler. She was not obsessed with the idea of seeing him again; rather, she was entertained by it. An amusement. She followed her progress the way another person might track a sports team, a political candidate, a popular band. Although it was true that she had been celibate since meeting him. Three years, two months; 1,153 days: she tracked her celibacy the way an alcoholic measured his sobriety.

"If you don't have sex for three years," she asked a friend, "are you a virgin again?"

In February, the new phone books arrived, and she found him. He had moved to the county. He had a landline. She took a drive that same afternoon, broke her lease in North City, packed her few belongings, and selected from Sunset North's many vacancies a third-floor efficiency whose balcony provided a view of the neighboring houses. From her angle, the complicated gray roofing of the fashionable houses looked like whole, elaborate structures seen from a great distance—the dilapidated remains of some lost culture. She was able to pick out the roof of Candler's house and a corner of his green lawn.

Weeks passed before she actually saw him. He appeared at the coffeehouse, standing in line, looking once again hungover. She left her book on the table and got in line behind him. She took a dollar from her purse and pretended to pick it up. "Is this yours?" she asked. He glanced from the dollar to her face and smiled, causing an intense vibration along her spine. "I don't think so," he said, betraying no sign of recognition. And why should he recognize her? He had seen her only once before, just another fucked-up girl in his office. She might have found a way right then to get to know him, but a woman sitting at a nearby table said, "That's my dollar." The look she gave Lise was so haughty. She had seen everything. Lise handed over the buck and left the line. She retrieved her novel and went to a table outside.

Candler's car surprised her, but not that he exited the parking lot too fast, the coffee cup pressed to his lips, sunglasses hiding his bloodshot eyes. He was damaged in ways that made him possible. He wasn't a floor rag, content to clean up the mess of other people's lives. He wasn't some bland professional friend. He was a man with demons, who helped others by seeing himself in them. And he had changed her life. Saved it, possibly.

Lise did not believe that she was stumbling again. *Okay,* she was a little obsessed, but she held a job, took classes at San Diego State, went to movies, read books, talked to her parents every Sunday afternoon. She simply had a secret pastime. A consuming hobby that added dimension to her life. A story that lacked an ending.

She shifted her position on the mattress, but the dream of having two heads continued.

You can't just switch me off, the nasty head informed her. *And don't* put too much faith in that exalted *fucking* voice. *That voice only* sounds *reliable.*

The other head cringed. *Please don't tell me what to think.*

Ha, ha, ha, the cruel head replied. *Haw, haw, haw.*

Lise sat up in bed. Her window was open. The highway below was half shadowed by the building, populated by a stream of vehicles in the shade, an oppositely moving stream in the light. She wondered what James Candler was doing at that moment, who he was helping, how long before he learned her new name.

2

Try as he might, Candler could not disappear.

In the long and colorful history of vehicles used in stakeouts, none was a poorer choice than his own. The Porsche was the red of holiday lingerie. To lower his head from view, he had to angle his body crookedly past the gearshift, his feet on the passenger floorboard, splaying himself like a man in a limbo contest. It did not help that his stomach coiled in accusation. Twenty-five years earlier in his family's living room, eight-year-old James Candler had swung a baseball bat at an imaginary pitch and the backswing knocked out his sister's front teeth. While their parents rushed his sister to the emergency room, he hid himself in a closet, arms wrapped around his tormented stomach. *Shame* was the name for his suffering.

A breeze passed over Lantana Avenue. The leaves in the immense trees lining the street fractured sunlight into millions of pieces. People emerged from houses and disappeared into vehicles, shadows swarming them like bacteria, and in Candler's gut, the flutter and flail continued. If his role in the accident became known, he would be instantly out of the running for the directorship. Nonetheless, he felt a powerful desire to tell someone. He had driven the remainder of the trip with absurd care, signaling a mile in advance of his exit, leaving the blinker on despite its accusatory sound, going directly to the client's street, parking along the curb behind an Escapade and just ahead of an Avalanche.

He didn't know which house belonged to Karly Hopper. No one seemed to know. Her intake papers had labeled Karly *mildly mentally retarded*. The therapeutic world no longer used the term *retarded*. Her file now read *mildly mentally impaired*. What made Karly unusual was that she was also attractive, the sort of woman that Candler might have called *drop dead gorgeous*. The therapeutic world wouldn't care for that term either, but Candler couldn't help thinking it. Beyond the street corner another young man waited in his car for the same girl. These two—the beautiful mentally impaired girl and the schizophrenic boy in his Firebird—were Candler's responsibility. They were his clients, and he had put them in a sheltered workshop together. Mick Coury picked up Karly Hopper each morning but not at her door. For most men, the corner pickup would have set off alarms but schizophrenia had left Mick naive. He had been a different kid before the illness: a good-looking teenager with a fast car and a cute girlfriend. Mental illness had made him innocent all over again.

The door to the house directly across the street opened, and Karly Hopper stepped onto the stoop. She wore a green T-shirt, jeans, flip-flops. Her hair and eyes were brown. She moved with an easy, loose-limbed grace. She stepped to the end of the stoop, aligning her toes with the edge of the concrete. She smiled—a lovely white smile—and walked back inside.

People believe intelligence resides in the eyes, but the body provides a thousand clues about a human's identity. Karly's clues were a muddle. She had possessed normal intelligence at birth but as a toddler she nearly drowned in a neighbor's pool. According to the Wechsler Adult Intelligence Scale, her IQ was 65. Yet neither in her appearance nor in her movements did she appear damaged. She had a wide range of vocal intonations, full of the subtle, musical shifts that suggest a complex, lively person is speaking. If her intonations were occasionally inappropriate to the subject of a conversation, she was inevitably forgiven. For a beautiful woman, Candler knew, such errors would come across as stimulating rather than improper. She was a provocative woman whose sexuality lived in her limbs and in her slender body. If she were dancing or sitting on a stool at a tavern or, he speculated, if she were unclothed and in bed, the average man would never guess that she was anything but fascinating.

In a certain way, of course, he would be right.

Never judge a book by its cover, the adage advises, but when humans encounter another of their kind such judgment is inevitable, and anyone encountering Karly Hopper or the boy waiting for her in his car would imagine that they came from the finest chromosomological clay, superior to that of James Candler, for all his personal charm, or Lise Ray, despite the allure of her recent metamorphosis. But for tiny acts of fate—a swimming accident, the mysterious descent of schizophrenia— Karly Hopper and Mick Coury would stride the planet like Titans, their agile, active minds the equal of their lovely, lithe bodies.

(Perhaps this is what those ancient gods experienced when they took human guise, their divinity evident but the expression of it limited by the mortal vessels containing them. Honestly, wouldn't it explain the foolish things they did?)

Candler waited for her to appear again. He had sent Karly and Mick to the sheltered workshop for different reasons. It was a protected workplace where clients packaged pantyhose for a local company, proceeding at their own rate, with the hope that they would improve over time and eventually take jobs at the factory. This was the goal for Karly Hopper. The workshop also doubled as therapy. The concentration it took to succeed on the assembly line should bleed over into other parts of their lives. And this was the goal for Mick Coury, that he could eventually corral his good thoughts and ignore the rest. Mick and Karly had nothing in common but the workshop; Candler had inadvertently played matchmaker.

Karly stepped again into the dappled morning light and paused at the edge of the stoop, a strategy Candler himself had taught her. She examined her shoes—the flip-flops were gone, replaced by sneakers— her jeans, belt, shirt. She patted her shoulder and smiled once more as she went back inside. Moments later she returned with her purse and went through it all again. This time she walked past Candler's car without a glance and continued up the street to join the patient Mick Coury and his burnt-orange Firebird, an anachronism from the life the boy led before the onset of schizophrenia. He drove so slowly now that he was a different hazard altogether.

As soon as the couple departed, Candler sat up. Karly's house was one-story and made of blond brick. The lawn needed mowing. Her family had placed her in Onyx Springs when she was eighteen, putting her in a halfway house, which was less expensive than the Center's dormitories. Men began appearing in her room—other clients, strangers, even members of the staff. Her family arranged this house for her. They didn't want anyone to know where it was, even the professionals at the Center. If Mick had not described waiting for her on the corner of Lantana Avenue, Candler would not have known where to look. He did not particularly care where Karly lived—though he copied down the address—but with whom she lived. She had run through a number of roommates, starting with a cousin and including an elderly woman who answered an ad the family placed in the local paper. If she was now living with a man, she had kept it secret from Mick Coury, and he was not a boy who liked surprises.

Candler rang the doorbell. A thumping of feet led up to the entrance but the door didn't open. Candler rapped on it. "I can hear you in there," he said and knocked again. He was running short of time. "I'm from Onyx Rehab. Just need a second or two."

That he could not get a response felt like defeat, as if the Road Runner had been sacrificed for no good reason, lives put at risk for nothing. Candler knocked on the door a few more times before grudgingly returning to his car and reaching for the glove box. He retrieved a Swiss army knife. The brownies' pan was still warm. He wanted a corner piece, comfort food, but the blade would not pierce the flat of brownies. He lifted the knife and jabbed, but it bounced off. The brownies were a solid tablet.

Those fucking eggs.

The curtain in the front room of Karly's house ruffled, revealing masculine fingers along the hem. Candler shoved the pan aside and leapt from the car. He flew across the yard and hammered on the door. This time it swung open. A rough-looking man, maybe forty, squinted from Karly's entry. He was barefoot, his thinning hair long on the sides. He sported a patchy beard. *Disreputable* was the word that sprang to Candler's mind.

"My supposed to know you?" the man asked.

"If you live here with Karly Hopper," Candler said, "you ought to know me." He heard the anger in his voice and pocketed his hands, which had made themselves into fists. As appalling as the situation might be, Karly had to have someone staying with her. Independent living was a goal of her work at the Center, but she was not yet ready.

"Where'd you come from?" the man asked.

"I'm a counselor at Onyx Rehab, and Karly, as you must know, is also a part of the Onyx Rehab family." Rules of confidentiality did not permit him to say that Karly was his client.

"What the hell's Ox Rehab?" The man held a toothpick, which he inserted like a bookmark between his teeth. His body gave off a sour morning odor.

"*Onyx* Rehab is one of the largest rehabilitation centers in the United States," he said evenly, "and it's right here in town."

"Karly's a drunk?" The toothpick waggled with each word. "A druggie? What?"

"May I come in for a minute?"

The man's head gave a quick shake, yanked by an invisible cord. "We can talk right here." He stepped through the door, pulling it shut behind him.

Discounting the unruly hair, he was an inch or so shorter than Candler and thin—an ashen thin that had nothing to do with exercise or hunger but was the product of self-imposed malnutrition. He was in sweatpants and a T-shirt that advertised an Oklahoma City radio station, its red tower making parenthetical waves across his chest. His feet were so white as to seem silver in the early sunlight, like beached fish.

"Karly's gone to work." The man spat the toothpick into his hand and inserted it in the hair above his ear. "She just left."

"I'm aware of that." A specific anger squeezed Candler's throat: he wanted to punch this bastard. "Let's start over." He introduced himself and offered his hand. "I'm a counselor at Onyx Rehab, and I'm here on home inspection."

The hand was ignored. "You got a warrant?"

"I need to know your name and the nature of your relationship with my client."

"What, you're a goddamn lawyer now?"

"I've already told you who I am." Candler put a finger to the man's chest. "You haven't told me who you are."

"A friend," he said, brushing away Candler's finger. He retrieved the toothpick from his hair. "I stay with Karly off and on. I don't got to give you my name."

"You do or do not live here?"

"I come and go. Drive a truck. Can't park it on the street 'cause of these stupid trees. Only part of town's got so many stupid trees." He stared angrily at the giants lining the street. "What's wrong with Karly that she's got to have rehab?"

"I can't discuss—"

"You mean that she's a dunce?"

"I can't talk about Karly without the permission of her guardian."

"She *told* me she was twenty-one." After a moment, his head gave a half shake. "It's not me you want. It's the guy who had this route before, you know? When I inherited it, he let on like Karly was part of the package."

"*Jesus*," Candler said, "what have you been doing?"

"I take care of her," he said. "When I'm here. Nothing wrong with it. She ain't so dumb. Can't cook or do laundry worth a damn, but who cares 'bout that shit?"

Candler's arms flapped once, like a bird's wings. "What kind of person are you?"

"Long haul. Got a place in Stillwater, so technically I don't live here. I'm a *guest*. You got a problem with that?"

"How many days a week do you—"

"None a your business." A wry smile crossed his face. "I can park my rig wherever I please."

The porch floor shifted beneath Candler's polished shoes. He closed his eyes, but the Road Runner elevated over the asphalt, the chrome grill a grimacing mouth laced with braces. He understood what the car's driver had said when he waved Candler on, what he mouthed behind the state trooper's back: *You win*.

"Don't shut your eyes," the truck driver said. "You're no better than me. Look it here." Candler felt a tiny prod against his belly. "You got a stain." The toothpick pushed against Candler's pristine tie. When he glanced down, the man flipped Candler's chin. He laughed. "Tell a truth, man. You're just here to eyeball Karly in her panties."

Candler swung from the hip. The punch caught the truck driver on the jaw, and he crumpled to the tile. He scooted on his back to the corner of the porch, raising one appendage protectively. "All right." His front teeth were bloody. "You made your point." He pulled in a ragged breath, crooking his elbow protectively. "She's *your* girl."

"Red makes blood," the new one announced.

He had only just started at the sheltered workshop and already Maura Wood disliked him. He was short with tiny hands and, generally speaking, she didn't like little men. She was tall and substantial. Puny guys made her feel all Easter Island. This one was a miserable-looking shrimp, with big ears, black-rimmed glasses, and the unmistakable stamp of stupidity dominating his face instead of the normal features. Nose, eyes, brows, lips—he had them but they were beside the point. Maura didn't need to look at the spider cartons to assemble them. She could stare at the witless stump and do her work. She could jaw with Mick and do her work. She had the feeling she could sleep and do this stinking work.

"If we didn't have red," the new one continued, "we wouldn't bleed."

"What's his name again?" she asked Mick.

Mick Coury finished packing the spider carton in his hands before answering, his fingers nimble and confident. Normally he was a sludge brain until noon, but today he zipped through the boxes, which meant he hadn't taken his meds. Maura didn't mind him slow-thinking in the a.m. It seemed like a kind of intimacy, like seeing someone in his underpants, but she preferred him like this—quick, loose, slightly out of control.

"Cecil," Mick said, whipping into another carton. "Cecil Something Something. Rhymes with Wednesday. Sort of rhymes. Like that rhyme when the nut's not on the bolt the whole way. Cecil Something Something."

The weenie looked up at Mick. "I'm Cecil."

"We're not talking *to* you," Maura clarified, "we're talking *about* you."

Cecil's smile was as twisted as the mangled spider carton in his hands. He was still on his first one. Daddy Long Legs packaged its pantyhose in an asinine box that looked like a tarantula. Line workers assembled the boxes (three folds, two tucks), inserted flat plastic envelopes that held the pantyhose, twisted shut the spidery arms, and placed them in a shipping container. To do a hundred in an hour took concentration, and even Maura, who found the work unspeakably boring, wanted to do it well. When she started out, a few months earlier, she had packaged five per hour—*a deliberate deliberateness*, she'd called it. She had hated the Center and expressed her contempt by doing nothing but bitch and talk about sex, which would force Alonso Duran to leave for the bathroom to masturbate.

But who didn't need money? Cigarettes, for example, cost plenty, and the water in Onyx Springs tasted green, which meant she had to keep bottles in her room. Besides all that, she decided to be faster than Karly Hopper, who had hit a plateau in the sixties. Maura averaged eighty-seven per hour. If she had been a chain smoker, she could have done a hundred. Eighty-seven got her what she had to have. Mick was a spider carton genius. He could box one hundred twenty per hour if he tried, but he wanted to stay in the workshop until Karly got up to speed. Once you hit a hundred, they sent you to the real factory. Maura liked that he put loyalty ahead of cash. It was loyalty to a ditz-brain but loyalty nonetheless.

The unpredictable one was the little fucknut Bellamy Rhine, a finicky, twitchy simpleton who stood too close to people and was exactly as tall as Maura's breasts. If she ever needed to, she could smother the little prick without even bending over. Rhine could go as fast as eighty early on, but as the day continued his speed fluctuated. He seemed to overconcentrate or would carefully spread the tentacles of a carton he had already packed, suddenly uncertain he had done the work. He was fine-featured and delicate looking, as if made of paper, and the part in his hair was so perfect it was like a crease. Some days his totals were as high as Maura's; other days, Alonso Duran made more money than Rhine.

Not counting this Cecil character, Alonso was the only one of them visibly weird. His eyes were too lidded and his mouth showed its tongue, and not just the tip. Each of his shirts had permanent drool stains from that open yapper. There was something else odd about his appearance, something she couldn't quite name, like his face was slightly askew on the front of his head. He barked when he talked, but he could package ninety boxes an hour. What kept his average down were his breaks, which he spent in the bathroom. Even though he had been around longer than anyone else, Alonso was still paid cash every hour. They had all been paid that way at the beginning. Immediate reinforcement and that bunk. After a while you were paid daily, then weekly, and then biweekly, just like the real employees of Daddy Long Legs.

Maura made a point of knowing where she stood with the others, but Mick was the only one in the workshop who interested her beyond freak value. He was also the only one who was faster than she was, and that suited her fine. She wasn't competing *with* Mick, she was competing *for* him.

The sheltered workshop was new enough to be an orphan, housed not in the shining white buildings on the Center's campus but across town in the cafeteria of a gruesome concrete-block composition known as the Onyx Springs Senior Citizens Facility, which smelled today of spaghetti. About half the time, the dump smelled of spaghetti. Down the linoleum hallway, old men and women learned dance steps or yoga or needlepoint or poetry. They painted landscapes, fox-trotted, studied German. The sheltered workshop only rented the space, and at noon the pantyhose assembly line was folded up and rolled to the corner so the old farts could eat their damn spaghetti.

The assembly mechanism looked like a butterfly on wheels. When rolled away from the wall and flapped open, it had a motorized conveyor belt onto which plastic packets were dropped from tall bins that their supervisor, Crews, filled each morning. It wasn't exactly like the real Daddy Long Legs plant (Maura had gone on the field trip), but it was the same basic setup. At the real factory, the assembly line was enormous and the workers stood on either side of the belt. They decorated their work spots with photos of their kids, maybe to remind them why in hell they had to keep their shitty jobs. There was no way Maura would ever work at a factory. She was missing her senior year of high school, but she had passed the GED without even studying. She knew she was smarter than nine out of ten people, which wasn't saying that much, given that the planet was teeming with dimwits. Still, she wasn't going to wind up on an assembly line.

Well, she *was* on an assembly line at the moment but it was temporary and meaningless, like most things in life. She was intent on discovering what those other things might be, the ones that were permanent and meaningful. There was death, but that could hardly be the whole menu. People had been around for fucking ever. Somebody had to have come up with something besides the bullshit stuff—god, country, family: a figment, imaginary geography, and a conniving crew of flesh eaters, respectively.

If there was anything that did matter, she suspected it had to do with Mick Coury, but when she tried to name what that *thing* might possibly be, she got stuck with crapola like *Whenever I'm around him, I feel great*. This was a disafuckingpointing line, and not just because it failed to capture the thrilling, enigmatic lunacy of hanging with him. *He made her feel nice.* Was that really the be-all and end-all? There were forty million songs and twice that many poems about love, and as far as she could tell it all dwindled down to some skinny schizo fucker who could put together moronic boxes designed to look like cartoon spiderwebs faster than the nearby completely incompetent vacuumheads, and yet this guy made her skin feel blistered and her breathing clog up. That had to be bullshit. Why, in the past million or so years, had no one got on top of this?

And what was she supposed to do about this age-old problem while she was committed to this swanky asylum? She might as well do what she liked. For example, she liked to be next to Mick, so she parked herself there. Worker ants at the real factory were permitted to talk, so they were free to natter here, too. This meant she liked coming to work. Karly could have taken her spot if she wanted. Maura knew this and had no intention of fooling herself about it. Luckily, Mick liked to be across from Karly so he could watch her. He was gaga for the twit.

"I've got an itch for *adventure*," she told Mick, but it was hard to speak over the noise of the assembly butterfly without broadcasting to the whole squadron.

Before Mick could respond, Karly spoke up. "I know what." She pulled a slip of paper from her jeans pocket. Karly liked to tell jokes and she was miserable at it. Some people could not be funny. She looked over her notes. This alone was a bad sign: *joke notes*.

"There are two cannibals," Karly said, "real ones that eat people. And they're eating people. They're eating a funny clown. I guess he would be dead before they're eating him. And one of the cannibals says to the other one of the cannibals, *Is this funny?*" She laughed. "Get it?"

Mick laughed, though clearly he didn't get it, assuming there was something to get. He laughed because it was Karly's joke. Alonso and Cecil laughed. Rhine never got jokes because he was the living incarnation of a joke. Rhine merely glanced anxiously from one laughing person to the next.

"That's so funny," Karly said.

Maura tried to figure out what the punch line was supposed to be. Cannibals eating a clown: what was funny about that?

Cecil the Shrimp piped up. "Mrs. Barnstone is old. She's going to die," he said. "Crews, is Mrs. Barnstone going to die?"

"Ms. Patricia Barnstone," Alonso brayed.

Crews was reading the newspaper. He didn't seem to have a first name. His bland, pale, bumpy face was like a sack filled with miniature doughnuts. "You don't talk to me," he said. "Talk to your pals if you got to, but not to me."

"One day Ms. Patricia Barnstone will die," Rhine said, "but almost certainly, unless you know something I or we don't, not today."

"Not no but hell no," Alonso said. He often said this.

"Not entirely certainly," Rhine went on, "but almost entirely one hundred percent, or at least ninety-nine percent, certainly."

"She's healthy as a horse," Maura said. Patricia Barnstone was her counselor, and Maura liked her. She was a no-bullshit person who actually enjoyed most people but wouldn't pretend if she didn't.

Alonso put his work down and coughed out some words. "It's the party at night at my house, if you're coming." The only time the drooler's mouth ever shut was with the *p* in *party* and *m* in *my*. "My house is over the garage at my house, if you're coming."

Alonso Duran lived in his family's garage apartment. Mick had told her about Alonso's parties but Maura had never been invited. They usually entailed food and a movie. According to Mick, the movie was always *Wayne's World*, which was Karly's favorite. What could possibly make more sense than to watch the same movie over and over because one idiot girl liked it? Every swinging dick in the room was in love with Karly Hopper, except maybe the new one, Cecil, who looked like too much of a mental-case retard to remember he had a dick. She predicted he would wet his pants before the day was out precisely because he could not find his dick.

"I'm invited, right? Isn't that right, Alonso?" Rhine said. "I'm invited?"

"You're always invited," Alonso said. "Karly's always invited." He pointed to people and made his way around the room. "Mick's always invited. Maura's always invited *now*." He looked at Cecil. "But not you."

Cecil dropped the crumpled box he was holding, stared at it forlornly, and bent to pick it up. "When goldfish die," he said softly, "they go upside down."

"Mr. Crews," Rhine said. "Cecil is making a mess of his box, which is really bothering us."

Crews sighed and put his paper down. "Over here, then. C'mon, Cecil." He took the clodhopper midget aside to teach him the procedure again.

"Like I said," Maura tried to speak confidentially to Mick, "some adventure?"

Mick snapped open another flat and bent the flaps at the folds. He was cute even when he was ignoring her. Something about his face looked edible. Her mother often described people as *sweet,* and now Maura got it. She would like to lick Mick's face.

Rhine spoke up. "Karly, I'm learning sign language. Karly? Karly, I'm learning sign language."

"What's the sign for shut your trap?" Maura said.

"I was talking to Karly."

"No kidding?"

"What kind of adventure?" Mick asked.

"The interesting kind. Like getting to someplace besides here. Up in the mountains or down to the beach or maybe," she lowered her voice, "getting some booze or pot or I don't know . . ." She involuntarily pictured Mick naked and blushed.

"This is *Hello.*" Rhine waved to Karly. "Get it, Karly? This is if you're cold." He rubbed his hands up and down his arms. "Get it, Karly?"

"That is so funny, Rhine," Karly said. "Isn't Rhine funny, Mick?"

"Very funny," Mick said.

"A riot," Maura put in. "A natural half-wit."

"Not no but hell no," Alonso said.

For months, Maura had been certain that Karly was a phony. She looked exactly like a girl from some hateful high school clique— skinny, perky, and cute. All such girls were actually heartless bitches, Maura knew, but Karly wasn't hateful or a bitch, and for that matter, she was more than cute. Way more. She had the perfect skin people called *olive,* as if it were green, and pretty brown eyes and a great face, and if that weren't enough, she had thick, shiny hair. She could shave her melon and the boys would still crawl across the floor to French-kiss her ass, but no, she had perfect hair as well. It covered an empty fucking balloon, but what difference did that make?

As much as Maura hated to admit it, Karly wasn't a phony. She was genuinely nice all the goddamn time. This fact didn't make Maura like her, but she couldn't hate her. A person had to be honest about her feelings, at least with herself. Barnstone had taught her that.

Crews returned with Cecil. "Do it that way on the line," Crews told him.

Rhine spoke up. "Maura told me to shut my trap, Mr. Crews."

"Smart girl," he said. To Maura, he added, "You and Mick keep an eye on things. I should be back in time to pay Cecil and Alonso for their next hour. Help keep this one on track." He indicated dwarfkins.

"No sweat," she said. This was one of Barnstone's expressions, and Maura liked using it. "Got you covered."

Crews worked evenings and weekends for a local lawn crew. Lately he tried to get in one yard during his day job. At first he had made elaborate excuses, but anymore he just gave Maura or Mick the heads-up and took off. When he returned, the cuffs of his pants would be green and he would smell of grass and gasoline.

Maura didn't mind Crews disappearing. She liked being in charge. She thought about lighting a cigarette, which would drive Rhine out of his mind. During her first week at the workshop Mick had given her a present. She already knew he was crazy for Karly, which meant it wasn't a romantic-type gift, and that made her suspect that he might be a geek or shithead or some other type of fuckwad. The present was wrapped in the Sunday comics, and when she ripped the funny papers off, she discovered a silver ashtray, the words CARLTON HOTEL stamped in the center.

"So you can smoke," he said.

Crews hadn't let her outside to smoke during breaks because she left butts in the hydrangeas. Now she would drag Mick out to watch her puff. Sometimes, he held the ashtray. She stored it in the assembly frame, on a rack next to the rollers. It was a great gift—perfect, in a way—and she tumbled for Mick that first week.

"I'm going to Alonso's party," he told her. "It's not too adventure, maybe, but it's pizza, a movie. Can you get away?"

Maura shrugged. She was not supposed to leave the campus unless Barnstone or some other official tagged along. "I might be able to make it. It could maybe be an adventure, I guess. A lame one, no doubt, but *some*thing."

Cecil completed his first spider carton and held it up to show everyone. The big hole in his face took on a shape no one ought to have to look at, like those chocolate candies that glop over wax paper, his teeth horrid cashews.

"Put it in the cardboard box, butter dick. The one with your initials on it."

Cecil obeyed. "The wizard in *The Wizard of Oz* isn't a real wizard." He shook his head as he spoke. "But the flying monkeys *are* real."

"You can zip it," Maura said. "I'm in charge. So shut the fuck up."

Cecil stopped moving and stared at her. His bottom lip began to tremble.

Rhine, master of the obvious, said, "He's almost certainly going to cry."

"You're doing fine," Mick told Cecil. "That's a good spider package."

"What's your last name?" Maura asked him.

"Cecil Fresnay," he said.

"That's your first *and* your last name, dipshit."

"Pack some more pantyhose," Mick said. "You're doing great."

Cecil reached for another cardboard flat, but he knocked the stack of them over. They slid across the slick floor. His eyes grew wide and he sucked air as if to wail.

"That's so funny," Karly said. "The flat boxes are on the floor."

Her laughter permitted the others to laugh. After a moment, Cecil joined them. That was all it took, Maura thought, *laughter*. It had to be the right kind, she guessed. It had to be friendly laughter, Karly's laughter.

Mick quit packing to help Cecil with the flats. Karly followed his lead, which meant that Alonso and Rhine helped, too. The four of them squatted down and scurried after the flats. Maura and Cecil watched.

"If animals could drive cars, it would be a *big* mess," Cecil said, nodding in agreement with himself. "Pooch couldn't because her paws can't reach the 'celerator or even the brake. She'd have to grab the wheel like this." Cecil bit into an imaginary steering wheel and turned it from side to side. "Crews, are there skeletons that are alive? Like in that movie with skeletons that are alive?"

"Crews isn't here, you freaky mushball," Maura said, still packing pantyhose.

"My dog's name is Pooch," Cecil said, nodding, smiling, oblivious, his black glasses rocking on his nose.

For no reason she could name, she finally figured it out. "Does this taste funny to you?" Maura announced. "The cannibals eating the clown, that's what they say."

All of the squatting people looked up at her and then returned to their task. Mick offered her a smile but no one laughed.

Figuring out the joke pleased her. What good it did, she couldn't say, even though she had got it right and Karly had garbled it. Getting it right ought to matter, she thought, as she watched Mick and Karly stacking the flats, wondering how in the world he had known to help and she, to laugh.

The site of the Onyx Springs Rehabilitation and Therapeutic Center had once been a ranch surrounded by other ranches, and it was still bordered to the north by an avocado farm. The old ranch house, made of river stones, had served briefly as a maintenance shed. When it was torn down, only the distinctive Onyx Rehab buildings remained. Each was five stories, covered with white porcelain tile, and no exterior corner was a right angle. The buildings were tightly clustered, and seen from above, the relation between the acute and obtuse angles suggested a single edifice shattered by a tremendous blow.

From ground level, there was a lot of glare. Shade trees planted among the buildings angered the architect's heirs but made passage among the behemoths bearable during the long summer. Onyx Rehab was a private center known for its pristine dormitories. "A great recruiting tool," John Egri had told Candler. They were talking privately, drinking scotch at dusk in Egri's office, staring out the floor-to-ceiling windows. "We simply *look* more professional than other places. Right now we have more referrals than we can handle." This conversation occurred some months earlier, in the fall, when Egri first advised Candler to apply for the directorship. "If the economy tanks, the rules change." Officially, Onyx Rehab served people with physical, mental, emotional, or psychological challenges. "What that actually means," Egri explained, "is during down years, we accept anyone who has the money or can nab the funding." He sipped the scotch. "The job's not for idealists. If you want to keep your dick clean, bow out now." Egri wanted Candler to succeed him and presented a typed list of things Candler should do before announcing his interest in the position. This conversation marked the beginning of Candler's unraveling. It was a slow process, but consistent in its progress, the small abrasion in the material widening, the threads eroding, until at last a rent in the fabric appeared.

Yet Candler deserved some credit: a lesser weave would have frayed overnight.

From the encounter at Karly's house, Candler drove to the Donut Hole, discreetly prying the brownies from the pan and tossing the chocolate plank into the trash—it *clanked* when it hit bottom—before claiming a box of the glazed. He could not say whether the pain in his stomach was from contributing to a freeway accident or socking a stranger in the jaw, but he felt tortured by his body and utterly out of control. He parked in the staff lot and began his daily wrestling match with the car's cover. The last time he slugged somebody was in high school, which was also the last time he raced on the highway. What was next? Cheating on exams? Hustling chicks?

Candler's pod was on the fourth floor of the Hahn Building. The office manager, Rainyday Olsson, greeted him at the elevator. She was standing on a chair to water a hanging fern—the same plant the gargoyles had brought to Candler's house. *Rainyday* was her legal name, as it appeared on her birth certificate. She was born on a rainy day. "Lucky it wasn't blustery," she liked to say, "or the sewers hadn't backed up." She was buck-toothed, rail thin, and freckled, with dark hair cut in a neat pageboy, a vivacious woman with a high school education and an unemployed husband who liked to hang around the office. Whenever a client she found particularly sad disappeared into the elevator, she'd say, "There but for the grace of god goes yours truly."

"Nice suit," she told Candler, stepping down from the chair. "You look like the Marlboro Man."

"I don't think he wears a suit," Candler said. "He wears a horse."

"Okay then, you don't look anything like the Marlboro Man." She snatched the box of doughnuts. "You happen to read the newspaper this week? Sports page?"

"Ah hell." Candler reached for his wallet. They'd had a bet about the opening day of baseball season and Candler had forgotten. Rainyday was a Yankees fan and Candler, a Yankees hater. "Take your blood money."

She folded the five and held it between her fingers. "What's got into you this morning?"

It was the opportunity he wanted, but she turned to go to her desk and the hem of her skirt was caught in its belted waist. Her freckled legs and flowered underpants had the air of sexual invitation, which kept him from tugging at the skirt himself.

He buzzed her from his office. "Your skirt is hanging funny."

After a moment she said, "Oh, my god." And then, "This is why I should start wearing pantyhose again."

Candler's office was roughly the size of a bank vault in a modest savings and loan, a cozy cave sandwiched between the offices of Clay Hao and Bob Whitman, with the Barnstone at the far end, and the evaluation floor beyond that. Each office had a single window, a mahogany-veneer desk, a filing cabinet, a bookcase, and two reasonably comfortable chairs. On the wall over Candler's desk was a painting by his brother Pook, and on his desk, a framed photograph of Candler and his fiancée at Trafalgar Square, their arms around each other, smiling like convicts straddling the opening to a tunnel. Candler's sister had taken the photo. A second copy was on the nightstand beside his bed.

As far as the Onyx Rehab board was concerned, Candler's bachelorhood was the only remaining drawback to his candidacy. John Egri had told him as much in February, by which time Candler had checked off everything else on the list. As luck would have it, Candler met Lolly the second week of March. This coincidence, if it was a coincidence, Candler thought of as good fortune. That it might be the product of his disintegration rather than fortuitous happenstance would seem to him absurd. He had planned the London trip to see his brother-in-law, who was dying, but the disease advanced rapidly and he was dead a week before Candler's flight touched down. His sister met him at the airport in a surprising spring dress. He had expected the darker shades of mourning, but her husband was buried and the slow progress of the illness had given her time to grieve while he was still alive. She had an offer on the business, she told him as they left Heathrow, and she had put the flat up for sale. Violet was readying herself to return to the States. She planned to stay with Candler until she decided what she wanted to do. Her front teeth had been replanted in her gums perfectly. Whenever Candler saw her after they were apart, he studied her smile to assure himself he had done no permanent damage. On the cab ride into the city, she asked if he minded a business stop. She needed to hand over papers to her assistant. "An American girl," she said.

Lolly Powell was comparing spreadsheets when they walked in, her head rocking from side to side, and she did not hear them enter. One of the papers slid to the floor, and she quickly retrieved it, her skirt's tweed hem rising above the back of her knees. Her white legs and the cascade of blond hair seemed somehow elemental, elaborately and foolishly so, like the slender trunks of aspen beside a mountain waterfall. She touched her glasses before shaking his hand, the lenses black-rimmed and rounded at the top, which made her seem both earnestly studious and perpetually surprised.

"Join us for dinner," he said, without consulting his sister.

"Those glasses are phonies," Violet told him when they were once again in a cab. "She only wears them at work."

Lolly arrived at the flat with a folder of contracts, each with a check stapled to it. She and Violet compared notes and signed checks while Candler opened the wine. As soon as the work was completed, Lolly pulled a clip from her hair and disappeared into the bathroom. When she emerged, the glasses and business suit were gone. She wore a sleeveless black blouse, short skirt, and patent leather heels. "I'm two people," she said, fluffing her blond corona. She had a mild British accent, though she was from New Jersey and had lived in England only a year. "Ask your sister if you don't believe me. I'm a total spod at work, but when the whistle blows I shed it like a second skin."

"I'm pretty sure I'm only one person," Candler replied, pouring the wine. "Sometimes barely that."

"Must be a lurker in there," she said. "Vi, who else is your brother?"

Violet, leaning against the kitchen doorway, her arms crossed tightly over her chest, said, "Lolly used to be a counselor herself."

"Another lifetime," Lolly replied dismissively. Nonetheless she told him about her counseling, which involved something called *fingertouch* massage.

From this exchange, Candler understood that his sister did not think he and Lolly were a good match. He changed the subject. "What is it you do for Vi?"

A long, sexy conversation followed, in which Lolly explained what she called *accountancy* in British publishing, ranging from the calculation of bifurcated royalties to the act of window-dressing foreign sales. "Vi covers the art end, choosing titles, editing those ungrateful whingers, that kind of thing. I'm the money end." In his memory, her bottom gives a shake as she says *money end*.

Violet excused herself to make a phone call and Lolly said, "You're quite the ripe bastard, you know. Why didn't you get your bum over here before Arthur died?"

"He went faster than any of us expected."

"You could have been here for the service. Your sister needed you."

"She told me not to change my flight." He did not reveal that he could not afford to change the flight because he owned an enormous stucco shed and a red sports car. In response to her silent glare, he added, "She seems okay."

"She's not *okay*. Vi is many wonderful things, but *okay* is not among them."

When Candler repeated the conversation to his sister, Violet was incensed. "That's the type of self-important blather I've come to expect from her. She badgered Arthur with massages and exotic meals the final months of his life. We were pouring his food through a tube, for Christ's sake, and she was bringing over samosas and sushi and edible flowers. I've never felt more ridiculous than filling a blender with flowers to pour down Arthur's belly tube."

"I'm sure she meant well."

"She'd spend twenty minutes with him while I ran to the pharmacy and then act like massaging his shoulders had prolonged his life."

Much of Candler's two-week courtship with Lolly involved concern for Violet. They took her to plays, to St. Paul's Cathedral, to a worldly variety of restaurants. When they were alone, Violet became their default topic of conversation—especially after sex. "I can't come to California until she's ready to leave," Lolly said after a particularly athletic bout. "Assuming you want me to come to California."

"Of course I do."

"I won't abandon Vi. She needs a friend."

Since returning home, he had talked to Lolly by phone each week and they emailed daily. They tried sex on Skype, but Lolly's movements on the screen became jerky and the computer lost connection. The image froze on her bent knees, her maniacal grimace. Candler had to restart his computer. By the time he reached her again, she was eating caramels, though still naked and willing to show off her goods to help him along. Later that night, he proposed by text message, inspired by her willingness to flaunt herself. It was just so damn nice. He was drunk and the message read:

> *i llove yo.u marry me*

It was noon the next day when she sent a return message:

Which meant it was settled. His long bachelorhood was at an end. His career as a counselor was almost at an end, as well. In both cases, he was moving on to something better, but big changes caused psychological strain. The Center had a stress calculator on its website, and both marriage and promotions were heavily weighted. He had recently purchased a house—more stress points. And that preposterous car, the death of his brother-in-law, a friend moving in. The accident was both the product of stress and a bonanza of new points. His score would be off the charts. He felt stupidly proud. *Proud to be a reckless bonehead out to destroy his own life?* If the trucker called the police . . . but he wouldn't. He was taking advantage of a mentally impaired woman. Candler would get away with his stupid, careless, juvenile acts.

His office window provided a view beyond the low rock wall that marked the Center's boundaries. In the avocado orchard that bordered the grounds, the rise and dip of the earth was visible as a rise and dip in the treetops. Near the wall, beneath the leafy limbs and between rows of trees, an old tractor with wide headlamps eyed Candler. Clay Hao had warned him that there would be days when his personal life interfered with his professional composure. He had offered advice but Candler could not remember it. Relax? Concentrate? Take a slug of whiskey?

He grabbed the phone on his desk and dialed his home number. Billy Atlas would be up by now. Candler had known Billy since elementary school and still thought of him with that childhood label *best friend.* Billy had been there, tossing the imaginary pitch, when Candler swung the very real bat and knocked loose his sister's teeth. A month ago, Billy had shown up at Candler's doorstep. His marriage had disintegrated and he had left Flagstaff. "Only after I told her she could have the house," he explained, "did it occur to me that I had no place to sleep." Billy was the perfect person to hear the story of the accident. He had a long history of bad decisions and, concerning Candler, he possessed not one judgmental bone in his body.

There was no answer at the house. Billy was either still asleep or riding the bus downtown, where he was a valet parker. Billy owned a car—the same Dodge Dart he had driven since high school—but it was in the shop, awaiting an alternator. Candler tried Billy's cell, got voicemail, and hung up.

Among his emails, he found a memo from the director's office advising that the term *patient* was no longer to be used officially or informally; the term *client* was now *mandatory and required.* The word *therapy,* while still appropriate for clients' monthly appointments with psychologists, was being phased out for appointments with counselors. *Esteem and direction sessions* was the new term of choice. Candler tried to imagine himself the director and worrying over such malarkey. He wanted the job but the thought of it made him weary—*energy challenged,* he amended. Forgetting the eggs for the brownies had displayed *poor sequential instruction comprehension.* Punching the truck driver had shown *impulse control impairment.* And racing on the highway? What was the official euphemism for mortal folly?

He opened the bottom drawer of his desk and pulled out his bottle of Mr. Clean Multi-Surface Spray, but Rainyday buzzed him. "The War Vet is here."

"Please don't call him that. Can he hear you out there?"

"He's at the window," she said softly, "checking for enemy soldiers."

"Send him in."

Candler put Mr. Clean away. He dashed off an email to the woman in charge of personnel, recommending Billy Atlas for any nonprofessional position at the center, noting that he had completed the requisite days of training. He took a deep breath and stared again out the window. The waxy avocado leaves lifted and fell in the breeze. The old tractor returned his stare, its headlights drooping slightly, as if in sympathy.

"Something happened to me today," Candler said. "It could have been avoided, but no one was hurt. After that, I struck a man with my fist, but from now on I'm okay."

If the tractor was listening, it gave no indication.

The dormitory supervisor used his key to let Patricia Barnstone into Maura Wood's room. Barnstone offered a quick thanks and closed the door on him. She hated this kind of thing, but the girl's parents were worried. She started with the unmade bed, lifting the pillows, the thin mattress, searching for what? Drugs, certainly, a flask, a beer can, knives or scissors, sure, but what else might give her away? A black leather jacket lay over the bedspread. When Barnstone lifted it to check the pockets, a skull painted on the back leered at her. Maura liked the punk scene, which Barnstone could not see as a cause for worry.

For the first thirty-eight years of her life, Patricia Barnstone had attempted to become a rock star. She came of age in the 1960s when the hard-core rock world was almost exclusively male. Her first real band was Stiff Warning, for which she wrote and sang songs, and played lead guitar. Everyone else in the band was a guy. They opened for Ten Years After in Phoenix when the scheduled band canceled after an overdose. They played a great set to a receptive audience and were invited to continue on the tour, but the drummer got an offer to join It's a Beautiful Day and split. While Barnstone tried to locate another drummer, her bass player was promoted to manager of a car stereo outlet and decided he couldn't leave town. Stiff Warning was silenced.

Barnstone abandoned Phoenix for the coast, founding a new band she called the Lawn Chairs. There were two other women, the rhythm guitarist and the keyboard player. She had the notion that mixing in women might up the sanity quotient. They became house band for a San Francisco bar and were discovered by Grace Slick, who arranged for them to open a Jefferson Airplane concert. They had a disastrous set. The rhythm guitar player had also been using rhythm as birth control and on the day of the concert discovered she was approximately four months pregnant. She spent the afternoon listing every drug she had taken, terrified she'd give birth to an octopus. On the same sheet, she listed the possible fathers of the child. The doctor had said he could only guess at the date of conception. "They can send a man to the moon, but they can't tell me when I got knocked up?" she cried and burst out bawling, letting the sheet of paper fall to the floor. The drummer was in immediate trouble with the keyboardist when she saw his name on the WHO FUCKED ME list.

The Lawn Chairs ultimately folded.

Barnstone drifted to Oxnard and continued her schooling. She found work as a studio musician and tried to reinvent herself as either a folk singer or a performance artist. She cut some small-label demos, and two of her songs were recorded by other singers. Jerry Jeff Walker did an acoustic version of "Butt Drunk and Blue" and Dolly Parton recorded "I Still Have the Suitcase You Gave Me." Neither was released as a single, relegated to the midalbum ghetto of a midlist release. Meanwhile, she waited tables, baked for a catering service, finished her degree, sold shoes, substitute taught, and pulled an unsuccessful stint as a real estate agent. In 1988, she was aimed in the general direction of Austin, Texas, when her aged Ford Fairlane broke down near Onyx Springs. She hiked from the freeway into town and then rode in the tow truck back along the interstate, only to discover that someone had busted the windows of her car. Three guitars were stolen, along with her suitcases, her record albums, and the briefcase that held the folders of her original music.

The Onyx Springs Rehabilitation and Therapeutic Center needed someone to stay weekends in the Minton Dormitory, which housed the severely retarded and brain damaged. Before the month was out, she was the house resident and on the path to her current job. She took a few courses at the local community college and every training session the Center offered, but she never earned a graduate degree. She simply became good at dealing with the clients. Her promotions were slow in coming, but she was persistent. Eventually, she became a level-one counselor. She was one of the rare few who had switched from the nonprofessional to the professional track.

Maura's desk was strewn with objects: ballpoint pens, tampons, a map of Onyx Springs, a couple of paperback novels, and photos of Maura's family, along with a Polaroid of Maura with Mick Coury and Alonso Duran. Maura Wood was an ordinary girl made to feel ugly by the beauty of the rest of her family. One of her sisters, the nine-year-old, was an actress and appeared briefly in a movie with Colin Farrell. The older sister was waiting tables in New York, trying to make a go of a modeling career. Her only brother—a full-scale prick, from Maura's description—was voted homecoming king at the same school where Maura endured daily humiliation. Barnstone believed Maura Wood required nothing more than separation from her pretty, petty family.

All the girl needed was a new life. Wasn't that what everyone needed?

In the Polaroid, Mick and Alonso were smiling, while Maura looked from the corners of her eyes at Mick. Barnstone seated herself and took from her jacket pocket the printout of the email Maura's parents had sent. It was one sentence.

> We're very apprehensive about Maura's current condition,
> even though there's nothing concrete, but we're concerned

about the tone of the letter she sent, not that we don't know our daughter's sharp-tongued wit (ha ha), but she talks about being sleepy, which may mean depression, which is the trouble that led to the incident, and then she says her heart races, which sounds like a symptom (doesn't it?) and there's one more thing because her sister says Maura emailed her and asked her to UPS a glass pipe and marijuana that Maura had hidden in a trunk and which we destroyed (pipe and marijuana both) because when Maura cut herself so badly (a night I'll never forget as long as I live!) she'd been smoking pot, maybe (her counselor here suggested) to get up her courage, but you can see (I hope!) why we want to put you on alert and ask you to look in her room and see if the other patients will discuss her frame of mind because we're not comfortable with this, thanks.

Barnstone put the slip of paper back in her pocket and examined again the Polaroid. Sleeplessness and heart palpitations sounded a lot like being in love. Mick seemed an unlikely boyfriend for Maura. Barnstone did not know him well, but she had made a point of eye-balling him. If there was such a thing as a god, it was likely she personally chose Mick's bones, skin, and eyes. His body was not especially athletic, but it was well proportioned. Only his confused mind undercut his looks, and yet that was all it took—the same god, having a joke. Mick had little manly presence because he had so little presence of any kind.

When Maura first came to the center, she was furious, suicidal, often stoned, and on the way to being seriously overweight. She was now only occasionally in a rage, no longer suicidal, and her body, though not fashionably emaciated, was in the healthy range. Barnstone took no credit for the girl's success. Maura needed only a safe place and some supervision. She was one of Barnstone's favorites and came to her house often, which was why this letter from her parents was so upsetting. If Barnstone had lived an ordinary life, she might have a granddaughter Maura's age. The thought was appealing but not over-whelmingly so. Those traditional comforts were not worth the expense of having embraced the mundane.

She pulled open the desk's drawers. Only once in the past few weeks had she seen Maura stoned, and Barnstone's response had been direct: "You can get kicked out of the sheltered workshop for that. You'll lose your privileges." She did not know how pot made its way into the Center, but there didn't seem to be any way to stop it. She wasn't so naive as to think the girl would never get high again. Nor was she so naive as to think a little pot was a big deal. Barnstone believed the unlikely route she had taken to her job served her well. Twenty years in rock and roll had taught her that people who give every impression of being mindless may yet surprise you. Many of the great rockers were basically idiots, and yet their music far surpassed her own. And she was not in the least an idiot. Whatever she might have been in the past, she was never an idiot.

She was not conditioned by advanced schooling to think she always knew what she was doing. This, too, seemed an advantage. It meant that she would make mistakes the others would not, but it also meant there were times the others would commit mistakes that she wouldn't. This made her a valuable member of the counseling team. That was not just her opinion. All of the counselors valued her—or they had until they discovered that two clients, at different times, had lived with her. Letting a client move in was not the type of error any of the other counselors would commit. She understood why they *claimed* it was a mistake, and she understood why they actually *thought* it was a mistake, and the two were not the same thing. They claimed it created ethical conflicts, but what they really feared was that they would be forced to scrutinize the ever shifting line between counselor and client—how much of your life to hand over to the clients and how much to hold back. As it turned out, inviting a client to live with her actually *was* a mistake but for a completely different reason: it had ripped wide a seam in her heart.

Mercy, she said, just audibly. It had become her preferred exclamation since she first heard Roy Orbison's "Pretty Woman." Maura had a box of condoms in one of her desk drawers. The box advertised two dozen prophylactics in a variety of colors, ribbed for pleasure. Barnstone counted. None was missing. A hopeful box, she understood, a rainbow of wishes.

Patricia Barnstone's life had not worked out as she planned, but it nonetheless pleased her. She had two decades of fierce fidelity to her passion, and then, by means of blind luck, she was permitted to make a new life. She had become a stubborn but amicable and able colleague, lumbering now into her late fifties, aware that old age was perched on her stoop and it knocked now and then at her door. She did not have a particular affinity for the mentally ill. If the Fairlane had fallen apart in a prison town, she might have become a reformatory specialist, or a parole officer. If she had been stranded in a university town, she might have become a tutor or an adjunct teacher. Sometimes she wondered what place she would have fled. A canning town? A home to the porn industry?

In the bottom drawer of Maura's desk, beneath a spiral notebook, she found a single domino stuck to a strip of silver duct tape. Barnstone had no idea what use this could be, but it certainly wasn't a legitimate one. Nor was it likely to be a life-threatening one, she reasoned, and she returned it to the drawer.

When the door to Candler's office opened, it was not the War Vet but John Egri.

"I told G.I. Joe out there to wait." Egri took a final bite of a doughnut and licked his fingers. He was a boy-faced man in his fifties, graying at the temples. "I said I'd be a minute, and I won't be more than twenty." He displayed a lopsided smile as he sat on the corner of Candler's desk. He had an absolutely commonplace face that people liked, the attraction having to do with the careless expressions that fluttered across it like burning slips of paper. "So . . . *no* to your internship plan. It's a good idea, boyo, and no way in hell's ten acres I'm agreeing to it. You want to get bombed at lunch? It's Friday, and I'm not coming back after chow—the lame duck advantage. Gives you the fifty-minute hour with Tommy Tonka-gun, an hour or so to clear your calendar, then we get an early start on the weekend."

"Hi, John," Candler said. "It's Thursday, actually."

Egri squeezed his eyes shut. "Okay, why won't I approve your internship plan? Because it'll *work*, that's why, and then you'll be fucked, my friend. See, if a man has one brilliant idea, he's generally regarded as lucky. That's what we thought about you and this evaluation hub. The lucky *schmuck*. But if a person has two brilliant ideas, hell, he's considered actually fucking brilliant. Okay, the sheltered workshop put you in that category. All the puffers and huggers on the board agree that the Candler boychild is *brilliant*. That's a good god-damn place to be, but here's the reamer: if a man has *three* brilliant ideas, he's *screwed*. They think he's a motherfucking *genius*, and every ordinary thing he does thereafter looks like failure. What I'm saying is, ride out what you've done, and quit having ideas."

"That's a definite no, then? Or are you just being colorful?"

"Wait until you're director and then pretend it's Hao's idea. Let him worry about being a genius. Now, how's 'bout that liquid lunch?"

"No can do." Candler took perhaps his first full lungful of air since seeing the flyaway pole leap into the air. "I've got this thing called *work*, and because it's Thursday, I have more work tomorrow, which means I don't want to start drinking at noon today." It was not Egri's friendship or good humor that momentarily settled Candler but the outrageous futility of him—yet he had been a successful director for eight years, and was stepping down to take a corporate position that would make him rich.

"If you quit having ideas," Egri said, "you're a shoo-in. Ideas make you controversial. Front-runners traditionally say nothing and kiss babies. Not *babes*, babies, though the board is crazy hipped on your getting married, correcting your only fault—this free-living lifestyle you got. Here's some advice: think of the board as an actual two-by-four and understand where they want to stick it. They want to see the proper preliminary chains on you before they offer you their cuffs. That's why I've decided to throw a party when your Dolly—"

"Lolly."

"—arrives, so the board members can imagine the little Candlers you two'll produce. It doesn't hurt that she's a knockout, assuming this photo is lifelike." Egri yanked the picture from the desk.

"I love her."

"Yeah, *love*," Egri said, "it's a swell golf cart but then you discover it won't take you but to one hole."

"Give me that." Candler took the photograph away. His chest rocked with the desire to confess his morning. "I could tell you something in confidence, couldn't I?"

"*In* confidence, sure. *With* confidence, forget it." His eyes shifted to the door and back to Candler—a *tell*, a giveaway, a revelation, but Candler was too preoccupied to notice. Egri did not want to hear any secrets.

"I'm serious," Candler said.

"Every man in love is serious. Science has proven that love is a toxin." Egri offered him another dramatic face. "It's released in the blood by the appendix, which is why thinking men have theirs removed. Want to see my scar?" He lifted the photo again and pretended to study it. "Now and then I try to revive the old blood with Cheryl the way a miser sticks dead batteries in the radio just to see if a miracle has transpired . . ." In Egri's public demeanor, he spoke so softly people had to lean close to hear him. Most of the Center's employees thought he was always that way, unless he was drinking. Candler knew better. When he drank, he could no longer hold in the insanely voluble person who hid in his professional manner. He was still talking. "I'd divorce Cheryl, but it'd be ugly, and I'd have to give up half her money. Does Lolly show some enthusiasm for it? Doesn't matter whether she's good in bed, that's all in your stinking head anyway. It's whether she shows some enthusiasm for it."

"Are you drunk?"

"Not even halfway there," he said, affronted, "which is why I came to sweep you away to a meeting of scotch and tongue."

"I've got work to do."

"What did you want to tell me?"

"It's about coming in this morning. I drove in early to check on a client—"

"Yeah, you're a good egg, boyo," Egri said. "That's the one big drawback to your candidacy. The board, those miserable numskulls, think it's a bonus." He offered an elaborate shrug and disappeared through the door without a good-bye.

Candler heard Clay Hao speaking in the hallway, but Egri would only talk to Hao in his professional whisper, and Candler could not make out the words. Hao was the person to tell about the accident, but Egri's visit made it awkward, even though Hao had been straightforward about the directorship. "You may be better suited to the job than I am." He had a patchy, graying goatee minus the mustache, which Rainyday had labeled a *Klingon*. "You're full of ideas and since you've begun putting the ideas into action, you've been not particularly gifted with the clients. I don't mean to criticize. But right now you seem to prefer projects to counseling. In all likelihood, you'll be a good administrator."

Despite the criticism, Candler had appreciated the reply. Hao *was* genuinely gifted with clients. The Barnstone was good with them, too, but she was no good at drawing boundaries or thinking like a professional. Bob Whitman was a processor with one eye on the clock and now one foot out the door. It was stupid for Candler to think he could talk to any of them. Until that fateful conversation with Egri in the fall, Candler had been studying to become a psychologist. He had started a special PhD program in Santa Barbara that required him to spend a weekend each month on campus. During the intervening weeks, he'd had a ton of reading and schoolwork to complete. Despite all that, he had liked it. Egri, though, had convinced him to drop out.

The Guillermo Mendez file was open on his desk. All that remained was the summary session, in which Candler would explain the tests that Mendez had taken and what the scores meant. Rainyday called him the *War Vet* because he wore fatigues every day, but he wasn't a veteran. He was still on active duty. Candler hadn't particularly enjoyed working with him, but Mendez was a boy. He had enlisted in the army right out of high school and done two tours in Iraq. Recently, he had received word that he would be going back and that the army had extended the tour to fifteen months. He was paying for this evaluation himself, and Candler was not sure what he expected to get out of it. Mendez had no physical disability and no discernible mental ailment. His psychological makeup was more difficult to measure. He regretted enlisting in the army, and he was furious with the military, the U.S. government, Iraqis, his father, women in general, and the able-bodied men who had not enlisted. In short, he was angry with everyone except his mother and a few buddies. He had done whatever Candler or the technicians asked of him, but he seemed always just a degree shy of boiling. Yet he had come to the eval hub for three days, and his Vesuvius never quite erupted.

He appeared now in the doorway to Candler's office, wearing his usual fatigues and usual scowl. The pink skin of his skull showed through dark, clipped bristles. Candler beckoned him in. They exchanged what passed for pleasantries, and then the War Vet demanded, "What do the tests say?"

Candler proposed that they sit. The IQ tests indicated that the War Vet was college material, and the interest evals suggested a predilection for the arts. A battery of psychological exams showed that he was easily annoyed with others and self-hating; however, none of the scores put him at risk. They merely implied he was bad company. Beyond these core matters, Candler had information about his fine and gross motor skills, abstract reasoning skills, and so on. Everything was in the average or above average range. The War Vet didn't have any great talents or glaring deficits. Usually this meant the client should simply pursue his interests. However, Mendez was committed to another year and a half of active duty.

"Before we discuss your scores," Candler said, "I'd like to know what you hope the results will say."

The War Vet colored and frowned. Candler feared he would finally see a display of the anger that floated just beneath the surface like a persistent snorkeler, but it turned out to be embarrassment showing in the War Vet's face.

"You want the long answer or the short?"

"We've got time," Candler replied.

"The smaller deal first. I'd like to hear that I could go to college. I want to do something with computers and design stuff. Like *art* things. My parents, my friends, my teachers are not so supportive. I wasn't the best student. Couldn't see the point. Your tests say anything about that?"

Actually, they did, Candler realized, though he hadn't put it together yet. There was almost no chance he could do this kid justice in his current state. He merely nodded.

"No one seems to think I'm capable of such stuff, like to be an artist you have to have the tap of an angel on your shoulder when you're a toddler. Otherwise, you're a *sap* to think it might be a way to spend your life."

"That's one of the small matters?" Candler asked. "Sounds like a big one."

"Everything's relative, no?" He launched into a story about a girlfriend who had once meant the world to him, and how one night in his bunk in Baghdad he had been unable to recall her middle name. "It's Iris," he said, "like your eyeball. I had to get out an old yearbook to find it. The weird thing is I don't even know what time zone she's living in these days. See what I'm getting at?"

"Things that seem terribly important to you at one stage in your life may later seem inconsequential."

"Bingo." He touched his finger to his nose. "I had it to do over again, I'd have a different line of attack for school. That's not an option, so . . . Another small deal would be what the tests say about me being . . . about if it's possible for me to get better, not so uptight, if I could be like I used to be. I'd like the tests to say that one day I could be *happy* and shit. Doesn't have to be soon. I'm no pansy-ass, gotta have it now. Just a possibility down the road."

"That's another small issue?"

"There's no guarantees, I know. I'm just hoping you're not going to tell me my head's screwed on so tight that the threads are permanently stripped."

"You want to hear my responses to these small matters, or you want to put the big issues on the table?"

"Only one big thing," the War Vet said, "and it can wait."

Candler displayed the results of the aptitude and interest tests, going over them category by category. It took a while. He was intentionally deliberate, not so much for the kid's sake but for his own.

"What's the gist?" the War Vet asked.

"You should do well in college if you can make yourself sit through the classes. A lot of them are dull and not what you care about but they're required. My best guess—it might be premature for you to leap into it. As for your interests, there's every reason to believe that you have a shot at being some sort of artist, particularly, it looks like, in graphic design, though people typically move away from their initial plans. I think you'd be better off in a specific art school where you're less likely to get restless. Whether you could be a successful artist depends on artistic growth, luck, economic intangibles, a lot of fac—"

"*Fate,*" he said. "I get fate. Jesus and Jonah, do I. But you're saying I got a chance?"

"Absolutely. You ought to be in individual art classes now, take the time to get some therapy, and then go to college."

The War Vet nodded, waited.

"As for the possibility of achieving happiness, I'd say the obvious stumbling block is your anger. A lot of it is self-directed, which leads to depression."

"If you're telling me to chuck the anger, I'll kick its ass out the door."

It was Candler's turn to wait. Rainyday buzzed to say another client had arrived. Candler acknowledged her and leaned back in his chair.

"I guess we're done then?" the War Vet said.

"I'll write a report and send it to you or to whomever you designate."

The War Vet stood and offered his hand but Candler shook his head. "We can take another minute or two."

Mendez dropped himself again into the chair. "The big thing?" He took a deep breath and exhaled through his teeth. "I'd like the report to say I can't go back to Iraq, that I'm unfit one way or the other, psychologically, physically, mentally, karmically, any goddamn way possible. That's the big thing, cause without it, the other stuff doesn't matter." He stood then. "I hate to keep people when I know they want me gone."

They shook hands.

"I know it's true," the War Vet said. "I *can't* go back and if I'm made to . . . I'm afraid I won't get through it." He rocked his head against his shoulders. "I thought maybe these tests'd tell me I'm right. Then maybe I'd have the courage to say no to those motherfuckers."

"That might mean prison."

He winced. "Not if the tests, you know . . ." He gave Candler a long look. "You'll email me the report?"

"I can do that."

"Thank you, sir." And he was gone, the door thoughtlessly slammed.

"*No*, you ugh-water, the song is called 'Summer Wind,'" Maura said, "not that I was talking to you."

"If the wind can choose when it blows . . ." Rhine continued but she cut him off.

"Shut the *fuck* up." She glared, a mock glare, really, but it did the job. It was almost noon, and Crews had not come back. He must be mowing a football field. She was telling Mick about someone in her dorm playing the same song over and over, a dorky Frank Sinatra song, but Rhine couldn't keep his nose out of it, and now Cecil Fresnay was upset.

"She's not talking to you, Cecil Something Something," Mick said. "You're doing just really fine. Good, fine work."

Cecil the human trout was on the verge of tears every five minutes. Maura had paid Cecil and Alonso at the hourly breaks. There shouldn't have been enough left in the cash box to continue paying them, but Cecil hadn't yet earned a dollar for the whole morning. He was hopelessly out of it. Crews had never been gone this long before, and she imagined him at the emergency room with a mowed-off foot in his pocket.

Mick calmed Cecil down and put him back to molesting spider boxes. The job was different without Crews around. Everyone in the room felt it, Maura especially. A thrumming vibration rattled her bones, demanding she take advantage of his absence. It was stupid to waste opportunity, wasn't it?

"My mom's car," Cecil said, dropping the spider box in his hands. He picked it up. "My mom's driving car is so big it can hold one mile of people."

"No car is that big," Rhine said, "except maybe an army car." His hands slowed as he pictured an impossibly long, light-green army truck, like the plastic toys he had played with as a boy; it had a square cab and a tentlike covering for the enormous bed, with rows of benches along either side. It wouldn't be called a truck *bed* if there were benches in it, he reasoned. "Is it a bed if there are benches?" he asked. The others looked at him as if he were nuts. He began explaining, which forced him to stop working. He couldn't talk and work at the same time. A ringing phone in the empty office had ruined his last hour. He could not block out the sound, and with each ring he flinched with the desire to drop everything and answer it. He had tried twice, but the office was locked.

Cecil picked up his elliptical, nonsensical monologue. "I was even born in California," he announced.

"You find out who was playing the Sinatra?" Mick asked.

Maura nodded. "The house attendant or whatever they call him— the fucking *guard*. He's trying to learn the words with his daughter. She's in a talent contest. Though why any normal kid would choose to sing F. Sinatra is beyond me."

"'Tectives follow people," Cecil continued, "and look for clues, like if you have any fingerprints in those boxes."

"It's *de*tective, moron," Maura said softly, almost to herself.

"And they have cars with special powers." His arms spread like wings, and he made a whooshing noise.

"You're an idiot," Maura said as she dropped completed cartons into the transport box. Cecil kept flying, calling now for mission control. "You mean the *control tower.*"

"You said the I-word." Rhine pointed at her.

That Rhine could not talk and work was one of the saving graces of the assembly line, but today he had done almost no work and a lot of talking. "Idiot, idiot, idiot," Maura said. "Get back to work."

Rhine counted with his fingers. "That's four I-words, total, Maura."

She did not reply but casually reached inside her purse, which was open on the assembly table. Her cell phone lay on top of the jumble. It took only a second to hit redial. The phone in the office rang again.

Rhine set his carton down. "Can't anyone hear the phone ringing?"

"I don't hear a thing," Maura said. "Karly, you hear anything?"

Karly was studying the carton in her hands with what looked like fascination, folding it so slowly you might think she had never seen a spider carton. When she got like this, she didn't hear anybody.

"Do you ever wonder," Mick asked Maura, "what people like that hear in their heads? What it's like to have thoughts and feelings that don't make you . . . like us?"

"People like what? Like Rhine or like Sinatra?"

"The dorm attendant who's got a daughter."

Maura quite literally didn't know how to think about the question. She didn't believe her thoughts were different from anyone else's, except the nimrods and dimwits for whom thoughts were like baths and a new one every few days seemed sufficient.

Mick Coury had been seventeen when schizophrenia unaccountably descended upon him, and he was only twenty-one now, but he didn't remember much about the fabric of his thoughts before his illness. It seemed to him it was something like the difference between color television and black-and-white. The basic environment of thought was recognizably the same, and yet some element was drained from it. He tried to explain this while he was whipping together cartons.

"Until we get better," he said, "the best we can hope for is like those colorized movies that make everything too bright and phony looking."

"Some things look better in black and white," she said.

"Chess," Rhine offered, as if he'd been a part of the conversation all along.

"It's not that I regret getting sick," Mick said reasonably. "I never would have met Karly if I hadn't gotten sick. Or you. Or everybody.

I'd be a totally different person, which means that the person I am wouldn't exist."

Alonso left the line for the men's room. Sounds of grunting and squealing quickly followed. He made loud noises when he jerked off, vocalizations, shouts without words. Everyone in the room was used to this rough music and ignored it. It was amazing what you could get used to. Amazing, too, what you couldn't get used to, like Rhine and the ringing telephone. What was it about this place that she wasn't yet used to? The green-tasting water. Confinement. She wanted to go to Alonso's party. She wasn't in any way suicidal. Shouldn't her desire to go out and have fun prove that?

Rhine left his spot to show Karly the wrapper to a McDonald's double cheeseburger that had no grease stain. He kept it in his wallet. He had quit eating animals several months earlier, a fact he announced to the group with some regularity. "I don't have any trouble being vegetarian," he told Karly, "as long as I know at the end of the week I can have thirty minutes of meat." He revealed that he could eat five double cheeseburgers in thirty minutes.

Maura's sophomore year of high school she had been in love with a senior, Skinner, who was addicted to amphetamines, which suited her fine since he was a bastard without them. Speed made him chummy and sweet. He wanted to give her things and have her jerk him off. The next day he'd want his stuff back. She would return it and jerk him off again. Maybe it hadn't been love, but she'd gotten used to him in a way that was more than habit. She didn't get off with him, speed or anything else, except to smoke a joint now and then, or drink some rum. They dropped acid together twice, smoked hash a couple of times, did ecstasy if they didn't have to pay for it, sniffed cocaine if it was around, and took downers if they didn't have money for booze. But that was it. She wasn't into drugs. She did the scoring, though, because Skinner had a wussy side to him that kept thinking he'd get arrested, which he finally did.

Maura got along fine with Skinner until his right leg swelled to the size of his waist. He passed out on the way to the hospital. She drove him there even though she didn't have a license. She saved his life, which no one seemed to notice. The doctors cut his pants off, and he got busted in the emergency room for the stuff in his pockets, right while they were rolling him into surgery to amputate. A tough day, no question, but he never did go to prison. Instead, he spent a few months in drug and no-leg rehab, a local, crappy place, not much like Onyx Rehab. The nurses there didn't like Maura, and neither did Skinner. She had nothing to do with the blood clot that almost killed him, and she didn't understand why he quit liking her, except that he wasn't doing speed anymore. A person would think if he lost his leg he'd be happy to have a girl who still wanted to jerk him off, stump and all. She smuggled amphetamines into the clinic, but he wouldn't take them. He wound up going to some college in the northwest his parents wouldn't name, as if Maura was the bad influence.

The last time she saw him, he had called her *fat* and a *bitch*, and—thinking she might have missed the substance of his mood—*a fat bitch*. She had thought: *This fight is going to be nasty*. It would include screaming and accusations. Each would bring up hurtful memories, and there'd be temporary truces, and when one of them broke the truce, the other would get to throw something or slam a door. Realizing this pleased her. It promised they would remain together for at least the duration of the fight, and if they made it that far, there would be make-up sex—just a hand-job, but sometimes she took off her shirt, and his mouth on her breasts was like the plucking of strings, as if she were a bass fiddle and he knew how to play. And she liked his cock, too, in her fist, how it grew and trembled, how it made their connection literal. They were denied their fight. His parents arrived and ushered her out. Thinking about it pissed her off, and she reached again into her purse.

"Sometimes," Mick said, "I wonder about those years when I'd think without thinking about it, and how I wasted all those ordinary thoughts, like I blew my sanity on *The Simpsons* or which shirt to wear with which pair of socks, and I wish I had some of that clear-headedness now, but then I wonder which thoughts I would have kept and how I'd know to keep them."

The unmedicated Mick liked to talk, the words building up speed until his tongue could no longer keep up with his brain. Right up to that point, though, he could sound like a philosopher. When the phone rang again, she had a moment of regret, thinking it might interrupt his train of thought. Rhine, that human dildo, should have guessed she was doing the calling. They were not supposed to bring cell phones to the sheltered workshop; therefore, she must not have one. She understood how Rhine's teensy brain worked. She also understood that she cared more about Mick, whom she had never even kissed, than she ever cared about Skinner.

"I know I'd keep the thoughts about serious things," Mick went on as the phone recommenced its ringing, "like love and being a good person and whether there's a god, but I can't actually remember ever thinking about those things, which makes me think that sanity is when you don't have to work hard to think nothing and it's not frightening to yourself or others to lie in bed and stare at the ceiling."

Rhine shrieked, "That could be a very important call!"

"I used to smoke pot all the time," Maura said. Rhine ran past her to the office and rattled the door. "It made me chill out, but maybe chilled out was bad for me. I was high when I cut myself up. You, on the other hand, could use some chill."

"When we get better," he said, "how do you think we'll remember being like this?"

At this moment she realized something she had long worked to avoid understanding: he was more fucked up than she was. Maybe a lot more, despite how he could talk, how he could be nice even to that Cecil character. She gave her head the tiniest of shakes. "I wouldn't mind if we were always just like this."

Rhine disappeared into the kitchen, which was off-limits, and he quickly returned, apologizing to the cooks, who didn't like anyone from the sheltered workshop. He returned to the line, but the phone rang again and he dropped his spider carton and jerked around, his agitation palpable to everyone in the room.

"It's not humorous, Maura," Rhine said.

"Look for Crews outside," she suggested.

"We're not supposed to go *outside*. It is forbidden for workshop members to go outside during working hours except for breaks or in case of emergency."

"If it's not an emergency, then just cool out."

"All right," he said and nodded convincingly. "That's the way to think about it."

Almost immediately, the phone in the office rang again.

Rhine picked up Crews's chair on the way to the office. He swung the chair at the window, which shattered. He stepped onto the chair and reached over the ragged glass in the frame to pick up the phone.

"Onyx Springs Sheltered Workshop," he said. "Rhine speaking."

A few things that have been omitted:

> The California Highway Patrolman who stood near the wrecked Road Runner was wearing the traditional high-domed, flat-brimmed hat, embellished with a metallic emblem (a golden eagle perched on the letter C), a blue hatband, and matching blue tassels. The front of the dome was dented on either side, as if from forceps.

> The best local weatherman, whose forecasts were never wrong, had predicted a morning shower, but there was no rain and there would be no rain for weeks. "Yesterday's precipitation," he would later concede, "was so light as to escape our instruments."

> When Candler was eight years old, after his sister came home from the hospital with a mouthful of wires holding her teeth in place, their father took him aside to say, "We know you're covering for Pook." Pook was the family name for Candler's big brother. Something was wrong with him—a form of autism, Candler now believed. Young Jimmy Candler had said nothing to correct his father, letting his brother take the rap. Certain acts and omissions one never forgets.

> In 1976 Ohio congressman Wayne Hays was forced to resign after it was revealed that he had employed for two years a secretary whose only apparent skills were in the bedroom. The secretary, a former Miss Virginia, famously admitted, "I can't type. I can't file. I can't even answer the phone." Though she was christened Betty Lou, by that time in her life she called herself Elizabeth—Elizabeth Ray. This woman, who capitalized on the affair by appearing in the buff in *Playboy*, is no relation (by blood or metaphor) to Elizabeth "Lise" Ray, who had not even been conceived at the time of the scandal. The two have no connection but the coincidence of names.

By all accounts, April 2008 was an altogether ordinary month. Witness: Frontier Airlines filed for bankruptcy; an earthquake struck West Salem, Illinois; Hillary Clinton won the Pennsylvania Democratic primary; global warming egged on tornadoes in the state of Virginia; and President of Russia Vladimir Putin while meeting with President of the United States George W. Bush asked privately what the commander in chief thought of Viagra. Bush confided that his mother crushed the pills and added the powder to cut flowers to prolong their blooms.

While Karly's IQ on the Wechsler Adult Intelligence Scale was duly noted (65), the IQ scores for the others are conspicuous by their absence:

Atlas, Billy: 111

Barnstone, Patricia: 113

Bush, George: 96

Candler, James: 118

Candler, Violet: 133

Coury, Mick: 130

Crews, Les: 102

Driver, Road Runner: 109

Duran, Alonso: 56

Egri, John: 111

Fresnay, Cecil: 68

Hao, Clay: 129

Hays, Wayne: 88

Mendez, Guillermo: 104

Olsson, Rainyday: 115

Powell, Lolly: 122

Putin, Vladimir: 77

Ray, Lise: 131

Rhine, Bellamy: 84

Sinatra, Frank: 97

Trucker, Long Haul: 103

Whitman, Bob: 91

Wood, Maura: 136

Billy Atlas, who had lived in Candler's house now almost a month, was the only one of Candler's friends who had been around long enough to recall Candler's big brother. Pook had shadowed James and Billy, a hulking and silent presence, but now and again he came in handy. Pook owned an old one-speed bike with no seat—their father repeatedly installed a seat that Pook repeatedly removed—but he could keep up with James and Billy on their ten-speeds. On one occasion, at a playground where James and Billy joined a basketball game, Pook caught kids trying to steal the bikes. He *roared* at them. The kids scrambled off, the basketball game fell apart, and Billy became hysterical with laughter. Pook laughed, as well, punctuating his high-pitched chortle with new roars. The moment was unforgettable for Candler, as it was the only time he could recall hearing his brother laugh. Pook would kill himself when he was eighteen and Candler, twelve.

Karly Hopper arrived for counseling in the clothing Candler had seen her assemble that morning. The T-shirt puckered slightly at her waist, creating a gap the size of a man's finger. "Good afternoon, Mr. James Candler." She had a smile from which one could not look away. "It's Thursday in the afternoon and here I am." She stuck out her hand. He was seated, and her arm was extended stiffly, directly over his head.

Candler ducked past her arm as got up from his chair. They grasped hands. "Good to see you, Karly. You're looking very chipper."

"Yes, I am. Very chipper this Thursday in the afternoon." She shook her hair, another piece of her limited but effective repertoire. "You look so good in that jacket."

The jacket to his suit was on the back of his chair.

"Well," he said, "the chair looks good in it."

They had routine questions to run through. She gave him her time sheets, and he calculated her productivity rates. He was in no hurry to get to his real subject. She crossed her legs, and he was happy she was wearing jeans. It didn't matter that she was impaired, she knew how to manipulate men. At least it seemed that way. In any case, Mick Coury was no challenge for her. Most of the schizophrenics Candler dealt with did not hallucinate—or not often—and rarely acted noticeably insane, what Hao called *TV crazy*. There were plenty of seriously delusional people in the world, but Candler rarely worked with them. Such clients weren't ready for the kind of evaluation he offered, and the Center no longer accepted severely damaged clients—a policy change Egri had instituted. A business decision. No one with the diagnosis of borderline personality was admitted and no seriously intellectually disabled clients. None of the recent schizophrenics had a history of violence, unless it was merely against themselves, and even then, no suicides who used firearms in the attempt.

Egri targeted adolescents in the Center's advertisements. An increasing number of parents, it seemed, were convinced they could not handle their children. Which meant the clients were getting younger and more docile, and Candler was more likely to see mild schizophrenics or kids who'd had temporary meltdowns, young people who actually had a decent chance of recovery. For the schizophrenics he saw, it was more like they overanticipated, responding to the imagined consequences of actions rather than what was actually said or done. They often became so supersensitive that their emotional responses lost connection with the catalysts. Their minds played tricks, crossing wires, like marionettes whose strings were spitefully misaligned.

Bob Whitman had once introduced Candler to a particularly bright schizophrenic with an interest in the theater, and Bob tried to show off by quoting Shakespeare: *To be or not to be, that is the question,* a quotation so familiar as to have the opposite effect. The schizophrenic immediately replied, "That'll cost you a penny." It was a crazy response, but Candler believed he could trace the logic. The quotation was from *Hamlet,* and Hamlet was the prince of Denmark, and a famous line from the play is *Something is rotten in the state of Denmark,* and rotten things smell, or have a *scent,* which has the same sound as *cent,* one penny. The connections were there. That the kid came up with the line in a split second was what made him insane.

Mick Coury's thoughts raced and his emotions did, too. His mother had described a morning when she asked him to pass the milk and he burst into tears. Candler traced that emotional curve. The request from one's mother for milk was a reversal of natural roles; in this reversal resides the passage of time and the altering of relationships. His mother was aging and their connection would one day end. Add to this Mick's sexual awakening and guilt is layered onto the sadness of separation. No wonder the boy was reduced to tears. Mick was an emotional freight train, and a single penny on the track could send him crashing into the landscape.

Enter Karly Hopper.

"Okay, another good week of work," Candler said, putting down the time sheets. Her supervisor was supposed to add observations, but Les Crews had merely written *Slow as molasses.* "Did you get your pay?" The sheltered workshop paid their clients every other Thursday and made a group trip to the bank on the subsequent Fridays.

"I have money in the three places," she said. He had given her a strategy for keeping track of cash. She kept spending money in her pocketbook, money to deposit in the bank in the zippered liner of her purse, and emergency money in her ID folder, which she wore around her neck. She patted each of the three places.

"You're getting good at this," Candler said.

"Yes, I am," she said. "I can make change, too." The smile faded. "Except for . . ."

"Still having trouble with nickels?"

She nodded seriously. "Why do they make them bigger than dimes?"

"Let's don't worry about nickels today."

That brought back the smile. "And I didn't break a window at the workshop," she said. "Rhine broke the window, but I'm not telling on him." She absolutely beamed.

Candler made a note to call Crews. "How are things at home?"

"My mother and sister are at home, but my father is dead and not at home. People die. Even people you know sometimes."

Candler nodded. Karly's mother and sister lived outside Los Angeles. "Good, but how about your house here?"

"What house?"

"The house you live in."

"I live in the same house that I'm living in for a long time." After a moment, she added, "Where I live, it's very . . . *treey.*"

"Yes, it is."

"How is your house, Mr. James Candler?"

"I have a few trees in my yard, but nothing like the ones on your block."

"The trees on my block are very treey," she said and laughed. "That's so funny." Then she added, "I'm sorry about your house."

"Oh, I like it all right."

"If you had a wife, she would live in your house with you."

Candler agreed.

"Mr. James Candler, do you have a wife?"

"No, but I'm planning to get married."

"Everybody knows *that.*" She made a gesture James had never seen her use before. He noted it in her file while she continued speaking. *Places one hand over heart, places the other hand on top, and presses against chest.* That brought the total number of gestures to twenty-one, which was also her age. Perhaps her personality grew by a single gesture each year. "When men and women grow up, they get married," she said. "My mother and father got married. I was just a baby. Now my father is dead, even though my mother isn't."

Candler glanced at his watch. He was getting nowhere. "But let's talk about the house you live in here in Onyx Springs."

"Onyx Springs is a hole with water in it, too," she said, "not just a town."

"I know, but let's talk about Onyx Springs, the city, where you live in a house with a man. What is the man's name?"

"What man?" she asked. "Your name is Mr. James Candler."

He offered a resigned nod. "What other men do you know?"

"I know Mr. Clay Hao," she said. "Do they have to be grown-ups? Because I know Mick and Rhine and . . . is Alonso a grown-up?"

"Let's forget about the people you work with in the workshop." *Knows how to duck a question.* Should he add that to her file? It was clearly a talent.

"I forgot my lunch today," she said. "I was supposed to put it in my purse, but it was so funny."

"What was funny?"

"I didn't put it in my purse!" She laughed. "Mick bought me lunch at the Kentucky Fried Chicken chicken place. I had chicken and he had chicken, and it was so fun." She laughed again. "Mick is not a grown-up but he can drive a car, and he keeps money in his billfold, which he calls his *wallet*, and he bought me lunch. Do you drive a car, Mr. James Candler?"

"Yes, I drive to work every day."

"Is it a long drive to work every day?"

"It is such a long drive that today I went too fast, and . . ." He stopped the story from spilling out and looked at her smiling, patient face. She really was beautiful, and the thump of his heart sprang from twin desires: to speak the truth, to hide it. He said nothing for several seconds. "Let's just say another car tried to keep up with me, and it had an accident, but no one was hurt."

"Was the car hurt?"

"Not my car, but, yes, his car was damaged."

"Could they fix it?"

"I don't think it can be repaired. It was going so fast that it flipped over. It flew in the air and hit a light pole and the driver could have been killed, but it was a special light pole, and he was fine." The dam was cracked, and words poured out of him. "We were racing, if you can believe it, and he didn't know when to stop. I found a seam . . . a wide spot between cars that made a diagonal like . . . a *slant* right across the freeway . . ." He demonstrated with his hands. ". . . but the traffic closed up after an instant, and the other driver just would not let it go. He *would* not let it go. He risked his life to keep up with me, to participate in that stupid, stupid race."

He told her the whole story. He spilled every bean.

"That's so funny," Karly said.

"Yes." He realized he was breathing heavily. "Funny."

"My sister tells her friends I'm a car wreck."

Candler swallowed hard, a lump in his throat. The sadness of this woman's life—no, not sadness. She was perfectly happy. The *tragedy* of her life was suddenly visible to him. It choked him up, and he flicked tears from his eyes.

"She calls me *Karly the Car Wreck*, which rhymes." She laughed and tossed her hair, gesture twelve on the list. She added, "I have a sister."

"I think I'll call you just plain Karly." He did not fully have control of his voice. "Karly's good by itself."

"I'm glad they could fix your car."

He nodded without trying to correct her.

"My sister says some car wrecks can't be fixed." She shook her head once more as she laughed, her hair swinging, her eyes seductive. "Isn't that so funny, Mr. James Candler?"

3

Rhine dropped the kickstand to his cycle—a motorized scooter but he called it his cycle—and checked his watch: 6:45. He did not trust his watch and dug through his backpack for his cell phone. If it was 6:45, he was early by a quarter of an hour, which meant he made the drive across Onyx Springs in less than three minutes, which was not humanly possible. His cell phone kept time by means of a satellite connection with a perfect clock in Greenwich, which, according to Wikipedia, was in three places: England, New York, and Connecticut. From this information, Rhine understood the perfect time was calculated by triangulation. His phone's window read 6:39, meaning he had crossed town in *minus* three minutes. Either there was a time warp or his bedroom clock was fast.

He adjusted his watch to match satellite time, removed his helmet, checked that he had his keys in his pocket, looked at the window over the garage where his friend Alonso Duran lived (window lit, curtains open), fingered the zipper to his fly (completely shut, lever down), and ran a finger over his teeth (clean). Still 6:39. Nothing he could do about it, he was going to be early.

He crossed the street and climbed the stairs. The door was open.

"Alonso!" Rhine called out, opening his arms. "Am I early?"

"You're so early every time," Alonso crowed, throwing his arms wide in a mirror gesture.

Their embrace was animated yet tentative, with much back clapping, but enough room between their chests to lob an apple.

"Is Karly here yet?" Rhine inhaled deeply. "You're cooking dinner? You can't cook, can you? Can you cook?"

"Every time early." A stranger might have thought Alonso's harsh expulsions indicated anger. Rhine knew better. Alonso was one of his best friends and Rhine knew. "Catching worms," Alonso continued, nodding enthusiastically, growling the words. "Healthy. Wealthy. And what's showing."

"If you were going to take my coat," Rhine said, handling his suit jacket, "I'm not wearing one."

"Karly is coming, all right," Alonso said. "I'm cooking garlic."

"It smells good," Rhine said, "but will it taste?"

"Just for smelling," Alonso said. "Mom called the pizzas."

Rhine tried to laugh and Alonso joined in to help, but for Rhine it always just came out *ha, ha, ha,* which didn't sound as much like laughter as people seemed to think. He was wearing his new suit, a color the salesman had called magenta, with thin blue stripes that crossed not like a checkerboard but like the wire fencing around the animals at the petting zoo. He had not removed the tag but tucked it inside the sleeve and taped it down with duct tape. His shirt was also new, a pink like the inside of lips. His tie was wide and yellow. "You could sell a *Playboy* subscription to a blind man in a getup like that," the salesman had said. Several fellow salesmen gathered to nod their approval. But after leaving the store, while he was waiting at the bus stop, Rhine wondered if the salesman said *"prescription."* Not *Playboy sub*scription but *pre*scription. He boarded the bus but immediately stepped off. He had a yearly pass. How often he boarded didn't matter. He walked back to the store. The salesman was with another customer.

"I'm kind of busy now, partner," the salesman said.

"It's *sub*scription," Rhine said. "Not *pre*scription. You can't have a *Playboy pre*scription, which means you couldn't sell it. *Sub,* not *pre.*"

What a look the salesman gave him! "You've got me there, bud." He shook Rhine's hand and waved as he turned away. Rhine waved back.

At the bus stop again, he wondered about the wave. You didn't wave to people who were right next to you. He boarded the bus, and then as it was about to start up, he hustled forward for the door.

"Rhine, you set yourself down," the bus driver said.

It was Mrs. Connelly. Just his luck.

"Yes, ma'am," he said, and that was how he got his new suit.

"Karly's not here yet, is she?" He could see the whole apartment, but wanted to be sure.

"You're early," Alonso said. "She's not even here."

Alonso's apartment above his parents' garage was one large room plus a bathroom. A broad strip of tape showed where a wall should be, separating the kitchen and living room from Alonso's bedroom.

"You didn't make your bed," Rhine said.

"Party doesn't go that far."

"I can see your socks on the floor," Rhine said. "And underwear."

"If there was a wall you couldn't."

"Noted," said Rhine, looking at his watch: 6:10. "What *is* it with the time around here?" he asked. He stared through the invisible bedroom wall at Alonso's alarm clock. Huge green digital numbers announced 6:45.

"I shouldn't do anything in the dark," Rhine said. "I adjusted my watch to match the Greenwiches in the dark, and I shouldn't do anything in the dark." It was only dusk and not close to dark, but he knew his friend would understand him.

"Movies," Alonso said.

"True," Rhine acknowledged, movies were better in the dark. "I'm going to make your bed. It's early and everyone knows you can't wait for time. Is your garlic burning?"

He crossed into the bedroom through the blank spot that indicated the door. He could make a bed with military corners. He had to or he couldn't sleep in it—not that he would sleep in this bed but it would be made with military corners. The doorbell sounded. Rhine picked up the pace. His first name was Bellamy. No one but his parents used it. He didn't look or feel like a Bellamy, and he had never actually seen his birth certificate. He grabbed the socks and white briefs and dropped them in the plastic box where Alonso kept his dirty clothes. The underwear fell between the socks, and flapped over one heel. Rhine bent down and quickly matched the socks.

"It's you!" Alonso said. "My garlic's burning and Rhine is making my bed in the bedroom."

"Hey, Alonso," Mick said. "I guess I'm early? Hey, Rhine."

"He's in the bedroom," Alonso said.

Mick Coury slouched in and offered a slow, slight nod.

Rhine stepped through the door path wearing an insane suit and tie. "I thought you might be Karly," he said.

Mick continued nodding. "Everybody wants to see Karly. You ought to turn that burner down."

"I know!" Alonso said, but he didn't make a move toward the stove.

Mick stepped past him. The pan held garlic cloves and a halved onion. He shut off the burner. "Is this for atmosphere?"

"I thought you meant Karly was a burner," Alonso said.

Mick stared blankly at him.

"She's hot," Alonso explained.

"She's hot," Rhine agreed. After a moment he added, "Of all the gin joints in all the towns in all the world, she walks into mine."

Mick Coury felt the slurring of blood through his body slow yet again. His head teetered under the weight of its monstrous mass. He settled himself in a kitchen chair, but got up and sat on the couch. If Karly wanted to, she could sit beside him. If she didn't want to, at least she would be in a chair and not beside Rhine or Alonso, whom he watched as they walked the smoking pan through the door, oven mitts on every hand. He heard them trammel down the stairs, the rush of water through pipes. They would be spraying the pan with a garden hose.

He wished Maura could have come with him to the party, though she didn't like Karly. Maura was smart and sarcastic; she put an edge on things that made them visible. Back in Minnesota, she took a knife to her wrists while she was bathing. When she described it to Mick, he asked, "How much water was in the tub?" And then: "Was the water warmer than the blood?" She liked those questions, and they became friends. She would be happy to be with him, even in his current sorry state. He had screwed up. He had skipped his meds this morning, revving his brain, the world brightening. *Polishing his shiny*, he and his brother called it. But his father showed up unexpectedly after work, having driven the thirty miles from Imperial Beach. "Look who's here," his mother said, and there was his father, buttoned up in a white shirt, standing in the doorway, saying Mick's name.

They sat in the kitchen, Mick and his parents and his brother Craig, who was fifteen now, two years younger than Mick was when the illness found him. Mick could barely stand to see how his father looked at Craig, searching for clues, afraid of what he might find. His parents' marriage ended because of Mick's illness. He knew this to be true, and not, as his mother liked to say, because of his father's *reaction* to the illness. Without the illness, there would be no reaction.

His father was born again, washed in the blood, saved by Christ, which made him unbearable. He was right across the table, grinning, and Mick could not bear to look at him; therefore, he was unbearable. Not that Mick blamed Christ, exactly, but his father's *reaction* to

Christ. He laughed inwardly, a sly smile showing on his face, but he didn't openly laugh, which was a symptom: laughing for no reason.

His father spoke to his mother in that singsong Christian voice, and the desire to laugh evaporated. Didn't it stand to reason that to be born again you had to first die? Wasn't he saying that Mick had killed him? Or killed off something inside him? It would take something like surgery to fix his father, make him give up the kneeling and that gawking smile, a smile like the bird in that cartoon who steals teeth from a glass of water beside a bed, a bed that angles out like the Van Gogh bed, a painting Mick saw once in a traveling exhibit in Los Angeles before his illness. He didn't like the labels for his illness. Wasn't it enough to say *illness* and not pollute the waters with terms no one could understand and so had to simplify like an algebraic equation: a boy's strangeness is equal to the sum of age + illness − (0 meds × 2 days)? Mick had gotten an A in algebra his sophomore year, and Leah Kasten, the smartest girl in the school, had cheated off his exam, he knew, because he had caught her in the corner of his eye. Caught her *from* the corner? Caught her *out of* the corner? Eyes don't even have—

"*Mick.*" Craig jostled his arm. "They're talking to you."

"You didn't take your medication," his mother said.

"I was going" *to but I wanted to be sharp for this party, where the woman that I love is going* "to choose between me and two" *goons who aren't bad—my friends, actually—but who have no more conception of the world than a rattling tin can filled with bottle caps* "making noise and calling it thought."

"You're doing the rag," Craig said.

Code, their fraternal code for Mick's ramble, when his mouth betrayed him, falling so far behind his thoughts that he sounded incoherent and, if the world was to be believed, scary and sad and dismissible, like a fire that burns so brightly and at both ends that its race to the middle is not only exhilarating but terrifying and explosive: his brain free of medication, blowing up his thoughts so that his mouth can only express the bits.

His mother, the pill: he had to take it. Weighted by the drug, he could barely put one word after another. That's how it felt. He was on their level: Rhine's level, Alonso's level. The doorbell made the light in the room quaver, his vision a sandbox, black around the borders, sand

67

spilling out, draining him. He looked to the door, but it was just Rhine testing the doorbell so they wouldn't miss Karly if it was broken.

Mick's meds made him like the blackened nub of an eraser on a pencil, while his mind without medication was like the pointed end, a needle-sharp pencil slashing across the page—too fast to be read, granted, but how could he compose with an eraser?

"We shouldn't do anything till Karly gets here," Rhine said. "It wouldn't be fair."

"I'll try not to be too interesting," Mick said.

"Not no but hell no," Alonso put it.

"She should be here any minute." Rhine studied his watch. "Any minute." He mouthed numbers, literally counting the seconds. "Not that minute, maybe this one."

"She should be here *every* minute," Alonso said and smiled.

"You made a joke," Mick said.

Thirty-nine, thirty-eight, Rhine continued silently, *thirty-seven, thirty-six . . .*

Why Candler decided to drive by Karly Hopper's house again, he couldn't say. Because it was almost seven p.m. and he was weary of the office but couldn't yet go home? He never quite reached his destination. A diesel truck and trailer was parked on a side street, a couple of blocks from the trees of Lantana Avenue. It had Oklahoma plates, and the engine was idling. Maybe his visit this morning had convinced the bastard to run, Candler thought. He felt a brief, ridiculous surge of pride. Of course, it could be the guy was scheduled to leave anyway. Evidently, Karly was able to manage during his absences.

It occurred to Candler that this arrangement was almost like a rehabilitation plan. The trucker would be away for periods, and Karly would see how she could keep up, what she could accomplish, what she would have to let go. When the driver returned, he would set her back up again. Candler might have logically pursued this line of thought and asked himself whether it had been smart to run him off, but he didn't go that far. Instead, he wondered what the guy hauled, how long it took him to get to Stillwater, whether he had a woman at every stop.

Candler parked the Porsche up the street from the truck and turned off the engine. What a strange day. That it was Karly Hopper to whom he spoke about the accident was weird, but she had most of the characteristics of a good listener—all of them, in fact, except for comprehension. The woman Candler used to live with was the opposite: she always knew what he was trying to say before he could get the words out. Saundra Dluzynski—Dlu—was the woman his friends and family expected him to marry. They had lived together six years, but he discovered that he didn't like being that well understood. He didn't think anyone would.

He remembered coming home with her one evening from a lecture—they met in college—and the cottage they rented had all but disappeared beneath the shadows of the neighbor's cottonwoods. Only the kitchen window, made silver by a nightlight, shone along the dark walk to the house, and it looked like a sheet of steel upended in the dirt where their house had stood. Later he would realize that a burnt-out streetlight contributed to the effect, but that night their place seemed foreign and beautiful and not like a house at all. Dlu knew not to turn on the lights after they entered, understood not only that they should make love but that the act should not be performed in their bed. They were magically elsewhere, and it was delicious.

The next morning when he stumbled into the kitchen for coffee, she was leaning against the table, her arms crossed, and she glanced at the clock over the stove. Candler understood they were going to have a fight. His mind searched frantically for a possible reason.

"Did it ever occur to you," she began, "that other people may not want to wake to your underwear on the kitchen floor?" That's where their lovemaking had taken them the night before. "You know I'm going to be up first," she went on, "and you simply expect that I'll clean up after you." She put her hands on the table behind her, her arms quivering with indignation. "You're the most thoughtless . . ."

Her angry monologue continued but he left the room, unable to argue with her because she was absolutely right—utterly petty, in his estimation, but unquestionably right. He got dressed, putting on sandals so he wouldn't have to return to the kitchen for his shoes, silently cursing her, regretting the night, regretting even the lecture. He had only gone to please her, but he enjoyed listening to the woman talk about her life among a primitive tribe, and then they returned to the mysterious house and made love on the kitchen floor. It had seemed perfect, and he now regretted all of it.

He went out to his car and she followed him up the same shady walk they had traversed the night before, calling him a coward for not engaging the argument, saying he was *a smug bastard even when he was in the wrong*. There were many passages she used that he could remember verbatim. He drove to a café, where he drank coffee, ate an omelet, and read the morning paper, furious with her, counting up the articles of clothing on the floor—shoes, socks, pants, underwear, shirt. Picking them up might have taken seven seconds. Kicking them into a corner, two seconds. At the same time, he knew her anger had little to do with the clothes. They had heard the speaker—her idea of a night—and fucked in the dark on the kitchen tiles, which was undeniably his kind of thing. It didn't matter that she was a willing participant, so aware of his desires that she could consciously pick up on what was as yet unconscious and unfolding in his own mind, an empathy so quick to materialize that it permitted her to step into the darkness ahead of him and lead him precisely where he wanted to go. She had to make him pay for that, show him that she could not only see what he wanted, she could also see how tawdry it was, how clichéd, predictable, sentimental, and stupidly male. She had to show him that she was above it, which meant she had lowered herself for his sake. She had lived among the primitive tribe of men long enough to know what they wanted and what expense to demand for acceding to it.

They didn't break up that day. They lived together another two years, but that episode stayed with him. It was still with him. When he eventually left her, it was not because she was in the wrong but because she was so precisely right. He wanted someone who was blind to his sentimentality, at least as it applied to her, someone who was not above any of it but up to her neck alongside him. He thought it might be more important to be heard than to be understood. It was almost certainly the greatest benefit of therapy: that someone was willing to listen.

Candler checked his cell phone, but Billy had not called. Les Crews had been fired, and Candler managed to get Billy Atlas an interview. They needed someone to start the next day, which meant it had to be someone who had completed the Center's three-day training session. The interviews were being conducted at the senior citizens facility, and Candler had agreed to give Billy a ride home. Counselors had no official sway over hiring, but they could recommend people as long as they sent forward two names. Personnel made the final decision, but the sheltered workshop was Candler's innovation and he guessed the two he recommended would be the only ones considered. He had sent a text to Billy Atlas—*get bus to onyx springs job interview haul ass*—before buzzing Rainyday to ask if her husband was still looking for work. If Billy couldn't outdo that anvil-brain, he would park cars forever.

Candler had been waiting for Billy to call since five. He used the first hour to study the Guillermo Mendez file. Nothing in the test scores showed the War Vet incapable of returning to Iraq. It occurred to Candler now, slumped down in his car and watching the diesel through his rearview, that maybe the question itself was ridiculous.

Near the end of their relationship, Dlu had entered a graduate program in behavioral ecology, specializing in the conduct of certain birds. She talked about things like *cooperative hunting, dear enemies, flock responsibilities,* and *territory pilfering.* "Some birds cheat," she told Candler and described a swamp bird that would give up a monogamous relationship with its mate to have another male around to defend the nest. "Others turn their back on their duties to get ahead," she said. "Birds and people, all the same." She branded human acts they witnessed on television or in the wild *flock behavior,* which rarely seemed like a good thing.

When Guillermo Mendez enlisted, he was exhibiting flock behavior, Candler reasoned, blindly following a lead bird—his father, the army recruiter, the president of the United States. What about Candler's consideration of the War Vet's request? Did he really believe that serving in an unpopular, unnecessary war fabricated by a dishonest, lame-duck president was reasonable? Or was Candler exhibiting flock behavior? If he refused to accept that being sent to war in Iraq was reasonable, then it might be easy—or at least possible—to write the recommendation Mendez wanted. Of course, that would be writing a professional report to suit his own political beliefs and a client's personal agenda, and not even Egri would support him on that, but at least he would be separating himself from the programmed thinking of the flock.

Karly and the trucker appeared at the corner. He pushed a red wheelbarrow filled with clothing, his wet hair plastered against his head. She was in cutoffs, a yellow halter, and the thought of the trucker's hands on her flesh turned Candler's stomach. Beneath the clothing, which the trucker tossed into the cab, were two suitcases, a clock radio, and several boxes of cereal. He piled it in the truck. He was leaving, Candler thought, and he felt gleeful. *You win.* Karly climbed in after the driver, and the truck offered a loud diesel mutterance. Candler let the truck turn a corner before starting his car. He would hang back and watch. He had no desire for another confrontation. The red wheelbarrow lay on its side by the street, a spilled box of Count Chocula beside it.

His cell phone tinkled, a text message from Billy Atlas: *dun.*

Billy would be in the senior center parking lot, and the diesel was headed in that general direction. There was no reason not to shadow it. Candler suspected that it was aimed for the freeway, and he feared the driver was taking Karly with him to Oklahoma. What could he do about that? She was an adult, according to the law, though her mother still had guardianship.

It should have been easy to track something so enormous, but he let himself fall too far behind and only caught up with the truck because they were headed to the same part of town. *Enter westbound ramp for Interstate Eight,* the omniscient librarian announced. Candler had punched in his home address to avoid hearing her complaint. *Recalculating,* she said as he followed the truck under the freeway. Passing the senior center parking lot, Candler spotted Billy leaning hands-first against the brick wall, as if to be searched. No one else was in the lot. He could be stretching, maybe, Candler hoped. He tailed the diesel to a residential street. The truck wheezed to a stop in front of a pale, two-story house. The trucker did not wait to see that Karly was safely inside. Candler watched her skirt the main residence and go to the garage, up the exterior stairs that led to an apartment. One of the sheltered workshop gang answered the door, Bellamy Rhine. They were having some harmless gathering.

He watched the shadowy figures beyond the curtains for only a moment before resuming his pursuit of the truck. He wondered again why he had decided to go by Karly's house. The encounter with the trucker disturbed him, he supposed. If he was going to be honest, it also bothered him that of all the people in the world to talk with, he had chosen Karly Hopper. The confession had taken place during a counseling session, no less. He unburdened himself to her, and now he owed her. That had to be it. *You're such a fucking coward,* Dlu yelled at his back as he walked to the car. He could hear the specific way she said it, with the emphasis on *cow*.

Rhine was lingering by the door, which made him the one to answer it, the tone of the ringing bell still alive in the room as he whipped it open.

"Wow, hi, Rhine," Karly said, her mouth wide and white with teeth that were . . . Mick tried to focus. Her teeth were as white as . . . as white as . . . a *smile*, he thought. Then: *God, I hate these meds.*

Karly had dark brown hair, brown eyes, skin that tanned and did not burn, a thin yet curving body whose shape made its own pronouncements, but it was her face, the bright eyes and smile, the beautiful way she took in the world, that made her irresistible, that made Mick's heart beat like a basketball dribbled up-court. He had played basketball in high school, not especially well, but he'd been able to immerse himself, to let go, to *play*. What an amazing thing.

"You look so good in that outfit, Rhine!"

Rhine nodded rapidly. "The man who bought it from me said *pre*-scription when he meant *sub*."

She wore cutoff jeans, very short, with white raveling strings that would drive Rhine crazy if he noticed them, if he could ever look away from her face, and a yellow halter top that showed off her shoulders. Mick loved her shoulders. She put her hands under Rhine's jacket, ran them up and down over his shirt. "I'm so lucky to see you in this. It feels so *pink*. You pink boy, you. *Pink*."

Alonso lined up behind Rhine. He could not take his eyes off Karly's neck, the notch at the base of her neck. He would like to slip his thumb into that slot. It would fit perfectly. It was made for his thumb. He put his thumb between his teeth and made biting movements to relieve the tingling itch: her neck, his thumb, the slot.

"Alonso!" she called. "Wow, hi."

"Hi, Karly," he said, removing his tingling thumb from his mouth. The skin that bridged his thumb to his hand tingled, too, and even, when he thought about it, his stomach. He realized he had an erection, dropping his hand to check. *Yep.* "Hi, Karly," he said again. He could almost make out the ridges of a thumbprint in her thumb socket.

"Isn't Rhine's shirt so pink? Have you felt how pink it is, Alonso?"

"I have my cycle outside if you need a ride home," Rhine said. "I parked it across the street, but I could drive over and pick you up if you don't want to cross the street." He touched his pocket to check for his keys, then, just to be certain, checked his fly, too. (Keys present, fly shut, lever down.) "I'll move it right now." He stepped to the door, which Karly had not shut. "Mick," he called. "You're going to have to move your car, Mick. Karly wants my cycle there."

"Mick!" she called out.

Mick raised his head to her, the shift in weight causing it to rock back. "Hey," he said. "I like that dress." He meant the cutoffs, her legs, her thighs, the way she tanned and did not burn, how the thighs paled slightly at the turning where they almost touched.

"Isn't it divine?" she said, meaning, he supposed, her shorts or the evening. Her legs were perfectly shaped, brown and sleek. That was a word, wasn't it? *Sleek?*

"Isn't Rhine's shirt divine? Oh, Mick, you look so good on that couch."

"Sit with me," he said and patted the cushion next to him.

Before she could sit, Rhine rushed past and sat so close to Mick his shoulder brushed Mick's nose.

"I thought you were talking to me," Rhine said, smiling at the ingenuity of his lie. "Karly, I thought Mick was talking to me."

"You almost knocked her down," Mick said.

"This place is so *divine*," she said, sweeping her head back and forth. She knew the effect her hair had on men whenever she'd sling her head from side to side. To her, it seemed like the same effect on any man. She could not know that the room became for Rhine a black-and-white movie, the world transformed by her movement. Not an old movie with bubbling static, but sharply outlined, hi-def, and digital, a great inaccurate clarity. What Alonso saw in the movement of her head and hair was a shift in the shape of her thumb slot, a wrinkling that wasn't pretty but was so *real* and womanly, a womanly indent of skin, that made him think: *This is a real woman.* And even through the medicated fog of Mick's brain, this gesture—one so familiar to him and yet so startling—caused a pain in his chest. He understood that the frequent and self-conscious repetition of a gesture should diminish it, should reveal the superficiality of its charm, and since it retained its power over him, it was he who was revealed, his own devotion to this lovely woman, which made him as much a goon as the others—and that hurt his heart because they were his friends and he did not want to be like them.

The big truck took the eastbound ramp onto the freeway and Candler circled back to the senior center. Billy Atlas was high-stepping up the building's white stairs.

Exercising, Candler supposed. Or just as likely: *Billy has lost his mind.*

Billy was disheveled and soft, chronologically in the prime of his life and yet he seemed never to have had a prime, his hair short and badly cut, the color of pine boards, his teeth too big and always showing—Billy was a smiler. He was capable of such insistently blank stares that people often believed he was putting them on. At the bottom of the stairs, he did squats, his hands thrust out like a Russian dancer. *Definitely exercise,* Candler decided, though that didn't rule out insanity as a sidebar. He was wearing one of Candler's suits. It was too small, Billy's pink hands emerging from the cuffs like sea creatures. *Exercising in one of my suits,* Candler revised. He and Billy were both overweight, but the pounds looked manly on Candler and chubby on Billy, and a list of tiny things like this accounted for the vast difference in their lives.

"Yo, Richard Simmons."

Billy high-stepped it to the car. "I was beginning to wonder if you were coming," he said, climbing in, huffing.

"Had to finish some things." He had them out on the street again quickly. "How'd it go?"

"I knew I'd get the job when I arrived and the other guy was arguing about whether he could play the radio while he worked. You send that clown?"

"Thought I'd keep the competition to a minimum."

"It worked. Where we going?"

To the consternation of the librarian, Candler turned onto the eastbound freeway ramp. He wanted to catch the diesel, which shouldn't be difficult through the Lagunas. *Exit freeway in point five miles.* "There's a piney place up ahead a few miles where we can eat," he said. "Have a beer and celebrate your employment." *Exit freeway in point two miles.*

Billy put his nose next to the GPS screen. He touched one corner with his index finger. He kept the finger there and the screen went blank. The omniscient narrator was turned off.

"How'd you know how to do that?"

"I'm a genius."

"Could've used a genius earlier. I've had a weird day."

"How so?"

"Driving stuff, clients, my secretary had her skirt tucked into her belt this morning so her panties were hanging out."

"This is why camera phones were invented."

"There are maybe a hundred reasons I wouldn't do that, starting with liking and respecting her, and moving on to her husband already thinks I'm trying to steal her away."

"That's the suit talking . . . Are you?"

"Am I what?"

"Trying to steal his wife."

"I'm engaged, and even if I weren't, I wouldn't go for Rainyday."

"Rainy Day? That's her name? I think I like that name."

"Her husband was the other guy I sent to interview."

"That guy has a panty-wearing wife?"

"Women pretty much all wear panties."

"Seems like it ought to be reserved to a limited few. The word has a special place in my head, and that guy shouldn't have a wife with admission to that special place."

"What should the others wear?"

"Boxers or something, like the rest of us."

"This is exactly the kind of speculation you can*not* make working at the Center—or any place else in the world, actually, but especially not at the Center."

"Don't worry. I won't talk about any underwear whatsoever. Except maybe teddies. You can talk about teddies in church."

"When was the last time you were in church?"

"I'm taking this job seriously. Time for a new start. I'm exercising these days, and—"

"When did this exercise regimen begin?"

"Maybe twenty minutes ago. You forget we're supposed to meet the Haos at the bar?"

Recalculating, Candler thought and exited the freeway. The Calamari Cowboys required his help. A decent guitarist played in an otherwise atrocious cover band Thursday nights at Toad's Tavern, a bar near Candler's house. Clay Hao and his brother had formed a country-and-western band that needed, among other things, a decent guitarist. Candler steered the Porsche through a burger joint before reentering the freeway. Egri would be appalled at their eating in the Porsche, but Candler was resigned to being a crummy sports car owner. He decided, too, that he didn't care about the diesel. It was gone for now, which made him feel like he had won a bet. As they were passing the last of the three Onyx Springs exits, Candler's cell phone rang.

"I've hesitated to call." It was Mick Coury's mother. "I know you have to have a private life, I just . . ."

Candler heard a clicking that might have come from her throat. "What is it, Mrs. Coury?"

She described her son's incoherent speech. "He's skipping his medication. If his father hadn't chosen this particular evening to visit, I might not have gotten him seated long enough to notice. His father insisted I call. He's in town one afternoon every other week, but he thinks he knows . . ." She let the sentence drift away. "I let Mick go out, anyway, to Alonso's. Mick's an adult, after all, and I try to respect his decisions. Besides, he took the pill at, oh, about five fifteen, and I thought I should let him go, but I've been fretting about it, whether I've inadvertently given him permission to cheat on his medication."

Candler guessed that Mick was at the same garage apartment where Karly Hopper had climbed the stairs. He could picture her taking those steps up to the landing, the cutoff jeans, the yellow halter top. "I'll see if I can have him called out of the party," he said, "at least temporarily. I'll phone you right back."

He didn't like asking favors of the Barnstone, but he only rarely hung out with the Hao brothers, and he didn't want to miss it. The Barnstone lived in Onyx Springs, near the Center, and she didn't seem to have any social life that his request might disrupt.

"Surprised to hear from you this time of the evening," she said.

"It's about Mick Coury." He explained the circumstances as he maneuvered freeway traffic. The morning's accident did not keep him from the fast lane. "The thing is, I've been drinking and shouldn't drive right now."

Billy Atlas smiled evilly at the lie.

"I could dictate a quick note," Candler went on. "The key is to make Mick leave the party temporarily, take responsibility for—"

"I catch your drift," she said. "You can owe me."

Her last sentence was almost enough to stop him, but he rattled off a message, called Mrs. Coury again, and by the time they reached the exit for Liberty Corners he had taken care of the business.

"Don't let me get drunk," Billy said, as soon as Candler clapped his phone shut. "I start my new job—and life—tomorrow." He put his palms together and pushed strenuously, his face turning crimson. *Isometrics.*

"I don't actually like Mr. James Candler," Karly said, making a pouty mouth and holding the expression while she took a bite of pizza. They were sitting in a circle on Alonso's carpet, talking about the counselors. This was a favorite topic, and it took many shapes.

If you had to be stuck on a deserted island with one counselor, which would it be?

Which counselor would make the best president of the United States?

If you could save only one of them from a terrible fire, who would you save?

Today's topic was marriage. Rhine brought it up. He wanted to marry Karly, and he reasoned this was a good step: the introduction of the general subject. He had an outline for approaching Karly, and the introduction of the general subject was the fifth step. Purchasing the suit had been step one, putting her name on his old cycle helmet had been step two, *hygiene* was step three, using his line from *Casablanca* was step four. Giving her a ride home on his cycle was step six. There were fifty-seven steps altogether, ending with *kissing etc. on wedding night.*

By this time, Mick felt better, not less medicated but more accustomed to it. He knew why Karly didn't like Mr. James Candler—he wouldn't flirt with her. Mr. Bob Whitman, who must be sixty-five or seventy, flirted in a grandfatherly way, and Mr. Clay Hao flirted in a distracted, friendly way. Even Ms. Patricia Barnstone commented on Karly's appearance in a racy, joking way. But Mr. James Candler would not flirt, and that hurt her feelings.

"What he is," she said, "is mean."

"If you can't say something nice," Alonso put in hoarsely, rocking back and forth on the floor, his head nodding, the pause growing long before he finished with, "say something else."

The pizza man had arrived while Alonso was in the bathroom masturbating. They heard him, but they were used to it—all but the pizza guy, who said, "You got an animal in here?" No one discouraged Alonso's frequent masturbation. His counselor was satisfied that he finally understood the requirement of privacy. Alonso had been at the Center longer than Mick, longer than any of the others. None of them, including Alonso himself, knew for how long. He was forty-two years old, but his face was unlined and open, and he looked almost as young as Mick and Rhine, who were in their twenties. Karly was twenty-one, but whether she looked older or younger, Mick could not say. She looked the age of actresses in movies when they were the stars of the show and every single thing about their lives mattered. What age was that?

Mick had paid for the pizzas. They did not talk about Crews disappearing and Rhine busting a window. If Maura were with them, she would make wisecracks and tease Rhine. The rest of them weren't teasers. Rhine had to break the window to answer the phone. What else was there to say? Someone from the facility had called the Center, and a counselor, Mr. Bob Whitman, showed up. All he wanted to know was the precise time that Crews walked out. He distributed their pay and let them go home early.

"Since there's just one woman counselor," Rhine said, "can we pretend the men are women? Otherwise, the men all have to choose Ms. Patricia to marry."

"Ms. Patricia Barnstone," Alonso said.

"Of all the gin joints in all the towns in all the world, she walks into mine," Rhine replied. It always got a laugh.

"That is so funny," Karly said.

"Go ahead," Mick said. "If all the counselors were women, who'd you marry?"

Rhine furrowed his brow and nodded. "I'd marry Ms. Patricia."

"Ms. Patricia Barnstone," Alonso put in.

"Then why'd you make the men into women?" Mick asked.

"To have a choice," Rhine said and turned to Karly. "Your turn. You never answered. You can make Ms. Patricia a man."

"Ms. Patricia Barnstone," Alonso said again. Then he added, "I'd marry Mr. Clay Hao."

"He'd have to be *Ms.* Clay Hao," Rhine said.

"He couldn't be *Clay* and be a woman," Karly said. "I know, I'm a woman."

"How 'bout we call him Janice Hao?" Mick said. "Jackie Hao?" There was a way to make this funny, but his brain wouldn't cooperate. This was his experience on his meds: he recognized the existence of a punch line but he couldn't name it. Some people, he guessed, were always like this. Which led him to think that the meds were designed to emulate stupidity.

"Which one?" Rhine asked. "Janice Hao or Jackie Hao?"

"It doesn't matter," Mick said.

"It matters what your name is," Rhine insisted.

"You aren't even marrying him," Mick said. "Alonso is."

"You have to pick a name for him before he can be your bride," Rhine said.

Alonso nodded, smiled. "Mr.—"

"Ms.," Rhine said.

"Ms.," Alonso agreed, "Ms. Karly Hao."

The room erupted in laughter. Alonso laughed especially long and hard, holding his belly. Only Rhine failed to find it funny. He reminded Karly that it was her turn.

"I'd marry Mr. James Candler," she said. "I'd be Mrs. Karly James Candler."

Mick was surprised by this. "You said he was mean."

"No, I didn't," she said, smiling. Those teeth. "You're so silly."

He couldn't contradict her. "It wouldn't work out, though, one of *us* marrying one of *them.*"

Alonso's phone rang.

"That's right," Rhine said. "Get that out of your head."

"Ms. Karly Hao," Alonso croaked again.

"Everybody knows that," Karly said.

"Aren't you going to answer that ringing?" Rhine asked.

Still laughing, Alonso shook his head.

Rhine leapt up and ran to the phone.

"Yes, Mrs. Coury," he said. "This is Rhine." He turned to the others, covering the receiver with his hand. "It's Mrs. Coury."

Mick got up so quickly that it made him lightheaded. He steadied himself and the room settled as well, the blurring of color reconciling into familiar shapes. On the wall, a poster of Britney Spears stared at him. She was in black leather, her breasts ready to burst from a vest, a portable microphone at her lips, held in place by a wraparound brace that hooked over her ears. Mick remembered not liking Britney Spears, back in the *before* days. Music, anymore, was hard for him to evaluate, even his own reaction to it. *Britney Hao*, he thought, but that wasn't funny.

"He's coming, Mrs. Coury," Rhine said. "He's crossing the room. Here he's stepping in. Not there! The doorway is the part that doesn't have tape. Good-bye, Mrs. Coury. This is Rhine." He handed the phone to Mick.

"How's the party?" she asked. Her voice was light, like balloons bouncing off the ceiling, rising, bouncing again.

"All right. Why are you calling?"

"Mr. Candler wants to talk to you."

Mick glanced over at the others. They were watching him. "What about?"

"I'm not sure."

"Now?"

"Yes."

"Did he call you or you call him?"

She didn't answer immediately. "We talked." Concrete had entered her voice. It became as heavy as Mick's head.

"You called to tell him I wasn't . . ." He turned away from the others and whispered into the phone. ". . . taking my medication."

"Okay, guilty. Call your lawyer. Arrest your poor mother."

"Do I have to go *now?*"

"He seemed to think it's important you see him tonight. He'll meet you at the Donut Hole. I suggested there so you don't have to drive to the Center and back. It's only a few blocks from Alonso's house. You can go right back to the party."

"Fine," he said, feeling miserable. His friends didn't know to look away. It was Alonso's nature to gawk, and Rhine was enjoying it. Only Karly was smiling. She did wish the best for him, didn't she? He returned the phone to its cradle. It was an old-fashioned phone with a dial. Alonso had trouble with push buttons.

To the group, Mick said, "I'll be right back."

"Of course, you will," Karly replied. "Don't be silly."

Before he met Lolly, Candler had gone to Toad's Tavern to dance and meet women. On two occasions a dancing partner walked home with him when the bar closed. He enjoyed the sex, but neither encounter led to anything. Each woman admitted after intercourse that she was already attached to a man. Candler's disappointment made him feel unsophisticated and a dolt. He had been raised in Arizona by a pair of Midwestern artists who were more Midwestern than artistic in their parenting, and moments like these made him believe he would never truly be a Californian.

To make things worse, Liberty Corners was so small he kept running into them. One was married. The other worked in the bank and had a boyfriend. She showed up at his house early one evening to make him promise to never talk about *their fling* with anyone. After he promised, she took his hand to lead him to his bedroom for a good-bye session. He declined the offer. "But I need to flush you out of my system," she said. Candler changed banks.

As a younger man, whenever he was not in a relationship, he actively pursued women. He was not shy and he enjoyed their company, but he was also by nature monogamous. He never fooled around during the years he lived with Dlu, and even in the early stages of dating, he didn't look at other women. He liked thinking about the woman he was seeing, imagining what it would be like to travel with her, live with her, what she would think of the books and movies and art he loved, and even, yes, what children they might produce.

Only three or four times had he wound up in bed with a woman when he had no intention of a possible future with her. Most recently, a woman from work—the technician, Kat—insisted he join her for dinner at her house. They had been working with a client who kept them an hour late, and Candler made an innocent comment about grabbing fast food on his way home. Kat was adamant. She retrieved her two kids from day care, and while she made pasta, Candler read to them. By the third book, they were sitting on his lap and resting their heads against his chest. He fell in love with her kids while they nestled upon him.

Kat had a boyfriend, an economics professor at San Diego State, who was not the father of her children. Candler later met this professor. He was young and black and had a narrow beard like a shoelace that traced his jaw and chin. He was not present for dinner, and when Kat returned from putting the kids to bed, she wore a terrycloth robe. "Cole and I have an open relationship," she said. She had braces on her teeth, and they took on significance Candler couldn't name when the robe loosened, revealing that she was naked underneath. "You want to spend the night?"

Candler followed with a string of stupid questions: "Me? With you? In the same bed?"

She nodded and smiled, and Candler wore one of Cole's shirts to work the next day. He and Kat had had sex a few times since then, and he drove her kids to the zoo one Saturday while she completed a training session. She liked sex with him and told him as much but made it clear that Cole was her real boyfriend.

After returning from London, Candler had buzzed for Kat to come into his office. He told her about meeting Lolly. She seemed happy for him until he explained that he could not sleep with her anymore. She wrinkled her brow and said, "You're so *serious*." She laughed. "It's just life, James." Her response upset him. He had practiced his speech for hours on the return flight, and he was prepared for almost any response except amusement. Before he could gather his wits, she put her hand on his thigh and rubbed the thin material of his pants. "I hope you two are very happy," she said and laughed again, displaying her braces. He still had her boyfriend's shirt.

He liked the naughty thrill of going to bed with a woman for the first time, but he wasn't cut out for casual relationships. He was good with women (meaning: *they liked him*) but he was traditional in his desires and conservative in his methods. The only married woman he ever slept with was the one he met at Toad's, and she had claimed to be separated from her husband. Later she said, "We were separated by a few miles, anyway." Her husband had been in the Laguna Mountains on a camping trip.

Another bit of mischief he genuinely enjoyed, which would soon end, was being a different person in the Corners than in Onyx Springs. No one who knew him from Toad's would be surprised to hear he had been racing a car on the freeway that morning or that he punched a guy on the jaw. He had a swagger when he walked about in the Corners, which evaporated when he got to Onyx Springs. He was a something of a flirt in the Corners, and there were women who stopped him in the grocery to say they looked forward to dancing with him again, to thank him for the drinks from the night before, or who ducked down aisles to avoid him.

As for the people he knew in Onyx Springs, their opinions of him varied. Kat (her full name was Katherine Eleanor McIntyre) might have thought he took himself too seriously, but she liked him; there were even times she imagined she could love him. She knew that he was the youngest of three siblings and believed this explained why he always wanted to please everyone. She was big on birth order. Rainyday Olsson might have conceded that he was stuck on himself, but she would have immediately added that he was her favorite co-worker, mainly because he took the time to talk and joke with her, and because he was smart and cute but also a mental klutz. Candler's clients, for the most part, appreciated him, and if one maybe wished he flirted with her and another wished he had not forced him to leave a party, they nonetheless believed Mr. James Candler was helping them, and they looked forward to seeing him. Even the War Vet, who had only worked with Candler for three days, trusted him as he did almost no one but the men in his unit, and he felt reasonably good about placing his life in Candler's hands. John Egri was pushing Candler for the directorship, telling anyone who would listen that he was levelheaded yet shrewd, a man full of ideas but with plenty of heart. Privately, he understood that his reasons for advocating on Candler's behalf were more complicated. Without any particular justification, he disliked Clay Hao, who was the natural choice, and placing Candler in the seat ahead of Hao felt like an appropriate final flex of his muscles. If he could free himself of his own propaganda concerning Candler, Egri might have called him superficial (by which he would have meant *childish*) and syrupy (by which he would have meant *naive, sentimental, soft*), but, *hell*, Candler liked to laugh, didn't he? He could appreciate a woman in a short skirt without calling out the political correctness police. He understood that scotch tasted best when you were supposed to be sober and working. He was an actual *man*, wasn't he? A rarer find in their line of work than most people knew. Clay Hao resented Candler's ascension but he did not let that affect his personal feelings toward Candler, who seemed to Hao a decent man with a good sense of humor. He had done well with the clients until Egri began privately advertising the directorship to him. Except for his sexual relationship with Kat McIntyre, he was thoroughly professional and pleasant to be with, especially away from work, at a bar or a ball game. One time they had gone to a concert, Clay and his wife, along with Candler and a woman who lived on the Haos' block, a setup that Clay's wife had plotted. Their neighbor was oddly intimidated by their conversation and unforgivably dull, but Candler was polite to her and he loved the Drive-By Truckers, and four or five times, he made Clay's wife laugh, and there were few things that Clay Hao liked better than the sound of his wife's laughter. Patricia Barnstone wouldn't offer a negative opinion of Candler unless he had done something recently to piss her off, but deep down she thought him narcissistic and bland, like some tepid soda that had lost its fizz. *Oh, he was okay,* but his roots were so shallow that one good breeze would knock him over.

Saundra Dluzynski, whom no one any longer called Dlu, and who had married a man with none of Candler's faults, a thoughtful and generous man who quit drinking during her pregnancy to share more completely in her experience, missed Candler most after dark, when the baby was asleep and her husband too was down, after she had knocked back a couple of Tom and Jerrys and come round once more to recollect the same night that haunted Candler, the night of the lecture and the ghostly appearance of their home, how they made love on the kitchen floor, how desire permitted her to fornicate on the linoleum, and (despite the extent to which it had shamed her) how she still felt that base longing to extricate herself from her nursing bra and suburban split-level and go back to that dark cottage with handsome Jimmy Candler and toss her bare body onto the kitchen linoleum, whose speckled pattern, she recalled, was designed to hide the dirt.

If some people had misgivings about Candler, no one thought ill of him. If he was not particularly tidy, he was very clean, smelling typically of Ivory soap and scentless deodorant, the naive, endearing fragrances of certain young men. If he was soft in the belly, he was otherwise reasonably fit for man with a running start on his thirties, his hair a brown that was almost blond and neatly cut. He had the sort of attractiveness that a casting director might look for in extras, easy on the eyes and yet would distract no one from the A-list actors. But there was something about him that photographs failed to capture, how he raised his head from his work when Rainyday entered his office, how mischief showed in his eyes when he teased Kat, how his body softened with resignation and friendship when Billy loped toward him, how his eyes zeroed in on Mick sitting across from him as if to view the words as they exited his mouth. Such traits win trust and love in others. Such traits merit love. Candler was loved by the people who knew him well. And the others liked him, even Barnstone, who mostly avoided him, and Dlu, whose heart he had broken, and none of them—with one exception—could have guessed what he would wind up doing this evening, how he would behave in a manner that contradicted the person they thought him to be.

The exception was Billy Atlas, who knew Candler best, and who understood, too, how circumstances could outweigh character. Billy's whole life, as Billy himself apprehended it, was an example of this. He had a vague belief that the ability to do the right thing and the ability to do the wrong thing were the same ability, and it existed like a great body of water on which floated your personality, and you could never tell just what might seep through, or in which direction a tide might take you.

Mick drove slowly through the milky darkness. The summer evening hovered beyond the windshield, bougainvillea blossoms waving in the automotive wind, and the grass in its evening clothes lingering greenly on the lawns. If this were a dream, he might know what the colors meant to tell him, how they seemed to hold true to the world he had once known, and yet how their dreamy disposition also captured this tumbledown way of living he had now.

Without his meds, he might be flying down the residential lane—colors blending one into another. With his meds, he was five miles an hour, and every blade of grass was a reminder that he was not the boy-behind-the-wheel he'd been before the illness, and he wasn't even the man he could be when his body wasn't lethargic from the heavy winter garments the meds insisted he wear. He had acquired his driver's license before the illness crouched in his chest, and he waited to renew it until he was having a good day. He wasn't a very good driver, but he never had accidents. His 1992 Firebird was the orange of lava, black racing stripes on the hood, a spoiler on the back. He could not lay hands on the person he used to be. Not that he had amnesia. He knew everyone's birthday and the theme songs to the TV programs he watched as a child. But what it was like to be a person who would hop into the front seat of a Firebird—he remembered *hopping*—he could not hope to guess. To recollect doing something but not recall being the person capable of doing it: how was that possible?

Nonetheless, he believed he was getting better, and one morning he would step into the world as it had been before—bright, solid, and full of meaning—and he wouldn't need to worry about meds or counselors or progressive treatment protocol or whether his father might drop in to force a conversation. He would stand up straight, and the world would once again part for him when he strode through it.

Despite his speed, the Hole came into view. It was open twenty-four hours, 365 days a year. Hole coffee tasted burnt and rubbery, as if they added pulverized tires to stretch the grounds. The Hole was near the sheltered workshop, close enough to the freeway to hear the scorching sound of traffic. At this time of night, he was able to park directly in front of the Hole's big window, which revealed a deep and well-lit stall in an old downtown building. Inside were three customers: a young couple cuddling in a booth and a single man who held a frosted doughnut to his nose as if it were a flower. The building was three stories high and made of brick. The second floor was a plasma donation center. A lot of people from the Center made some cash there, and Mick had given some of them lifts. He didn't know what was on the building's third floor. He thought people might live up there, smelling doughnuts and blood and listening to traffic.

Mr. James Candler was nowhere in sight. Mick had been taught to relax himself whenever he believed he might have made a mistake. He dropped his hands from the steering wheel and took twelve deep breaths. Step two required him to consider possibilities.

Was he supposed to have gone to the Center to meet Mr. James Candler after all?

No, he recalled his mother saying *Donut Hole* and that it was near Alonso's.

Was there another place near Alonso's?

There wasn't. He had not made a mistake. He had simply beaten Mr. James Candler to the building—despite driving very slowly. Perhaps that meant his counselor had to come all the way from his house. He lived somewhere in the county. Mick supposed he should feel guilty about making him drive all that way. He took twelve more deep breaths and the anxiety receded.

Faith Hao, that was sort of funny.

A car pulled in behind him, an old green Toyota. The woman who got out was short with a solid build. She carried a slip of paper. He climbed from the Firebird to meet her. Ms. Patricia Barnstone paused on the sidewalk to study him. "How are you this evening, Mr. Coury?"

"I was at a party."

"I didn't expect you to be driving. That's quite a car, a beauty. It all cherried out?" She bent down to stare through the passenger window. "I dated a NASCAR driver way back when I first moved to Onyx Springs. He was always talking about *making the cut,* and what a tense life it was if you didn't have the big backing. You follow racing at all?"

Mick shook his head. "I got a ticket, though, when I was seventeen, for going forty miles over the speed limit. It was in the Lagunas, the freeway through the mountains, and it was a plane that caught me." His girlfriend had been with him, her bare feet in his lap. They had been in high school together in Yuma, Arizona. He remembered the details perfectly, but he could not remember the experience of doing it. "I had to go to safe driving school."

"You were quite the hell-raiser."

He and his girlfriend had committed intercourse that day, after the ticket, on the way back through the mountains. They stopped in a tiny town with an even tinier mountain lake. They ate at a park on a picnic table, and then they lay together on the table, one beside the other. She said, "If we're going to do it, I want to take off my dress."

"I have a note for you," Ms. Patricia Barnstone said and handed him a sealed envelope. The note within it was handwritten.

> Mick,
> You have to take your meds. Do I need to tell you
> why? Your mother is freaking, and I have another
> engagement. Counselors have private lives, too,
> you know. We'll talk in my office, regular time.
> Take your meds, doofus.
> James Candler

The *doofus* made Mick smile, followed by a surge of anger that he had left Karly for nothing but this flimsy wing of paper. The anger quickly dissipated. He was not an angry person. He turned to Ms. Patricia Barnstone. She was dressed in drab pants and a man's shirt. He felt the odd sensation that there ought to be a picnic table, pine trees. His girlfriend's name was Peggy Stein. Her family had moved to Yuma from Miami, and when she was naked in the dark, lying on the table, a gold Star of David had dangled from a tiny chain around her neck and glimmered in the moonlight. That was a few weeks before it happened, before his illness skewed the world, before his family left Yuma and moved to the other side of the Lagunas for his rehabilitation. *You're like a Gatling gun*, Peggy Stein said to him, meaning the sex. They were in the same American history class, and he knew what a Gatling gun was.

"What party were you at?" Ms. Patricia Barnstone asked.

"A friend from the workshop. We were going to watch a movie."

"I won't keep you then. I was watching a movie myself."

"I remember driving this car fast," Mick told her. Peggy Stein seemed to be there too, watching him, smiling slightly—something he could tell about her even though he couldn't see her. "But I don't remember being the person who drove this car fast."

"Like what? Watching a video of yourself?"

He shook his head. "It's like being the person in the video instead of yourself."

"You feel flat? Limited?"

"Maybe," he said, but he couldn't make her understand him. "I know I'm the same person, but I've lost . . . something."

"Lots of people feel they're not the person they used to be. Count me in the club. It's a crap feeling."

"I feel I've lost . . . I've lost my *atmosphere*," he said, nodding, happy to name it, despite the meds, despite having to leave the party. He remembered that night in the mountains with Peggy Stein, and the moment was lingering, staying here with him, letting him think like the boy he'd been when he was with her. Here was the proof, the best proof yet, that he was improving. Yuma wasn't so far away. He had lived on one side of the mountains, and now he lived on the other. It should be easy to go back.

Ms. Patricia Barnstone patted his shoulder. "I'm watching *Key Largo* at my place. If you'd rather come over there, you're welcome to. I can start it fresh from the get-go. Bogie, Bacall, a hurricane. Hard to beat."

The invitation so surprised him that Peggy Stein, her moonlit body, and the golden star slipped away. "Thank you," he said, "but my friends are waiting."

"No sweat." She slapped his shoulder this time. "You ought to do exactly what you want to do."

On the way back to Alonso's, Mick realized that Ms. Patricia Barnstone must have written the note. Mr. James Candler would be at home out in the county. He had dictated the message. He tried to imagine what Mr. James Candler would be doing at his home. Reading, maybe. A book with hard covers, thick and important. When he went to work the next day, people would say, *Have you read that important book that everyone is talking about?* And Mr. James Candler would nod solemnly. *I finished it last night. I didn't go talk to one of my clients to finish it.* What might the book be about? It was an election year, but Mick couldn't quite imagine Mr. James Candler reading a thick book about politics. The book was definitely thick. It might be about the important issues in every person's life. How to do the right thing, for example. How to be good to the people who love you. How to love people yourself. How to take care of others. How to make decisions that are smart and that do not hurt people. Really, Mick thought, he ought to get this book himself.

Rhine's moped was in the space where Mick had parked earlier. He pulled in across the street. At the top of the exterior stairs, he stared through the window. They were watching *Wayne's World.* Alonso, Rhine, and Karly sat on the carpet, Alonso with his hand down his pants, Rhine in his gaudy suit, one hand tugging covertly at a stray thread from Karly's cutoffs, and Karly, lovely Karly, sitting with her legs crossed and feet tucked beneath her legs. *Indian style,* it was called, to sit that way. Was it a racist way of sitting? Could there be mean-spirited postures? He would defend her right to sit that way, he thought, and was almost immediately aware that he had gone off on a tangent. People can sit any way they want. She shifted, her knees rising, her thin arms wrapping round her legs, one wrist held in the other hand.

Oh, he loved her, all right.

He slipped in quietly and took his place on the floor. *Grace Hao,* he thought, *Blanche Hao, Felicity Hao.* When the time came, he sang the two-word theme song with the others. No one asked where he had been or what he'd been doing. By the time the movie was over, they had forgotten he was ever gone.

Maura played her boom box at top volume until the attendant tapped on her door. She put on an oblivious smile, as sweet as she could make it, and opened the door.

"It's after ten," the attendant said. He was her father's age, the same guy who had played Sinatra over and over to sing it with his daughter. He spoke kindly and without condescension, and she felt bad about fooling him.

She punched the stop button on the boom box. She was in a flannel gown she never wore, and the smile got away from her—a phony, patronizing grin, but *fuck it*. "I'm so sorry." So saccharine it embarrassed her. "I was just turning in, anyway."

The guard wished her good night, raising his fingers to an imaginary cap. As soon as the door shut, she whipped off the gown and slid a chair to the door, fully dressed. She pressed an ear to the louvered vent. She could not hear his feet on the linoleum, but she would hear the door to the stairs swing open and clink shut. Making him knock was the only way to know for sure that he was on her floor.

The metallic clank of the door set her into motion again. She had to be fast. She shut off the light and eased her door open. Over the latch, she applied a domino held in place by duct tape. It had taken experimentation to find the right size block, sanding the domino with a fingernail file. The piece permitted the door to close without locking. Bedroom doors on this floor automatically locked at night. For safety reasons, clients—*inmates*—could leave their rooms, but they could not reenter without the assistance of an attendant. This wasn't true in all of the dorms and not even all the floors of Danker Dormitory, only the at-risk floors.

She padded down the hall to the stairs and pressed her ear against the door. When she heard another door close, she knew he was out of the stairwell. She let herself in. There was a monitor on the ground level, sitting at a desk by the entrance, but she went down to the basement, which held offices and storage rooms. No one was there this time of night. A dusty desk was centered beneath a casement window, right where she had shoved it. In less than a minute, she was walking across the grounds.

She didn't have directions to Alonso's place, but it was near the workshop. The party would be winding down by the time she got there, but the only thing that interested her was getting Mick to give her a ride home. She had studied the route the van took to the Center. She wasn't stupid. *Too smart for your own good*, her mother liked to say. A lot of the clients at the Center were plenty smart, and just as many were dumb as cheese. Alonso was dumb, but she didn't mind him. She liked to brush her ass against him so he'd hightail it to the john to jerk off. She didn't have that kind of power in the real world. She wasn't a girl men looked at with sugary eyes or that predatory stare that seemed to come as naturally to boys as menstruation to girls. Maura was ordinary, and her personal plan for mental health required her to be honest about it. *Accept your mind, accept your body.* She was smart and looked as ordinary and dismissible as a tree stump.

She reached the edge of the Center's grounds and hopped the low brick wall. This wasn't a prison or a real asylum, just a private retreat for fucked-up-in-the-head people with money, like herself, or people who had turned over their lives to save their kid, like Mick's family, or people who needed someplace to store the family problem. She crossed the highway, which was obviously the old route through town, full of gas stations and rundown motels. She didn't want to walk beside the road. It was not a walking sort of street, and someone from the Center might spot her. She headed to the backside of the buildings, a gravel alley, and picked up the pace. It was a long walk, but Mick would have his car. All she wanted was to ride in that hideous contraption and talk to him. She was wearing a loose-fitting T-shirt and short skirt. She never could have worn the skirt at any other stage in her life. She had nice legs now. Her body wasn't extraordinary, but she had to use what she had. Bodies mattered. The crochet-brained therapist she had seen back home tried to tell her it was what was on the inside that mattered. "You mean my liver?" Maura had asked. "My gastrointestinal tract?" The bitch was wearing a Danskin and there was an exercise step beside her desk.

Barnstone just said, "Some of that weight ought to go. You'll be happier."

She smelled garbage. It was hard to see where to put her feet. Mick's car was a grisly, macho, gearhead car. Not that it mattered. He was no longer the person who'd buy such a car. He was sweet and beautiful, blond in a California way. Maura was from Minnesota and knew something about blonds. He wasn't a Nordic blond, his hair and skin had more color, and he carried his shoulders with a western attitude. If he could get past this mental whatnot, he could have the world. Maura would not then be a candidate for girlfriend. If you can have the world, no fucking way you choose Maura Wood. She wanted him to be well, and she needed him to be ill.

His attachment to Karly Hopper was both baffling and obvious. Karly was none too bright, though she was more dingbat than flat-out stupid. Here was the honest part—Karly Hopper was incredibly good looking. Every day Maura wound up acknowledging this. Good looks were an advantage that no amount of cleverness could overcome. You're born, and you've either got it or you haven't. Karly had it. She was dumb and fucked up in some meaningful way to be going to the Center, but what did it matter? All the boys threw themselves at her. Maura had to admit that if she were a boy, she'd do the same. *Fucking honesty.* She was better looking than Maura's sisters, better looking than her brother, her mother, that girl at the high school who supposedly fucked the vice principal. Karly was a beauty. There. Said and done. Enough already.

Some of the motels—or whatever they were—had back fences. Most were dark. One had dogs in a wire enclosure, big black dogs with enormous heads. They barked and trailed her to the end of their lot. Their black bodies had dollops of brown, like rust spots. After a quarter mile or so, she turned where the van always turned, a road that angled through a residential neighborhood. No one was walking on this street either, but there was less traffic and she didn't feel conspicuous. She had never been trouble to her parents until she was fifteen—a straight-A student, reasonably honest, a favorite of her teachers. One day in a secondhand clothing store with friends, she decided she wanted a flowery psychedelic miniskirt from the seventies, and she didn't want to pay for it because she knew she'd never wear it—she just wanted it. She took it into the changing booth and stuffed it down her pants. That was the beginning, that stupid skirt she never wore because it made her thighs look like beer kegs. Later that week she ripped off cigarettes and became a smoker. She stole beer from the fridge and tried to drink it. She ditched her old friends and dressed like the lowlifes who convened in the park. She liked that word *lowlifes*

and used it often. *How's my favorite lowlifes?* They got her high and she
stole an entire canister of Slim Jims from a convenience store. She let
the air out of the tire of a parked police car. She climbed a fence, shed
most of her clothes, and jumped from the high dive into the community pool at three in the morning. She learned how to give hand-jobs
and took up with Skinner. Her junior year, she called a history teacher
a *cunt-eating cunt* and got suspended.

The suspension led to trouble. Her family lived in a house outside
of the city, near the woods, and some nights she could see from her
window deer that wandered in to eat their flowers and chew bark from
their trees. But there was nothing to *do* in that fucking house. She
made some calls and ran away. Friends picked her up, and they spent
three nights in downtown Minneapolis—sleeping in some man's bath-
tub the first night, a parked car the second night, an alley the third.
They were caught in the alley, she and the four boys with her.

Her parents wouldn't say it, but they feared she'd pulled a train,
not that they'd use that language: *sexual relations with multiple partners.*
Her parents were dense beyond words. Maura was a virgin. Hand-
jobs and one boy had stuck his pointer finger inside her to the second
knuckle. Nothing else. She told all this to the Danskin counselor as
well as the next therapist her parents dragged her to, a woman with
a white house in St. Paul that she had turned into an office. She was
friendly—there's the tough honesty—and unbelievably dull, a fairly
young woman with gray hair she refused to dye. Maura's hair had
been purple at the time, and they spent a good portion of several fifty-
minute hours talking about hair. The friendly bitch wound up telling
Maura's parents they had to separate her from her peer group. Her
parents would never have the same sway, the counselor said, as this
group of kids. "Would they, Maura?" she asked, and Maura said, "Fuck
no, gimme a break," without even thinking about it. The gray-haired
twat insisted her lowlife pals were headed for serious trouble.

Maura liked thinking of her friends as a *peer* group, as if their
job was to look at things other people didn't want to see. The rest of it
made her furious.

"If you make me leave my friends," she said, "I'll kill myself."

That night she slipped down the stairs but her father was lying on
the couch, prepared for her. He put his arms around her and would not
let go. When he started crying she quit struggling. She went back up-

stairs, ran a bath, smoked a joint, and slit her wrists with a box cutter. They had to break down the bathroom door to get to her. Her father cut his shoulder on the splintered wood. Her mother was crying in the ambulance, but Maura hadn't sliced herself deeply enough for any real damage, except to the bathroom rugs, which were ruined. Her father's shoulder took more stitches than her wrists. The day she was released from the hospital, her parents drove her directly to the airport. They sold their home to pay for her treatment.

Thinking about it this way, she supposed an outsider would think her family was like Mick's, giving up their house and all, but from the inside, Maura understood the difference. Her parents were only doing it for show, to keep up appearances. Well, not her dad. He cared, but her mom resented her. Selling the house made her look brave. Though, Maura had to admit, her mother would miss the deer. She loved those fucking deer. Whatever her parents did was their own responsibility. Maura hadn't asked them to put her here, and the place would be a complete wash if not for Mick and Barnstone. She refused to feel responsible for any of it. Were deer responsible for gnawing so much bark that the trees died? Creatures had to live. They had no choice about it. There was only one thing that Maura felt guilty about: *she wasn't crazy.* She wasn't in any jeopardy anymore, if she ever had been, and her judgment was as solid as a heart attack.

She had been at the Center almost a year, starting out in Cagin, the high-risk ward. It had *insane* security routines, from which adventures like tonight's trek were impossible. After six months, she was moved to Danker. All of the interesting girls were on the at-risk floors—cutters, nymphos, kleptos, addicts, you name it. One girl set fire to her chemistry teacher's desk *during class* and wouldn't tell her counselor why. She told Maura, though: *He broke up with me.* All of those girls needed to be in such a place, but Maura didn't. She was over her bad patch.

Okay, her common sense had been spam quality, and she got carried away with shitty influences. To be absolutely fucking honest, that *peer* group of hers was into meth now and had been expelled, arrested, and one was in a coma the last she heard. *Her parents had done the right thing*—Barnstone made her admit that. Her dad had, anyway. Her mom hardly visited and her phone calls were always indirectly about how much nicer things were now that she was out of the picture. Fuck that bitch. But her dad visited and wrote letters. Twice, her little sister came with him, and her big sister called with gossip. As for her fucking brother, he wouldn't even take a turn on the phone. She had snapped a picture of him jerking off and emailed it to a dozen people. So, okay, *honestly* then, the fuckwad had reason to be pissed.

All that sewage was behind her. She'd tell her parents as much and let them off the economic hook if not for Mick. She loved him. Or whatever *love* was a euphemism for, she felt *that* for him. She wasn't going to act like some sad-sack missy lying on her bed whining about it. She was going after him. A vehicle slowed beside her, and she turned her head away, afraid it was someone from the Center. The voice that called to her, though, was far from professional.

"Hey, sweetheart, want a lift?"

The pickup truck was shiny, possibly new (how could you tell with a truck?). The men were adults, thirty-forty-fifty years old—who could say? The passenger had a day's growth of beard and straight brown hair, long enough to sheath his ears. His face had about it the emptiness of a snowscape but not the beauty. His clothes were nice, though, and she liked *sweetheart*. The driver was bulky but almost good looking, a drinking straw that he chewed on while he stared protruding from his mouth. He wore a gold chain around his neck, which made him a certifiable ass, but he was otherwise acceptable. The passenger did the talking. "Where you going?"

"Downtown."

"Jump in." He opened the door and climbed out. The truck had a bench seat, and she slid to the middle. Girls always had to ride in the middle. There was some unwritten rule. When they were back on the road, the passenger produced a short, flat bottle of copper-colored booze. "You look like you could use a drink."

She swigged enough to show them she'd had a drink before. It tasted like lighter fluid.

"I'm Bert," the passenger said and laid his hand on her bare thigh, "and that's Ernie."

"I guess that makes me Cookie Monster," she said.

The men laughed, and the driver gently took her other thigh.

"You want to party with us?" Bert's hand was already sliding up her leg, under her skirt.

"My friends are expecting me." She was not afraid. She didn't like these particular men putting their hands on her, but she liked that she was out on her own and that grown men were feeling her up. Bert's hand found its way to her underwear.

"I'm not going to fuck you," she said to him. "I'm a virgin."

"The hell you are," said Bert, but then he reversed himself. "I'm a virgin, too."

"I'm fifteen," she said, a statement meant to provide her some protection, while at the same time she thought enough of her blossoming body to feel it was a transparent lie.

The driver took his hand away. "Where downtown?"

"Let's not be in a hurry," Bert said. He had his finger pressed against her. At the *gateway*, she thought, the *portal*, the *threshold*. "Give her another taste of that whiskey."

She turned to look Bert square in the face. "You can finger fuck me, but only till we get to where I'm going." She took another swallow of lighter fluid and stared out the windshield, while the finger wormed uncomfortably inside her, like the scrubbing side of a kitchen sponge.

Toad's Tavern was a converted feed store with bad acoustics and a big dance floor. It was a landmark in the Corners: the first building constructed on the county road, dating back to the late fifties, an unattractive brick box with almost no parking. Candler, drunk and dancing with a stranger, did a spin move and then could not determine which of the nearby women was his partner. He had maybe overspun, which he took as a signal to sit down. He danced to the edge of the gyrating crowd and headed back to his friends. Clay and Duke Hao were leaving the table as he arrived. They wanted to watch the guitarist up close. Billy, hunched over the table and smiling like a donkey, poured his friend a glass of beer from the pitcher.

"You oughta dance," Candler told Billy. "You're never going to meet a woman sitting here."

No sooner had he spoken than a thin woman with stringy hair emerged from the crowd and walked barefoot across the concrete, her shoes in her hand, a walk that was obviously a journey for her. Her hair was a light shade of brown and seriously tousled, her face young and, if not for the slanting drear of alcohol, pretty. She did not stagger, but liquor informed her gait. Her blouse was transparent with sweat, revealing the white triangles of her bra. The modesty of a bra might have affected Candler had he noticed her approach at all. The short skirt covered bare, smooth thighs. Her toenails were maroon. She was aimed at Candler's table, but he did not see her coming. He finally turned to see what Billy Atlas was gawking at, and he had a moment to think that she reminded him of someone before she pivoted on the naked balls of her feet and seated herself on his lap. Candler startled and sloshed beer on the table. Billy Atlas smiled even wider. He liked to believe this type of thing happened to Jimmy all the time.

The woman raised one of the shoes as if to drink from it. "The strap broke," she told Candler. "That's why I fell."

This was the woman with whom he had been dancing. Evidently she had fallen. He was a reckless dancer who did not so much dance *with* someone as *at* her. "I guess I missed missing you," he said, his hand riding gently up her spine. Her dress was wet with perspiration and he didn't want her to lean against him.

Lise Ray teetered on Candler's bony knee. She had been nursing her third Jack-and-Seven when she saw Candler step into the bar with his tubby friend. She immediately downed the drink and ordered another. She watched as he and his pal joined two Asian men at a round table, and somehow her new drink was gone. It was no coincidence that she was at the bar. Toad's was near Candler's house, and there was only one other bar in the Corners. A couple of weeks earlier, she had stumbled upon him there, sitting on a stool at the bar, facing the tap, his glass of beer as golden as a chalice. Sweat in his hair told her that he had been dancing. She had touched his shoulder and rocked her head in the direction of the dance floor. He acquiesced without a word. He was a surprisingly good dancer. When the song ended, he smiled at her but did not introduce himself or offer to buy her a drink. In another thirty minutes, he left the bar with an overdressed woman from a table of full of overdressed women. A woman he preferred to Lise.

That night, she was tempted to go home with the bartender, a balding, goateed man who flirted with increasing seriousness the longer she remained at Toad's. What was the value of three years of celibacy on the open market? She was curious to find out, yet she resisted, even after the bartender let her drink for free.

Tell me about yourself, he said.

She offered him an unhappy smile and the minimum biography possible: she came from Missouri and sold clothing for a living.

I've seen you in here before, he said and she mentioned the proximity of her apartment.

I live in the sticks, he told her and left to pour a round of shots for a gang of middle-aged cretins in matching polo shirts.

I dropped out of law school, he said upon returning.

I have season four of The Wire.

Lise asked for stuffed olives.

My family owns a ranch, but there's nobody left out there anymore but me.

Amid the pressure of great events, a general principle gives no help, he said. *That's Hegel. You ever read Hegel?*

That guy doesn't know you exist. He isn't worthy of you. He's just some clown who can dance a little and puts mousse in his hair.

He's sweating, she explained. It isn't mousse.

I'm going to fire up the grill, he said. *This job encourages eating funny hours. My freezer is loaded. Steak, hamburger, venison. Fresh tomatoes in the hothouse. The guest room has a private patio. I inherited an Otto Mueller, a nude in a landscape.*

I'm not bringing up nudes to make you think of sex. I just like talking to you.

Well then, he said after a while.

Nothing great in the world has ever been accomplished without passion. Hegel, he added.

The same bartender was working again, but he was too busy to flirt—or perhaps he had written her off. It didn't matter. She ordered one more Jack-and-Seven and finished it while Candler danced with a woman who did not look old enough to legally drink. Lise advanced to the general vicinity of his table. "Do you want—" She pointed at the moving bodies, and "Sure," he responded. They danced to three songs before the measly strap that held her upright gave way.

As for Candler, he did not know that he had met her before. He did not recognize her—or did not fully recognize her. Some part of him laid claim to her, but he could not consciously touch it. She had grown a little heavier and a lot smarter since Los Angeles, and Candler was not the only one who might have failed to recognize her. She thought her friends from Missouri or her associates from L.A. (none of whom qualified as a friend) might not recognize the less slender, healthier-looking, working woman she had become. Her parents would still be able to pick her out of a crowd or ID her body, if it came to that, but they, too, would be surprised by her appearance. Her face carried her features more generously now, and she had greater confidence and was more at peace. Her eyes had lost the desperation that had long been the source of her trouble. She was at once more comfortable in her body and less obvious. People saw what she wanted them to see— her clean face, her strong body, her manicured nails. Every part of her body was under her control, except perhaps her heart, which would not give up its single-minded pursuit of James Candler.

Candler could not place her, distinguished nothing beyond a nagging déjà vu.

"I like the way you dance," she said, putting her hands over her heart. She had boldly plopped down upon him, but she didn't know what to do with her hands. Once upon a time she provided strangers with lap dances, as many as a dozen in a night, and never worried about what to do with her hands. "Most men don't dance worth a damn."

"It's my only talent," he said.

"We'll see about that."

Candler introduced Billy Atlas, saying, "We've been friends since grade school."

"You'd know then," she said to Billy. "He have any talents besides dancing?"

Billy Atlas displayed his oversized teeth, happy to have a woman speak to him even if she was perched on another man's thighs. "Let's see," he said, *"talent."* His eyes worked the bar's dim stratosphere for a moment, as if the details of their long friendship hovered there. Finally he said, "He knows the words to the preamble to the Constitution. We learned it in American history sophomore year."

"Just the preamble?" she said and whapped Candler's chest with her hand. "For once I'd like to meet a man who can get to the actual amble."

Candler laughed. Though he could not have articulated the thought, the woman's witty line reminded him of Karly Hopper. It was the kind of thing she might have said without irony or the intention of humor. This moment of cleverness pushed open a door in his mind to the cubicle bearing the label *an interesting woman.* His mind held many such rooms, and the one labeled *a worthy person* held Jane Goodall, Clay Hao, Cornel West, and even the Barnstone. But no one ever entered the room labeled *an interesting woman* but women he found both attractive and compelling, and they never stayed there long. They were either tossed out after he discovered their entry was in error, or they were ushered along to the next space, this one with the label *a fascinating woman*. With one exception, no woman ever made it to *fascinating* without first residing in *interesting,* and that exception was Lolly Powell. She burst through all of the barriers and splashed down in *fascinating* in the first moments of their acquaintance.

"What do you want to know about me?" the woman asked him.

"Not one thing," he said. "I'm happy to have you sit anonymously on my lap."

She squirmed, and the movement of her thighs sent a charge running through him.

"What if I want to know something more about you?" she asked.

"He's a psychologist," Billy said.

"No, I'm not," Candler said. "Just a counselor."

"Close enough," Billy insisted. "He talks to people."

"Tell me about it," she said.

It was his turn to stare at the ceiling. He could not tell a total stranger anything substantial about his clients, but he decided he could tell her something. "I have this client we call the War Vet, although he's really still in the army."

"How old is he?"

"Twenty or so. I don't remember exactly. Been in Iraq two tours already."

"I like the story fair to middling so far. What's happened to him?"

"He came to my office today to finish his evaluation." Candler described the conversation he'd had with Guillermo Mendez and the man's impossible request.

"And what have you done?"

He hadn't done anything, but that made for a lousy ending. He shrugged. "I'm not supposed to talk about clients," he said and she rolled her eyes as if he were teasing. He thought to look about for the Hao brothers. He ought to get this woman off his lap.

"Too late," she said. "You have to tell me what report you wrote."

He told her what she wanted to hear. "Against my better judgment, I recommended that he be kept out of Iraq and finish his duty in the U.S." He told himself that he could actually write the report that way if he so decided. Simultaneously, he understood that he *wouldn't* decide to do it. As long as the report was still unwritten, he wasn't lying, merely pleasing this barefoot, damp-thighed, *interesting* woman. "I'm probably going to catch hell about it later."

She kissed his cheek. "That story is completely self-serving. It makes you the hero."

"Got him a kiss," Billy said. "You expect him to tell stories that make him look bad?"

"I've regretted doing it." Candler was extemporizing now. "I like the kid, but it's going to blow up in my face. Could cost me a promotion." He wasn't so much working the story now as thinking aloud. He imagined making a deal with Mendez, requiring therapy in exchange for the report. Such things could be done, but he would not do them. Nevertheless, he believed he had made an impression on this barefoot woman, which must be what he had wanted to do.

"Don't you want to know my name?" She put her free arm around his neck, her mouth close to his face. She set her shoes on the bar table and drank from his beer.

"I bet we can guess it," Candler said, flashing Billy a conspiratorial look. "It's Agnes, right? Agnes of the Beautiful Legs."

"I'll give you a clue," she said. "It's unusual. Not weird, just unusual."

Candler could think of only one name that fit the bill. "Karly?"

She rolled her eyes and looked to Billy. "You have a guess?"

"George Bush," he said. "I know that fucker must be out here somewhere in disguise."

"You remember Gorgeous George?" Candler asked. He and Billy had been fans of a professional wrestler who went by that name when they were boys.

"She's *not* Gorgeous George in disguise," Billy said. "I guarantee it."

He wasn't impressed with her, Lise decided. Even with her sitting on his lap, he'd rather reminisce with his friend. She felt a pulse of panic, which made her bold. It opened up the old bag of tricks. "Did you say George Bush or *Gorgeous* Bush? 'Cause people do have nicknames."

Candler and Billy both reacted to this, Billy by rocking back in his chair and widening his eyes, and Candler by a hardening pulse in his cock, which rested beneath her bare and shifting thighs. It was the opposite of what he had felt this morning, hiding in his car, watching the house of the impaired girl while his body revolted against him. He had felt like a child caught in a disgraceful act. He could almost feel the movement in his mind, as she walked barefoot and with a drunken sashay into the chamber of *a fascinating woman.*

Candler was drinking but he was not especially drunk, and he was not simply a mindless male driven by sexual craving. He was flattered by this woman's attention, and he felt a distinct sexual charge from her, but he did not believe he was in any danger of infidelity. Only this morning—but this morning seemed ages ago, and if the Road Runner had found the seam in the traffic instead of Candler, maybe it would have been the Porsche crashed by the side of the road, and he might not have been as lucky as the other guy . . . What was he thinking?

Billy was speaking, but Candler interrupted. "I punched a guy in the face today."

"Did he have it coming?" she asked, while Billy said, "You didn't tell me about that."

"He was a jackass, but it was a stupid thing to do."

"How was he a jackass?"

"He was taking advantage of a client, someone who can't take care of herself."

"I think you're full of shit," she said. "I think you spent the whole day in your office prowling the internet for porn."

He nodded. "*That's* where I've seen you before."

She laughed but the statement was too close to home, and she felt a sudden appalling fear. She leaned in close to him. Her breath pulsed against his cheek as she spoke.

"Take me out of here," she said.

Then: "I need shoes."

The heavily slurred, delicately tinkling imperative and declarative sentences might have marked the end of his body's controversy; after all, he certainly wanted to go to bed with her. But some marginally sober part of him resisted.

"I shouldn't," he said.

"You shouldn't let me get shoes?"

Billy, looking for a way back into the conversation, said, "Barefoot women are unbelievably sexy."

She put her arms around Candler's neck in order to stretch her leg and drop a foot in Billy's lap. "Your friend likes me," she said. "Why not you?"

Candler eyed her leg and didn't reply.

"Why really did you punch that guy?"

"He did the old joke . . ." He put his finger on her stomach, and when she looked down, he ran the finger over one breast and up to her chin.

"Not great humor," she said, "but I can't see hitting him. What are you leaving out?"

"He sort of accused me of something."

"You must be guilty of it to get that angry."

"Not possible," he said, but his throat tightened and he barely squeezed it out. To cover, he put his hand on her thigh. When she stood, he stood beside her. Though he did not recognize this woman, he knew her, and that connection, because he could not name it, seemed like something else, possibly something profound. He did not know that the meeting was no accident, and her audacious placement of herself in his lap and her dogged persistence in the face of his resistance were the product not of some general passion or stubborn pathology but of the popular delusional state known as *love*. She had loved him for years. She had followed him to Liberty Corners. Her hair was a different color now and her body was no longer cocaine skinny or silicone voluptuous, but some part of Candler's mind identified her, situated her in relationship to him, recognized her as a former client—he had called them *patients* back then, and the term better fit her, as she had taken her time seeking him, a patience that was either heroic or preposterous, and this night would go a long way toward saying which. He knew all this and did not know it. Why she spiked certain of his erotic chords remained mysterious to him, but the spikes hit their target. She had been in his care for only an hour, a forbidden, lovely client making eyes at him from across a desk.

Ignorant of the deepest movements taking place inside himself, he became dismissive of his resistance. Why was he pretending that he was anything more than just a man? Why, he asked himself, was he acting as if he were not subject to the follies to which men have always succumbed? Why not have a final fling before the yoke? A tiny, expulsive laugh escaped him, a clank of a laugh like a pin slipping from a hinge, at the absurdity of the rationalizations, as he took her hand, leading her unsteadily to the exit.

At the door, as Mick and Karly were leaving, Rhine reminded her that she had promised to ride with him on his cycle.

"Oh, that," she said, laughing and touching his pink shirt. "I didn't mean *that*."

"I brought an extra helmet for you, Karly," Rhine said, a despondent tremor in his voice. He held it out to her. On each side, neatly printed in Magic Marker, it said: KARLY'S HELMET FOR RHINE'S CYCLE.

"That's so sweet," she said, and hugged him, taking the helmet with her as she gripped Mick's arm.

The spring night reminded Mick of thunderstorms even though the sky had only a few slight clouds—a terribly distant sky and the same purple-blue of the hydrangeas that lined the walk of the senior citizens facility. He breathed in the lush air, and because Karly was beside him, descending the stairs with him, he discreetly tucked his nose in her hair. She smelled incredibly fresh. It was mint, he realized. She must have a mint shampoo, but when they reached the concrete drive and she spat into the hedge, he realized it was her gum he had smelled.

In the car, she became exuberant. "That was so *fun*. Wasn't it fun, Mick?" She crossed her legs and took off her shoes, placing them on the floor, beside the helmet.

Mick recalled Peggy Stein, her bare feet in his lap, her knees bent, the skirt riding up her pale thighs. As if she could read his mind, Karly pivoted and touched his knee with her toes.

"Wasn't it so much fun, Mick?"

Mick agreed that it was fun.

"I like everybody so much," she said. "I like Rhine. I like Alonso . . ." She ran down the list of guests, ending with Mick. When she said his name, she rubbed her entire instep over his knee.

A thumbprint moon found the piece of sky directly above Onyx Springs and lit the few windblown clouds. The cloud's light, in turn, backlit the tree limbs that arched over the street above the black asphalt and the moving car, the wobbling leaves casting nighttime shadows.

Mick took his foot from the accelerator to let the car coast through the complicated light. Cars parked in driveways seemed like mottled messages, as if the general design of automobiles was a means of cloaking in metal their vehicular secrets. Some nights, such cagey cars would have made him uneasy, but this night he understood the city was like a storybook forest: alive and mindful and willing to guide him. He understood that his encounter with Ms. Patricia Barnstone—even her name sounded like an enchantment—had helped him see the forest, something in her ordinary friendliness had opened the window, but it was Karly, riding beside him, her bare arches against his thigh, who had made the world come alive. And the living world gave him courage. But was it enough courage? He wanted to tell Karly that he loved her. He wanted to propose marriage. *You ought to do exactly what you want to do,* Ms. Patricia Barnstone had said. How had she known precisely what he needed to hear?

A block before Karly's street, Mick said what he had wanted to say for months. He told her he loved her. She was describing her session with Mr. James Candler, and how he had been racing his car on the freeway. The story sounded improbable, but Mick had decided to believe every word she spoke, and that faith—along with the night, having talked to Barnstone, remembering Peggy Stein—led him to finally speak his heart. He had been dying to say it for so long.

"Oh, Mick," she said. "That's so sweet."

She unbuckled her seat belt and leaned over him, as if to kiss him, but instead she put both her hands on his chest, her face just an inch from his cheek.

The car bounced onto the curb.

"Excuse me," he said.

"Oh, that," she said, raising a hand to wipe the air clean of his mistake. As he bumped back onto the asphalt, she said, "Mrs. Karly . . . What's your last name?"

"Coury," he said.

"Mrs. Karly Coury." She put her hand over her heart and then put her other hand on top of the first. "That's so pretty." Then: "You have to let me out at the corner."

He pulled over. She didn't like anyone to drive her to her door. She lived with family, Mick knew, but not her parents. A cousin, perhaps, an uncle or aunt, maybe grandparents. She wasn't supposed to tell anybody. Her family worried about people taking advantage of her. Yet he knew which house was hers. He had watched her walk and counted the houses. Later he coasted by and memorized the number. Late one night, when his mother thought he was sleeping, he circled her block twelve times to stare at her black windows. He thought, *I'll do this every night,* but he had never driven by again. It was enough to know it was there.

"It's dark," he said now. He wanted to show her that he knew which house was hers. It seemed proof of his love. "You shouldn't walk alone in the dark."

"Everyone knows *that,*" she said, opening the Firebird's door.

He didn't know how to respond. "So it's settled then?"

"Of course, silly."

"We're engaged then?"

"You and me?" she asked.

"You and me," he said. "We're engaged to be married. You'll be Mrs. Karly Coury."

"And you'll be Mr. Karly Coury," she said and laughed.

He laughed, too. When she got out of the car, she said, "That was so fun." Then she sang, *"Wayne's* World, *Wayne's* World."

He watched her form retreat into the darkness of the street. Her hair disappeared first, and then her cutoffs, and then her legs and arms, and then the straps of her halter top. For an instant, he could see the white fringe of her cutoffs, riding up and down like tiny, incandescent teeth. And then she was invisible.

"Mr. and Mrs. Karly Coury," he said, and burst into laughter again, but this bout didn't last long. He was engaged to be married. He needed to take his life seriously.

"Later," Billy Atlas called, as Candler and the woman made their meandering way out of the bar. Billy wondered whether they would miss the doorway and bounce off the wall like the cartoon characters he and Jimmy had loved as boys. The band went on break, and Billy looked at women's legs—a scrutiny unlikely to call up their scorn, as he seemed to be staring at the floor. He missed having a woman around. His ex-wife married him to get her citizenship, a fact he had understood and verbally agreed to from the outset. He had a year of sex, good enchiladas, and frequent bouts of kindness, and now he had the allure that went with being a divorcé.

Before Pilar, he'd had exactly one girlfriend and never had sex with anyone but prostitutes and once, years ago, with Candler's longtime girlfriend Dlu, who had been trying in her way to encourage Billy to see himself as worthwhile. After Candler dumped Dlu, Billy attempted to get rebound action, but she told him very definitely there was no chance. He and Pilar had had sex twice a month. Exactly twice. You could (and he had) set your calendar by it.

The Hao brothers, whom he hardly knew, returned to the table, bearing the prized guitarist, a balding Chicano with a massive frowning mustache, as black as three a.m. Both the Haos had grown beards for their country-and-western band. Really lousy beards. Billy was reminded of his mother's incompetently frosted cupcakes. *That's a bunny hutch,* she'd explain. *That's mud wrestling.*

Clay introduced the guitarist as Enrique, who offered a long-fingered delicate hand. "You in the band?" he asked.

"*God* no," Billy replied. Fearing he'd insulted the Haos, he added, "I have no musical talent whatsoever. I couldn't carry a tune in a suitcase." Their polite smiles were on Candler's behalf, Billy understood. They were being well mannered with Candler's boring friend. He had already made the mistake of saying, *I didn't know Calamari was Chinese.* They had let him know the band's name had nothing to do with their ethnicity. "I hang out with these guys to feed off the leftover groupies," Billy said. This earned him a laugh from the Hao brothers, which doused the momentary hopefulness that had crept into Enrique's black eyes.

"Jimmy took off," he added.

Clay and Duke Hao exchanged a look. They'd seen him leave. Billy wished some pair of brothers somewhere had, once upon a time, shared such a look over Billy's departure with a pretty girl when he was engaged to another pretty girl. No such swap of looks had ever happened on his behalf, and he suspected it never would.

"Whatta you do?" Enrique asked him.

"Nothing at the moment," Billy replied. He explained that he only recently moved to town. "Starting tomorrow I watch over this workshop for differently empowered individuals." He said this carefully because Clay Hao worked with James, and he wanted to sound like a professional.

"That's worse than me," Enrique said, sounding genuinely surprised. "I'm cleaning swimming pools. Of course, I'm twenty-four. If I'm cleaning pools when I'm your age, I'll off myself."

"Yeah," Billy said, "I hear exposure to chlorine makes you simpleminded and in the long term renders people suicidal."

The kid responded by wagging his head vaguely and drinking from his beer. If he understood that Billy was needling him, he gave no indication. Much of Billy's wit went unnoticed, flung over the head of the intended like an errant—but very sharp—spear. This was the curse of being Billy Atlas. One of many curses.

The impassive oaf's gaze that fixed his expression did not genuinely express his character, Billy believed, and yet it was the look he most often gave the world—or at least the masculine world. For as lame as his life with women was, his way with men was worse. Even when he needed nothing from them, he wanted their acceptance, and the role of fool was one men would willingly accept. They generally liked having him around, and they demanded very little of him, only to serve as the constant reminder of what they had surpassed, no matter how measly their circumstances. Billy did not know why he was this way. It had taken him a decade to finish college, and not because he was dumb. It didn't require a lot of smarts to get a degree, but he kept coming up against blockades—all stemming from his screwed-up self. He'd forget deadlines, sleep through exams, work furiously on a paper for weeks but only half finish and have to tack on a conclusion at the last minute. Why? Because that's what it was to be Billy Atlas, and it was relentless. He wasn't a nice-looking guy like Jimmy, but who was he kidding? He looked okay enough. A lot of absolutely goofy-looking men had women, and sometimes they were babes. It wasn't so much what you looked like but how you were perceived, and that stemmed from some cave of personality so deep down in your soul it was like pulling teeth to change it.

He loved women, but—this was something he could never tell anyone, not even Jimmy—he wanted an attractive girlfriend mainly as a ticket into the world of men. Men respected men who were able to get attractive women in the sack. Not that he didn't appreciate sex. He did. He liked it, even though it made him nervous, all the what-do-I-do-now stuff, and the questions he couldn't ask. *Are you getting anything out of this? Does this finger do something for you? Up and down or sideways?* Most disgraceful of all, he could not come unless the woman came first, or if she was at the very least having a good time. This meant that prostitutes were a waste of good money. The pity fuck, which had seemed like a decent target for a while, was also a no-go. Pilar figured this out about him early on in their year together, and to her credit, she quit putting a pillow over her head. She learned to pretend, and he learned to accept her fake moaning as the real thing. He thought—he was still sure—she had grown to like the whole rigmarole. He'd even imagined that maybe she wouldn't want to break up after she passed her exam. That hadn't happened, but she had given him an extra, off the calendar, adios plunge, which had to mean something.

Billy wanted these men at the table of this overwhelmingly mediocre bar to like him. Oh sure, he had matured a lot in recent years, but the approval of these three strangers touched on that remnant feeling from his boyhood, and hadn't it, after all, been the principal source of all the vitality in his life? Anything that he ever accomplished—he wasn't going to ruin the thought by trying to make a list—he owed to that desire to be accepted by other men.

He speculated on the thoughts going through the Haos' heads. They were likely thinking about noble things, like art and beauty and naked women. Or maybe they were just as disposed to make a good impression. Billy had no way of knowing. The sole exception to all this was Jimmy Candler. The one person who saw him for who he was and said *good enough for me.* Billy sipped his beer and imagined Jimmy with the barefoot woman. They'd be at the house by now. They might be sitting side by side on the couch. They might be in the kitchen, leaning against the counter while they drank water. They might be in Jimmy's bedroom. Or maybe he was giving her a tour of the place, his hand on the small of her back. She would see Billy's room then. She would look at the bed where he would sleep tonight. He should have made the bed, but still, it was nice to imagine her there.

Item One:

> You can't live in a goddamn garret over some lawyer's office if you want to be the director of a giant operation. Get out

of Onyx Springs but not all the way to San Diego. Maybe a place in the foothills or out in the county? A place with class? Someplace where you could entertain if you had to?

Item Two:

Forget about this matchbook PhD program. They aren't going to hire a *student* to direct a multimillion-dollar organization. Once you're top pooch, you'll make more money than the psychologists, anyway, who are a bunch of whack-jobs who spend all their time thinking about other people's boners. You'll come to despise and distrust them, take my word.

Item Three:

Ditch the truck. You can't drive around people with deep pockets in a beat-up Tacoma with a hundred thousand miles on the ticker. Get something with flair, a little style, some class. Notice how that word *class* keeps coming up? Don't be afraid of standing out. The bossman ought to stand out.

Item Four:

Does your office always have to smell of Lysol?

Item Five:

Your hair gets shaggy. Do not let that happen. Keep in mind that most of the board members still think if they can't see the top of your ears, you're a hippie. Look the part, and you'll become the right actor for the part.

Item Six:

Quit dipping your stick in every warm piece that shakes her butt at you. Settle down. Or at least appear to settle down until you're officially anointed. I'm dead serious about this. Nothing will screw the pooch faster. You've got to remember this basic fact: no one on the board has had sex with a woman in five or six decades. They see you having fun, they're gonna take it personally.

Item Seven:

Be yourself. Otherwise.

The pickup truck pulled into the parking lot of Congregation of Holy Waters Museum, which was downtown, across from the Onyx Springs Old Farts Facility, and Maura got out. She had visited the museum on a field trip—a dull local show-n-tell with nothing to look at but old clothes. Alonso's place was nearby, and she had a general idea how to get there.

Ernie, the less gruesome one, volunteered to drive her farther to look for the street, but she'd had enough of them. Bert asked if he could have her underwear, and though she liked the idea of telling Mick that it cost her the very panties off her bottom to make the trip, she didn't let Bert have them. That act was in the one-thing-leads-to-another category, and she had already made such a mistake by letting his finger have the run of her vagina.

"You okay here?" Ernie asked.

She told him she was fine. As they drove off, the stereo in the pickup was suddenly turned up loud, some predictable thumper rock, but the truck accelerated slowly. Ernie, driving, wanted to draw no attention, while Bert, wailing up the tunes, was celebrating. She had made Bert's night, she understood, while frightening the hell out of Ernie. She was their adventure: Maura Wood, the human personification of adventure. She watched the truck disappear with the combined feelings of relief and pride—and something else, a slippery something she couldn't name that swam her body and rested in the marrow, making her bones feel alternately bloated and hollow.

Alonso lived on Lapin Avenue, and she knew from the map in her room that Lapin crossed Main Street not far from here. She was confident she'd find it. The street name reminded her of something Mick had told her. His mother was the niece or grandniece or second cousin or *something* of an actress from the black-and-white days: Ida Lupino. It sounded like a made-up name, like Anita Peter, or I. P. Freely, but one time at Barnstone's house she looked her up online, and Ida Lupino was beautiful just the way Mick was. She liked going to Barnstone's. Besides the workshop and the occasional field trip, her visits to Barnstone's were her only legit trips off campus. A freaky ex-patient lived with her, some scary-looking guy who hardly ever talked. Maura's mother liked what she called *a tight ship;* Barnstone's ship would sink like a cement block. But the house was comfortable. Maura didn't have to worry about ruining a veneer. She needed to find some way to make Barnstone her ally in the recruitment—seduction? Was she the kind of person who could seduce another person? She needed Barnstone's *advice* about Mick.

Lapin Street was just far enough from downtown to be residential, a typical Southern California neighborhood with a combination of green yards and cactus fiascos covered with orange rocks. There were trees here and there, and lots of bougainvillea. She spotted Rhine's scooter parked by the curb and checked the address of the house. Alonso's place had grass in its yard. She knew he lived in the garage apartment. She didn't see Mick's car, but the street might have been full of cars earlier, and his ridiculous humper was probably parked around the corner. She checked her watch. Not even eleven o'clock. He'd be here, and he'd be happy to see her.

If she was still in school and a teacher offered a class in "Maura Wood Climbs the Stairs," and the teacher was actually good at his job and it was Maura's only class, she might ultimately be able to account for the weird flux of emotions that made her big and then small, wide and then narrow, as she stepped up the dozen stairs to the lighted windows over the two-car garage. It seemed to take a long time, that climb, as if she were on a rickety ladder that leaned over a dark precipice. The image embarrassed her, and she might have slowed even more to come up with something less melodramatic. Shadows appeared on the curtains, elongated and not quite human in shape. Her climb of that flight of stairs was like a condemned man climbing to the gallows, where maybe the governor waited with a pardon but . . . *Crap*, there was no way *that* was less melodramatic.

At the same time, despite the excitement and trepidation that carried her up the steps, she also understood that she was a teenager with a crush on a boy who liked but didn't love her, and despite how large Mick Coury loomed at this moment in her mind, he was just a boy with nice eyes and a brain that had to be tuned daily with medications to keep it operating. Which meant what? That even as she felt this was one of the most important nights of her life, she also understood she was embracing the role so tightly that it was slightly phony, like a girl playing house but with details from a specific movie, so she was playing Scarlett Johansson playing house, and she herself was suddenly the least important element in her own play.

She knocked on the door.

Alonso swung the door open. "Maura!" he barked out. "Rhine, it's Maura!"

Rhine appeared next to him in a freaky suit like a bad carnival ride. "You just missed Karly," he said sadly. "She was supposed to ride home on my cycle."

Maura understood what that meant. Mick's car was gone and Karly was with him.

"Maura's crying," Rhine said. "Maura, are you crying?"

She thought to say, *Somebody raped me,* but she didn't want anyone to know, and it wasn't even true, was it? It was just a finger, and she didn't even mind, did she? She had told him to go ahead, and if Mick were here, she wouldn't even be upset, would she?

Alonso rocked from one foot to the other, staring at Maura. Crying made her into someone he didn't know. Rhine understood, though. He might cry if he went to a party and just missed Karly. He had almost cried when she left with Mick.

"I didn't cry tonight, Maura, but I'm a man," he offered, as words of condolence. "I can give you a ride on my cycle, Maura. It's parked on this side of the street. You can see it from the porch. Look, Maura. See my cycle?"

Candler and the barefoot woman walked the few blocks to his house, the giant frame-and-stucco ranch-style job with a fatuous front room— *the great room,* the real estate agent called it. The high ceiling had a dopey chandelier that looked like an oversized bird's nest made of glass. He didn't turn on the light for fear she would comment on the thing. He had not done much with the place: hung framed prints by the Impressionists, kept the sheets clean, dishes washed. Every other week a Guatemalan woman vacuumed and scrubbed. Before too long, a plague of mortgage failures would cause the value of the house to drop ninety thousand dollars below the amount Candler owed, and he would walk away from it. By that time, the circumstances of his life would be radically altered.

"Home," he said.

"I've got to pee," the woman replied.

He took her through his bedroom to what the real estate agent had called *the master bathroom* and he had thought *masturbation room,* and even now he wouldn't let himself say *master bathroom* for fear of saying *masturbation room*. God, he was drunker than he'd thought. He nabbed the framed photo of Lolly and him in Trafalgar Square, tucking it in his underwear drawer. He was ridiculously pleased with himself to have this woman here and have the bed made and condoms in the nightstand. If there were going to be doubts and self-recrimination, they would have to wait for sobriety and daylight. It was, quite obviously, the kind of night that might cause him trouble. Or maybe it was a freebie, a night he'd never have to fret about. He might treasure it as a secret rebellion against the promise of fidelity for the remainder of his life. The message light on his answering machine was blinking. Probably Mrs. Coury, or possibly Mick himself. But, no, it was his cell phone he used with clients. It was likely Lolly then, and he certainly did not want to hear her voice at this particular moment. What was it she called a condom? *A French letter.* He laughed aloud. In the bathroom, the medicine cabinet door creaked. Candler pushed open the bathroom door.

"Looking for something?" he asked.

"Evidence of a wife," the young woman said. He still did not know her name. She had a nice, slightly crooked smile. She turned away from him to flush the toilet.

"Ain't got no wife," he said. After a moment, he added, "Does it matter?"

"Yeah," she said, "sure it does."

She put her arms around him, leaning against him so that he backpedaled to the bed, falling onto it with her on top of him. Their heads bumped.

"I have a riddle for you," she said, settling on him, her hands in his hair, his hands lifting her skirt. "How does the Venus de Milo scratch her butt?"

"I don't know," he said. "How?"

She shook her head. "It's a fucking mystery."

They kissed and the clothing came off.

Long after the Haos left and the band quit playing, Billy Atlas and Enrique drank together. When their strength was fortified to the point of falling down, they picked themselves up and approached two women sitting alone at a nearby table.

"*Men*," one of the women said, as they advanced, "who'd've thought we'd meet *men?*"

The other woman laughed.

"So charm us," the first woman demanded.

She was likely forty, Billy guessed, almost a decade more experienced than he, and the top she wore, which was made of a shiny turquoise material, was too tight, squeezing her breasts up and out as if they had just bubbled to the surface of a mountain lake. Enrique immediately chose the other one, leaving Billy with the talker.

"I'm Billy," he told her.

"Like the goat," she replied, adjusting her glossy top. "You've got big teeth, don't you?"

"I guess so, yeah."

"You could use some sun, too. We're both drinking piña coladas."

"I'll get this round," Enrique said. He knew Billy was out of dough.

"Yours is cuter," Billy's gal said to the other woman.

"Yours is better dressed," she responded, which made Billy look appraisingly at his clothing: the suit he had borrowed from Candler's closet.

"I'm pretty drunk," he said. "I'm not much of a drinker."

"I assume you know how things work." The woman's mouth had a natural frown. Her whole face seemed defined by lingering disappointment. "You have to pursue me, buy me drinks, give me compliments, put out for a few meals, maybe some flowers if you're a real catch, and, I don't know, let's say a bracelet, and then I let you in my bed."

"That sounds about right," Billy said. "Or we could skip that long first part."

She snorted. "Fat chance." After a moment she added, "Don't bother being funny unless you absolutely have to. I'm not all that impressed with *funny*."

"I'll try not to be," he said. "Sometimes I can't help it."

"After we go to bed a few times," she said, picking up the thread, "you'll act like a shit, and I'll start feeling bad about myself. We'll get into an argument at some revolting restaurant where you've taken me to save a few stinking pennies. We'll make up, break up, see a counselor, and so on until we can't stand the sight of each other."

The way she looked at him, it was clear he had to contribute something. Her eyes were hopeful while the remainder of her face was steeped in a combo plate of cynicism and low expectations. It occurred to him that she hadn't offered her name.

"I'm Billy," he said again.

"Like the fucking goat," she said.

Her name was Alice, and she worked at Neiman Marcus in leather goods and travel commodities. Enrique made it back with the drinks, but Billy could only stare at the frosted glass of beer, a pretty color but he had passed his limit. He was starting a new job in the morning. Alice had siblings, parents, a condo, a cat, a 401(k) with a hefty number of zeros, a used Rabbit, and plans to take a cruise to Alaska. She thought it likely that she could spend the rest of her life working for Neiman Marcus because she liked leather and had no larger ambitions. That statement came off as a challenge, but Billy let it slide. He offered but she did not want to hear anything about his peyote vision.

"Hearing about somebody's psychedelic trip is like listening to another person's dream," she said, "boring as *hill*." She wanted to know what he did for a living.

By this time, Billy understood the futility of the truth, and yet he was reluctant to commit an out-and-out lie. "I'm not a psychologist, exactly," he said. "You want to hear about a patient?"

"As long as it's not a long story. I don't like long stories."

"There was this boy in the army, and he wanted out," Billy said. "So I wrote a report that got him out."

"That *was* short."

"Actually, it's my friend who's not a psychologist, not me."

"You're not not a psychologist?"

"Not even close to not being a psychologist."

"What does that make you?"

"I'm not not anything," he said. "Not yet."

"Well then," Alice of Neiman Marcus said cheerily. "Fuck off, why don't you?"

Billy nodded and stood. "I need to throw up anyway."

In terms of the physical movement and the specific sensations of the body that accompanied such physical movement, the sex between James Candler and Lise Ray would have fallen into that great, wide, generous category of *so-so*. But a participant's evaluation of intercourse is never merely a measurement on some orgasm scale, and despite everything that pornographic movies have taught us over the years, the corporeal whatnot is rarely first in the hierarchy of sexual pleasure, and this was definitely true this particular night for our participants. Candler loved the wicked mischief of finding a willing and attractive woman and bringing her home to his bed just a couple of weeks before his fiancée would arrive and permanently end his wandering. The whole business was just *so* not him and yet he had pulled it off. And Lise felt the liberation that comes from accomplishing a treasured goal of long standing. That may seem a prosaic description given how lengthily she had imagined the encounter, but rarely is it possible for any event to equal such a buildup. In the release from long-held aspiration, there is also an element of wonder, like the virgin thinking, *I'm doing it, I'm doing it;* which is both rousing and a distraction. She enjoyed the sex more as an event than as a passionate act, a marker on the road that proved she was making progress.

The sex, then, had been thrillingly adequate for both.

The lights were out, the sheets a mess, and their naked bodies were perched on the mattress like fallen figurines on a game board. He weighed more than she had imagined but she did not particularly care about his body. Her hip bones showed sharply, much like her cheekbones, and he liked this anatomical symmetry.

She said, "Are you ready to know my name now?"

Some rather elemental part of his personality did not want to know her name, but he could not say that. He nodded, and she told him.

"Lease?"

She spelled it.

"What brings you to live all the way out in the county?" He was suspicious of any woman living alone in the Corners. Women out this way tended to have husbands, and while he had no intention of seeing her again, he nonetheless hoped she was not another woman hiding a relationship.

"I wasn't wild for San Diego," she said. "The whole beach culture, it's all body nazis and dimwits, or Elmer from Bumfuck, Kansas, with his wife and their three paleface blobs in swimsuits advertising Corona beer or Johnnie Walker or Microsoft."

"You're hardly being fair to Bumfuck," Candler said, "or Microsoft."

"Oh?" she said. "You like 'em corn-fed?"

All at once he realized that he hated this conversation.

"Let's not be so entertaining," he said. "Let's just talk. Tell me something about yourself."

She pulled the sheet over them. He had no idea that she had loved him for what seemed to her a very long time. She intuited that she would have to continuously forgive him for that ignorance, or she would not be able to be with him. She liked that he had stopped the exchange, that he wanted them on a more meaningful conversational road. When they first entered the room, she had noticed the photograph of him with an attractive woman, younger than Lise and prettier, though overly cutesy in her frilly dress and skillful smile. While she was in the bathroom, he had hidden the picture and she appreciated that. (That he was cheating on someone had been evident from the start.) After sex, when it was his turn to duck into the bathroom, she opened the drawer by his nightstand, where she found a stash of mild sex magazines: *Penthouse* and something called *Naked Volleyball*, the porn of generations past. This find also pleased her. It made him seem upstanding in a retro way, without being a complete stooge. When Lise liked somebody, she accumulated evidence that supported her estimation of his character. No matter what the evidence happened to be, she managed to find it endearing. Now he wanted to know something about her. Her evidence would make him flee. She had reinvented herself, turned her life around, become a new person. That might impress him, but it required her to divulge the past, the thorny mire from which she had emerged. Those thorns were sharp.

She leaned down and touched her lips to his chest, a quick kiss, and said, "I like men who can dance. Your turn."

"I like women who like men who can dance."

"Now who's being entertaining?"

"All right, let's see. I'm a counselor at the rehab center in Onyx Springs. I've been there three years."

"I work in a clothing store, a nice place. Expensive, but not the dreadful stuff you usually see in shops like that." The boutique was called *Whispers and Lies*. Lise worked on commission. Her colleagues offered customers nothing but compliments, but she knew better. *It's not that you look bad in it,* she would say, *but the way it emphasizes your hips isn't flattering.* Women asked for her by name. She made a decent living, picked up college classes here and there, had a group of friends.

How could she convey all of this, the terms of her new life, and indicate how precious it was to her? He had no idea that he had made it possible. She decided she was less curious about whether she could win him away from the cutesy dish in the photo, which seemed unlikely, than about whether in the best of circumstances she might have been able to love him. She decided this, and immediately wondered whether she believed it. "Beautiful clothing," she went on. "I think I might like to open my own shop one day."

"See how easy this is?" He reached for pillows to stall. All he could think to say next was that he was engaged to be married and his fiancée was arriving in a couple of weeks to live with him, and he was a complete shit for bringing another woman to his bed. The thought crowded out all others, even though he did not *feel* like a shit. He should, but he didn't. "I drive a stupid car," he said, "a Porsche. My boss owns a Corvette and told me I ought to get a Corvette, which was out of the question and not my obsession but his, and then this opportunity for the Boxster came out of nowhere, and I went after it as if I *had* wanted a Corvette. I bought it used and got an amazing deal, and my car payment is nonetheless greater than my house payment."

"You own this place?"

"For better or worse, yes. I guess I could have said that, too: I live in a stucco warehouse. Too big and people tell me it's not so attractive, and I guess the front is overwhelmed by the garage. But the unincorporated parts of the county are having hard times, and I got it cheap, considering that it's four bedrooms."

"It's kind of big for one person."

"My friend Billy has moved in. You met him." He hesitated and it showed. "And my sister is coming to stay with me pretty soon." In a burst of bravery, he added, "And my girlfriend."

She did not let herself show any reaction, entering his honesty as another point in his favor. "I chose you because you look so square-johnish but you dance like a mad genius. It made me think there must be a couple of things to you. Typical guys are, at most, one-thingers. Some can't quite even cut it at the level of one." After a moment's hesitation she added, "When does your girlfriend get here?"

"Couple of weeks."

"Two weeks," she said. "You want to be with me for two weeks?"

"Then what?" he asked, but he slid his hand over her hip as he spoke, the tips of his fingers finding the divide in her ass.

"Then I disappear from your life like the bubbles from a beer you leave in the sun."

"I've always wondered where those bubbles go."

"Ocean Beach," she said. "One of my girlfriends is looking for a roomie. I'll be on the opposite side of this thriving metropolis."

"Two weeks," he said. "Maybe." Then, "Can I trust you?"

She kissed him.

Neither had the perspective to see that their congress would never have happened had Candler not come unglued that morning, racing on the freeway, punching a stranger, telling a mentally impaired client all about it. Likewise, Lise would not have been impressed with Candler had he not entered her life when she was falling apart. Neither had the whole story.

To review: both parties were delighted with the tepid, drunken, utterly unexceptional sex. They followed it up with another bout— slower this time, pleasanter. And then, after another brief interlude of chatter and resettling, they slept. They were sleeping when Billy Atlas stumbled into Jimmy's big house and quietly shut the door. He took off his shoes to tiptoe past, falling heavily against the wall while removing each shoe. Did he hesitate by the door to Jimmy's bedroom? Did he listen for sounds of lovemaking?

Well, did he?

PART TWO

Two-Week Time Machine

> You were a stranger to your sorrow;
> therefore fate has cursed you.
> —EURIPIDES

4

DAY 1:

Friday morning, Mick parked as usual on Juniper Street, at the corner of Lantana Avenue, to wait for Karly. Nirvana performed on his CD player, a band he'd loved before his illness. He could understand why he used to like this music, but he couldn't say he liked it now. It was insistent in a way that made him anxious. A part of the chorus of one song, though, stuck with him.

> *Here we are now, entertain us*
> *I feel stupid and contagious*

Because he'd taken his meds late the previous day, he'd taken only a quarter this morning, and yet he felt precisely stupid and contagious. It had to be a good song to nail that down.

He believed if he listened enough to the things that used to please him, they might please him again. They might make him well. Something was going to make him well, and it was impossible to say exactly what it might be. Kurt Cobain could maybe do it.

He didn't want Mr. James Candler calling him out again, embarrassing him in front of his friends, but he didn't want to go through life a zombie, either. He needed a balance between ragging and dragging. His therapist had twice lowered his dose, but she wouldn't go any lower. So it was up to Mick—partial doses, skipped days, experiments.

Earlier, before leaving the house, he had told his brother that he and Karly were engaged. "She's pretty," Craig said. He had met her twice but only briefly each time. "What's wrong with her?" he asked. "I mean, why is she at the Center?"

Mick admitted that he had no clear idea. She was friendly to everyone, and she was forgiving of people; it was hard for him to think that she might have an emotional problem. Maybe she had trouble concentrating, but he was pretty sure she didn't take meds. Sometimes, if she didn't want to talk about a subject, she'd act like she couldn't understand, which was more polite than cutting somebody off. Sometimes she genuinely didn't understand, but no one understood everything. Some would say she wasn't bright, but even acknowledging what others might think felt like a betrayal, a denial of the woman who made his heart swell, his veins throb, his thoughts swirl. Karly was his love, and he would not indulge in the transgression of imagining that she could be better.

Karly lived in the leafy part of town, and a lot of the sunlight was lost in the leaves, especially on the sidewalk where she would soon walk. There was something about the distance that sunlight traveled only to be stopped by leaves just a few feet before the concrete where Karly Hopper—*his fiancée*—would momentarily walk, that million-mile journey of the light impeded by the implausibly transient leaves, no thicker than magazine paper, with their wobbly inconstancy that randomly blocked some rays and permitted others to reach completion: it seemed so heartbreaking to Mick, that such an incredible passage could fall short of the earth just a few feet before—Karly! She appeared up the street, on the walk. She was possibly late. It was hard to tell. He was invariably early, and he never thought to look at his watch once he caught a glimpse of her. She wore a black dress with high black boots, more like a party outfit than work clothes, a space between the top of the boot and the hem of the skirt, an interval of leg, bare flesh-colored legs in locomotion. He did not look away to check the time, but watched that winking of flesh on one side and then the other. She passed through the patches of light and moving shade, oblivious to the celestial tragedy surrounding her. The passenger door flew open.

"Hi, Mick!" she said, as if they had not seen each other for weeks. "You look so good in that jacket."

Mick had decided to wear a suit and tie to work. He was in a suit and she, a party dress. They were on the same page, weren't they? He worried that he was maybe inspired by the suit Rhine wore last night to Alonso's party, but now that she had dressed up too, he felt jubilant. He had thought a long time about how to greet her this morning, how to convey their status as engaged people without making her uncomfortable.

"How are you, my betrothed?"

"I have a new joke for you," she said. "I can read it while we drive." She showed him two sheets of lined paper. The scrawl of ink on them was enormous, and he thought her disability might have to do with muscles and motor skills. "What did the reindeer—it's a Christmas joke. I know it isn't Christmastime. Do you still want to hear it?"

"Of course, my betrothed."

Her handwriting was large and crude, which had to reveal something. She must have a neuromuscular disorder. None of clients at the Center talked about their diagnoses, if they even knew them, but this guess made sense to Mick. Karly had some problem with her muscles or with her brain's control over her muscles. This problem could get worse. Maybe, as an old woman, she would have to be in a wheelchair, and he would have to push her. He imagined himself carrying her from the wheelchair to their bed, pausing to feel her personal heft. Weight was a measure of a person's attractiveness to the planet, wasn't it? The melancholy image made him unreasonably happy. He put the car in gear and pulled into the street.

"I heard it on a movie," Karly said, "and rewinded the DVD nineteen times to get it on paper." She paused then, studying her penmanship or something else about the lined sheet. She seemed to be counting. "Yeah, nineteen times." She turned one of the sheets sideways. "What did—*do*—what do the girl reindeer do while the boy ones are out with Santa Claus?" She looked up from the paper and smiled at him.

Her smile made it difficult to drive. Men had been blinded by less. The trip to the sheltered workshop required changing lanes, merging, signaling. Her smile was like another sun right here in his Firebird.

"So it's Christmas Eve, right?" Karly said. "Do you want to guess? Don't peek at the writing on the paper."

"Knit?"

"What do you mean?"

"Prance?"

"No, silly. But that's a good guess, *pants*."

He slowed the car, as if to help with his concentration. They were almost to the sheltered workshop already. What would be funny? The male reindeer were making deliveries, and giving birth was called a *delivery*, but only females could give birth and so if the males were making deliveries . . .

"Pass out cigars?"

Karly shook her head, delighted. "Not right."

If he hadn't taken any of his meds whatsoever this morning, he would have the answer. He was sure of it. The meds would let thoughts reach the tip of his tongue, just close enough to tease his mouth. Yes! He could literally feel the answer resting on his tongue, like a tingling lozenge, but his tongue was bloated by the meds and only marginally connected to his brain.

"All wrong answers," she said. "Give up, Mick?"

"I can't think of anything."

She raised the papers and read the punch line. "They go to the town and blow a few bucks." She laughed, leaning so far forward that her forehead brushed against the dash.

"That's a good one," he said and laughed with her. Sexual jokes—her way of confirming their engagement, so much subtler than his attempt. Sometimes he worried that she was too sophisticated for him. Not that she was too smart but that she knew the ways of the world. There were lots of ways of being smart.

"That's so funny," she said, "shopping on Christmas Eve."

He took a second and got it again, how she was turning it around to make yet another joke. He laughed harder.

"That was the workshop street turn," she said, "wasn't it?"

"I missed it," he said, nodding, imagining all the work it would take over the years to keep up with her.

The sheltered workshop was suddenly way different. For instance, the new supervisor worked alongside them. He wasn't very good at it, Maura noted, but she liked that he was trying it out. He was going to completely fuck up their progress reports, as if they had all suddenly become master packers, but that meant more money. Free money. He told them to call him *Billy*, just *Billy*, and during their morning break, he shared his lunch, flattened sandwiches with greasy peanut butter windows showing through and not even any jelly, but it was nonetheless unprecedented. He was not at all like Crews. If anything he paid too much attention, smiling and nodding, with big teeth, like a horse. A big nodding horse. He was a moderate fatso and had too much action in his face, like a reasonably cool piano piece played way too quickly. Both of Maura's sisters played the piano, and her little sister was actually good at it. Why was this portly dweeb making her think of her sister? He was trying to see what they were like, this crew that was suddenly his charge, as if it was his intention to find a way to fit in. *You're the boss*, she imagined saying. *We have to fit in with you.*

Unless Billy's cheating brought it up, her work score was going to be crap. She was bugged, bummed, bushwhacked—anything but *depressed*. If she was depressed, she'd have to spew to Barnstone about sneaking out of the dorm and accepting a ride from perverts and missing Mick anyway—Mick who hardly had the time to say hello to her today. Except for getting through the basement window, which was trickier from the outside, she hadn't had trouble sneaking into her room. But she slept badly. She had cried in front of Rhine and Alonso, and that fucking ride in the pickup was a stupid thing to have done. If she told Barnstone about it, Barnstone would have to narc on her, and she'd be in lockdown and totally fucked. If she told Mick about it, he'd think she was pathetic and loose and unbelievably stupid. He'd have to think it because it was *true*.

She wasn't a *chickenshit*, at least. She did what she set out to do. Letting that guy finger her had been dumb, but it was the type of thing she used to do all the time. Now at least she felt fucked over by it. That meant something, didn't it? How could she measure her progress when she didn't know what it felt like to be anyone but herself?

Mick's whole deal with Karly had bumped up a notch, the way he cozied up to her, like he couldn't leave the ditz alone for ten minutes. Maura tried to concentrate on the insipid spider cartons. Who on earth bought all this pantyhose? She'd worn pantyhose maybe twice in her life. Once for her cousin's wedding, and once when she had a role in a play as *the mother*. She'd been in the school theater club and was always cast as the mother or some part meant for a man because she'd been fat. Part of the reason she was willing to put up with this place was that she had lost so much weight. Barnstone's sessions were always outside and they walked while they talked. The cafeteria only served healthy food, and the whole craving, the daily filthy desire to stuff her mouth, had vamoosed. Who knew the reasons? Maybe there was something in the water. Not that she drank the water.

Mick, not even beside her today on the assembly line, worked at a furious pace. He had cut down on his meds or quit using the stuff entirely. This was his ongoing drama—to take the dope or not. He was definitely more fun without it. She wanted him to drop the meds but smoke pot, which ought to slow him down just enough to keep him in the sane spectrum. If she could keep him stoned, he'd be fine.

"It's not just the cash register," the supervisor was saying. This Billy used to run a convenience store in Flagstaff, Arizona, and he was telling everybody about the requirements of the working world. "I stocked the shelves, kept the cooler filled, mopped the floor, cleaned the toilet, did the inventory." He counted on his fingers. "There's a lot goes into it."

"That's so great," Karly said. "Mick, isn't that so great?"

"I bought lunch at the Pic Qwik last Tuesday during lunch break," Rhine said. "That's a convenience store. The Pic Qwik."

"Do you get a lot of nickels?" Karly asked.

"Nickels, dimes, quarters," Billy Atlas said expansively, "ones, fives, tens, twenties, and the occasional fifty- or hundred-dollar bill."

"I know who's on the hundred-dollar bill," Rhine said. "Karly, do you know who's on the hundred-dollar bill?"

"I like stores," Karly said. "I make a shopping list before I go to the grocery store." After a second's pause, she added, "But I hate nickels."

Billy shrugged. "You get used to them."

"Karly, do you know who's on—"

"Just fucking tell us, will you?" Maura said.

"Oops," Billy Atlas said. He smiled at Maura, showing his horse teeth and that dopey smile that would not stay off his face. "They discourage swearing at the factory, so I have to discourage it here." He shrugged expressively. "Them's the rules."

"Tom Cruise is on the hundred-dollar bill," Rhine said.

"Everybody knows that," Karly said happily.

"Are you genuinely an idiot?" Maura directed the question to Rhine. "Or are you trying to be funny?"

A tinkling alarm sounded, indicating it was time for their morning break.

"*Idiot* is one of the words the Center doesn't want you using," Billy said. "They don't want a lot of labels tossed around." He showed her his fat teeth again. You could crack walnuts with teeth like that. He examined the transport boxes. "I think all of you made more than me."

"We been here longer," Alonso Duran said, his voice today like a locomotive. "I been here longer, Rhine's been here longer . . ." He continued his list as he headed for the bathroom to masturbate.

Maura grabbed her ashtray and led Mick to the parking lot. She had to pull on his arm to keep him from wandering over to make moon-eyes at Karly. "You can't make me smoke alone," she said. "It's inhumane."

The day was sweltering. When had it gotten so hot? She rarely noticed the weather since coming to California. In Minnesota, people talked about it all the time, checking the Weather Channel and sometimes, before a trip, calling the Highway Patrol. Were the roads open? Was the street passable? Out here, there was hot, warm, and not particularly warm. What difference did it make? She lit up, thinking about words for *hot as hell* that made the temperature appealing—*sultry*, for example, *sunny*. She didn't feel quite right. She'd had the opportunity to ream Rhine, but her response was halfhearted. He had given her a ride on his scooter back to the Center from Alonso's house, telling her whenever he was going to turn or slow down. He was a fuckberry, but she had appreciated the ride and liked the wind in her hair.

"You're going to die." Cecil Fresnay had followed them outside. He was pointing at her cigarette.

Maura blew smoke into his face. "Now we're going together, numbnuts."

Cecil laughed. He liked the smoke. "Do it again."

"What's that?" Maura said, cocking her head. She put her hand to her ear. "I hear Billy calling for you."

"Crews doesn't work here anymore," Cecil said.

"Billy's going to be angry if you don't hurry."

Cecil moved his mouth around—smiling, slobbering, about to cry, some damn thing—and left them. The roach stub had a hideous mouth.

"Don't you think it's insulting to be on the same work line as that drooler?"

Mick needed no time to think. "No. Nope. Unh-uh."

"I'm insulted enough for the both of us."

"We're all different. Effervescent," Mick said. "Dance to your own whatev you call it."

"Cecil's practically a four-year-old."

"I like four-year-olds." He nodded at the cigarette. "I used to smoke. Puffed at parties, my car. Before the wheezus, of course."

"Before you got loony?"

He nodded again. "Tried to quit. Couldn't. Tried. Couldn't. Too craving, like it was inside my skin."

"But you *have* quit."

"The want to smoke went away with . . ." A tremor ran through him, as if he were cold. "Rhine keeps a surgical mask in his scoot scoot scooter for in case people're smoking."

"Rhine has a pinecone shoved so far up his ass he smells the mountains."

Mick laughed. "He can be irrigating, but I like Rhine, dig that boy, also Alonso and of certainly Karly, and not to mention, but I do mention, the incomparable Maura Wood, who chimneys and wheedlesque humor."

"I know who skipped his morning cocktail."

Mick's smile disappeared and he nodded. "Half skipped. Ski-doodled. Less than half. Less I forgot the half."

"Go ahead and jabber if you want. I can't make sense of it, but I don't mind."

Mick laughed, harder than he expected, harder than was called for. "It's just this wrinkling in the words going from here to 'ternity in their cable cars, and what do I care if I can't get every single one to line up like we did—'member?—in grading school with the pink skirts that you weren't supposed to, if you were me, touch and that time after dance class when I stuck my head through the dance curtain where the dance girls were dressing and they giggled and covered and stars were shining in their hair."

"You have the wildest mouth," Maura said.

"We're engaged," he replied. "Me. With Karly."

"You're what?"

Mick tried to slow his tongue, but there seemed to be mercury flowing over it, as if from a busted thermometer, and he could not stop the metallic flow. "I wanted to tell you" *earlier but* "the others" *were there and those clowns . . .*

"You told the others and not me?"

"No. No. No. I didn't tell because the others were, and everyone, with that one saying rudely, and I didn't want with them."

"You proposed?"

He nodded and breathed deeply.

"You asked her to marry you? Karly?"

He nodded again.

"She said she would marry you?"

He kept nodding.

"That's why you've been so . . . why you've been hanging with her so much? That's . . . that's wild." Her voice caved at the end, her chest having developed a hole that was widening, like the top of a tornado. *Hey, sweetheart, want a ride?*

"What's wild?" Billy Atlas had come outside to advise them that the break was ending.

"Mick is getting married," Maura said. To Mick, she added, "No shit?"

"No shit whatsoever," he said. "I'm going to engage a bride in the aisle."

"I used to be married," Billy said. "Who's the bride?"

"Karly Hopper," Maura said, "the complete bingo head."

Mick laughed again.

"She's a hottie," Billy said. "I've promised to teach her nickels."

"Yeah yeah," Maura said. "Teach her pocket change." She colored, embarrassed by her anger, but what would Mick be to her but pocket change? She charged past the men and through the door to the assembly butterfly, surprised to discover that she was not going to cry. Surprised and proud. And devastated. She was such an ass. As stupid as any of them.

DAY 2:

The front porch of James Candler's childhood home was made of wooden planks all in a row, like piano keys, and painted a soft off-white, also like piano keys. It faced north, making it the coolest place in summer for the boys to play if they had to be outside, and they almost always had to be outside. May Candler did not want them in the house, which was old and made of adobe, impossible to keep clean, the exterior walls as thick as a grown man was wide, with fine dust, like the ash of a paper fire, continually descending from the walls to the furniture and floor. May didn't want the boys adding to it with their grime. Sometimes they were even given their dinner on the porch.

The Candlers lived west of the freeway on what was, at that time, the unfashionable side of Tucson. Their street had mesquite trees, oleander hedges, and old houses that had been tacked on to over the years and that spread out unevenly across the sandy lots like unfolded luggage. Their home had once been the bunkhouse for a ranch and was set far back from the residential street, connected by a long sandy drive. Behind the house ran a crooked yard, the lot so lengthy that three cross streets would dead-end along its border. The entire property was enclosed, the quality of the fencing deteriorating the farther it got from the road, a handsome wooden fence turning to chain-link, which connected to a crumbling concrete-block wall. The back of the property had posts of upended railroad ties connected by crimped field wire, into which were strung vertical ocotillo stalks, most of them alive and taller than any man. The fence bloomed in the spring, the tips of the stalks engorged with the nectar that brought the hummingbirds the boys loved, their nearly invisible wings propelling them through the wholly invisible air.

"I've got three Wade Boggses," Jimmy Candler said. He kept his baseball cards in a shoebox covered with comic book stickers. The cards within were habitually bundled in rubber bands, segregating them into teams.

"I got three bogs to wade," Billy Atlas replied. His cards were in a faux-Tupperware box, which he always brought when he spent the night but this day was reluctant to open, a curling crack in one of its transparent sides, over which he had applied a long strip of tape, now yellowing, a big-mouthed frown, an indignant catfish of tape. He clung to the box and to a residual understanding that he always got the short end of the stick in their deals.

These two were sitting on the floor of the front porch, Jimmy in cutoff jeans and a blue T-shirt, Billy in long green pants with cuffs and holes in the knees, a white T-shirt that stretched unappealingly over his gut. They both wore sneakers and white socks. They were twelve years old.

"And I've got two Danny Tartabulls," Jimmy said.

"I'm not making any trades," Billy insisted.

"What's the point if we don't make trades?"

"Baseball doesn't have to have a point," Billy said, "it's baseball."

Nineteen eighty-seven, the middle of June, 8:22 in the morning, and they had been up since 6:00. The expected afternoon temperature was 104 degrees. In those days, the morning had several stages and each stage could hold a dozen surprises and the distance between waking and sleeping was too great to be measured by anything so flimsy as hours. So far they had eaten breakfast, played catch, run through the sprinkler, watered the garden, raced sticks in the irrigation canal, imagined the end of the world by fire, eaten a snack, wrestled with the dog, and examined Jimmy's baseball cards. It was one of many broad-handled summer days that could not be grasped by a single fist or contained in a single sentence, and it was just beginning. They decided—abruptly, for no evident reason—to take their first dunking of the day.

At the rear of the property was an old cistern, an uncovered brick rectangle the size of a truck bed with which, by means of an elaborate system of canals and culverts, the Candlers watered the yard, and into which the boys dipped themselves during the long Arizona summer. The big trees on the lot—sycamores and mulberries and oaks—had never been trimmed, except for the haphazard cuts made by the boys to accommodate their tree houses, which permitted them views of the long stretches of high grass, a fenced garden tended erratically by Jimmy's mother, the shallow concrete irrigation canals, the adobe rubble of smaller dwellings behind the main house, and in the far back, a stretch of unmolested desert, with ocotillo, creosote, yucca, barrel cactus, prickly pear, and two giant saguaros—and beyond that, the living fence.

The boys took off their shoes and socks and Jimmy shed his T-shirt. They leapt into the cistern, sinking to the depths, the sun on the surface of the water above their heads like tossed coins of light floating uneasily on the waves. Though the water was clear and they could see far into it, the cistern seemed to have no bottom. They had tried, numerous times, to swim to the base of the well, and never succeeded. They imagined that it had no floor, that it continued indefinitely through the center of the earth and up to the surface on the other side of the globe, a rectilinear tube of water connecting disparate continents. They imagined surfacing in Africa or the Soviet Union or some island populated by smiling girls who wore flowers instead of shirts.

The desert, Jimmy's father taught them, had ephemeral rivers on the surface and covert rivers beneath the surface, and cracks and caverns down below, along with arroyos and mesas and crags and cliffs above. The cistern was fed, Mr. Candler had explained, by an underground stream, whose irregular passage caused the water to rise and fall, as did the metal gate the boys raised by means of a wheel—like a horizontal steering wheel—to fill the shallow irrigation canal, which would flood the various patches of grass, the garden, the dirt around the trees, according to which of the gates were lifted and which were lowered, a miniature mechanical system of locks and troughs and dams. If the water in the cistern was low, they worked the handle on the metal pump, which would shoot water into the canal. The pump was painted green, the same shade as the big cacti in the yard, and bare metal showed like wounds beneath the flaking paint, lesions the color of steel.

When the water was more than a few inches from the top of the cistern, it could be difficult climbing out, hands on the top bricks, muscles straining in the forearms. They each managed it without assistance, though Billy had to lie on his belly and roll forward, his wet clothing picking up long slashes of dirt. They put on their shoes and socks, once again, and Jimmy thrust his head into his shirt. Even though it was not yet nine a.m., they were almost dry by the time they reached the porch. Their damp pants left ovals on the plank floor, like mouths, like the wet places lips were always making, like the coloring on a topo map that indicated forests or high elevation or great swamps.

On the west end of the plank porch was a card table with folding chairs, and on the east end, a formerly maroon, once-velvet couch beneath a wide window, which was unscreened and cracked open all summer, the evaporative cooler pushing cool air out through the gap, over the ledge, and down onto the couch, where the dog, who was not permitted in the house, perpetually lay, a fat brown corgi, slightly cross-eyed and sternly proud, often accompanied on the couch by one of the boys, who would pause on the hairy cushions to catch some of the cool air bleeding through the window and pet the dog, whose name was The Dog—his parents' idea of humor and Jimmy thought it was funny, too, and further evidence that his family was extraordinary. (A boy didn't need much proof to think his family was like no other, better, smarter, braver, stronger, more beautiful, more kind.)

The Dog would settle on the left cushion, always that same cushion, would bark at you if you sat there. The windows had no screens and yellow curtains fluttered in and out—an image that Jimmy's mother had painted, managing somehow to capture the motion. Whenever she set up her easel on the porch, the boys knew they had to leave. Jimmy's father might set up his easel in the yard, in the long grass or the shade beneath the trees, and the boys would make loops around the man and the tall transparent pitcher sweating on the tiny table that Frederick Candler would park next to his easel. He would fill his glass from the pitcher, that bubbling, sweating pitcher with an indefinable smell, which, years later, Jimmy—by then James—would identify as tonic, a pitcher of gin and tonic, and the adult James could be carried back by that slight smell to his youth, the rambling house in the high Sonora, and the expansive sense of possibility, as wide as the desert sky.

The house was flat-roofed and sometimes, after a rain, Jimmy would see his father, his white hair and white beard, on the roof with a broom, sweeping the puddles into the gutters, and once, after a rare snowfall, his father was on the roof with a shovel, as if he were going to tunnel through the roofing and adobe insulation, down into the dusty rooms. Snow came flying over the side of the house, Jimmy and Billy positioning themselves to be pelted by the shovel-loads of it.

"I'll give you a Wade Boggs, a Tartabull, and a Steve Sax," Jimmy said.

"Steve Sax sucks, and you've got extras of the others," Billy said. "I'm not making any trades."

"You don't even like Dawson," Jimmy accused. "You just want him because I like him."

"He's a good player," Billy said. "Let's eat something."

"We already had a snack."

"What was it?"

"Pimento cheese on that bread you like."

"Oh, yeah, how could I forget that? I'm still hungry, though." He looked past Jimmy. "You're hungry, aren't you?"

Pook shook his head. He was sitting on the couch with The Dog. He had been with them all morning. He'd eaten breakfast beside them, pointed at the flying ball while they played catch, turned the horizontal wheel that raised the metal dam to water the grass and then shut it and opened the gate for the garden, watched the sticks in the irrigation canal, eaten a pimento cheese sandwich on that same bread, and pinned The Dog onto its furry back when it was his turn to wrestle. He had run with them to the cistern but had not jumped in. He had offered nothing about the baseball cards, as he did not play baseball or watch it—unless Jimmy or Billy was playing—and while the boys discussed the possibility of the world burning to a cinder, he had stared at a spider on his shoe: *one leg, 'nother leg, one leg, one leg.* Pook wore a white shirt with sleeves buttoned at the neck and wrists, jeans, white socks, and work boots. He had not said a word since climbing from bed.

"All right," Jimmy said, "I'll give you Boggs, Tartabull, and any Pirate of your choice—except Bobby Bonilla—for Andre Dawson."

Billy, for reasons no one understood, was a Pirates fan.

"Keep Boggs. I've got a rookie Boggs already, and I hate Boggs anyway—he's bowlegged. I'll take Tartabull and any two Pirates I don't already have."

"Boggs is a great hitter."

"Two Pirates."

"Not Bonilla."

"I've got a Bonilla."

"You've got a Bonilla with the White Sox."

"Doesn't matter. I *know* he's a Pirate now, I don't look at the uniform and think, *Gah, I wish he was a Pirate.*"

"I've got a Bonilla *with* the Pirates."

Roadrunners lived on the property, despite the feral cats and the fat corgi, who was really two corgis, the first The Dog, who was put to sleep when Jimmy was six, and the second The Dog, who would survive Jimmy's childhood and was still hobbling around when Jimmy left for college. The current The Dog leapt from the couch and ran, in its short-legged hopping fashion, after a roadrunner that neither Jimmy nor Billy had noticed. They laughed at the suddenness of The Dog's departure and the comedy of its gallop and how, when it became clear the bird would escape, The Dog switched to a cat lounging in the shade of a palo verde, as if the cat had been his target all along and the roadrunner was merely a ruse or an unlikely partner. There was no better dog than a corgi and no better corgi than The Dog; on these facts, the boys agreed.

Pook watched without laughing. He had felt the dog tense beneath his hand and followed the dog's gaze to the yard where the roadrunner was standing, its head turning from side to side, as if it were about to cross a busy street. The Dog leapt from the couch.

It's after it. It's not catching it. Trees' dark blotches. Lines.

The secondary target scampered to the sycamore and up the side of the tree to a branch beyond The Dog's reach, where it turned and stared, without hissing, amused at the attention of the barrel-shaped dog, whose short legs could push its snout within inches of the cat but no closer. Jimmy and Billy had given the feral cats names and tried, unsuccessfully, to tame them. Some had more than one name, as who could be sure with cats whether it was the same as the one they'd seen the day before? The cat in the tree was named Scooter and Lonesome and Thor and Fat Albert and Hunter and Andre Dawson. Giving each of the cats many names multiplied them, and the number of felines on the premises seemed to the boys enormous, and often they wondered how it was that the majority were always hidden. Such crafty animals. So much of the world was just lurking. It gave their lives a sense of theater, the secret audience of creatures no one—not even neuroscientists or space engineers—could understand.

When The Dog returned to the porch, the boys petted him elaborately, celebrating his failure.

"Good dog, The Dog," Jimmy said.

"You weren't even close," Billy added enthusiastically. "You did good, though. Fine and dangly."

The Dog let them salute him for several seconds and then returned to Pook on the couch.

"We should give Same Man a dog," Billy said.

"That's a great idea," Jimmy agreed.

Pook understood what they were saying and got up from the couch. He was allowed to go inside any time he wanted, while Jimmy and Billy were supposed to wait at the door until May Candler evaluated their request to enter. Needing a drink of water would not get them in, as she set out a cooler filled with water and each had a plastic cup with his name on it. Needing to pee didn't cut it, either, as she knew the boys routinely peed in the desert and in the grass and in the cistern and from the tree house. Snacks she put on a tray and set on the porch. Injuries required blood or unconsciousness.

Pook returned with the folder labeled *Same Man*. It was a comic book that the three of them were creating together. He placed the folder on the card table. Jimmy and Billy made up the story, and Pook drew the comic's panels. "How was it possible," Jimmy's father, Frederick Candler, had wondered aloud, "that two artists could procreate and produce a child who cannot draw or paint or sculpt?" He was talking about Jimmy, who could not draw or paint or sculpt, and who came up with an answer for his father's question. He imagined the streams of being flowing from his mother and father, combining into a single river that branched and branched again, and all those streams flowed through his sister, but for himself, one of the streams was blocked—he pictured a horizontal wheel as red as emergency vehicles and screwed down tight, and it was this stream that permitted drawing and painting and sculpting, and for his brother Pook, that particular stream was undammed but some unnameable others were blocked. "You've got that much right," Frederick Candler said when Jimmy described his vision, "your brother's damned all right."

Jimmy planned to write comic books for a living, which Pook would illustrate. The problem was that Pook only drew himself, and how could you have a comic where all of the people looked the same? Jimmy had asked Billy about this, and he suggested that the main character could have a disease that gave him superpowers but it also made everyone look to him just like everyone else, and the comic book would display exactly what the hero saw. This was unquestionably a good idea, and Jimmy decided that he and Billy would write the comic together. They named their hero *Same Man* and a big part of Same Man's job, given his problem, was to keep the good guys and the bad guys straight. Dating, too, was complicated, as he liked girls, even though they all looked like men and the men all looked like him.

"We're going to have to get real psychological with this," Jimmy said.

"What if the girl takes her clothes off?" Billy asked. "You can't have a naked girl that looks like Pook."

"People in comics keep their clothes on."

"But *what if*," Billy insisted.

"He only draws what he draws," Jimmy said.

Billy shook his head sadly. "I feel sorry for Same Man."

Jimmy concurred. He and Billy shared a strong interest in girls—specific girls from school and nonspecific females out there in the bright radioactive sunlight or in that feminine falling time of evening or hidden, like the cats, in the night, their numbers impossible to know. Girls in skirts. Girls in tight jeans. Girls in bathing suits. Girls walking in shoes with thick heels. Girls on one knee. Girls pointing. Girls turning. Girls making their hands into phones and waggling them at their faces. Girls stepping sideways. Girls making faces. Girls lowering their eyes. Girls backing into the ladies' room. Girls covering their surprised mouths with their hands. Girls twisting in their desks as they raised their hands. Girls doing elaborate slapping, chanting routines. Girls dribbling a basketball. Girls in those funny shoes just the size of feet. Girls shading their eyes. Girls coming up from chairs with their backs arched. Girls with a skip in their stride. Girls snapping their fingers when they remembered. Girls with their arms raised and crossed, their fingers holding to their shoulders, and twisting at the waist.

DAY 3:

The boys returned to Same Man early the next morning, unable to recall how they'd lost track of the project the day before. They quickly settled on the images they needed, describing them in detail to Pook. While he drew the panels, they climbed to the sycamore tree house, which had three levels: *base camp,* where the massive lower limbs initially spread, maybe seven feet above the ground; *hideout,* several feet above base camp and out on the thick limb that also held the rope for their tire swing; and *lookout,* high on the main trunk, among a spread of thin arms, a height the boys felt in their lungs and in their arms and in their tingling testes.

They climbed the sycamore several times a day, working their own limbs feverishly, as if all the monuments they had to scale could be made literal and by reaching lookout they were becoming men. Base camp had a floor of lumber, constructed with the help of Jimmy's parents and Pook (working from the ladder's top rung) and even Violet, who sometimes climbed up there to read. The other perches were unofficial, and except for a single board they had nailed themselves at the hideout level, which served no purpose, and a single thick nail at the lookout level, around which they would hang the binoculars, there was no construction but nature's spread of limbs.

One day from the high lookout perch, Jimmy had seen green leaves floating on the cistern's watery ceiling, as tiny as fingernails. And that same evening, with Billy, after skimming and swimming the cistern, and lying in the grass and then climbing to the lookout, they saw Jimmy's parents holding each other and kissing within the confines of the garden, a commonplace event, and yet his father had been painting shirtless that evening and his mother's blouse was pulled by the embrace to reveal a naked slash of pale flesh below her neck, and Jimmy remembered this image the way an android might remember the first time he was plugged in. Sometimes he even dreamed it.

It was in the hideout a year earlier that Jimmy spied his father and brother emerging from a dented Ford Maverick, parked not in their long drive but on the street, and driven by a young woman with blond ringlets (he had the binoculars), whose head projected through the driver-side window to watch them walk away, her lips moving without (he could tell) making a sound while she watched Jimmy's father or Jimmy's brother walk away from her. *Pook has a girlfriend,* Jimmy thought, knowing it could not be true and yet holding tight to the thought, unable to take the leap to the most reasonable approximation of the real—that this pretty girl in a dinged white car loved his father and her infatuation had been encouraged or even provoked by his father, that she was likely a college student, a painter, one of his father's protégés, his lover. *My* how that mouth of hers had taken on so many shapes, and this active mouth, too, would return to him from time to time for the remainder of his life, and he would not understand why he was unable to take his eyes away from the woman whose mouth had roused the memory.

The trees in the yard held the light the way his father had held his mother, and Jimmy understood, without the interference of words, that he wanted to hold a girl in just that manner, a girl whose mouth was like the mouth of the girl in the dented Maverick. And later, during that summer, after his brother killed himself, Jimmy would recall that embrace, which was no longer associated in his mind with his parents, and that girl's mouth, which was the same mouth and the same girl sticking her head out of the same car window but she was no longer looking at his father or his brother, and he would realize this about Pook: he almost never had to deal with the interference of words.

And still later, an autumn afternoon when Jimmy was sixteen and up in the sycamore with his first serious girlfriend, whose flowered blouse hung on a branch beside her white bra, and whose tiny skirt would slip from the gray boards and drift like a giant leaf to the leaf-strewn ground, he would see a cat sleeping in the shade of a ruined wall and the bent knees of what had to be his dead brother watching the sleeping cat, and as he pulled free of the girl to ejaculate on the soft skin of her tummy, his eyes would close and the image would be lost, and when he opened his eyes, even the cat was gone.

"Fished," Pook said, by which he meant *Finished*. He stood beneath them at the trunk of the sycamore. They made their way down to him.

Before looking at the new drawings, they reread the comic from the beginning. The first panel showed Same Man—before he was a superhero—in a baseball uniform, standing in the outfield, eating a flauta as a baseball flew past him. The next panel showed him in a hospital bed, sweating, sick with a high fever from eating too many flautas. The next panel was all words. Jimmy had the best penmanship, and he did the word panels.

YOU LOOK BETTER,
THE NURSE SAID,
HOW ARE YOU FEELING?

A panel showed Same Man looking up at a nurse in a white dress who looked exactly like Same Man.

OH NO!
SAME MAN THINKS,
EVERYBODY LOOKS
THE SAME!

Same Man's dog, which looked a lot like The Dog, they named R. Budd Dwyer, after Frederick Candler's favorite politician, the Pennsylvania state treasurer who, this past January, had held a press conference to say that he was innocent of the kickback charges of which he had been convicted and then pulled out a gun and stuck it in his mouth and killed himself on camera. It took three panels of words to explain who the dog was named after, and then the dog vanished from the comic because it had no superpowers.

Jimmy and Billy had had a lot of trouble deciding what powers the illness had given Same Man. Flying was the best, but too many superheroes already flew. The same went for running fast and seeing through things. They decided to give him a powerful sense of smell. He could sniff out bad guys like a dog, but he could also smell lies and schemes and tricks and shady deals.

"I'm not sure being a good smeller is enough to call him a super-hero," Jimmy said.

"How 'bout also he's real strong?" Billy said. "And wears a costume?"

THIS IS HOW THE WORLD
REALLY LOOKED TO HIM.

They argued about whether he could remember people from before he was sick.

HE COULD REMEMBER
BEFORE HE WAS SICK,
BUT THE MEMORIES
ALL LOOKED LIKE THIS.

Pook's drawings for the comic book—he did them in colored pencil—shared something more substantial than style, which neither Jimmy nor Billy could name.

"Like if you could eat them," Billy said, "they'd all taste from the same food group."

"Mangoes," Jimmy said, agreeing, and they decided on a name for Same Man's nemesis.

MANGO FORTITUDE
WAS NAMED BY
HIS MOTHER,
MRS FORTITUDE.

-

SHE NAMED HIM
MANGO AFTER HER
FAVORITE FRUIT,
THE MANGO.

In Pook's room, the wallpaper had red carnations, faded to the color of watery blood, the paper yellowing and curling along the seams. And he put this wallpaper in Same Man's hotel room, where Mango Fortitude arrived, offering to sell the entire city of New York. Same Man and Mango Fortitude stared at each other. They looked identical except for their shirts. Same Man's had green vertical stripes and Mango Fortitude's had tiny sea horses or possibly shrimp.

SAME MAN
SMELLS TROUBLE.

"Why is he even in a hotel room?" Billy asked.

SAME MAN
WENT ON A TRIP
TO MIAMI.

"But why?" Billy insisted.

FOR BUSINESS.

"Show him having an idea," Jimmy said.

Pook drew a close-up of Same Man's face, his eyes slightly askew, and his lips open, as if about to speak, and another identical pair of lips floating in the air next to Same Man's ear.

FOR SALE?!?!
NEW YORK!?!?!?!

"That's perfect," Jimmy said of the drawing. "How'd you come up with that?"

Pook offered one of his rare responses to a direct question: "My brain told me."

"Now they fight to save New York," Jimmy said.

"He has to change into his outfit," Billy said.

"*Costume,* not outfit. We never decided on a costume."

"Let Pook decide," Billy said. To Pook, he added, "You're the artist. Give him a cool superhero outfit."

"We have to get him out of the hotel room first," Jimmy said.

EXCUSE ME,
SAID SAME MAN.
HE WENT IN
THE CLOSET.

"Show him busting out of the closet in his superhero costume," Jimmy said.

"But Mango will know it's him," Billy pointed out. "There couldn't be anyone else in the closet. He'll blow his secret identity."

They were stuck.

DAY 4:

Lise was on the kitchen side of her Corners efficiency, a paperback novel in hand, dressed in her work clothes. She had read two hundred pages of the novel and could not have named one of the characters or even come up with the name of the planet on which the characters connoitered. It had three moons, she remembered that much, and the main source of protein for the inhabitants was a vine that had the properties of water, bubbling up from underground wells, but who was the main character and what was at stake? How was it possible to read without paying attention?

James Candler was her lover. This thought interjected itself between the sentences and wrecked the narrative's continuity. *James Candler was her lover.* She had to leave in ten minutes for Whispers and Lies, giving herself half an hour to make the drive, which always took forty minutes, but she had to wait that long in case he actually called as he said he would. She hadn't insisted, hadn't made him promise. *James Candler was her lover.* She hadn't trusted herself to give him her cell number, imagining the phone vibrating in her lap as she negotiated traffic. No, she needed to be still, in this single room, which still smelled new, and in which she and he had made love—on the bed, on the couch, bent over the kitchen counter, on the carpet by the door to the bathroom. *James Candler was her lover.* The kitchen counter had been uncomfortable for both of them, its edge made of particleboard that pressed sharply against her abdomen and at her ribs, and she had knocked over the sugar bowl, and sugar had gotten on her hands and her arms to the elbow and her chest and then her lips and cheeks and the tip of her nose, and he'd had to put one foot on a kitchen chair to keep balanced and thrusting, his messy breath damp on her back, and why, if they both were uncomfortable, did they feel obliged to continue their awkward humping when her bed was less than four feet away, not even a wall separating them from it, its quilted cover still on the floor from their last go-round?

The phone's ring interrupted her thoughts. "Call me tomorrow," she had said, "during lunch, if you think of it, and tell me a secret." She let it ring twice.

"Good morning." A man's voice, mechanical in tone, someone taught to sound like a robot. "I'm looking for . . ." A brief pause while the robot read the next name on his list. "Elizabeth Ray. Am I fortunate enough to have found her this fine morning?"

"I'm not buying anything or willing to participate in a survey," she said, "and I'm expecting an important call. Please remove my name from your list." She hung up, staring at the phone as if it had betrayed her.

He had licked the sugar from her arms. His tongue was wider than most tongues, it seemed to her, and if it had hurt, that fucking on the counter, it had nonetheless been necessary, an act of exertion to prove a point—having to do with desire, or with not yet being too old to fuck wherever, or maybe, possibly, conceivably, with love. *James Candler was her lover.* They had fucked all weekend, even when it hurt them to fuck, when every bit of every portion of every involved genitalia was red and raw and shrieking, and yet they managed to reach orgasm, or come close, and the hell of it was: she didn't even care about the sex, particularly, but she cared terribly about the effort, the coming together, the urgency, the nerve and verve of it. *James Candler was her lover.* For two weeks, they would be teenagers again, but also not teenagers. They were separate from the constraints of time, all ages at once. It sounded like the plot to one of her sci-fi novels: *Two-Week Time Machine.*

Not that he was much like the man she had imagined. Or like the man who, in his clean office nestled in that decrepit building, had altered, redirected, and revived her life. That man, too, she had more imagined than encountered, his imperfect excellence the product of her need. If he had been waiting for her when she returned to that old building for her second session, the real him might have spoiled it. Oh, he could be crass, going right for the buttons on her blouse when he walked through the door, handling her ass with what he imagined was discretion while they waited for a table in Ristorante Arrivederci, and he could be insensitive, relaying the details of his trip to London, how he had expected grief and the uneasy requirements of its expression, but found instead a mindless ecstasy in Miss Cute-em's bendy body. But his insensitivity meant that he was not careful around Lise as he had to be around his patients, and that was paramount: he must not think of her as one of his patients. Even though she had been exactly that. He must not see her as she had been in that cheap plastic chair, her hair the color of taffy, and sometimes, in her memory, it seems that she was wearing nothing but Saran wrap. Not true, she knew, but not inaccurate.

The phone rang. She let it ring three times.

"Hey," he said. His voice was nothing special and she liked it.

"I thought that might be you," she told him. "How was your morning?"

"The usual—clients, work gossip, reports to write, and now pastrami on rye. Yours?"

"I put new sheets on my bed. That's an invitation, if you're slow on the uptake."

"You want my secret?"

"Should I sit down?"

"I lived with a woman for six years. I guess that's not a secret, exactly, but I don't usually talk about it."

"Hmm," she said.

"Everyone expected us to marry, including me, but I cut it off. She wasn't right for me, and I found the . . . the . . . the *courage* to cut it off."

"I guess that's a good talent to have," she said. "Heartlessness."

"Not how I'd put it." He laughed. "It was more that I'd painted myself into a corner, but when I realized it was not right for me, I managed to get out of it. Maybe it was severe, I don't know, but . . . Your turn."

She had invented several secrets in anticipation of his call, but she chose to tell him something real. "I used to—this is humiliating. I used to pay to have my pubic hair trimmed, cut in the shape of a heart." It had been her signature when she was a stripper, that bleached-blond heart. "The guy I was seeing at the time liked surprises. It cost me a hundred bucks every trim."

"Where do you find that kind of professional in the grooming business?"

"I thought about it because I just took a shower." She wanted him to picture her naked body. She understood that this was the old her, this was Beth Wray using the most familiar of manipulations. But he was a man, wasn't he? Out there just waiting to be manipulated?

"You're saying you've right now stepped out of the shower?"

"And I'm shaving."

"Shaving your . . ."

"It was dumb to spend a hundred bucks on such a thing, such a *trim*. Not as dumb as the eighty grand you spent for that silly car, but still dumb."

"It was only sixty grand. I got a deal. Don't shave it all off."

"You don't like the bare look?"

"It's all right, I guess, for some married couple in their twentieth year, and they need to shake up the routine. But it doesn't turn me on. It doesn't look *womanly* to me."

"We don't have twenty years or even twenty days. I've already started though. I'll just do a landing strip."

"You're shaving right now?"

"Are you jerking off during your lunch break? What kind of counselor are you?"

"You want to see me tonight?"

"Every night for two weeks. Even if we start hating each other, it's every night until your lady arrives."

"Why? Why do you want to?"

"Another of Lise's experiments in human behavior. Don't think it has anything to do with you. You're just a volunteer, a human subject. I'll debrief you after it's all over."

In the telephonic silence that followed, she could hear her heart beating in its sugar-coated cage, and on his side, a rustling of paper, a squeezing sound—he had taken a bite of his pastrami sandwich. Let him eat, she thought. How long could she happily sit here in silence, knowing he was on the other side, the phone to his ear, listening to the hush of her life?

Finally, he said, "You like Thai food?"

"Mmm-hmm. There, just a rectangular strip. Ninety-degree angles. I may get some tiny runway lights."

"Your secret was better than mine."

"Yours was a pretend secret," she said, and as she spoke the words she understood that she believed them. He was still protecting himself, padding the space between them. Why, if he wasn't the person she had imagined, not the person she had fallen for, why did she still want him? Why did she still thrill to his voice or even his semiattentive silence? "It means you must have a real secret that you won't talk about."

No pause. Not even a beat. "A dark secret. Every romantic hero should have one."

I was a stripper, she thought. *I went to hotel rooms with strange men. I did two guys at once for three hundred dollars cash. I snorted cocaine off the erection of a real estate broker who did not bother to remove his socks or wristwatch to screw me. How romantic is that? What kind of hero am I?*

"I don't know about *dark* secret," she said, "but there's something back there."

He took a breath. He seemed to be thinking. He said, "I have no idea."

In the next silence, she felt the urge—a sliding shudder that resembled panic—to extricate herself, to hang up and let him go. What was he selling, really? Why should she want to remain on his call list? He was fucking around on his fiancée, and she was having a fling with a fantasy. To choke back these thoughts, she said aloud, "James Candler is my lover."

Following another pause, he said, "For now."

Only after they had ended the call and she was sitting in the kitchen chair alone, happy and unhappy simultaneously, a bell just rung that cannot hear its tone only register the vibrations, did she recall it: *Tristan.* The name of the planet with three moons. She looked for the paperback but could not find it. Hadn't she held it in her hands? How could it have disappeared?

She glanced at the kitchen clock, grabbed her keys and purse, and hurried for the door. The paperback lay on the floor, beneath her chair. It had been invisible to her because it had landed on its spine and leaned against the chair's legs. The characters on the cover—a man with desperate hair and a shiny V-neck shirt and a woman in what appeared to be space age underwear—watched Lise leave her apartment, disappointed not to be found, wondering what in this tepid world of hers could be so important that she would leave them and Tristan and Tristan's moons on the carpeted floor.

DAY 5:

Candler left the evaluation floor and hurried to his desk, holding the words in his head. Some years ago, while he was at the clinic in L.A., he began transcribing certain lines spoken by clients. The kid who got him started was homeless and undiagnosed—a recent college dropout—who tried to explain how it felt to sleep under the freeway: "The loud beneath the image sketches, but also there's the buttoned-up absence we don't need to distill." Candler transcribed the words later, from a tape of the session, into a fresh notebook, which he labeled *Cabbage*, a title he'd stolen from one of his father's paintings. Now he had thirty pages of quotations. During his first week at Onyx Rehab an elderly client asked, "Why do you keep shooting me veiled looks?" A stroke victim, brought to the Center by his teenage son, told the boy, "I know your name, I just don't know the word for it." And there was the tiny woman who seated herself across from Candler just as he spilled coffee, and said, "I disorder you." He might go a month without adding anything, and then he'd hear a sentence that would get him started, and he might add a dozen new lines over the course of a week.

He was working with Lowell Darringer, a long-term resident initially diagnosed as *schizophrenic* and later revised to *borderline personality*. Candler thought the first verdict was closer to capturing the enigma of Lowell Darringer. There might be no adequate label for what was wrong with him. In his midfifties now, Darringer was essentially cargo at the Center. His intake evaluation, done seventeen years earlier by a psychologist named Bucheole, included a scribble in the margin: *He's like a sturgeon on the subway*. From the day he arrived at the Center, Lowell Darringer was deemed hopeless. These days his treatment was handled almost completely by techs. Even this evaluation of work skills was a farce, merely a requisite entry in the man's file. He was an anachronism, the vestigial tail of an evolving giant.

Candler transcribed the man's utterance in the notebook: "Eve was the apple peddler, but men got twice the sin in one ball as women's got in box and brain combined." Many of the pages of *Cabbage* belonged to a single, madly voluble schizophrenic named Jack Cartwright.

> *Because there's so little in our lives we actually get to choose, we become violent over crunchy versus creamy and wax eloquent about the girl up the street instead of the one down the street while a biologist with a lot of time on his hands couldn't find a molecule of difference between them.*

Cartwright was a constant talker, always in complete sentences, often fascinating, rarely incoherent. With a tiny bit of self-control, he could have been a writer, an analyst, or *something*, if he could only close his mouth long enough to write down his thoughts. There was no topic he could not talk about with amazing fluency, but he couldn't turn it off. His IQ was the highest Candler had ever measured, but intelligence was no help. He was one of Candler's most disturbing failures. After a two-week evaluation, Candler knew only that Cartwright could not shut up.

Beneath *Cabbage* lay the unfinished report for Guillermo Mendez. For the first time in his professional career, Candler could not finish an evaluation. The Jack Cartwright report had been weak, but at least he'd written the damn thing. The Mendez eval was a different matter. Admitting defeat would put the kid back in combat, and yet what could he legitimately do about it? He had to write something. Tomorrow, maybe. He left his desk. This weekend at the latest.

On the evaluation floor, Kat McIntyre observed Lowell Darringer on the station called *full body range of motion*, a tall platform with three differently angled planes. Each plane held a pattern of bolts and the client had to move plastic templates from one plane to the next, screwing them off and on. The exercise was meant to measure the ability to work in different physical positions—squatting, hands above head, and so on. The eval hub held twelve workstations, spaced evenly about the room like trees with great root systems. Kat casually showed Candler her stopwatch: forty-five minutes and counting. The task usually took no more than fifteen minutes. Some clients could do it in eight.

Clay Hao joined them. He asked Kat about another of the clients, a bone-thin man across the room who called himself Vex.

Candler answered for her. "One of Bob's clients."

Hao smiled. "A floater."

Bob Whitman had a few months yet before his retirement, but in most ways it seemed that he had already vacated the premises. His client worked at a furious pace, as if the floor beneath his feet were electrified.

"Mr. Vex is focused, but a wee bit *combative*," Kat said. "That's the term I'm going to suggest to Bob." She put her hand on Candler's arm to ask if he agreed. She smiled, displaying her braces. He'd never had the nerve to ask about them. She'd had them the whole time of their acquaintance, more than two years. Could they be merely decorative? Jewelry for the teeth? How out of touch was he?

"Vex is wound a little tight," he agreed.

"When does your lady get here?" Kat asked. A playful, nervy light animated her eyes.

"A week from Saturday."

"Last few nights of freedom," she said. "Soon you'll be an old married man."

It sounded like an invitation. He pretended to miss it. If he weren't already cheating on Lolly with Lise, would he find himself over at Kat's house again? She seemed to want a final fling with him before Lolly arrived for the same reason that he had wanted to sleep with Lise—the wicked thrill of it. Half-remembered lyrics to a song played in his head: *Kicks just keep gettin' harder to find . . .*

"You'll meet her," Candler said. "Egri is throwing a party."

"I heard." She displayed that decorative smile again. "The Calamari Cowboys ride again—for the first time."

"Hee-haw," Hao said and swung an imaginary lariat.

Darringer laboriously checked and double-checked the templates. He inevitably turned the nuts the wrong way and offered a semi-continuous rumbling commentary: "Think you can stop me, widget?" Across the room, the one called Vex banged on the table that held the mechanical aptitude workstation—either in frustration or excitement, Candler could not say which. The tech observing him took a tiny step back. Kat's body brushed against Candler's, and he understood how easily he would have tumbled. Only the fact of Lise kept him from a good-bye fuck with Kat. What kind of man did that make him? Certainly not one belonging to any of the first several ranks.

At long last, Darringer finished his task. Candler listened while Kat asked him the standard series of questions. He answered with affirmative or negative grunts, and then Candler stepped in. "That looked like a tough one."

"Not so bad," Darringer said, "but I want to know something."

"What would that be, Lowell?" Candler made a point of using clients' names, establishing rapport, encouraging intimacy. He had to decide what recommendation he could write for this unfortunate man.

"Not sure it's proper protocol to ask publicly," Darringer said, eyeing Kat and Hao with suspicion.

Hao took the cue. "I'd better get back to my reports."

"I've got to run, too," Kat said.

"All right, Lowell," Candler said after they were gone, "what do you think of this workstation?"

"It was tolerable in terms of the physical body," he said and leaned in close, putting his mouth to the back of Candler's head. He spoke softly. "But why do you have me working on this spaceship?"

He was utterly sincere. Candler decided to respond to the offer of confidence rather than the detachment from reality. "You can never tell," he said, "when you might need to escape."

Darringer nodded. "Least you're honest about it."

"It doesn't fly so well, anymore. I'd only use it in an emergency."

"Fuel prices, too," Darringer said. "Fuel companies are gouging our hearts and eyes out."

"That's right," Candler agreed. "It's not cheap to operate a spaceship, and they're not as safe as they used to be. I don't know what it would take for me to get into one. What about you? What would it take for you to step in and fly away?"

"Just between us?" Darringer checked over both shoulders. "If it would take me to the mountains."

"You'd go if . . ."

"I'd spend my last Demerol," he said. "I grew up among mountains. My mother and what remained of my father. That was Montana. I was younger than that one." He aimed a finger at Kat. "Waking in the pines, my mother and father and me, chilly winter air, and feeling, you know, like that . . . feeling *mountainous*."

Candler nodded attentively but his mind slipped back to the *Cabbage* notebook, another of the Jack Cartwright entries.

> The past doesn't adhere to the same rules as the present. Amazing things are possible. People know themselves. They understand their desires. It's a whole different planet, and we show the signs of transport—gray hair, wrinkled skin, the distance in our eyes that tells you where we'd rather be. Only you can't get there from here, and it never existed.

"What if I arrange a drive for you?" Candler said. "Montana is a long ways, but the Laguna Mountains are practically next door. I could arrange a van."

"Just like that?" Suspicion resided again in Darringer's eyes.

"You identified the spaceship."

He nodded and his expression softened. "That I did."

"I'll ask for a van. I'll get you a drive to the mountains."

Darringer let out a big breath. Tears rimmed his eyes. He placed his hand gently on Candler's shoulder, saying, "Give me another one to do, boss."

DAY 6:

Even though Billy had worked less than a week at the sheltered workshop, he understood that this was the best job he'd ever had. There were only six clients, and they all liked him. They were nice people. They paid attention when he spoke. All he had to do was set up the assembly machine, track their work, take a few notes, pay them, and talk to them. He *enjoyed* talking to them. Especially the babe, Karly, but he tried not to let his preference show. He joined them on the assembly line to see what the work was like, tossing the boxes he made into one person's pile and then another's. He didn't play favorites.

And it would be no trouble with this job to keep up his exercise regimen. While he was looking over their shoulders as they folded boxes, he secretly went up and down on his toes, an exercise that had an impressive-sounding name he couldn't recall. He needed to lose eighteen and a half pounds. Not that he was fat. No one would call him fat. Well, one girl had called him fat, but that was in a fit of jealousy, or not jealousy exactly, more like *dislike*, and it was meaningless—though it had been, come to think of it, the reason he began exercising. She was one of his regulars at the U-TOTE-M, the convenience store in Flagstaff he had managed, and she came to the store and talked to him every day for a year, but when he finally asked her on a date, she said she wouldn't go out with him because he was fat and married and stuck in a dead-end job.

"I'm not fat," Billy replied. The worst part was that she wasn't even upset, just stating the facts. As for being married, he told her (withholding her change to make her listen) his wife had filed for divorce, and that was why he never asked her out before. He thought she might've been pissed that he waited so long to pull the trigger.

She pursed her lips in the most dismissive act of lip pursing Billy had ever witnessed and said, "Dead-end job still holds." She had a gold nose stud but no earrings, and a tattoo on her back, just above her butt, of a Native American–type sun.

"I'll quit," he said.

"Don't quit on my account," she told him. "I still won't go out with you." When he remained reluctant to hand over her change, she sighed.

"I have buttons and you don't push them." She left the store without her change and never returned.

What would she think if she saw him in this job and witnessed how he was rising on his toes even as he thought about her? He weighed just eighteen and half pounds more than he had in high school. Not that he was exactly slim back then, but still. And this job had benefits, a retirement plan, and a title: Technician, Level Three, Probationary.

He had already diagnosed all of the clients under his watch, which wasn't even required. The easiest to peg was Bellamy Rhine, who was a clinically measurable nerd. Billy'd had plenty of association with nerds, many of whom were nice guys, though all were utterly hopeless losers. Rhine was a nice guy, but his head was so far up his ass he had to stare out his belly button. Not that Billy himself hadn't gone through a period or periods when he was almost as much a goof as Rhine. He had a thing for chess briefly, flying the old nerd flag. And twice he noted that certain losers in high school seemed to be wearing the same shirts he wore, which Jimmy explained was because they were hideous shirts that appealed only to buffoons. Billy took the shirts to Goodwill to keep from accidentally wearing them again, and he bought shirts identical to Jimmy's. How else to know what was okay? Jimmy got all annoyed, and for a week they called each other to make sure they weren't dressing alike, until Jimmy quit noticing.

Billy made a mental note to bring to work some book related to science or math to give Rhine. Had he packed his chessboard? It might be in the trunk of the Dart. He would find the kid's strength.

Maura Wood's diagnosis was also cake. She was a *rebel without a cause*. She had a nice face with some evil and some kindness in it, which made him think she would grow out of her trouble. A nice face meant something, and women grew out of the rebel stage faster than men, considering that some men never grew out of it. Maura carried around a lot of anger, mainly, he reasoned, because the phase demanded it. Billy knew not to take her comments personally. It was just the rebel in her. She didn't think the world was fair, and who could argue with that? What she'd decided to do about it was carp. Her whole therapeutic deal, he was fairly certain, was just learning to act instead of carp. Billy was often attracted to women rebels, who tended to keep things lively. Male rebels tended to get everybody's noses broken.

Logically speaking, what a rebel without a cause needed was a cause. He had to find something for her to believe in. Nothing as obvious and overpublicized as the environment or civil rights or children. It had to be specific, like when he read that porn actors were going on strike for better working conditions. That turned out to be a publicity stunt but Billy read maybe twenty online articles about it. Maybe that wasn't a cause, exactly, but he needed to find something that would light up Maura's brain the same way his had been lit.

As for Alonso, he was as dumb as a sack of stupid. Not his fault, and he had a very healthy libido, but he was no Einstein. Billy had plenty of friends who weren't the sharpest wrench in the tool kit. Pook came to mind. He'd been strong and basically kind, even though he sometimes liked to hit things and/or Billy. But he couldn't think his way out of an elevator. He was a very loyal friend, though, and Billy thought that he would add a comment about Alonso saying that he was undoubtedly very loyal. This would impress everybody. *It took us years to figure that out.*

The genuinely stupid people he'd known all liked (1) chewing gum, (2) comic books, and (3) television. Actually, Pook hadn't liked television, and Billy crossed that one off. He decided to keep working on the list and use it to motivate Alonso.

Karly was a sad story, a fantastic looker but none too bright. Smarter than Alonso but several of her crayons were missing from the pack and none of them held a point. Not that smarts were everything. Intelligence was way overrated. Handy now and then, but what had his brain gotten him? Mostly into trouble, like for thinking up comeback lines that got him punched or kicked or laughed at or stuffed into an old refrigerator for what seemed like an hour. Guffawed at? Had he ever heard a laugh that sounded like *guff-aw?* Was the bee sound really *buzz,* or more like *enn-n-n-n?* Where had he been going with all this? Oh yeah, Karly's diagnosis and how intelligence wasn't always the cat's meow. Also, beauty could be a hardship. From the way Karly moved about in a constantly sexy way, he deduced that she had maybe been raped or molested. Possibly not literally raped but she'd been taught by the behavior of others that there was nothing to her but her beautiful body and beautiful face, and they *were* impossible to ignore, and—true—she wasn't ever going to be one for big ideas or even lengthy conversations, which meant maybe there was no one to blame for people seeing these obvious qualities and missing what was on the inside. But that had to be what was wrong with her. Too much attention to her hot bod and not enough to her not-so-bright but still (he could tell) *nice* insides. Which meant she just needed personal time, and he was glad she was taking it in the sheltered workshop. She was great to look at, no denying that, and he would find out about her inner whatnot—he promised himself to do it—and he'd be careful to do nothing to make her afraid of him.

Billy had only ever known one woman who was actually raped, and that was Dlu, who called him from the hospital looking for Jimmy. It was a couple of years after they broke up, and Jimmy had moved to L.A., but Dlu didn't know that, and she wanted Jimmy to come be with her. Billy went instead. Someone had pried open her apartment door and raped her in her own bed. Billy stayed with her through the hospital and police episodes, and he put in deadbolts. He spent the night with her, sleeping on the carpet beside her bed. He wound up spending four nights on her carpet because she didn't want to be alone in the dark. Finally, Dlu told her parents, and her brother flew in and Billy thought he ought to go home even though he didn't want to leave her. He liked sleeping beside her bed. He felt useful, as if for once he knew exactly where he should be, and he understood that he was competent to do what was asked of him—sleep beside her bed, put in deadbolts, check and double-check all the windows and locks, let her talk when she wanted to talk, hold her when she needed to cry.

Karly probably needed some of the same—deadbolts, a guy on the carpet, family. Maybe some gum and comic books, too.

Dlu had sent Billy a card, maybe a month later. She thanked him for staying with her during *my personal trauma*. This was such a weird way to put it that he understood it was still going on. He went by her place but she had moved out. He thought about taking the deadbolts back. The card had no return address, and Billy to this day had not seen her or heard from her. Dlu had gone to bed with him that one time, back when she and Jimmy were a couple, and he thought that put a bad spin on his caring for her. Made her nervous or feel beholden, sexually beholden. And sure, he would have loved to go to bed with her again, but he wasn't thinking about that while he slept on her carpet. Maybe he wasn't all the time thinking about her, either, more what he should be doing for her, what another person—someone more used to intimate human behavior—would do. Recalling all of this saddened him, but he had done the right thing that time, hadn't he? And wasn't it better that he got nothing in return?

Cecil was about the size of a fireplug with a fireplug's IQ. He was a chatty little retard, and according to the papers that came with the job, he was only there on a temporary basis. There was no way he could put together more than maybe five boxes an hour if he stayed in the workshop till kingdom come. He'd be shipped out and taught something simpler, like counting cars on the highway. If he could count. Some of the things he said, though, resembled thoughts Billy himself had had but had known to keep to himself. Like Cecil said his dog Pooch could sing some song, and several years ago Billy tried to teach this dog Jimmy and Dlu owned, Flannery, how to keep time with her paw. *It's a dog's life, baby,* Billy would sing, *a dog's life from head to tail.* Billy had been into the blues, and while he couldn't play any instrument and his singing voice required a dog for distraction purposes, he imagined a career for them that included, at the very least, a visit on Letterman. *Go to sleep in dog heaven, wake up in dog jail.* Flannery's paw kept perfect time when he sang it, but Billy figured out that she wasn't listening to the music but watching his head nod, and that took the wind out of his sails. The point being, it was a bonehead idea but while he pursued it he didn't let on about his Letterman plans to anyone but Jimmy. He could maybe try to teach Cecil discretion. It would be a challenge.

Mick was the only one actually crazy. But it was only a half-assed craziness. Billy knew a lot of guys who were half-assed crazy. Most of the time they were okay, but they'd get pissed about money you owed them or the way you pronounced their girlfriend's name or the deodorant you were wearing that made them sneeze. Not that Mick was the angry type. Billy remembered a guy whose name was something like Belltower, a guy he knew from college, the third time Billy tried college. They were in a sociology or anthropology or one of those kinds of classes together, and this guy Belltower knew way more about whatever –ology it was than Billy, but he completely blew the test, and Billy saw him hiding his face in the hallway right after the exam. Billy led him to the Brick Tavern so the guy could at least hide his face in a bar.

Belltower had been so nervous about the test that he didn't sleep all night, and he was so wiped out that he couldn't come up with the right answers, and he said, "Swear to god you won't tell," but the letters on the test page had folded in on themselves and then unfolded and become notes of music, and Belltower, as it happened, could read music and recognized "Candle in the Wind." He burst out bawling in the Brick Tavern. Billy consoled him by saying that was the kind of suck-ass song that would make anyone flunk.

What Billy did for Belltower—was that his name? what the heck was it?—was talk to the teacher, who let Belltower do the test over the next class without telling him in advance, so the guy could get some sleep, and with no time constraints, so the guy wouldn't fret, and Belltower got a 100 on the test. Billy, ironically, got a 56 and dropped out of school for the semifinal time. He never went full time again, anyway, eking out a degree after ten arduous years.

Not Belltower, *Hornblower.* That was it.

Anyway, to help Mick, Billy decided he had to find some way to loosen up his strings and get him to sleep better. He heard Maura tell him to try smoking pot. That made good sense. Just a joint or two per day at the beginning.

This was a job he could sink his teeth into.

DAY 7:

Maura wouldn't have thought it possible that she might miss having Cecil Fresnay, but Thursday morning Billy announced the twerp was gone, replaced by a foaming-at-the-mouth feral creature who insisted on being called Vex. To make things worse, Mick was still giving her the oblivious shoulder, though not unkindly. Mick didn't know how to be unkind. He was simply more interested in Karly than he was in Maura. She could hardly blame him. They were getting married, for fuck's sake.

Vex was a bony, gaunt, scary-skinny guy who, on day one, told Billy Atlas, "You're full of empty and don't fake it very well." He looked late twenties with black close-cropped hair and a beard that hid just below the skin. His eyes were light brown, like a dinner table with a cheap stain, and his face seemed fashioned out of something harder than skin and bones. Maura had an ugly desire to flick her fingers against his cheek and see if it clanked. He assembled 112 boxes during his first hour of the workshop.

"You're certainly catching on, Mr. Vex," Billy said, that cow grin of his like a saddle on his face, as he paid him at the end of the hour.

"It's just Vex," the man said. "No mister here. I'm not titled. Not entitled to a title. *Vex.*"

The guy exuded violence the way Mick radiated intelligence and sweetness. How the holy fuck had he ever gotten accepted into the Center?

"Vex it is," Billy said, patting him on the back.

Vex stiffened, his back bunching up beneath his shirt. "Don't touch Vex," Vex said.

Billy opened his mouth to respond to the freaky nutcase but he quite clearly could think of nothing to say.

"He's a fruit bat," Maura said, loud enough for everyone to hear. "They don't like human people touching them."

"That's so funny," Karly said. No one laughed but Billy, a phony and frightened gargle, and tension squeezed the air out of the room, but Vex did not look up from his manic, depraved box folding, and they all got back to work.

Maura's diet did not permit trips to fast-food restaurants, and she ate her sack lunch in the parking lot, sitting on the concrete with her back against the wall. Sometimes Alonso sat with her, but he often rode with Mick and Karly to the KFC or McDonald's, trailed by Rhine on his scooter. After eating, she smoked a cigarette, and now Vex joined her. She balanced the Carlton Hotel ashtray on one of several short concrete poles designed to keep people from crashing into the building. The Carlton Hotel teetered on its perch, sunlight winking off it, flashing in their eyes as if to convey meaning: *SOS. I'm smoking with a maniac.*

"We supposed to use that?" Vex nodded at the ashtray.

Maura returned his nod and lit a cigarette.

"You smoke what they put in packages," he said, "and you inhale what filler they can get away with." Vex rolled his own cigarettes. He had an unusual voice: the words seemed to be compressed out of him. Maura flashed on her mother writing on a birthday cake with a big metal hypodermic. "What's a hundred percent beef?" he went on. "In a wiener, maybe sixty to sixty-three-point-five percent. And cigarettes? You don't know what you're sucking in."

"Like tobacco is good for you anyway," she said.

The cigarette he rolled was fat in the middle, and the paper was wrinkled in an unappealing way. He kept licking it, displaying the purple underside of his tongue. He was wearing a T-shirt advertising the Bitter Hole Hunting Lodge. A bad transfer had given the deer or elk or whatever it was on his chest big rosy cheeks. A Goodwill shirt, a twenty-five-cent-max piece of apparel.

"Nothing's good for you," Vex said, lighting the veiny thing by sucking hard and fast with several quick repetitions, a frantic urgency to the act. "Not even breathing."

His weird lighting ritual reminded her of a time the lowlifes had stolen gasoline by siphoning, and a boy had sucked on a tube shoved down a car's tank, sucked and quit, sucked and quit, hoping not to get gasoline in his mouth.

Vex pointed to the sky. "Clouds make me think of garbage, white garbage in the deep blue. They ever make you think of garbage?"

"No. Never. Not once."

"There are worse things than garbage. A lot worse."

"What is it you're smoking? It smells like mold."

"Least I know what I'm smoking." He gestured with the repellent cigarette again, this time to indicate her. "Clothes, you know what I mean, they're making them flimsier all the time. Clothing research now, they got all these scientists trying to make clothes out of what? What is it we got no shortage of? *Talk*, that's what."

"You're so full of shit."

"This time next year you'll be wearing a murmur. You'll be wishing you had a declaration or some pleading."

"I hope to god you're putting me on."

"Putting you on my ass. You ever had a dream? At night? When you're supposed to be asleep? Huh?"

"Everybody has dreams."

"Trained myself out of them. That's how they get inside your brain. You don't believe me? Why is it I'm different, huh? They can't get their commercials inside my head."

"You can't train yourself not to dream."

"Set an alarm for every three minutes. Not three-oh-fucking-one. Three minutes. All night. Every night."

"No wonder you're crazy as a fucking butt-faced elk."

He laughed. "Butt-faced elk. I like that." He surreptitiously glanced at his T-shirt.

"How are you so fast on the assembly line when you only just started?"

He rocked his head and stared at the floating garbage above him. "Mind stuff."

"I should have guessed."

"I could teach you. Ever caught a mosquito with your tongue? Hunh? Put out a flame with your eyes? Stopped a moving stream with your concentration? Quit peeing in mid-pee?"

"I'm going to pass on the lessons. I prefer not to eat chicken heads and lick my own ass."

"Chicken head soup, sister. Delicious if you're hungry enough. Gotta get the feathers off is all."

"Don't forget asslick soup, yum."

He laughed again. "Ain't easy to make me laugh like this. You've achieved something."

Billy Atlas threw the door open, and they went back in to work.

"You've achieved something," Vex repeated.

"So bring me a trophy," Maura told him, aware that she was flirting.

"Artists invent their own traditions," Frederick Candler told Jimmy. The family was packed into the old station wagon, touring the neighborhood on garbage day—Frederick and May in the front, with Jimmy sitting between them. Pook rode alone in the back because Violet was working. Once a month residents set out for removal items too big for the trash can, and the Candler family ritually inspected the booty the night before. On this particular tour, they investigated a rocking chair and a slightly cracked birdbath, but they scavenged nothing. Summer was the wrong season for discards.

Jimmy's favorite family tradition involved Christmas. The family went out every Christmas Eve in search of a tree. Whatever misshapen evergreen they'd find in a tree lot, they would prop up, decorate, and celebrate, no matter the foliage gaps, bent trunk, or drooping branches. "No one could love this tree but us," his father would say. Jimmy adored this practice, which made Christmas uniquely theirs. It wasn't until he was twenty and overhead his father telling a friend how he'd never paid more than ten dollars for a tree that Candler understood the family ritual was about being cheap.

Oh, *cheap* was not the right word. It might be the right word if it was applied to another family, but not to his. It wasn't *frugality*, either, or *parsimony*. It was not wanting to be taken in by a capitalist cultural event—Christmas as commercial enterprise—yet not wanting to deny the children the pleasure of the holiday. Their father found ways to celebrate Santa without completely caving in. Coincidentally, they didn't cost much.

Frederick Candler's paintings appeared in museums around the country, though rarely more than one work in any particular museum, and he was excluded from the list of important American artists as often as he was included. He was known for a quotation: "Art does not exist in nature. Art is a repudiation of the natural world." A middling-famous artist was Frederick Candler, recognized by anyone serious about contemporary art but such recognition did not always mean that he was admired or revered. Some of his paintings sold for six figures, but he could never anticipate which, and it usually took several years for the work to accumulate that value. By the time the paintings earned any real cash, they were no longer his and the profit belonged to some lucky bastard who had purchased Frederick's work early on for next to nothing.

Little wonder that he distrusted capitalism.

He could have held on to certain paintings and let their value accumulate, but he was always short on cash. This was inevitably true despite his university salary and his wife's community college salary. Money simply evaporated.

He had been a reasonably successful artist all of his adult life, and sometimes he thought this was a fatal limitation, that he could not draw on the years of frustration and difficult economic times that other artists bitched about. In such moments, he would seem to himself like a watchdog who knows the route around the fenced property so well that he can take no pleasure in it, and what he wishes for is an intruder, an enemy, a justification for all this circling, and he comes to love the imagined intruder that would give him reason to bark and attack, and in his misery he comes to mistake those he loves for those he hates and he wants to bite their heads off. In particular, in the summer of 1987, his patience with Pook was giving out, like the flickering, rolling screen of an old television that would soon go black.

In their family, not counting the animals, only Jimmy and his sister Violet were not artists, and they were not artists for different reasons. Violet had the talent but did not envy the life. Jimmy had no talent and even his stick figures were wobbly and uncertain, like television with bad reception. Though Violet was closer to him in age than Pook, Jimmy saw a lot less of her. They did not become close until after Pook died and she went away to college. But she was there, too, that summer, sixteen years old and in her room or off at her summer jobs— scooping ice cream or shelving books at the library or taking tickets from the sweating patrons who wished to escape the heat in the dark of a movie theater. Three jobs, but it was the one at the cineplex that defined the summer of 1987. She made a new set of friends at the theater and they got to see movies free, plus a discount on popcorn and sodas. She did not see every movie released that summer, but she kept a list of the ones she saw: *Creepshow 2, River's Edge, Ishtar, Beverly Hills Cop II, Ernest Goes to Camp, The Untouchables, Harry and the Hendersons, The Witches of Eastwick, Roxanne, Dragnet, Revenge of the Nerds II: Nerds in Paradise, Robocop, Full Metal Jacket, Jean de Florette, Adventures in Babysitting, Summer School, Superman IV: The Quest for Peace, La Bamba, The Lost Boys, No Way Out, Dirty Dancing, The Big Easy, The Princess Bride.* She could have sneaked the boys in, but then they'd be there every night, Jimmy talking about some inane action figure or baseball player, Billy-the-Blob blubbering happily alongside him, and Pook, her sweet and silent and ultimately scary big brother, for whom movies were a torture, shadowing the younger boys and bothering her new friends with his size and silence and the hibernating violence that now and again woke within him.

Because he had flunked two grades, Pook was in Violet's classes during her freshman year of high school, and she had seated herself beside him and whispered to him, and guided him as best she could, losing most of her longtime friends in the process. He still did not pass and still got into fights, and she never had close friends again while she was in high school, except for a boy at the cineplex, whose name was Armando Sandoval, two years older than Violet and from the other side of town, already enrolled at the University of Arizona. Armando was handsome and funny and homosexual, and he had a car. He drove her to work and bought her presents, just like a real boyfriend, but without the pressure of romance and disrobing and sex. Except with Violet, he pretended to be straight.

Violet was legitimately straight but a virgin, and she liked having Armando as a boyfriend. "Keep in mind," May Candler advised her, "all the things that attract you to him now will eventually drive you crazy." They went to a lot of movies together. Armando preferred big hits and liked to analyze their success—not what the movies were about but why the public lapped them up—a love of commerce over art that Violet found entertaining. She dragged him to one dark, artsy film *(River's Edge)*, which he *absitively loathed*. "The director is showing off how serious he is," Armando argued, "like those boys who wear capes to parade their suffering." Any movie that wasn't at least trying to be a blockbuster didn't interest him.

What Jimmy had in common with his sister: they both liked to read. In 1987 Jimmy had a strong preference for comic books, baseball novels, and the Hardy Boys (though Frank and Joe's hold on him was giving out), or books with sexy covers and descriptions of girls putting their slender arms around boys' muscular necks. Violet gave him *On the Road*, but he never got beyond the first few pages. She loved Jane Austen, rereading three of the novels that summer *(Sense and Sensibility, Emma, Persuasion)*, and the Brontës *(Wuthering Heights, Jane Eyre)* and Edith Wharton *(The Age of Innocence* twice), but she also read *The Exorcist*, which she found in a stack on the floor of her parents' closet, and *Valley of the Dolls*, which was also in the stack, and *The World According to Garp*, which her mother checked out of the library and lined up on the lowboy in the hall, along with her other library choices *(The Prince of Tides, Crooked Hearts, It, A Perfect Spy)*, all of which Violet read before her mother completed *Garp*, and the only hardback her parents purchased new: *Presumed Innocent* by Scott Turow.

Violet and Jimmy both imagined that they'd be writers, the creators of worlds within worlds, but Violet had turned her back on comic books (it was Armando who insisted they see *Superman IV*) and Jimmy wasn't yet reading the novels she loved. The only time this shared interest provided them with a moment's intercourse was when each agreed to cast the other as a character in a single sentence involving a simile. This was Violet's idea, and she had to explain to her brother what a simile was. Her goal was to teach her brother the difference between the books she loved and the junk he read.

Description of Jimmy, as written by Violet:

He charged about dirtily from one meaningless undertaking to the next meaningless undertaking like an unquenchable hummingbird in a store that sold nothing but plastic flowers.

A description of Violet, as written by Jimmy:

She combed her hair and made up her face with the precision of a watchmaker and so became invulnerable to the passage of time and the things she touched with the fingertips of her left hand got younger instead of older and she knew in her heart she had to use her power for goodness instead of evil.

"That's more than one sentence," Violet said, annoyed, because anyone could see that if he cut out the comic book elements his description would be better than hers. "I'm so sick of superheroes," she went on. "Why can't you accept the world the way it is?"

"I do," Jimmy said. "But think about it. In the whole world there are billions of people, right? Billions and billions and billions, to be accurate, and surely one of them must have powers that he keeps hidden. I mean, what are the odds that no one would have any superpowers? Not even one out of the ten hundred billion who are alive or used to be alive?"

"One hundred percent against," she replied.

"No way. Like what about Pook, who can talk to animals in *their* language?"

"He cannot."

"Then why do the animals like him?"

"That's not a superpower, that's just—I can't talk to you. You need a bath."

"Here we go with the bath again. I was in the cistern like ten minutes ago."

"*Soap.* Shampoo. Scrubbing. Why don't you become Mr. Superclean?"

"If it'll make you happy."

After that conversation, Violet decided she did not want to be a writer but rather a librarian or bookseller or editor, and Jimmy took a bath. The contest took place the last week of July of that fateful summer. At this point in their shared life, Jimmy and Violet would both have described the family as *happy*, despite Pook's getting kicked out of school, despite Frederick's intermittent anger, despite May's distance.

Later on, of course, the children would hear about their father's indiscretions and May's bouts of depression, how he would get drunk and insult his colleagues at the university, how she would go months without letting him into her bed, but these adult secrets did not tarnish the narrative to which the children held tightly—that everything had been good until Pook died.

5

DAY 8:

By the time lunch came around Friday, Maura and Vex had a routine. Overnight, he had fashioned a giant rubber gasket that fit over the end of the stubby concrete pole and connected perfectly with the Carlton Hotel. When break time came, she grabbed the ashtray and he, the gasket. He lit her cigarette and she lit his, using his flip-top lighter that produced several inches of flame. He taught her how to roll cigarettes, how to tie various knots that were superior to the traditional figure eight, and how to tell time by the concrete pole's shadow.

"What if it's nighttime?" she asked.

"Then you're off the clock," he said.

He told her about mental exercises that permitted him to look around corners, vaginal exercises that permitted women to make themselves impenetrable to men, and an insane but systematic reason why no one should have hair more than a quarter inch long. "The Samson story was reversed, see, to keep people in the dark. It's growing hair that makes you weak, not cutting it off." In the workshop, he threw fits, yelling terrible red-faced curses. Crews would have given him the boot, but Billy just made him sit in a corner until he could pretend to be rational. Vex hated to lose assembly time and squirmed in the seat, but obediently sat when he was told to and stared at his hands. When he was alone with Maura in the parking lot, he never yelled or threatened and she enjoyed his company.

"Why don't you want anybody to touch you?" she asked him.

"Says who?"

She made her voice low and ridiculous. "Nobody touch Vex!"

His laughter was sly and skittish. "I got a few topics of nobody's business. Chaos in the hacky sack." He pointed with the cigarette at his head. "Chimney up your thoughts long enough and see for yourself. Like when you were in there sparking at that boy Whine."

"His name is Rhine."

"Nobody's name is Rhine. Another trick, you gotta wise up. What've I been saying all day?"

"A lot of incoherent loony-ass shit."

"A loon shits, that's guano." He coughed out a laugh. "I can joke, too. See? But serious here, a man's got clefts in him, woman too, and gorges and deep, deep divides. You think you can build a bridge? You think this here is bridge-building school? Pack life into a box of your own making is it. But how do you do it, right?"

"Which leads me to the obvious question," Maura said, stubbing out her smoke. "Were you born a muddle-headed trout or did something happen to you?"

Vex offered his sly chuckle. "I'd let *you* touch me."

"I'd rather chew on electrical cord."

"If I still had a thing for women, I'd have a thing for you."

"Switch over to household pets?"

"I'm making my mind pure, like the deep down in the planet water that takes days to get to the surface, even with a high-efficiency submersible pump and the horsepower of a Silverado. Pure mind can see inside the mechanics of anything. You walk from here to there, I see ball joints, bone pistons, hinges. Go ahead, walk. You'll see me see you."

She tried it. It was a lot like being naked. He nodded appreciatively and she blushed.

"Built exactly right," he said, "balanced and sturdy and strong, like a perfect backhoe."

It wasn't an ideal compliment but she blushed again.

"Sex is all about practice." He gestured with his cigarette. "Like pistons and rings. You have to run the engine high and low, vary the RPMs, or the rings don't set right. You follow?"

She replied by crushing her cigarette in the Carlton Hotel, noticing that she had only just lit it. The words *virgin smoke* popped into her head. *Here I am crushing my virgin smoke*, she thought. Smoking, too, had required practice, as had drinking beer.

"Having too much sexual bounty has been a mixed dressing." He lifted his hand-rolled cigarette to her face. "Look how evenly that burns."

Billy Atlas took her aside that afternoon to ask her if Vex was a problem for her.

"He's weird," she said, "and creep city half the time. I maybe like him, though. In small doses. He's okay enough."

"He told me I could lose weight," Billy said, "by imagining bees pollinating soap bubbles."

"That sounds like him, all right."

"Maybe he meant I was supposed to do that instead of eating. Karly says he doesn't bother her."

"He doesn't bother me either," Maura said. *Except he's a metaphor,* she thought. He had arrived to make tangible the difference between her life with Mick and her life without him. Subtract Mick and she would wind up with some monster truck like Vex.

The van arrived and took her into the weekend.

DAYS 9 & 10:

"He'll live with me," Jimmy always replied to the question his parents often raised, usually without quite saying it and sometimes without saying anything, one merely catching the other's eye, a specific look of concern reserved for this topic:

What would Pook do when they were no longer able to care for him?

Or: What should Pook do with his life?

Or: How would Pook get by in the world?

Or: What to do about Pook?

To Jimmy, Pook seemed uncomplicated, without pretense or artifice of any kind, but that didn't mean he was predictable. He could surprise you. Boy, could he.

One day early on in that same summer, following an angry tirade by Frederick Candler against Pook, Jimmy and Billy decided to resolve the problem by making a list that would explain Pook to other people, including the family. This was needed, they understood, because Jimmy's father had gotten upset for the reason that Pook would not get on the roof and sweep the rain, meaning Frederick Candler had to do it. (Jimmy and Billy volunteered but no one wanted those two on the roof.) "You're so goddamn stubborn," Mr. Candler accused Pook. "And selfish."

The boys knew that Pook was not selfish (there was no arguing with *stubborn*), he simply did not do certain things, and while he would happily climb a ladder, he would not step off it onto another surface.

To expect him to do so was like asking a cat to swim or a dog to walk on those metal grates they can see through. They made the list to define and explain Pook.

1. *Pook is enormous.* This was not, strictly speaking, true. His actual height was six feet two inches, but he seemed much larger, partly because of the way he would stare and partly because of the quiet he kept. His hair was short—his mother ran a battery-powered clipper over his skull every Sunday morning—and he shaved himself daily with an electric razor. He had broad, muscular shoulders, and he was fierce when angered, and these things also increased his size. The source of his anger was not always evident, and he could rarely, afterward, explain what made him angry, but he was protective of his siblings and parents and Billy Atlas and all animals everywhere, and to Jimmy and Billy, he was enormous.

2. *Pook doesn't like to talk much.* He carried his silence with him the way another person might carry a briefcase—one with a lock and full of papers no one would ever see. Jimmy and Billy, at least, believed there were papers inside. Others, including Frederick Candler, seemed to think the briefcase was empty. Conversations with Pook were never long.
    "Is this your sock on the branch?"
    He nods.
    "Is it supposed to be there?"
    Nothing.
    "Do you want it there?"
    He nods.
    "Why do you want it there?"
    He says, "It fits."
    Or he says, "If the wind moves it."
    Or he says, "I thought daytime."
    "What do you mean?"
    Nothing.

3. *Pook stays on one level.* He would not climb trees or dive into the cistern, but he would go up a ladder and stand on the

top rung, or he would lean over one of the canals and dip his face or some other part of his body into the water. But he would not step off the ladder and into the tree house, and he would not slide off into the cistern. The roof was out of the question.

4. *Pook makes sense in his own way.* By which they meant he was consistent and logical within the terms of his own understanding of the world, but (unfortunately) those terms were not evident and were completely mysterious to others.

5. *Pook likes shaking things.* This was an erroneous generalization. He enjoyed shaking martinis for his parents because he liked the way the jigger turned icy in his hands. He did not particularly care to shake other things, and both of the boys were dimly aware that they were not quite hitting this one on the head. Nonetheless, they left it in.

6. *Pook doesn't like to have no clothes on.* He took baths in his underwear. He slept in pajamas. He wore layers of clothing, even in the Tucson summer.

7. *Pook doesn't do one thing after another.* By which they meant that he had trouble with sequential tasks. He would willingly turn any of the horizontal steering wheels when directed to by a parent or sibling or Billy Atlas, but he could not, on his own, water first the distant green patch, then the trees, the garden, and so on. He used a push mower to trim the front patch of the Candlers' lawn every week without being asked and whether it needed it or not, but he would not cut any of the other splotches of grass on the property, no matter the extent to which their father directed him or yelled. Jimmy believed that Pook would mow the other, scattered lawns if there was a mower for each different patch, but he never brought up this idea with his father for fear of inciting Pook-directed rage.

8. *Pook can't digest with talk going on.* He did not like conversation when he ate and he did not like visitors, except Billy, and when conversation at the dinner table reached a certain—

never to others—identifiable point, he would take his plate
and drink and flatware into his bedroom, where he would
put the plate on his desk, which faced the wall, and eat
in silence. (He never asked for seconds, and May Candler
learned to overfill his plate.) Yet he would not begin a
meal in his room. Even if guests were over, he would not
start dinner at the desk. A plate of food set there would go
uneaten and seemingly unnoticed. He had to begin at the
table and then slink away.

9. *Pook likes doing the dishes.* He washed the dishes every night
with his siblings or alone, and he knew where to put every
pot, pan, plate, cup, and utensil.

10. *Pook doesn't like TV.* He had no interest in television, including
cartoons or shows that featured comic book characters. He
liked comic books, but it was never clear whether he was
reading the panels or just looking at the pictures. He would
accompany others to the movies, but he never enjoyed them,
sometimes openly moaning during them, sometimes falling
asleep, and one time lying on the carpet between the rows of
seats with his hands over his ears (*Crocodile Dundee*).

11. *Pook is not a picky eater but he is a picky drinker.* He drank water
and milk and nothing else, but he always cleaned his plate,
even when Frederick Candler made the dreaded onion
enchiladas.

12. *Pook is never sick.* He never got the flu or colds, and when he
had the typical childhood illnesses, he stayed in bed as his
mother directed but didn't seem to understand that a fever
made him feel bad. He would just lie there.

13. *Pook walks in his sleep.* This item on the list was inaccurate. Some
nights, for reasons no one could determine, he would leave
his bed and sleep on the porch or in the yard or in the station
wagon. He was always awake when he went out the door.

14. *Pook sees himself and is surprised.* Mirrors made him turn to
look behind him, but after that requisite gesture, he might
stare at himself or he might not.

15. *Pook only draws Pook when he draws people.* Same Man was Pook and Pook was Same Man and everyone looked the same as Same Man.

16. *Pook doesn't like noon.* He would go inside no matter what they were doing at or near noon. Later that summer, Jimmy would figure out why, but at the time they created this list it was merely an unexplainable fact, like the existence of black holes or the nature of evil.

17. *Pook doesn't like seats on bikes.* Pook would permit no seat on his bicycle. Their father insistently put the seat on, and Pook insistently took it off. The sight of the bare post would send Frederick Candler into a rage, and he fit the seat on with locking nuts, using a giant plumbing wrench to tighten it down. Discovering the seat once again on his bicycle, Pook would begin working it off. He never used tools, just waggled the seat back and forth until it loosened—a project that might take an hour. He approached the task calmly and never complained to his father about the seat's recurrence. When Frederick Candler took the bike to an auto shop and had the seat welded on, Pook quit riding his bike altogether until Jimmy and Billy sneaked a hacksaw out of the garage and sawed off the post—a project that took most of a day. They rode their own bikes to the Safeway and tossed the seat into a dumpster. No one—not Pook and not Frederick Candler—ever said a word about it, although Mr. Candler must have known that it had not been Pook who sawed through the post. The battle of the bicycle seat came to an end.

18. *Pook is liked best of anyone by animals.* The Dog preferred Pook above all others, and the cats, who would have nothing to do with the remainder of the family, ran to him and let him stroke them. Several times, Jimmy and Billy came across Pook in the shade of one of the ruined outbuildings watching the cats sleep. He would be on his haunches, like a catcher in a baseball game, watching.

19. *Pook knows something about shadows and colors.* Some mornings Pook would stand or crouch on the porch and watch the

sun grab hold of the yard in increments, coloring the pump handle and pump, the low wire fence around the garden, the tomatoes hanging on the spindly plants, the white of the concrete canals. The light progressed like a slow wave, washing the yard, sweeping away everything, even the house, flooded and looted by the light. And Pook liked to watch.

20. *Pook loves the people he knows and they love him.* The summer sky in Arizona was the size of eternity, and within every cubic inch of that floating transparency—secured to each constituent of the Candler relations, bound to them and trailing them like the smoke of existence—was the enigma of Pook, in whom their sense of the world did not reside in any recognizable form.

ONYX SPRINGS REHABILITATION AND THERAPEUTIC CENTER
VOCATIONAL FITNESS EVALUATION

CLIENT	Guillermo (Memo) Mendez
DATES OF EVALUATION	April 21–24, 2008
EVALUATOR/COUNSELOR	James Candler
SUPERVISORY PSYCHOLOGIST	Dr. Jules William Nelson
EVALUATION TECHNICIAN	Katherine McIntyre
REFERRED BY	Self-referral

TYPE OF EVALUATION
A three-day evaluation of abilities, needs, talents, and shortcomings. (See full description of the three-day evaluation in *Addendum A*.) Assessments that require a psychologist's input and interpretation were administered by the evaluator under the tacit supervision of the supervisory psychologist. (See *Addendum A* for details of counselor-administered psychological assessment.)

REASON FOR REFERRAL
Client articulates as follows: "I want to see what's possible that I could do at some point down the road, and the sh_t that no way can I do, now or ever."

In concert with the evaluator, the reason for the referral was refined as an examination of vocational and educational aptitude, as well as a measure of emotional and psychological predilections and readiness.

CLIENT BACKGROUND

Guillermo Mendez is a twenty-one-year-old male of Hispanic ethnicity. Both parents are living and are second-generation immigrants from Mexico. His father is employed as a foreign-car mechanic by Griffin's Auto Repair Services in San Diego; his mother is employed as a cashier at Big O Tires in Imperial Beach. Client reports that his family life as a child was loving and busy. He has four younger siblings, all of whom live with the parents in National City, California.

Client has a high school education (Sweetwater High School, National City) and is currently employed by the United States Army, holding the rank of private first class. His grades in high school, by his own admission, do not reflect his intelligence or aptitude. Client reports being a "lousy" and largely unmotivated student in high school: "I was pretty *crapadaisical [sic]* because I couldn't see the point. Now I see the point. Jesus and Joseph, do I see the point."

Client reports no history of arrests or substance abuse.

Client worked part time during high school at a number of businesses, including the following: Burger King, Von's, Griffin's Auto Repair Services, Subway, and Big O Tires. He enlisted in the U.S. Army during his senior year and began his service immediately upon graduating.

Client has never been in therapy.

EVALUATION METHODS

Review of Medical and Employment Records
Counselor Interviews
Standardized Assessments

ASSESSMENTS ADMINISTERED

American Identities Artistic Aptitude (Full Inventory) Assessment
American Identities Personality Inventory
American Identities Spatial Aptitude and Reasoning Assessment
American Identities Systemic Work Values Inventory
American Identities Vocational Aptitude and Interest Assessment,
    Advanced
California Psychological Inventory

Minnesota Multiphasic Personality Inventory-2

Novak Mental Status Examination, third edition

Otis-Lennon School Ability Test

Stennis-MacLean Anxiety Inventory

Strong Interest Inventory

Wechsler Adult Intelligence Scale, fourth edition

Valpar Component Work Samples

    VCWS01 - Small Tools Mechanical

    VCWS02 - Size Discrimination

    VCWS04 - Upper Extremity Range of Motion

    VCWS10 - Tri-Level Measurement

    VCWS12 - Soldering and Inspection

    VCWS15 - Electrical Circuitry & Print Reading

    VCWS17 - Pre-Vocational Readiness Battery

Valpar Whole Body Range of Motion

(For a full description of each assessment, see *Addendum B*. For the client's individual scores for each assessment, see *Addendum C*.)

INTERPRETATION OF RESULTS

In terms of Guillermo's general physical mobility and strength, he . . .

As far as Guillermo's general intellectual skills go, he seems . . .

Guillermo's grooming and dress were . . .

Results of the mental status assessment show . . .

His interests and talents coincide with . . .

The possible personality traits that might conceivably hold him back
    include . . .

Guillermo stated his vocational goals as follows . . .

In terms of Guillermo's willingness and ability to resume life-threatening
    violence at the behest of his country's major oil interests, he . . .

CONCLUSIONS AND RECOMMENDATIONS

Guillermo's personal desire to discontinue active combat should be thoughtfully considered by the appropriate person or persons in charge. Even though there is nothing in Guillermo's assessment that shows definitively that he is physically or psychologically incapable of continuing his duties as a soldier, the assessment is far from infallible, and the client's own statement of preference should . . .

An examination of the Social Introversion subscale of the MMPI-2 may not seem noteworthy unless one adds personal observation to the analysis. The term *alienation* or *social alienation* is frequently . . .

It is within my purview to recommend a full psychological evaluation even though none of the assessments point in an obvious fashion to . . .

How does one assess the ability to continue doing that which no one should be asked to do . . .

Hell no, he won't go . . .

I have been asked to write—in the crippling language of this discipline—another man's memoir, and end with a life or death recommendation. To do this, I need not only weeks of examination but something like an omniscient understanding of his psyche, and I would need the same all-knowing comprehension of the conditions of the war, and, for that matter, the reasons *for* the war. While I am accustomed to assuming this type of role, in terms of this client's situation, I am feeling a tad uncertain or unreliable in this specific case, as if I have bitten off more than . . .

Guillermo Mendez is a man of integrity. He approached each of the assessments honestly, even though he had a private agenda (which he did not reveal until the exit interview) that could have been advanced by a dishonest approach. *I must not cheat,* Memo thought, *despite the dire circumstances of my life.* Even in the final interview, he did not reveal all of his thoughts, but you need to hear them before you decide to send him back to Iraq, and my measurements permit me to offer an articulation of those thoughts with a degree of precision that . . .

Jesus, god, help me write this thing . . .

DAY 11:

Over the weekend Maura read a book Barnstone had given her about a man who went to Alaska, deep in the sticks, and died there, and she got into a long, unbelievably tedious conversation with another girl on the at-risk floor about ways to release bad energy from your body (the girl had scars up and down her arms), and she read a second book Barnstone had dropped off about biologists measuring the beaks of finches to prove the theory of evolution. It didn't sound like a page-turner, but she got into it, finishing it at three Monday morning, reading with her lamp under the blankets because it was way after lights out. A few hours later, at the sheltered workshop, the assembly butterfly jammed, and Billy Atlas could not get it to run. Maura wanted to roll out a cafeteria table and take a nap. Her work scores were shit without sleep, and the broken assembly machine seemed like a wish come true.

"You want it fixed?" Vex asked.

"Don't let him touch it," Maura said.

"Thanks for offering, Vex," Billy said. "I appreciate your offer, but I need to make a call." To everyone, he added, "You guys take a break."

Billy had trouble, as he often did, finding the right key on the facility key ring, and before he could open the door to the office, Vex had the machine running again.

"Vex stuck his arm in the assembler machine," Rhine said. "We're not supposed to stick our arms in the assembler machine, Mr. Atlas, and Vex did."

"Mr. Billy Atlas," Alonso said.

"Just Billy, guys," Billy said.

"It'll jam again," Vex said, having already resumed his relentless box assembly.

It did jam again, and this time it took Vex almost a minute to get it running. "Once I'm off the clock," he said, "I'll fix it permanent."

It jammed twice more, and near the end of the day, it made loud rattling thumps, like gym shoes in a clothes dryer, and then an almost dental grinding. It smelled of burning rubber. Billy unplugged it.

"The only thing is take the motherfucker to pieces and put it all back together," Vex said. "I need tools, a hookup, and some chicken or beef sandwich, no condiments."

Resisting Vex's offer once again, Billy Atlas pulled out one of the cafeteria tables and gave them each paper and a pencil. "Write a story," he told them.

"Can't we just sleep?" Maura asked.

"Not no but hell no," Alonso said.

"What sort of story?" Rhine asked. "There are very many sorts of stories."

"Whatever kind you like," Billy said.

"I like different sorts of stories," Rhine said.

"You're going to have to tell him what kind," Maura said. "Why are we writing stories?"

"I like stories," Karly said, reaching out to Billy, who did not take the hand but patted her on the back. She reached around and patted him on the back, too.

"A fairy tale," Billy said. "Here's how it starts: Once upon a time . . ."

Remarkably, all of them started writing even though it was obviously busywork. Maura understood why they did it: they all liked Billy, even Vex. Who wouldn't like him? He was like a tub of butter that even the meanest alley cat would lick.

Besides, there was only a half hour before the van arrived.

Maura retold "Little Red Riding Hood," moving it to Minnesota so she could have some snow on the ground, which provided her with tracks in the white landscape, which tipped off Hood that the fathead wolf was in the cabin with her granny, and Hood peeked through the window (why don't characters in stories ever shut the damn shades?) and observed Granny and Wolfy getting it on. Maura spent a paragraph describing this action explicitly, especially the wolf's furry loins and wolfish cries, and then the van driver honked and she didn't get to finish.

"It's like we're all dogs," Jimmy said.

"We're dogs now?" his mother asked, and at the same moment Billy Atlas said, "What kind of dogs?"

They were at the dinner table, Jimmy and Billy at the far end due to the filthy condition of their clothing. Pook had begun the meal with them but conversation had driven him away. He had taken his plate to his room: pot roast, yams, green beans, which was what everyone was eating except Billy, who would only eat boxed cereal, bread, pimento cheese, and potatoes. He had a bowl of Cheerios and a yam. May Candler insisted that a yam was the same as a potato. With his fork Billy poked the yam, which was the orange of traffic cones. There was no way he could eat a yam.

"Any kind of dog," Jimmy said, "and we live by dog rules, like we jump around and flap our heads when other dogs come by and bark and play and chase each other and growl."

"I don't much care for thinking of us as dogs," his mother said.

"Couldn't we be emu or something more elegant for your mother's sake?" his father asked.

"Let him finish," his sister said. Was she really there? Was it one of those rare nights when she wasn't working or out with Armando Sandoval? Or had memory—Jimmy's and Violet's both—put her there, insisted that she had been present that momentous evening? The most true statement: she was both there and not there.

"I wanna be a Lassie," Billy said. They had seen *Lassie* on Nick at Nite at his house earlier that week—they did nothing at the Atlas home but watch television since the Candlers did not have cable—and the boys hated the show, especially the apple-cheeked Timmy, but Billy refused to be prejudiced against the beautiful and amazingly well trained dog who could hardly be held responsible for the butt-stupid show. "What kind of dog is that?"

"A lassie is a girl," Jimmy's father said, and at the same moment Violet, if she was present at all, said, "Collie."

"It's just a comparison," Jimmy said. "I don't mean we're really dogs."

"What do you mean then?" his mother asked.

"It's just that dogs see the world like dogs."

"Thank you for that insight, son," his father said. "Pass the yams."

"I'm not done," he said and passed the yams to his father. "Now I have to start all over."

The groans came from multiple sources.

"Make us collies this time," Billy said.

"I'm just saying that it's like we're all dogs, everyone here sitting at the table."

"Can I still use my fork," his father asked, "or am I meant to bend over my plate and . . ." He lowered his head and took a lick of the roast.

Jimmy and Billy laughed appreciatively.

"I rather like being a dog," his father said, gravy sticking to his nose.

"You're pandering," his mother said.

"That's disgusting, Dad," Violet might have said, but she would have been smiling and would have laughed aloud after she spoke. One of her roles in the family—a wholly unconscious role, though one she relished—was defender of their father against their mother. In her supple hands, the part did not require her to turn against their mother, and most of the time, she merely used laughter to undercut the tension.

"Don't be a prig," Mr. Candler said and cleaned his nose with a napkin. They could tell he was talking to Mrs. Candler because he did not look up from his plate.

"Will you finish?" Violet said or might have said to her brother. "So we can get back to a normal dinner?"

"It's like we're all dogs," Jimmy repeated, "but Pook's a cat. He doesn't make any sense to dogs, but that doesn't mean he doesn't make any sense to anybody. He doesn't like barking and chasing balls and dog stuff, but if we could see him through cat eyes, he'd make perfect sense. It's just cat sense."

No one said anything for several seconds.

Finally, Mr. Candler said, "The only problem with that hypothesis—"

Mrs. Candler cut him off. "That's very creative. Let's just leave it at that."

"The only problem with that hypothesis—"

"Fred, please."

"—is that there is no other member of his species. He's in a dog's world, all right, but there are no others like him. No one has ever seen any cat quite like your brother."

"We are changing the subject," May Candler demanded. "The subject is changed."

"Your mother doesn't like to talk about the problems of our eldest—"

"Billy, tell us one of your—"

"Your mother lives in a world disconnected from the rest of us. Not a cat world, exactly, more a—"

"Billy, damn it, you're always interrupting us with some ridiculous story. Tell us one this minute."

Violet leapt up from the table and left without a word. Or, if she was never there, her absence was suddenly felt.

"Now see what you've done." Which parent said this to the other? They were both thinking it. Perhaps they spoke identical words at the same time. The remainder of the meal was consumed under the toxic cloud of accusation that often visited the family during those years. But this conversation became important to the boys and eventually to Violet. In its colloquial and nonscientific way, it filled a substantial gap. Except for the cat argument, Pook existed without diagnosis, as he might have in another century. Frederick and May Candler refused to permit one. Why hadn't their parents had Pook seen to by professionals? This was a question Violet and Jimmy would talk about a great deal after his death. It was a mystery neither felt they could bring up with their parents. It was impossible to ask without acknowledging the implied criticism, and there could be no denying that Pook's suicide was the most damaging moment in their shared life. To point fingers was to behave monstrously. It remained their secret topic.

"In cat world," Billy Atlas said after Mr. and Mrs. Candler had left the room and the boys were alone at the grubby end of the table, "bicycle seats are forbidden."

"Talking is only for when you have to," Jimmy added.

They worked up their list of attributes. It was probably as close as anyone ever came to understanding Pook while he was alive. And after he died, the family rarely talked about him, though occasionally Violet would tell a story of a bully following her home, taunting her, threatening her, and how Pook appeared from nowhere and leapt onto the boy's back. How she had to get on her knees and beg her big brother to stop choking the kid.

"He was fierce," she would say. "He loved us."

That recollection would inevitably lead to the story of his roaring at the boys on the playground. "He wouldn't let kids mess with us," Jimmy might say.

Billy, when he wasn't with one of the Candlers, told stories about Pook with some regularity. How Pook had pinned a smart-aleck varsity wrestler. How Pook could open a Coke bottle with his belly button, but he would not drink Coke. How the one and only time Pook played baseball with them he caught a high fly and then refused to give up the ball. How the Candlers' feral cats would follow him around, stopping and going as he did, as if on a leash. How under the influence of peyote Billy had a vision and animals spoke to him, and the whole hallucination was ultimately about Pook—a fact Billy would perpetually intuit and forget. He told the story of the peyote revelation frequently, and during each recitation there would be a moment in which he thought *Oh yeah, they were trying to tell me something about Pook.*

During his sophomore year, after a half dozen suspensions, Pook was expelled for fighting. He was eighteen by that time, and he never returned to classes. The summer of 1987 was his first summer after the expulsion and the final summer of his life.

That night, after dinner and a bath, Jimmy sat out on the porch couch. He was in an odd mood. Pook had walked with Billy to Billy's house to wait (he would stand outside, on the concrete stoop, hands in his pockets) while Billy took a bath and changed into clean clothes. (Jimmy's mother required Billy to do this before spending yet another night.) Jimmy had not wanted to accompany them. He didn't like Billy's mother, who would rush up to him with an unhappy smile and a mad barrage of questions. *What have you two been up to? When is my boy going to learn?* Pook went because she would never say a word to him.

The yellow curtains flittered in the window's narrow opening like a tongue speaking all the words of a language at once, and Jimmy studied the drawings Pook had completed for the comic book. He had drawn the panel they asked him to, but it had not turned out as Jimmy imagined it—Same Man exploding out of the closet, dressed now in his superhero costume, to attack the cringing Mango Fortitude. Instead, Same Man was hunkered down in the closet, whose door was open a sliver, pulling on pants, and he looked up in embarrassment at the intruding light. This drawing seemed to prove what Jimmy had said at dinner. Here was a cat drawing despite the doggy request. The thought excited him, and he decided to show his father.

"Pook drew this?" Frederick Candler didn't merely look at it, he studied it. They moved to the dining room, and he held the drawing under the bright light over the table. Jimmy felt the specific thrill that children love and long for, the delight of having engaged a parent beyond the parent's expectation. He had discovered something about Pook that his father had missed, and now, at this very moment, his father was recognizing that fact. Frederick placed a big, rough hand on Jimmy's shoulder—a gentle, grateful placement—pulling the boy incrementally closer to him while he continued to examine the drawing, the boy's pleasure like a mountain spring inside him, bubbling at the surface but pure and deep at the source. After another moment, his father said, "Let me see the other things he's drawn."

Almost no other moment in Jimmy Candler's existence pleased him as much, and he would cling to that pleasure later, even as he came to understand that it made him complicit in Pook's undoing, that it led to Pook's death. Pleasure and pain and sadness and guilt, his father's warm hand on the back of his neck, the best and the worst of his young life.

DAY 12:

The assembly mechanism was in working order, and Maura believed it was the most ordinary and dull day of her ordinary and dull life. That changed when a man in coveralls arrived with a work order to fix the butterfly.

"It's already working," Billy told him.

"Fix itself?" the man asked.

"I don't know," Billy said. "How would I know? Sorry."

"No skin off my nose."

Only Maura knew to look at Vex, who had not slowed his manic box folding but cast a glance in her direction, his head down but those dark eyes rolling up to meet hers. "I can fix anything made by man," he had said to her, "and any woman fucked over by man." This grown man, this grown wolf of a man, wanted to fuck her, specifically her. An adult male, handy with his hands and all blown gaskets upstairs, desired her. Vex wanted her in the same way that she wanted Mick. Or as close to the same as Vex was capable. He suddenly shouted something, eyeing her again, a millisecond of contact, before resuming his yell.

"Practice," he screamed. "Practice, practice, practice."

His hands on the boxes were a blur.

It was a small-town museum located in a pioneer church house built in the early nineteenth century by a now extinct religious group. The building had a peaked roof but no spire; a porch ran along the front and another filled a corner of the back. During Candler's campus interview three years earlier, an attractive young woman from John Egri's office had given him a tour of Onyx Springs, including a visit to the Congregation of Holy Waters Museum. Candler had been impressed not with the museum but with the woman. When he later asked after her, Egri revealed that she'd been employed only for the interviews. He explained: "She was supposed to keep you from noticing what a crummy town this is."

Candler's rationale for meeting Lise at the museum was simple: *no one ever went there.* It cost five dollars to enter, a trivial price to pay for privacy. He had promised to meet her for lunch after making a mess of their plans the night before. Kat had needed an emergency babysitter, and Candler volunteered. The chore had taken longer than expected, and by the time he got to the Corners, the door to Lise's apartment was locked. He had slipped a note beneath her door, proposing lunch at the museum.

Although there was no one else in line, gaining admittance to Holy Waters took forever. The florid middle-aged man behind the desk operated a sleek new computer with the pointer finger of his left hand. He had the appearance of a man born without a nose, and when they tacked one on they used whatever was handy—the tongue of a shoe, by the looks of it. He laboriously entered the numbers from Candler's credit card. He fingered in another dozen bits of information—name, address, phone number, the expiration date of the card, and more new boxes continued to illuminate, demanding still more information. Candler could not imagine what. His weight? His shoe size? His IQ?

When the printer would not come out of hibernation, the screen cleared and the man had to poke in the information all over again. He never looked directly at Candler and never removed his white earphones, a book playing on his iPod. (Candler could hear the thrum of the narrator but not the words.) The cashier displayed enormous patience, never doubting the rationale for all those numbers.

At one time the province of the gods and later the dominion of science, omniscience was now the property of technology. Evidence of this was endemic in the culture: Sherlock Holmes and Philip Marlowe displaced by the omnipotent, if ersatz, technology of *CSI;* Achilles and Agamemnon vanquished by the mythology of hi-tech laser-targeting systems that produce surgical strikes; human memory and folding road maps supplanted by GPS. If you require further evidence, consider the following: a three-chord rock song turned into elevator music and·

played through a speaker the size of a tear duct indicating the arrival of an all-caps, almost certainly clichéd message, to which the minion, no matter the circumstances, eagerly responds in kind—this is as close as we come to bowing before something greater than ourselves.

The printer lasered out a ticket of admittance, and the cashier handed it to Candler without ever meeting his eyes.

"Thank you," Candler said, but the man still did not look up.

"What is it you want me to see here?" Lise stood in the doorway to the room beyond, hips canted, her colorful striped dress and complicated shoes making her seem like an altogether different species from the guy at the desk or Candler himself, who had abandoned his jacket and tie—it was ninety degrees out—and who lugged a white bag of carryout.

"You look nice," he said. "When did you arrive?"

"Maybe thirty minutes ago or possibly a year." She displayed a pamphlet. "I've read this twice, looked at the clothing, the memorabilia, the antiques, the photographs." Though the museum was located in the church, it did not limit itself to the history of the congregation. "I read the fine print on every placard, took the trivia test. I like the rock paintings best. They ought to be in a better museum."

"You're so audience," he said. He had been reading again from the *Cabbage* notebook. A young woman with Tourettte's had said this to him. He explained the origin of the line while she steered him to the room with ancient artifacts. A stone roughly the size and shape of a backyard barbecue dominated the floor. It was covered with pictographs—human hands, arrows, what might be deer, lizards, boxy people, pointy mountains, and curving lines thought to represent water. Local historians—meaning a schoolteacher and a self-educated anthropologist—had translated the rock, and their interpretation, elaborately printed on parchment, was situated beside the boulder.

Ages ago, when the native inhabitants of the region left the comforts of the ocean to explore the mystery of the inland, Onyx Springs became a cheerful respite on that journey. The natural spring provided an endless supply of fresh water. People rested here. The weak or ill were left here to recover. Deer and lizards romped abundantly.

Candler wondered which of the pictographs meant *cheerful.*

"I picked up lunch," he said. "We can eat on the back porch. It's shady and shouldn't be crazy hot."

"You didn't answer my question."

"What question?"

"Why are we here? What is it you want me to see?"

"It's private." He shrugged theatrically. "A public private place. I just wanted some nearby location where we could be alone."

"We could have gotten a motel room if you simply wanted privacy."

"If I have other motives," Candler said, "they're hidden even from me."

The back porch was fully shaded by the house and more comfortable than he had any reason to hope. There was a round metal table and matching chairs on which to perch themselves, as well as a view of the rock garden and its few plants—sagebrush, prickly pear, ice plant with yellow blooms, pink bougainvillea. The backyard was the best thing about the museum. He had brought Vietnamese baguette sandwiches and chips. While he parceled out the food, she examined him silently.

"Are you upset with me?" he asked.

"Just trying to figure you out."

"I swear to god I had no ulterior motive."

Her look was suspicious, but she put the pamphlet down and picked up her sandwich. "I've driven through Onyx Springs a dozen times, but I never got off the freeway."

"Not a lot of reason to stop," Candler acknowledged.

"No offense, but it seems like the worst of both worlds."

Candler understood what she meant. The elevated basin in which the town resided was boxed in by hills that introduced but failed to suggest the Laguna Mountains. It was too high to benefit from the coastal rains and too low to accept the cooling advantages of altitude. It was a desert town that separated the forested mountains from the lush ocean, a sore in the landscape that would not heal.

"No offense taken," he said. "It's a nowhere place with nothing to recommend it."

"And yet you've taken me to a museum to read about it."

"I just thought it would be nice not to worry about being seen together. No one comes here. I've been to the museum just once—three years ago—when I was here to interview for the job, and we had lunch on the porch. So I thought—"

Lise gulped air noisily. "That's it then," she said. "That's why we're here. You came here during your interview and now you're here again with me." She paused, staring at him. "You know who I am, don't you?"

"A big part of my job is giving tests," he replied, "so don't be surprised if I ace this one. You're Lise Ray of that other local nowhere, Liberty Corners. Haberdasher to the wealthy few that have taste. You're the woman who conducts mad experiments on willing men, making them her temporary sex slaves. Am I close?"

She smiled weakly, words seeming to gather in her mouth, but she said nothing and unwrapped her sandwich. They ate for a while. Hummingbirds bothered the ice plant. A fly circled low over Candler's sandwich, and he flicked at it.

"You think you can know something unconsciously," Lise asked, "without knowing that you know it?"

"You mean how supposedly we use only ten percent of our brain? That's been proven baloney."

She shook her head. "One time—this was in Missouri and I was maybe fifteen—I decided out of the blue to go see a girl I used to know. She'd dropped out of school because she was pregnant. It had been a long time, and I didn't want to come empty-handed. I stopped at the drugstore and bought a cheap box of chocolates, and bicycled to her house. Her mother burst into tears when she saw me. It was the girl's birthday, and I was the only person from her old life who remembered. Only I *hadn't* remembered, even though I was there and I had a present for her."

"I guess I've probably done things like that," Candler said, "but I still don't think I have a secret reason for choosing this place."

"Maybe you know more than you think you know."

"Christ, I hope so, 'cause I think I know just about nothing whatsoever."

This confession pleased her. For an instant she recalled the evening she first investigated Liberty Corners, how she had droned repetitively by Candler's tasteless house like a housefly appraising a new cadaver.

They ate for several minutes without speaking. A hummingbird inoculated cactus blooms. Candler swatted at the fly dive-bombing his sandwich.

"This church was mean-spirited," Lise said to end the silence. "The older men were treated like gods. They had multiple wives, and they'd cripple the young men who stood up to them."

"I didn't know that," Candler said. "I don't know anything about the church."

In the early part of the nineteenth century, Lise told him, a religious cult seeking holy land had claimed the northern end of the basin. According to the writings of the congregation's leader, the combination of the spring and the defined borders—the box of craggy hills—inspired him. He saw it as a place of modest and well-delineated expectations. Another diary, left by one of the women, claimed that they were simply too weak after the trek through the mountains and the sudden explosion of heat to journey beyond the spring. Her journal also documented the sexual slavery of the women to the elder men, and the violence against the young men who challenged the elders.

When Lise finished, Candler said, "*God's will.* I'm sure that's what they must have told the young men as they were breaking their legs or while they were holding the young women down on the bed. God works in mysterious ways."

"If there is a god," Lise said, "then *mysterious* doesn't quite cut it. It's way beyond mysterious."

"We all have our secrets," Candler said. "Only makes sense if you know everything, then your secrets are gonna be whoppers."

"God is hiding things from us?"

"Unless he only pretends to know everything. He could be bluffing. Or maybe he's just indecisive, and what seems like mystery to us is just god changing horses in midstream." Candler swatted the fly with the pamphlet. He had finished his sandwich and chips. "We're running out of time."

"I know," she said, "less than seventy hours to go."

Candler wiped the fly carcass onto a napkin. "I meant my lunch hour."

She was silent for several seconds before rapidly standing, the striped skirt swinging. "I've got to pee," she said and was gone.

Even a blind man could tell that he had upset her. These final days were going to be tough. But hadn't he been clear at the beginning that he was engaged to marry another woman? Close to the beginning. Right after they'd had sex, he'd told her.

Between his sophomore and junior years of college, he had back-packed through Central America. On his way home, somewhere in Mexico, he met another American, a girl maybe three years older than he, her dirt-encrusted face the result of a month in the Oaxaca jungle. They were in a bus station, waiting for different delayed buses, a storm raging outside, the afternoon turning dark, and the time they had to-gether was doubled by the storm, by the unpredictable natural world, by the luck of running into each other in such an unlikely place, and then it was tripled by these same forces, and then quadrupled, and they had a moment to believe the multiplication would never end, that each had stumbled onto the person who would matter more than any other. He took her into the lone bathroom and washed her face with his last clean shirt. He opened her blouse and washed her small, per-fect breasts, and when the loudspeaker announced the arrival of his bus, he almost let it go by. Months later, he showed up on her campus— half a continent away from Flagstaff. They ate Indian food together, but the only thing they could find to talk about was that bus station. He spent the night with her, and the perfunctory sex put an end to any hope one had for the other. "We should have left it alone," she had said.

Candler was determined not to repeat the mistake with Lise. The deadline that numbered their days also sweetened them. Its hovering finality kept them from openly arguing, permitted them to ignore the spitting and roaring of the other aspects of their lives.

Oh, well, this much he had to admit: when he was with her, he could breathe. Really breathe. But some things were meant to end, and because of that they might seem more beautiful than the things that lingered. He finished his sandwich and picked up the pamphlet.

In the 1940s, Onyx Springs became briefly famous for the Spotted Horno Rhinus, a false genus of lizard discovered by recluse biologist John Rhinus, who had moved to the city after failing to get tenure at one of the state universities. With purple spots and incomplete rear legs that forced its end to wriggle like a snake, the Spotted Horno Rhinus represented the missing link in the reptilian evolutionary chain, claimed Rhinus. The local newspaper ran a photograph of

Rhinus holding the creature by the tail. The discovery became na-tional news though no reputable biologist understood what Rhinus meant by a missing reptilian link. It turned out that Rhinus had been an English professor, not a biologist, and a neighbor was quoted in the newspaper: "Most of us believe John's suffering from a mild form of a serious mental disorder." The lizard—there was only one—was merely a genetically damaged gecko.

Candler put the pamphlet down. Why the hell had he thought this place was a good idea?

Lise finally returned, smiling and self-consciously cheery. "You never told me why you were out so late last night."

Kat's daughter had fallen from a swing at her preschool, and Candler picked up Kat's son from his afterschool program, fed him at Little Caesars, and drove him home. "She thought she'd just be an hour or so," he said, "but her daughter had a concussion. They had to run tests. The boy and I played some awful video game and then I put him to bed." He had called Lise with the gist of this information the night before, but she knew that Kat used to be his lover. "I went to your place as soon as Kat and her boyfriend made it back from the hospital with her daughter."

"What awful video game?" Lise asked.

"A bunch of robo-guys shooting aliens. I don't remember what it's called." Most men his age had grown up playing video games, but most men hadn't been raised by Frederick and May Candler. "Blood and guts—a gory game." There had been a moment during the ordeal when Candler thought he had a way out. An alien got the drop on them and blasted Candler's avatar in the back before the boy's character could whip around and obliterate the assassin.

"All right, I'm a goner," Candler had said. "You go on without me. Be brave."

"Just wait a second," the boy told him.

Sure enough, Candler's character came back to life, swiftly up on his feet and humping down yet another dim roadway.

"Isn't that cheating?"

"It's part of the game."

"But it's not like life."

"It's like *this* life," the boy said, aiming his finger at the screen.

Candler still wanted to object. What was the point of tracking your progress if even death didn't stop you?

"You don't want to be killed," the boy explained, "even though you don't stay dead."

"Why not?"

"'Cause it costs you. You're weaker now."

He'd definitely felt weaker, but he didn't go into detail with Lise about the video game, and it occurred to him in a flash that he should break it off with her now, even though they still had a few days to go. He liked seeing her, but the end was going to be difficult and possibly ugly. This lunch was a sign, a signal, an omen. Encounters like this one marked the beginning of the end—this kind of disjointed unhappy conversation, full of missed connections and the little misunderstandings that would lead to the big, ridiculous fights.

"I've got a client at one," he said.

"I like that we came here," she replied. "Honestly, I expected some motel quickie. I'm sort of surprised, given the nature of our relationship—"

"Less than seventy hours to go," he said. "I know."

"—that it would turn out to be about something more than sex."

"To be honest, I just didn't think of a motel. If I'd thought of it . . ."

"There you go. Some part of your head decided this would be better, figured out that I'd like it more than a motel, and it kept the other part of your head stupid."

Oh well, he thought, people weren't really so complicated, were they? Humans didn't do all that much but seek out people to hold and fuck and talk to, people they might like to eat with and argue with and lie next to. But what he said was: "My head is always at war with itself. Lately, anyway." And then, for no reason that he could articulate, he didn't want her to go. He thought about canceling his one o'clock. He could claim an upset stomach. They would sit here and talk until they made real connection, until they corrected the misunderstandings. He said, "You know what Kat's son told me last night? He was in bed. I'd read him a couple of books, and he was telling me about his school, how his teacher said that an ant colony is a type of intelligence. It enacts thinking. I can't remember how he put it, but that's the general picture. And this boy—he's only eight. I could tell he liked that a lot.

He liked lying in his bed and thinking about it. I get a kick out of that kid."

"I'm going to kiss you on the cheek," Lise said. "Then you take off. I'll stay another few minutes, and then I have to get to work, too."

"You're just going to sit here."

She nodded and shooed him with her hands.

He felt queer leaving her there and oddly awkward as he crossed the porch, as if he were walking on mice. The strange man was not at his desk but the iPod was, and its face was illuminated. Candler bent over to peek: *The Death of Ivan Ilych.*

"It's good to see you, Mr. Candler." The cashier stepped from the hallway. "I didn't want to embarrass you before. With the pretty girl waiting and all. I'm doing real well these days, and grateful for all you did for me."

Candler smiled uneasily, trying to place him. "I'm glad to hear that. I'm genuinely glad to hear that."

"My life was like the guy in this story." He indicated his iPod. "Except I didn't have to die to figure it out. I had the help of people like you."

"Nice of you to say that." He could not come up with a name. "So nice." The man didn't look in the least familiar. As Candler turned to leave, the pocket of his pants caught the corner of the desk and pulled him back.

"It's a good story." The man fitted the earphones back in place. "I've listened to it more times than I can count. He starts off dead and then he lives his whole life and then he dies again."

Candler could not remember the plot or the man, but he knew the story was one of those dreary Russian things. "You take care of yourself," he said. "Don't be a stranger." He stepped carefully away from the desk, through the door, and into the heat of the day.

DAY 13:

Despite the dumb corporate name, Lise felt Petco Park had the dignity of a train station, one of those elegant old buildings that called to mind women in long dresses and men in hats. She had purchased tickets down the third-base line, a good location for foul balls, with a clear view of the field. The Padres were terrible, and it was easy to get good seats.

She had moved in with her friend in Ocean Beach and given up her apartment in Liberty Corners, and soon she would have to give up James Candler, as well. But not this evening. On this evening, she and James and Billy were in downtown San Diego, in the red brick ballpark, and the Padres actually scored a couple of runs early, and she had sneaked in a bottle of scotch—not a flask but an entire bottle smuggled in under her skirt like a spy with a bomb.

Her father had taught her to love baseball, but it hadn't entirely taken. She recalled fondly going to major league games with him in St. Louis and twice in Kansas City and once at Wrigley Field in Chicago, where Sammy Sosa hammered one off the scoreboard in right center. But her father had failed in his efforts to make her love the sport, and his work had merely made her love him. She hadn't followed baseball since leaving Missouri, but it was easy to revive her interest after watching Candler study the box scores with a scrutiny usually reserved for the dark spots on X-rays or mysterious passages of scripture. He and Billy slouched on the ugly gray couch in Candler's living room and watched games together, talking to the players on the screen. "Come on, Hairston," Candler would say. "How 'bout a clutch hit for a change?" She had squeezed between them on that gruesome couch for a couple of games, and when the opposing team had the opportunity to score, Billy Atlas would start chanting and Candler would join in: "Hey batta batta batter, hey batta, *swing*." She got the tickets online. A present.

It was a Saturday, a fine June evening, the Padres already out of the pennant race, impossibly far behind the Dodgers, twelve games out in the loss column, and Lolly Powell, that exotic frilly creature from the photograph, would arrive at San Diego International Airport in less than forty-eight hours. There was Lise's loss column: forty-eight and counting down.

They drank scotch from Coke cups. Scotch was Candler's favorite, and she was developing a taste for it. He was talking to her—to her and Billy both—saying that the shortstop for the Padres, formerly their star but now struggling, suffered from nervous attacks and was having a terrible season. Candler explained that social anxiety disorder was a disaster for anyone habitually scrutinized by others.

"Like strippers," Lise said without thinking, the scotch and the balmy night making her tongue too quick. Candler and Billy laughed, and she asked them what a shortstop's scrutiny was compared to a woman who six times a night took off every shred of her clothing and squatted before the audience like a catcher but without even a mitt?

"At least there's no box score for strippers in the paper," Billy pointed out. "Nothing saying she went oh for five or whatever a stripper would go oh for. Not the paper we get, anyway. Maybe we subscribe to the wrong paper."

"I used to do that, you know, dance in a club," she said, terrified by her own boldness, but with only forty-eight—forty-seven now—hours left, what did she have to lose? "This was when I was kid, of course. A dumb kid."

"I had no idea," Candler said at the same moment Billy Atlas said, "Marry me."

There was no point now in not being brave. "I moved to California after high school. It wasn't the only work I could get, but it paid more than anything else, and . . . I don't look back on it with pride, but I don't blame that stupid girl I was for doing it." She was making it sound like it was ages ago, but otherwise she was telling the truth. "You think I'm some skank now?"

"Of course not," Candler said.

"No wisecracks?"

"I could come up with some if you want, but—"

"No," she said, and took his arm. She added scotch to their cups. "I like this better."

"I always wanted to date a stripper," Billy said. "Or any other woman."

"Some men get ugly about it," she said, "and I keep it a secret. But sooner or later, it feels like there's this dark patch that I have to avoid, have to work my way around. Unless I fess up about it. And the timing, you know. If I mention it right off, that sends the wrong signal too."

Candler put his arm around her and pointed to the Astros' right fielder. "That guy throws like a girl," he said. "I mean, he can throw farther and with more accuracy than nine out of ten men, but watch him warm up. It's like his arms are webbed and he can't fully extend."

"Some girls throw perfectly well," she said slapping at his chest.

"And he's one of them. He's a helluva player or will be. In a year or two."

"Remember that game," Billy began.

"You know I do," Candler replied. "I was just thinking of it."

"What game?" Lise asked.

"Just a ballgame played in a dirt lot," Candler said. "Maybe twenty years ago."

"For some reason we both remember it perfectly," Billy said, "as if it happened last week."

"Did something bad go on?"

The both shook their heads. "It was a good game, close score, a few nice plays, though nothing spectacular."

"We both had hits," Billy said. "Just singles, but still."

"We played after school, and it was fall weather, dusk by the late innings."

"I was the first baseman," Billy said. "Jimmy was shortstop. It was just a pickup game but we managed to get seventeen kids to play, eight on a team, and this kid Pumper caught for both teams."

"Any girls playing?"

"Three or four girls," Candler said. "Vi played, my sister."

"Three girls." Billy counted with his fingers. "Vi, Bobby Orton's little sister Meg, and that beautiful Mexican girl you dated in junior high."

"Delia Almadova," Candler said. "Isn't that the most musical name?"

"She was a terrible left fielder."

"Not in that game."

Billy shrugged and nodded simultaneously. "Caught that fly all the way out by the mesquite bush. I remember."

"I don't get it," Lise said. "Why do you guys always think about this one game?"

"Hard to say," Candler said. "It was just one of those days when you loved playing ball."

"When there wasn't any fight," Billy said, "or argument over a call, and no sad plays."

"*Sad* plays?" Lise asked. "What are sad plays?"

"Sometimes even if you hit the ball hard, the way it's caught makes you happy," Billy said. "Other times there's a collision, bleeding elbows, and temper. Or the game's so sloppy it's no fun. You know, we lost that game—Jimmy and I were on the same team. We lost by a run on a ninth-inning rally, but it's still the game we always think about."

"That's why you remember it, because you were teammates."

"We almost always were," Candler said. "We didn't like competing against each other."

"Too intense," Billy agreed.

A foul ball lifted from the bat of the Padres' center fielder and came flying their way. They all three stood, but it fell several seats short of them. The person who retrieved the ball—after it bounced off several hands—waved it grandly above his head, and he was cheered. He had spilled beer down his shirt.

"My dad used to take me to the ballpark," Lise said. "We listened to games together on the radio when I was really young, and he had these funny things he'd say."

"Like what?" one of them asked.

"A player would get a hit against a good pitcher, and he'd shake his head and say, *You could shoot that ball out of a cannon and some of these boys'd hit it.*"

Her boys laughed.

"I remember the shortstop for the Cubs," she said, "Sean something."

"Shawon Dunston," Billy said, spelling his name. "Arm like a catapult."

"He fell down going after a grounder, and my dad said, *He fields 'bout like a pig on ice.*"

Her boys laughed again.

"Bobby Orton was the shortstop on the other team," Billy said, and she understood they were talking again about the sandlot game. "I hit a grounder past the third baseman, and Bobby ran over, gloved it, spun around, and threw without bracing himself. I wasn't super fast or anything, but I could not believe that wasn't a hit. It was amazing."

"It doesn't exactly sound *amazing*," Lise said.

"Bobby Orton wasn't all that good," Candler explained. "It was one of those times when you play better than you're capable of playing."

"I would've had a rare multihit game," Billy said. "Rare for me, anyway, but for that play."

"Bobby wasn't even close to being good enough to make that play."

"It was the third out," Billy said, "and I shook his hand when he ran in."

An Astros batter connected, making that distinctive sound, bat and ball in perfect alignment, an almost metallic snap, and the ball arced into the bleachers in left-center. They all watched the flight. *He hit that one so hard, it put a dent in the sky*, her father would have said. *By the time that one comes down, it'll have a white beard.* She could hear his voice so clearly it brought tears to her eyes.

"I love baseball," Candler said, his arm around her, his breath rich with the decaying sweetness of scotch, and she could almost believe he was saying that he loved her. "I don't know why. It's the only sport I watch anymore."

"We could get season tickets," she said.

And then no one said anything for a long while.

DAY 14:

Frederick Candler set up an easel for Pook in the yard, and Pook, to everyone's surprise, decided to paint. The Candler children had all grown up painting, but Pook had not picked up a brush in years. After a week or so of dilatory work, he painted five canvases in a single day, one after another. He would not look at a painting after he finished it. The capacity for revision never had any place in his personality.

Pook's interest in painting marked the end of the comic book, though Jimmy and Billy failed to understand this. At first Jimmy thought his brother could simply paint the images they needed, but the paintings were stranger than the drawings, and Pook didn't seem capable of doing the scenes they requested, as if this new work was beyond his control. The boys approached Violet, and she drew a few panels for them. But her people all looked different from one another, and they didn't have the same authority as Pook's characters, and the comic book project drifted away. Yet Same Man was not gone. He appeared now on canvas.

The paintings were hard to describe. They were not good, but they were undeniably great. Pook's sense of perspective was funny, as if there was a ripple in his vision that skewed the relationship of one thing to another. His colors were bold, and he covered every inch of the canvas with several coats of paint, creating shapes by adding new colors to define the old: he'd paint over a brown background except for a section in the center, and the brown would turn out to be shaped like a man's pants. These uneven coats contributed to the weirdness, the earliest layers evident in the gaps like something that flashes by when you're not quite looking.

His subject matter was always the same: they were all self-portraits. He would set up the easel outside, sometimes facing the house and other times facing the yard, but he was always painting himself. Frederick propped up a mirror for him, but Pook turned his back to it. His paintings were about representing not the exterior world but his interior vision—and it was this that made the paintings great. Even Jimmy understood that Pook's paintings were better than his drawings, and he speculated that this had to do with the size of the canvas. The more space he had, the more extraordinary the paintings would become. That was just logical. Jimmy discussed this insight with Billy, which led them to stretch a canvas themselves—Jimmy had known how to stretch a canvas since he was ten—three times the size of the canvases their father supplied.

"Can't leave well enough alone," Mr. Candler said when he saw it. "You're just like your mother." He and Pook had set up in the shade of a mesquite tree at the far end of the property. Frederick was painting the living ocotillo fence. Pook had painted a canvas entirely green, except for one oddly shaped patch where the previous coat of pink showed through. The pink, Jimmy understood, was the sun, an oddly shaped blister in the green sky. Frederick sent the boys away, and when they thought to look in on the painters again, the big, blank canvas was gone.

Like his drawings for the comic book, Pook's paintings had strange shadows. Often the shadows were up to something slightly at odds with the figures casting them, and sometimes the shadows seemed to have volition while the humans were merely attached at the heel. One of Frederick Candler's most famous paintings was a portrait in which the shadow and figure traded places, set in the backyard near the cistern, and Jimmy understood that this idea had come from Pook's work, and perhaps that was why the figure in the painting was Pook himself—not Pook as he appeared in his own paintings and not Pook as he appeared in real life, but a version of the real Pook, in which he looked much the same but with squared shoulders and an expression one might associate with ordinary life, the way Pook might look if he were just anybody. When Pook saw the painting, he gave no indication of recognition, but he never saw himself in Frederick's or May's paintings or even in photographs, though once he had pointed at himself in a family picture and said, "My shirt." Only in his own drawings and paintings did he seem to recognize himself, and these, while clearly of him, did not exactly look like him but rather captured something about him—they captured precisely what Frederick's painting missed, the utterly unique quality of being Pook.

By noon Pook had moved his easel to the front porch, and Jimmy understood, at last, why his brother did not like to venture out at midday. At noon, the blister cast no shadows, making the earth, for his big brother, unbearable.

Besides his own image, Pook's paintings included two recurring elements: flowers and cats. The flowers sometimes resembled a daisy but no petal was the same size or quite the same shape and the parts had no visible center, as if the pieces were a flower in the process of being rebuilt or reborn and the receptacle that might hold them did not yet exist. The cats had heads like deflating soccer balls, and their features were not feline but almost human, insane heads of no recognizable creature and yet identifiably cats. Their bodies were large, sometime stretching across the canvas. Their bodies were nations, hemispheres, worlds. Along the continents of their bodies, the cats were often missing territory, fur scraped loose or ripped out in fights, which Pook represented by some previous coat of paint—and this process amazed Jimmy.

"He's a sedimentary artist," Billy had said, referring to their sixth-grade geology lessons. "You know, how sedimentary rocks can have layers of stuff. But he's also kind of volcanic." There was one other type of rock, but they couldn't remember it.

Jimmy thought Pook's method of composition had to reveal something about him. Why did he have to paint the whole canvas pink in order to have that pink sun emerge when he failed to paint over it? It was like having a hundred guitars each playing a different note, and then mixing and silencing them sequentially to create a song. Or if you were writing a book, you'd have to write a single word over and over and over, and then cover most of the words with new words, and then cover most of the new words with newer words, until a story emerged. He got out the typewriter and Wite-Out from his dad's study.

First Layer:

```
THE THE THE THE THE THE THE THE THE THE THE THE
THE THE THE THE THE THE THE THE THE THE THE THE
THE THE THE THE THE THE THE THE THE THE THE THE
THE THE THE THE THE THE THE THE THE THE THE THE
THE THE THE THE THE THE THE THE THE THE THE THE
THE THE THE THE THE THE THE THE THE THE THE THE
THE THE THE THE THE THE THE THE THE THE THE THE
THE THE THE THE THE THE THE THE THE THE THE THE
THE THE THE THE THE THE THE THE THE THE THE THE
THE THE THE THE THE THE THE THE THE THE THE THE
```

Second Layer:

```
THE
THE
        THE                                    THE


    THE                          THE

    THE
```

Third Layer:

```
THE DOG DOG DOG DOG DOG DOG DOG DOG DOG DOG DOG
THE DOG DOG DOG DOG DOG DOG DOG DOG DOG DOG DOG
DOG DOG THE DOG DOG DOG DOG DOG DOG DOG THE DOG
DOG DOG DOG DOG DOG DOG DOG DOG DOG DOG DOG DOG
DOG DOG DOG DOG DOG DOG DOG DOG DOG DOG DOG DOG
DOG THE DOG DOG DOG DOG DOG THE DOG DOG DOG DOG
DOG DOG DOG DOG DOG DOG DOG DOG DOG DOG DOG DOG
DOG DOG THE DOG DOG DOG DOG DOG DOG DOG DOG DOG
DOG DOG DOG DOG DOG DOG DOG DOG DOG DOG DOG DOG
DOG DOG DOG DOG DOG DOG DOG DOG DOG DOG DOG DOG
```

He gave up. He shouldn't have started with THE. Pook always started with the deepest thing, and there was no way THE could be very deep. That meant you had to know what was deep before you knew anything else, which Jimmy didn't know how to do.

Many paintings hung on the walls of the Candlers' house, but not the paintings of Frederick and May. It was a point of honor not to hang their own work. They traded with other artists. Periodically, some came down and others went up. When Pook painted from the porch, the inside of the house became the setting for the portraits, and the paintings on the living room wall appeared in the background but they were transformed. Abstract paintings became representational, portraits became landscapes, and landscapes became flowers or wallpaper or slabs of meat. Pook painted everything from memory and each item was not merely altered but remade. Even the objects that were identifiable—the piano, for example—were made unspeakably odd, and Jimmy had not been able to say why.

"There're no black keys," Billy pointed out.

Frederick and May did not immediately trust their estimation of Pook's work. They knew art and they had both taught for years, but this was their son and he was damaged. They were prone to compliment his few successes excessively. And this time it mattered in an entirely different way. If Pook was as talented as he seemed to be, the question of how he might spend his life was finally answered.

Frederick placed a few of Pook's canvases in the station wagon and drove to Phoenix. He was acquainted with an art dealer who had connections to galleries in New York, Santa Fe, and Los Angeles. Frederick did not tell the dealer that the artist was his son but claimed the paintings were the work of a student. The dealer flipped for them. He sent slides to the owner of a New York gallery. Plans were made. The gallery wanted to stack the paintings three high on its walls and augment them with paintings on easels. Fifty versions of Pook staring at the customers. They set a date that gave Pook several months to finish the remaining portraits.

Pook was told nothing of the plans, and for days all he did was situate and resituate his easel, paint canvases brown, set up and take down his easel. Then one day he painted four canvases, and the next day, he painted three more. The following week, he had a day of seven completed pieces. He had more than fifty paintings by the time of the opening.

And still, Pook knew nothing. As long as he had a window seat, he liked to fly in airplanes. It was easy to convince him to fly to New York with his parents. They planned to stay at an inexpensive hotel in New Jersey that Frederick and May often used, but the gallery owner lived in the high-rise across the street from the gallery, and the three Candlers stayed in an apartment on the fifteenth floor owned by a family spending the year in Europe.

Violet was seventeen by that time, and she remained home to look after Jimmy and, of course, Billy Atlas, who was spending the night despite Violet's protests. "Couldn't you two spend one weekend apart?" It would be years before they would see pictures of the show, the paintings stacked like windows, one upon another, all of the images of Pook staring out, staring back. In every painting, the figure peered out directly, as if to look the observer in the eye. They were unnerving and powerful. *It was impossible,* one art critic would argue, *to say that one of Paul Candler's pieces was better than another.*

Some had background objects—trees, the house, a car, Pook's idea of a horse or goat or pumpkin. There were never other people. In most, Pook was standing, but he squatted in some, reclined against a fantastically polka-dotted chaise, stood on tiptoes. There were no nudes, but his clothing changed, and most of it was either imaginary or based on his memory of actual clothing. For one shirt he painted dark blue trains against a yellow background, and Jimmy realized the shirt was modeled after a pajama top he wore, which had no trains but cowboys with lariats. He asked Pook about it, taking the pajama top to show him. Pook pointed to the raised lariat and its perfect circle of rope. "I remembered smoke," he said. "That made a train."

Frederick and May dressed up for the opening, but they saw no reason to ask Pook to change from his habitual jeans and T-shirt. He was the artist and eccentricity was expected. They ate first, bringing food to the room since Pook did not like restaurants. After the first few bites, he took his plate to the bathroom and finished eating there. They timed their entrance, as the gallery owner requested, to coincide with the height of the crowd.

"We have a surprise for you," his mother said to him. "I know you don't much care for surprises, but this is one you'll like, I promise."

At first, it did seem that he liked it. He ran in a quick circle around the room, his head turned up at the paintings. He knocked one patron to the floor and splashed wine on another. "This is the artist," the gallery owner told them, and even the knocked-down man laughed it off. This part of the story, Jimmy and Violet pieced together from their parents' accounts, and they had not thought to wonder about the detail of the man laughing until later when they discovered how the paintings had been marketed. Pook had been offered up as something of an idiot savant.

When Pook finished his lap, he walked out the door. May ran after him, leaving Frederick to explain. The opening was a mild success, but the show would turn into a fantastic triumph the next day when the world learned that the artist had leapt from a balcony on the fifteenth floor to the sidewalk, dying on a spot directly across from the windows of the gallery, expiring under the gaze of his creations. The paintings were snapped up quickly, and the gallery owner would one day admit that he should have raised the prices but the death had so befuddled him that he'd missed the opportunity of a lifetime.

What Violet remembered most was Jimmy's reaction when she told him Pook was dead. She had been watching a movie when their parents called, and she had not wanted to answer the phone. Her mother's voice trembled when she spoke. Violet leapt up and turned off the television. She was crying when she called her brother into the living room.

"Pook's dead," she said. "He jumped out a high window."

Jimmy dropped to the floor on his bottom, simply sat on the rug with a thump. He was not crying but staring off into space. Billy, who had come into the room with him, got down on his knees to put his arms around his friend.

"Mom said the exhibit upset him," Violet told him, kneeling next to her little brother. "He didn't know what he was doing."

"Pook always knew what he was doing," Jimmy said.

"Not this time," she insisted. "He wouldn't have killed himself if he'd known."

Jimmy shook his head. "He didn't like people seeing him. Seeing him in the pictures. Seeing so many of him. All of him."

Later, Jimmy cried in her arms, but it was this conversation on the floor that stuck with Violet, how the boy was so utterly certain about his brother's indecipherable act.

Candler remembered it differently. He and Billy had been in Pook's room while Violet watched television. They were playing a narrative game, a running dialogue, where one and then the other would invent plot. The secret treasure—the narrative always included a secret treasure—had to be in Pook's room, they reasoned. They were not normally permitted to enter his room, and so it only made sense that the elusive treasure was in there.

Unlike the rest of the house, Pook's room had no paintings, nothing on the walls but scraps of lined paper, taped in place, in even intervals. The scraps were all at the same height. Nothing was written on the bits of paper. Pook's dresser was neat and his desk was clear of clutter. In his closet were empty hangers on the rod, and below, a neat stack of pants and shirts on one side, and a neat mound of dirty clothes on the other side.

They found the treasure between the mattress and the box spring. Jimmy held up the mattress, and Billy pulled it free. A painting. The painting on the large canvas that Jimmy and Billy had stretched. Unlike any of Pook's other paintings, it was set in the very room in which they stood. It showed the pieces of paper on the wall. In the painting, each scrap held letters: *mon, two, wen, thrus, fry*. To show all the scraps, Pook had painted his body only in outline, a ghostly absence. There was something about those painted pieces of paper, how the whiteness of them seemed to vibrate. They were the deepest layer, the gesso that covered the canvas before any paint was added.

Then the phone rang and Jimmy's sister shut off the movie and began to cry.

The boys did not show the painting to Violet. They did not show it to anyone. They hid it, first in Jimmy's room and later at Billy's house. It hung now in James Candler's office. It was the only one of Pook's paintings that any of the family still owned.

And years later there was a night when James Candler was in bed with Saundra Dluzynski, asleep beside her, dreaming that he was a boy and wearing his cowboy pajamas, which had transformed into a shirt with a pattern of trains billowing steam. And both Jimmy in the dream and the sleeping James in bed would recall how Pook's head was angled in that painting, and in his left hand there was an object—a ball? an apple? What had he held? Candler shifted in bed, rolling his head along his pillow, half awake. And then he woke with a start: a pinecone. Pook, in that self-portrait, held a pinecone as if he was ready to toss it. The tiny clouds of steam on the shirt. The trains. The lariats. The bicycle without a seat. The scraps of paper on his wall. The big brother who goes away on a trip and never returns. What made Pook different from other people, Candler realized, if vaguely, as if he were still dreaming, was that Pook was just one person, and always the same person, and all those images of himself made it impossible to continue with his single life. Yes, Candler thought, at last that mystery . . . but he drifted off and lost forever the thread.

Billy Atlas remembered one other detail from the night Pook died. When Jimmy fell to his butt on the carpet and Billy went to his knees to put his arms around his friend, Jimmy whispered, "We didn't save him."

PART THREE
Once Pond a Time

Even the gods cannot change the past.

—AGATHON

6

She killed the car. She had stopped again at the tiny local museum to sit on its porch, peer through the darkened windows, and compose herself. She had not expected America to be so utterly unchanged when she had been through so much. Only her name was the same. She had kept her maiden name when she married, and she carried it now as a widow: Violet Candler. She was thirty-eight years old, and her husband had been twenty years older, which meant they had expected him to go first. Just not so unreasonably soon.

She climbed from the ugly, dirty, decrepit, perfectly adequate car, and returned to the comforting porch. She had her brother's cell phone, which meant she could not think of herself as lost so much as misplaced. The party in their honor—hers and Lolly's—was going strong and she would have to return, but she'd also had to escape it for a while. She enjoyed parties, generally, but not with loud, bad music and dozens of strangers, all wanting to shake her hand and tell her how much they liked Jimmy yet having nothing real to say about him—or perhaps nothing they were willing to say. He was evidently in line to become their boss, and they were careful, which rendered them tedious.

The porch was modest and tidy, its painted wooden planks solid under her shoes. Through one of the black windows she made out an enormous wing, rising from a great and oddly shaped body. She wondered about the nature of this museum and the treasures the house might hold. A fantasy of strangeness presented itself but vanished when she realized she was staring at a piano, a baby grand, its black lid raised as if to fly away.

She had left the party with the excuse of going to see the Congregation of Holy Waters Museum, and though she had tried to follow her brother's directions, she had gotten lost. She only managed to find it because Jimmy said it was practically under the freeway. It was impossible to drive in Onyx Springs without running into the freeway, and she tried every exit until she saw the modest blue sign for the museum.

It was closed, of course, but she parked and examined the old building. The only part of the evening she genuinely enjoyed took place in the squeaking porch swing.

She had driven off to return to the party and didn't know how thoroughly lost she was until she realized that she was driving by the museum again. After circling for half an hour, she was back on that tempting porch. The swing was soothing and the interior of the car smelled bad. Out in the relative dark, she could ignore, for the moment, her navigational incompetence.

The car was not hers and not her brother's. A rust-laden ancient Dodge Dart, it belonged to Jimmy's hapless friend Billy Atlas. It was the only car he had ever owned, a fact that struck her as deeply pathetic. He had driven it since he and Jimmy were in high school. On the one hand, she admired her brother's loyalty to his friend; on the other, Billy Atlas was an incompetent. She didn't dislike him, exactly, but she never looked forward to seeing him.

They were all, for the moment, living together in Jimmy's house: her brother and his fiancée, Billy Atlas, and Violet. The house was fairly new and (thankfully) had plenty of bedrooms and Jimmy kept it clean, but it was a drafty, unattractive barn that managed to be ostentatious and cheap at the same time. Why Jimmy would buy such a place baffled her. He owned a fancy automobile, as well. It was a pretty object, much the way an ashtray might be pretty, but why would he spend a fortune on a car?

Jimmy had changed. They had been close when Violet was in college and Jimmy in high school. She had driven home regularly to see him, and they phoned twice or more each week, talking about the people they were seeing, their colorful array of lovers. They had been frank about sex and desire and the attendant feelings of uneasiness and fear, but their real topic had been the future, what they were going to do, how they were going to make their lives interesting and bold— *meaningful*. They planned to have meaningful lives. Their conversations bolstered her when she decided to live in Europe. She left for England young and excited and full of the electric heat of possibility, and now she had come home, her youth spent, her husband dead, and her brother was neither the friend he had once been nor any man she knew.

Oh, she missed Arthur. Not the way he was at the end. She was not sad to see that final, diminished version of him disappear. She missed the man she had married, the gentle, absentminded man who wanted nothing more from life than to spend it with her. She flipped open Jimmy's cell with the intention of calling him. Only while she was examining his contact list did it occur to her that, of course, she had *his* phone. Who was she meant to call? Ideally, it would not be someone at the party. She didn't like the idea of her ineptitude becoming a joke to pass around like a bowl of dip. She had only been back in the States for ten days, and she wasn't ready for even a minor humiliation. Unfortunately, Jimmy's contact list was merely first names. Lolly was one of the few she knew, and she was the last person Violet wanted to call for help. She had inadvertently introduced Jimmy to Lolly, and there were few things in her life she regretted more.

Lolly Powell drove her mad. She was a woman who shaped her identity to fit the immediate circumstances of her life, a talent she must have discovered at some point in her youth, and she clearly had never gotten over the astonishment of her adolescent success. All of which left her bereft of an actual personality. She simply did not make sense as a person. She was an enormously competent child, and now she had no outlet for that competency except as it concerned Jimmy. They were in that stage of romance where they could not keep their hands off each other, which meant Lolly spent her time being a sex object, and Violet had to admit that she was terribly competent at it. *Terribly competent.* Violet had almost changed her plans to stay with her brother once she understood Lolly was coming, too. If her parents hadn't divorced she might have gone to Tucson.

More to the point: Lolly's cell, like Violet's, didn't work in the U.S. She didn't particularly care to ask Billy Atlas for help either, but he, at least, would be discreet if she requested it of him, and his was the only other name on the list she recognized.

The call went directly to voicemail: "This is Billy to the B—" She ended the call, folding her arms over her chest and pushing with her toes to rock the swing. She was going to have to call a stranger.

As she thought this, something brushed against her leg. She stopped swinging and shifted her feet. She felt it again and lifted her legs, folding them onto the swing. Her heart hurtled beyond reason into something resembling terror. The open phone provided a nimbus of light, and there on the painted planks was a cat, a tabby, her head cocked away from the phone's illumination.

"You gave me a scare, kitty," Violet said, lowering her feet slowly, displaying her free hand in the phone's light as she neared the cat. Curling its head to accept the offering, the cat revealed the opposite side of her feline face, which was matted with blood. Violet startled and the cat bolted. She called after it apologetically, but the opportunity had passed.

One of the entries on the phone's contact list had *at home* written after the name, and she tried that one. At least, if he answered, he definitely wouldn't be at the party.

"Coury residence."

"Is this Jimmy Candler's friend Mick?"

A long pause ensued and then a tentative "Yes."

"I'm terribly sorry to bother you, but I'm Jimmy's sister and I know it sounds ridiculous, but I don't know my way about Onyx Springs and I'm lost."

"You need directions?" He asked for her location, and she told him.

"I'm trying to get to a bar . . ." She realized that she could not recall the name of the place. "It's out on a highway . . . I . . ."

"I can be at the museum in five or five and a half minutes," this Mick Coury said. "If you don't mind the porch? If it's not too dark."

"I like the porch." She almost added that she liked the dark and winged things hidden inside, the dark and damaged things that prowled the deck, but she held back. She already sounded stupid; she didn't want to sound crazy.

Mick had been upstairs, barefoot in his bedroom, shifting his weight experimentally from one foot to the other, when the telephone rang in the hall. He went to get it. His mother didn't like to answer the phone if both her boys were in the house. The two greatest inventions in the history of humankind, she liked to say, were the answering machine and disposable diapers. "What about the wheel?" Mick had asked her.

He had a plan for the evening: hanging out with Maura at the only place she was permitted to hang out—her dormitory. Not in her room. Boys couldn't go to the girls' rooms because they might layer together in a dormitory bed and ladle kisses along the length of their bodies. On the ground floor were Ping-Pong rooms and board games and a TV like a great rectangular mouth—no eyes or nose, just the mouth, as if instead of mounting the head on the wall, the taxidermatologist had cut everything away but that enormous mouth, which hung on the wall and people stared into it, the monster's immense mouth, from which no one could look away.

He had showered. He had toweled off. He had rubbed the towel over his hair briskly. He put on black socks but felt funny naked in black socks and took them off. He combed his hair. It was still damp, and he toweled it again. He rolled deodorant on his pits. He couldn't decide whether to put on the shirt first or his underpants. How do people make such decisions? What is the underlying basis for such decisions? He went with the underpants. He put on the same black socks, but they sheathed him from the carpet's sly tickle. He took off the black socks. He sat on the edge of the bed and simultaneously lifted his legs while with two hands he waved the pants. He shot his feet into the pants' oval openings. *Who says he puts his pants on one leg at a time like everybody else?*

He was buttoning his shirt and thinking about balance, the carpet licking his bare soles, when Mr. James Candler's sister called to ask for help. Such an unexpected call, but it had been a day for the unexpected. For one thing, Maura finally got to ride in his Firebird. "Thank god your brain wires fried," she said upon climbing in. "You were definitely an asshole before."

He had taken her to lunch. She wasn't supposed to go anywhere without an official chaperone, but Billy Atlas gave her special permission to ride with Mick while he ferried the others to KFC. Maura's diet didn't permit fast food, and Mick escorted her to a diner. That was another unexpected thing, eating at a diner, whose chairs had padding and silver legs, and the utensils were not made of plastic. Also, Karly had all day not wanted to make wedding plans with him. Could something be repetitively unexpected? Routinely unexpected? A daily unexpected thing that he could count on?

After he finished talking to the lost woman, he reunited phone and receiver. He put on his socks and shoes. He didn't examine himself in the mirror, which always took longer than anyone might suspect. He couldn't afford the time when there was a woman waiting for him, a stranger who needed assistance. Had Mr. James Candler advised her that Mick was the one she should call if she strayed off course? What other answer could there be?

Downstairs, he dipped into the living room to say good night to his mother, who was spread over the couch buns like a condiment. The room would have been dark except for the television, a black-and-white movie offering a shifting, grumbling light. His mother wore sweatpants and a T-shirt, her after-work uniform. Today's T-shirt was red with yellow lettering: I CAN RESIST EVERYTHING BUT TEMPTATION. He knew that was funny, though it didn't make him laugh. Her eyes left the screen long enough for her mouth to say, "Call me if you're going to be late."

"I'll call you if I'm going to be late," he replied.

She looked at him then. "You didn't comb your hair."

Mick ran his fingers through his hair, the ravines between tingling much the way his bare feet had against the carpet. He counted backward from twenty to appease her, to prove that he had taken his meds, which he hadn't. Not a whole pill, anyway. His mother had read an article in a magazine about how to tell if a person was crazy: have him count from twenty to zero without a mistake. Only people not at the moment out of their minds could do it, evidently. Mick could do it. Sometimes he got the perfect amount of medication in his bloodstream, and tonight was such a sometime. He felt light and alive and free, and not in danger of levitating out of it. Firmly rooted and all that.

"All right, I suppose," his mother said. "Have fun."

The reliable Firebird roared to life. On the way to the diner, Maura had told him that he drove at a *glacial* speed. That had made him laugh. The lunch had gone well until near the end. The waitress, her short sparse hair like electrical filaments, had said, "How does everything taste?" Mick considered how humans tasted things, and how animals had specialized tasting abilities, and how every creature, even something such as a halibut, which was what he'd been eating, must have the ability to taste, and how did the hook taste when it bit into the fish's mouth? He could not answer, staring dumbly at the waitress, but Maura saved him.

"Z'all great," she said.

How it was possible that he could not come up with such a simple, generic line? A waitress was not interested in philosophical truth-saying. She was checking in, being polite, protecting her tip. It seemed to him that all he needed to do was memorize a few rote sayings, latch on to a handful of clichés, and he'd be sane.

"Have a nice day," he practiced as he steered, not zipping along as he would when he had taken no meds. Sane driving, though slower than any other car on the road. "Take care," he rehearsed. "Keep your head up."

The Firebird ducked under the freeway's dark awning and just beyond, the unlit museum crouched by the side of the road. The car in the lot was older even than his own, and he felt a sudden kinship with this mislaid woman. A shadow on the porch rose from the swing and descended the steps, gaining color and human dimensions as she approached, shedding her shady existence, utter transformation. How magical life was when you really saw it. She had blond or maybe light brown hair, a willowy build, a woman older than Karly or Maura, but no older than his mother. He got out of his car to greet her.

"Are you Mick?"

Obviously, he was different from what she expected. He wondered how it showed, his illness. He had studied himself in the mirror, compared himself to men passing in the street. He could not see the difference but others could. He said none of this, merely nodded, a heaviness with him just that quickly, ready to flatten him.

"I'm so grateful to you," she said, and in a second the heaviness lifted. "This is beyond the call." She smiled, which changed the shape of her face. A striking smile but it made her unattractive—which made him understand that she was pretty when she wasn't smiling. She was wearing a light-blue dress belted low on her waist. Her arms and legs were bare. *Beyond the call? Beyond the phone call?*

"Hello," he said.

She extended her hand, and Mick shook it, a gentle handshake, a careful handshake, telling her his name, which she already knew. She was definitely not brown-haired but blond, so blond that he felt uncomfortable, and with that deforming smile. *Jimmy?* This was Mr. James Candler's sister. *Jimmy?*

"You work with him," she said, "don't you?"

"I work with him," Mick said.

"I thought so," she said. "I'm—this is so embarrassing, but I'm easily turned around. I left the gathering to . . . just to get away, but I wanted to see the Holy Waters place."

Easily turned around: he knew what she meant, but some part of him resisted knowing. Mr. James Candler was trying to get him to be what he called *mindful,* which meant being aware that his mind was going to offer up junk, and he had the power to ignore it.

"It's not open at night," he said, glancing at the museum, which was taller now, darker now, and more solid.

"I didn't think it would be, but I'm not much for bars, and I needed a getaway. I've been driving in circles forever." She laughed gently. "I have no idea how to get back to the bar, or the name of the bar. Oh, can you rescue me?"

Mick wanted to straighten out her error, tell her that he was a client of Mr. James Candler, not a colleague. He *worked with* her brother, but they were always working on Mick. At the same time, he liked her mistake. A fabulous mistake, and the picture snapped back into place. It was just a parking lot, a woman he didn't know, a simple task to perform. Just like that, the world was clear again, the magic gone.

"I didn't grow up here," he told her, "but I know the way around pretty well. I drive a lot. If you can't remember the name of the place," he didn't want to say the word *bar,* for some reason, "can you tell me what that part of town is like?"

"There are so many chapters in my stupidity that I might have a complete and completely preposterous book. It was on a highway, and there were a number of old motels."

Mick raised his hand to cut her off, but it made him think about school, raising his hand to answer a question. What question? He couldn't remember any questions from school, but here within him was the urgency to respond. Mr. Clay Hao was in a band with his brother. Mick knew they were playing in town tonight. Why else would Mr. James Candler be in Onyx Springs on a Saturday night? He said, "Is it the Phantom Limb?"

She smiled, that disfiguring expression of pleasure, and nodded. "How could I have forgotten that?"

I've forgotten who I used to be, he thought to say. He told her how to find the Phantom Limb. He gave excellent directions. He had a logical mind. His problems did not involve logic, exactly. Not street-direction logic.

"Do you want to follow me there?" he asked.

"You're going?"

She seemed excited by the possibility. Was it possible to go to a bar where the counselors would be? He imagined this as a topic for the crowd at the sheltered workshop, but he didn't seriously consider going and at some level he understood that her eager response was merely relief. It had been that way in the restaurant, too. Even as he was imagining the tasting apparatus of a halibut, some part of his brain knew he was on the wrong track. All he had to do . . . he let the thought go. He had been a little loopy, he realized, but now he was better. This woman, her kind way of talking, was making him better.

"I'm not going to the party," he told her, "but if you're worried about finding it, I could lead you."

"You're very kind, and I am a moron with directions."

Mick flinched. *Moron* was one of the words they were prohibited from using at the shelter. "I don't mind."

After a second, he added, "Z'all great."

"I'd feel better if you'd let me buy you a drink, at least."

"I have another . . ." He had to search. ". . . engagement."

"I may be moving here," she said. "To this part of the world, any-way. I'm just visiting right now, but I'm at loose ends and I like the ocean—not that Jimmy has taken us to the beach yet. You coastal types take the beach for granted."

"When I was a boy, I would say take it for *granite*."

"You wouldn't want a beach you could take for granite."

She again tendered the complicated smile. It revealed her in such an odd way, as if it showed the person beneath the face. What was underneath wasn't pretty in the simple way her unsmiling face was pretty. Her smile made her ugly in order to reveal her deeper beauty. This made sense to him, although it was the kind of thinking that made his counselors worry. Did logic have to apply to everything?

"Please don't tell Jimmy I had to beg directions off you. He already thinks I'm a dimwit."

"I know plenty of dimwits," Mick said. "Many of them are my friends."

She laughed at that and said, "Now you know another."

Before they drove off, she called, "Don't drive too fast."

That would not be a problem.

The boy drove so slowly, he must think she was an utter nincompoop. But it was generous of him to guide her across town, and Violet found herself once again on the old highway that led to the bar. She had not driven much when she lived in London. She would ride the tube or take buses and taxis, and when she and Arthur had taken out their car, he had done the driving. She never adjusted to being on the left side of the road, and now, back in her home country and with the car on the right side, she still felt tentative behind the wheel.

The two-lane blacktop that had once been the main thoroughfare for Onyx Springs was lined with failed motels from the 1950s. Jimmy had told her that the city council, back in the day, had worked to preserve the neon signs advertising the motels, even as the buildings themselves were demolished or transformed into low-rent mini-malls, seedy apartment houses, a salvage yard and parts store. Only a few survived as motels. Jimmy provided all this information on the drive in, an apology of sorts to his fiancée, Violet thought, for their destination. The Wayfarer's Inn sign showed a neon car from the fifties parked beneath a neon palm, but the building housed a drinking establishment and band venue, the Phantom Limb.

Violet liked the history of the old highway. It was so supremely American, the road culture of motels, the preservation of the signs instead of the buildings. Ludicrous, but she liked it. She understood that she had been homesick. Arthur's illness and death had overshadowed her own desires, and she was happy now to acknowledge her feelings.

The young man pulled into a gravel lot, and she followed. He didn't stop to let her thank him, but waved as he drove off. She wondered how he knew her brother. He seemed too young to work at the Center. Or perhaps he merely looked young. Maybe she had grown so old that young men looked like boys, but she suspected that he was one of Jimmy's patients. What would have happened had she dialed someone who was seriously disturbed?

She had to pass through a lingering group of people at the door. They eyed her with curiosity and suspicion. The Center had reserved the place for the night, and one had to be on the guest list to enter. She could not guess why people were surrounding the entrance as if to catch a glimpse of a celebrity. None of the doctors or counselors at the Center was famous. Violet had researched Onyx Rehab when Jimmy took the job three years earlier. Arthur had helped her. He had been fine then, as far as she had known. Just three years ago.

An immense, pudgy security guard in matching blue pants and cap, and a white shirt so thin that it was virtually see-though, stood at the door. He had a fat silver badge pinned over one nipple.

"I'm Jimmy Candler's sister." She took her passport from her purse. "I just left to get some air."

"I remember you," the guard said, declining to look at her identification. "I'd have to be a gooney bird to forget you. You're Candler's sister."

She had just said as much, but she smiled anyway. "That's right."

"My wife works with your brother," he said. "I'm glad he's finally getting married." He winked at her. "This job is only temporary. Somewhat demeaning, given the work I'm accustomed to, but what the heck, anything to help out. You know?"

"It's nice of you," she said.

"I'm not pretending I can't use the feed besides." He abruptly turned to stop a young woman from entering the bar. "Hold it there, missy. This is an invitation-only thingy." The woman mumbled something and turned away.

Violet leaned in close to him. "Who are these people you won't let in?"

He put his lips against her ear. "The *crazies*," he said, softly. "The long-goners. The three-bolts-and-only-two-nuts, the the-cab-looks-fine-but-where-are-the-wheels. In other words, the loonies. What they call their *clients*, the ones that live out in the open. My whole job is to keep 'em out."

Inside, the scene suggested why. What patients could trust therapists who drank so much and danced so badly? Violet rubbed at her ear, which was moist from the guard's breath. The front lobby had a quiet bar, while the band played in what had once been the motel's restaurant. The windows were blackened, but otherwise the place still had the rundown charm of the Wayfarer's Inn.

She made her way to the lobby bar, passing two young men waggling their heads and beer bottles to the music, eyeing the hypnotic buttocks of a dancing woman. She was surprised to find Lolly in the lobby. She would have thought Lolly the type to dance until she dropped. She was a bit tousled and damp from dancing, but she did not look close to dropping. Several young men gathered about her, but not Violet's brother. When Jimmy had come to London to visit, Violet introduced him to Lolly because she was an employee. It was not her intention to throw them together. She tried to talk to her brother about the danger of falling for someone while abroad. He and Lolly were two Americans in London, which might make it seem like they had a lot in common.

Jimmy misunderstood her intent. "I'm sorry about Arthur," he said, "but his illness had nothing to do with where you met him."

That flummoxed her. Her husband of nine years died of a rare disease of the muscles, known in the U.S. for a baseball player who had suffered from it. Arthur's muscles one by one burned out until in the end he was wholly immobile. It was true that she had met him in London, but she couldn't otherwise follow the circuitry of her brother's logic.

Lolly called her over. Arthur had liked Lolly. She reminded herself of this fact often. Arthur had liked Lolly and so there had to be something worthwhile about the woman. A half dozen men surrounded her. Lolly was pretty, but it was the way she flaunted herself that attracted the men. She was all candle flame, and the moths inevitably lined up to be charred. It had been a joke between Arthur and Violet, how obvious and predictable Lolly's provocations were, and how a certain type of man was made powerless by them. By that time, Arthur could not speak or actually laugh, but his eyes would flare with wicked delight. Nonetheless, he had liked Lolly. In one of the painfully slow messages he had managed to type on his computer—a filament was attached to his eyebrow, which served as a mouse—he typed:

You re tooo hardon her.

That was possibly true, she admitted, but that didn't mean she wanted Lolly as a sister-in-law. Violet could not believe that her brother was one of the moths—the head moth, prepared to be stuck in her hot wax forever.

"Where'd you disappear to?" Lolly asked.

"I drove around Onyx Springs." Instead of revealing that she'd been lost, she told Lolly what the guard had said, that the bunch outside the door were all patients.

When one of the young men stuck his head between them for an introduction, Lolly said to him, "Don't you wish they let the patients come to this? It seems so bloody callous to lock them out."

Violet winced at *bloody*. Lolly affected a number of British phrases. She had lived in London merely a year, and the expressions included most of the clichéd lines that Americans imagined Brits spoke. The men stared earnestly at Violet, waiting for her view. She offered them a smile. She had met them earlier but could not have named a one. She said, "I can understand wanting to be free of responsibility for a night."

"There you go," one said. He shook a cigarette from a crumpled pack and offered it to her. "It's a private party," he said. "Smoking's cool."

Perhaps she was through with parties. She would live alone for the remainder of her life to avoid small talk. She'd have to get a cat. She would return to the Holy Waters and find that poor kitty. She and the damaged feline in some snug cottage.

"It's just so dull, don't you think?" Lolly said, adding, "No offense, gentlemen."

"It *would* be dull," another said, "if you two hadn't come."

Lolly showed him a wide, rectangular smile. She was twenty-six, a few years out of college. Jimmy was thirty-three, and he'd been more mature than Lolly when he was in high school. Or perhaps that was merely a sister's biased assessment. Violet was only just getting comfortable with the idea that she'd soon be forty. She was a widow and middle age had stopped like a cab at the corner to wait for her, but she was still attractive to men—when she wasn't standing beside someone like Lolly.

There was another reason she had doubts about Lolly, one that sounded self-important, and she never voiced it. She believed Lolly's desire for Jimmy had to do with Violet herself, with joining Violet's family. Violet had hired her, and Lolly had been so grateful for the job. She wanted to *hang out* with Violet and help with Arthur, and at first, she and Arthur enjoyed her company. There was no denying that Lolly was helpful. Violet leaned on her at times. But there was always an expense.

Once, when the two women were in a specialty grocery, delighted to find several cases of the high-calorie nutritional drink meant to keep Arthur from withering away to nothing, Lolly sought out a clerk to help with the toting, and the young man, an Ichabod type, all elbows and Adam's apple, said to Violet, "Your sister's grand. She have a bloke?"

"You told that boy we're sisters?" Violet asked after the gawky creature finished loading their car.

"Aren't we, though?" Lolly responded. She had dated the clerk for a couple of weeks—that gangly, ungainly stork. And now these men that crowded about her—given the chance, would any of them resist Lolly's charms? Was Violet absurd to think her brother ought to know better?

Lolly was telling the boys about her own history as a counselor—the absurd massage idiocy—a recollection that Violet could likely have repeated word for word, and so she knew when Lolly was winding down—yet the final sentences surprised her.

"Do we get to meet some of them?" Lolly asked. "The patients?"

Of course she'd want to meet them, Violet thought. She'd want to display her own therapeutic skills, and god help them if they failed to applaud her talents.

The young men looked earnestly to a somewhat older man whom Violet had met earlier and she did remember his name: John Egri, the departing director. He fit in well with the twenty-something crowd, despite his age, chubby-cheeked and cheerful. All of the men were handsome, or at least well groomed and inoffensive in appearance. She found them difficult to tell apart. For the moment, men did not particularly interest her, not romantically, not sexually, and only rarely intellectually. It was as if the whole gender had lost their verve during the years she was married, and they didn't seem to be making much effort to get it back. Maybe this was why she could not connect with Jimmy. Maybe it was her fault.

"If you'd like to have a tour of the facilities," John Egri began, speaking so softly everyone had to lean toward him.

"Not another bloody tour," Lolly said rather dramatically. "Before I joined Violet at the agency, I worked on a tour bus in London. I had to fake an accent. No one on vacation from Idaho wants to hear about Westminster Abbey from a Jersey girl."

She still had that fake accent, Violet thought. "We took a tour this morning," she said. They had strolled the grounds and eaten in the cafeteria. They had not even seen Jimmy's office. "It was interesting, but we didn't meet any of the patients. I understand that might be impossible or inappropriate."

"Oh, well, it's not that," John Egri said, and he seemed to say more, but Violet couldn't hear him. He was so soft-spoken that she wanted to take him by the shoulders and shake him.

Lolly, quite sensibly, ignored him. "You were gone so long," she said to Violet, "I thought maybe the Calamari Cowboys had run you out of town."

At some point during their acquaintanceship, Violet had confessed to Lolly her shameful secret: she did not like rock music. The secret had been exposed while she was in high school, and the revelation had led to endless invitations from well-meaning boys to listen to one hateful song or another. *I guarantee you'll like this one,* they said, and along came Guns N' Roses or Beck or Nirvana or Radiohead or "Freebird" or "Cowgirl in the Sand." She had been a quiet girl, which many of her peers and teachers misinterpreted as shyness. She was actually fairly comfortable with herself, by teenage standards. She was pretty but not popular, and while she was a good student, she had not joined any of the clubs or societies. She had a few friends. She dated. But she never went in for that *gushing* quality that seemed quintessentially teenage. Much of her senior year, she had dated a boy who was gay—great company and he didn't mind that she hated U2.

And yet she went off with one of the boys—just the one. *Give it a spin,* he said. *You don't have to like it.* Robbie Kearns. She tried to remember the song he played for her. Not that it had anything to do with choosing him. She was ready to have a real boyfriend, and he adequately fit the bill. Brave enough to slip his hands beneath her clothing and reasonable enough to accept directions.

Oh, yes, the Beatles, "I Am the Walrus." She had not liked the song but it had been an unpredictable choice, at least.

There was never a long silence when Lolly was around. Violet had told her about her desire to see the Pacific Ocean, and Lolly used it now in the conversation. Here was another annoying trait of Lolly's, her appropriation of another's desires, dreams, even words. Not to mention family members.

"I'd like to see the sun set in the ocean," Lolly said. "I grew up on the wrong coast for that. And I want to get inside the heads of these patients—the kind James works with. I want to know where he's putting his energy."

"He'd better reserve some of that energy for you." It was the same fellow who had been speaking all along. The American capacity for crassness was stunning, as was Lolly's terrible gift for flirtation. She gave the fellow a long look and then smiled, displaying her gleaming bank of white teeth. "Bloody right, he better."

Billy's peyote vision involved creatures from the natural world speaking English, though he could never quite catch their lips moving. "Always behind my back," he said, "as if they knew I couldn't handle seeing where the words were coming from." He inhaled deeply on the joint and passed it to Mick Coury.

Mick liked the smell of marijuana, especially from a distance. He took in another lungful of smoke and tried to hold it. They had all heard the peyote story before at the sheltered workshop, but they enjoyed listening to Billy Atlas. He had an expressive face, and he loved going over every detail. Mick passed the cigarette to Maura, and immediately coughed smoke in her face.

"Secondhand high," she said, and laughed before sucking on the joint herself.

Mick and Maura and Billy Atlas were sitting on the cool concrete floor in the basement of Danker Dormitory, with Vex and Billy Atlas's girlfriend making it five. Billy and the girl were on their way to the Phantom Limb, and Mick wanted to tell them that he had been there—at least in the parking lot. He considered describing Violet Candler's complicated smile, but she hadn't wanted people to know that she could not follow directions, and anyway, he was practicing not saying things that made him sound stupid.

For the past few weeks, with Karly, he had been hinting about engagement rings. She wouldn't give him a clue about the type she preferred, and he'd made several idiotic comments about rings and gold and diamonds. He had visited a dozen jewelry stores and listened to strangers tell him about Karly. "A diamond will thrill her," said one. "Every woman longs for a big rock," said another. "She'll want gold," a young woman in a black jacket said, "even if she preferred silver in the past—gold means forever." One of the clerks told a joke. "Heard this on the radio," he said. "A standup guy doing jewelry humor. So the new diamond slogan is *Diamonds, they'll take her breath away.* And last year's was *Diamonds, they'll leave her speechless.* You get the message they're trying to tell you? *Diamonds, that oughta shut her up.*" Mick had laughed hard and then escaped. Stoned, he could not recall exactly why he had been in such a hurry to get away from the guy. How long had he been thinking about all this? Was everybody in the basement staring at him?

"Gold means forever," he said aloud.

"Not even close," Vex said. "Diamonds are forever." He had supplied the pot, a ziplock baggie, like the kind Mick had kept in his glove box back when he was his real self. He tried to think what else was in the glove box back then. Not gloves, he knew that much for sure.

"James effing Bond," Billy said.

"Dope used to make me cry," Vex said. "I know you won't believe that. It was embarrassing." He looked like he might break down while he was admitting his tendency to break down. "Makes me think of my dad, how we'd get high together."

"Your dad dead?" Maura asked.

"Almost," he said, nodding. "He's like sixty and he has a mole on his neck." He pointed to his own neck.

Maura pretended to bite his neck. Vex had blown the lid off the assembly scores—135 boxes in an hour—but there was no way they'd send him to the factory. Two or three times a day he got furious and terrorized people, especially poor Billy. She loved his threats. "I'll rip off your foot and stick it up your nose," he'd said. When Maura laughed, Vex turned on her. "You think I won't beat the shade out of you just because you've got a motherfucking vagina?" That had made her laugh harder. Billy had said, "It's time-out time," and Vex had hung his head and trudged to the time-out chair.

"This is primo leaf," Billy said. Anything he said made everyone laugh.

"Generalissimo Atlas," Maura said, "tell us, please, kind sir, what's in our files."

Billy made like zipping his lips, but they cajoled him into it. "Officially," Billy said to Maura, "you're a major depressive disorder, single episode, severe without psychotic features." High, he could not hide his pride at having memorized this. "In my opinion, my *professional* opinion . . ." He took another toke and spoke the remainder while holding his breath. ". . . the better diagnosis is rebel with no effing clue whatsoever."

"I like that a lot better," Maura said. She did a rebel yell. "Do him."

"Mick?" Billy said and exhaled.

"Not the official one," Mick said. He hated that word.

Billy shrugged. "Okey doke. My diagnosis is . . . *thoughtfulitis.*"

"Oh god, did he nail you," Maura said. When the laughter subsided, she demanded to know all the others: Rhine was a kindly geek, Alonso a moron with erotic tendencies, Cecil a squeezebox retard, and Karly? He hesitated and smoked to cover his caution.

"You can skip her," Maura said.

Billy had seen Karly's records. He knew she was officially *mildly mentally impaired,* which meant *retarded* and made him think that a lot of the people he'd known were likely mildly retarded. Karly was one of the sweetest people he'd ever met, and she wasn't dumb about everything. She was on Facebook, posting jokes she had heard and commenting on videos. She often got the jokes wrong, and the posts were simple, but Facebook intimidated Billy—the busyness of the page made him feel itchy and overwhelmed. Karly was also on the fifth level of an online video game that he had looked into on Candler's home computer. It had to do with farming on alien planets, which sounded interesting, but the movement of the characters through the world made Billy carsick. Was it carsick if you weren't in a car? "If my dad didn't die," Karly had said to Billy, "I'd still live at home. He couldn't help dying, and my mom couldn't help if it was all too much for her with me there without him." They had been talking during the lunch break. He had taken her and Alonso to the KFC. After a moment she added, "Everybody can't help something." That had stuck with him, and he could hear her voice whenever he recollected it. He said, "I think Karly's got some complicated stuff in her past that she's working through, is what I think."

"That's not a diagnosis," Mick said.

"What about Mr. Psycho?" Maura asked, indicating Vex. She wanted to ditch the subject of Karly Hopper.

Billy looked directly at Vex. "That's easy," he said. "You're a *dick.*"

The laughter resumed.

"Good thing I'm on the reserve tank from this kickass weed," Vex said. He was crying and laughing both. "Hate to spoil the party by bashing in your fat face."

Billy cautioned them against mentioning the dope to others. "It's only legal in this state if you've got glaucoma or cancer or something," he said, "and I'd hate to have to give you a tumor."

"Ha ha," Maura said and then actually laughed, something about forming her lips into the *ha* shape forcing real laughter out of her. "Your jokes are so dumb it's funny that you think they're funny."

Billy Atlas nodded. "So you tell me some funny *smart* stuff. Jokes about quarks and black holes and deconstruction and symbiosis."

Vex doubled over laughing. He had the joint and smoke came from his mouth in place of language. Mick could almost read the smoke.

Billy Atlas's girlfriend wasn't smoking. She was sort of pretty and seemed content to be there, smiling and moving her head, but she wasn't getting high or making jokes. The room held a stack of metal chairs against one wall, and there was a single grimy window over which they'd draped Billy Atlas's dark shirt. Billy had a belly that wiggled when he laughed and changed shape when he inhaled. It wasn't a huge stomach, but it filled his undershirt in a lively way.

"That old car of yours," Maura told Billy, "needs a quark of oil."

They all laughed, which told Mick the pot was working. He had smoked pot before his illness but this was the first time since. He was pretty sure he was enjoying himself.

"That proves my point," Billy said. "It's funny because it's dumb. But did you see the car I'm driving tonight?"

"A smart-looking car?" Mick asked.

"Okay, all right, look," Maura said, still burping up an occasional giggle as she continued. "Here's something incredibly smart that's also funny. Hysterical. When I was in high school, back about an hour ago, I had a physics class at the crosstown high school because there were only enough brainiacs in the whole town for one physics class, and I had to ride the bus with these completely genius boys who were hopeless to comprehend the idea of sex, and I was the only girl, and one day when we were riding the school bus to the class, I told one of the boys that I'd show him my tits if he'd tear up his homework."

Laughter in the basement ricocheted off the walls, and Mick caught himself trying to see the echoes. He lost track of Maura's story while he was trying to identify which of the many things that seemed to be bouncing about in the nether regions were echoes. He heard them all laugh again, but he didn't know whether Maura had displayed herself to the dumb geniuses or not.

"You didn't think that was funny?" Maura asked, her elbow whacking his ribs.

Mick explained about watching the echoes, and they all joined him.

"I saw a thought once," Billy Atlas said, "a whole string of thoughts, actually. They were spilling out of this guy's ear and circling his head. I mean, sure, I was doing acid, but that doesn't mean thoughts can't sometimes be seen."

More laughter and echo hunting ensued. Whenever the hilarity slowed, either Maura or Billy would bring up something else they had seen or done, and another round of laughter would start. Even Billy's girlfriend was laughing. Maura told about shoplifting a monkey wrench, and Billy said he made a *witticism* during a party in junior high and some bruiser held his head down in a punchbowl until he almost drowned, and Maura said she once slipped on the concrete around a public swimming pool and knocked herself out, and Billy revealed that he once peed in the open window of a car in a parking lot and then realized it was his car. When the two of them wearied of carrying the weight for the whole crowd, Mick felt he had to say something.

"When I got my mental illness, I drove my car into another car that was parked in a Burger King parking lot because I thought the other car was also my car and the two had separated and needed to be rejoined." No one laughed. After a second, he said, "No, not Burger King, *Taco Bell!*"

Laughter ricocheted about the basement again.

It had never been a common occurrence and it hardly ever happened anymore, but there were moments in Candler's life when the flesh of the world evaporated and he became privy to the bones of things.

He was seated in a wooden chair at a wooden table in the Phantom Limb, his friends' band spanking through "The Shape I'm In," a cold beer sweating circles on the round table, but he was also stepping onto the porch of his personal silence to look out through its screen. He understood that the bass line of the music was meant to beat along with the listener's heart, so that the fast songs made one lively and the slow songs brought on tender feelings. This was not a profound thought, and yet its arrival at a loud bar that smelled of beer and feet *seemed* profound, and memory fed the feeling—not episodes from his life, but the body's recollection of how those episodes felt, coursing through him in 6/8 time.

The substance of his working day was spent listening to other people. In moments such as this, he felt he was listening to himself—not to what he had to say, exactly, but to the rhythm of who he was. When he stepped out of himself, the world seemed to shuttle back, and he might gaze through that screen from a safe distance or he might consider the space between himself and the remainder of the human landscape, that hazy mystical trough. He was aware that he was in a bar with a concrete floor, and his work for the evening—parading his fiancée around for the board members, dancing with her long enough to make her happy—was done. He was waiting for Billy Atlas to show up. Billy not only knew about Candler's moments of separation but claimed they were petit mal seizures. Billy had briefly majored in psychology in an attempt to prove as much, but he had never been much of a student.

Candler felt he knew better. The spells were not a disability but the distinctive thing he identified as his own. He had tried to explain this to Billy before, and in a moment of weakness, he'd called it *his deeper self*. He still hadn't heard the end of that.

"If that's your deeper self," Billy had said, "then Pook was the deepest guy we ever met."

Candler's deeper self examined the women at the next table, how furtively they moved, women with ponytails, one two three of them, their golden beer in glasses gilded with frost. Like spies, they signaled with cigarettes, engraving the air with the secret text of the female. Smoky characters from the forbidden alphabet dawdled above their table, curling from their cigarettes, from their painted mouths, announcing themselves and vanishing in the same moment, like almost any act of beauty. It was so rare, these days, to see smoke in a bar, he thought, and yet it did so much for the atmosphere. It was a private party and smoking was permitted; his spells sometimes seemed to him like exactly that: a private party.

Thinking this took him off the porch and he was back in the bar once more. It sounded to him like that old Gene Autry song: *I'm back in the ta-vern again.*

God, he thought, *I'm drunk as a skunk.* He was drinking scotch. He had introduced his fiancée to so many people that *Lolly Powell* had begun to sound strange to him. He spotted Billy out on the floor, doing the crude, jiggling bounce that was supposed to pass for dancing. How many times had he tried to teach Billy how to dance? "You don't have to be talented," Candler had told him, "just confident." He looked for Billy's mystery date, but the crowd had closed around them. Candler had traded cars with Billy so Mr. Atlas could impress this woman, his first date since moving to California, the first since the divorce.

It was already clear that Billy was an improvement over Crews. His weekly reports—Candler had seen three by this time—were thorough and detailed, if also presumptuous and flowery. The clients liked him, and production rates were up. He had noted a few things that surprised Candler, including a detail that was undoubtedly important: Karly Hopper had come to the workshop in soiled jeans and a bulky sweater even though it was ninety degrees out. That meant the trucker was gone for good, and no one had moved in to help with things like laundry. When Karly came for her counseling appointment, she wore a clean white shirt with creases from packaging, but her pants were a mess. He asked her if she was living alone. She did not want to answer, seeming to think she might be in trouble. He had not pressed her; the evasive maneuvers were answer enough. After she left, he phoned her mother in L.A. and left a message, saying that he was concerned about Karly's living arrangements. He was proud of Billy for noticing something most supervisors would have missed.

The song ended and Candler thought Billy might bring his date over to the table, but a new song began—a slow one—and Candler let out a laugh. Billy would seize this opportunity to hold the woman in his arms. The floor emptied out a bit for the slow song, and James was sure he would spot them. A hand touched his shoulder and Lolly spun into view. She knelt theatrically before him.

"Let's waltz," she said. "I want you to hold me." She raised herself up just enough to kiss him quickly on the lips before tugging him out of his chair. He spun her around and pulled her close. She put her mouth to his ear. "Your colleagues are all hitting on me," she said, clearly not complaining. "I left so they'd direct their attentions to Violet. I'm worried about her."

"Don't worry about Vi. She's—"

"She's in emotional peril, I think."

"Peril?"

"It's a perfectly good word," she said and laughed.

Over the exuberance of Lolly's hair, he recognized not Billy or

Billy's date, but a dress, the dress he had purchased the day before Lolly arrived, a fantastically expensive and elegant dress. He focused so sharply on the garment that it took him a moment to realize that the woman in the dress was Lise and that she was dancing with Billy Atlas. He spun himself and Lolly away from them. His heart pounded farcically. He should have known something like this was coming. Reflexively, he told himself that it was stupid to blame Billy. If a pretty girl asked Billy Atlas to do something—almost anything—he was helpless to do otherwise. But god*damn* him anyway. Where's his fucking brain? Of course it was Lise who had promised to disappear. Instead, she was pressing herself against his best friend, moving in approximate time to "I Wish I Were Blind," trying to dodge the clod's big feet.

"I'm getting dizzy," Lolly said. "I'm going to swoon." After a second, she added, "I always wanted to say that."

He stopped spinning her. They were on the other side of the floor now. She leaned up to be kissed again, which he obliged. He believed the night he met Lise to be one of the most extraordinary of his life, although why he felt that way was mysterious to him. He and Lise had spent two weeks together—about the same amount of time he'd had in London with Lolly. Lise had given their interlude names: *The Days of Beer and Dandelions, The Year of Living Dangerously in Two Weeks, The Fourteen Days of the Condor with Sex Involved.* The names weren't all that clever, he realized, but when she'd popped them off, they'd made him laugh. He had gone to see her at Whispers and Lies and pretended to be shopping for his wife. The place had intimidated him. It was an old house made over for retail, and both the prices and the garments were out of his league. Lise tried on one thing after another, helping him shop for this supposed wife, and finally he purchased what seemed to him a simple black dress but he came to understand that its fabric and cut made it special, made it emphasize the wearer's beauty while the dress itself seemed to disappear.

Lise had known what was happening while it was going on, how he had cornered himself into buying something for her, and he realized later, after looking at the credit card receipt, that she had shown him the least expensive options, which were nonetheless more than he had ever spent on a gift for anyone. He didn't care. He owed her a parting souvenir.

The song ended and Lolly wanted a drink. "You go ahead and

dance," she said, pronouncing it in the English fashion, *dahnce*. Once, years ago, when James was a boy traveling in Europe and trying to pick up girls, he had ruined an opportunity for himself when the Danish blonde he was squiring had ridiculed his U.S. pronunciation of *dancing*, and each time Lolly said *dahnce* seemed to him like a slap in the face. She was from New Jersey, after all.

"I'm going to find your sister," she continued. "I'm genuinely concerned for her. You should be, too."

"I'll come with you," he said, confident she would turn him down. She liked the attentions of men. James didn't blame her. He liked the attention of women. He didn't think Lolly was in any danger of falling for one of his colleagues.

"No, you want to dahnce," she said. "Go ahead, but not with any of the pretty ones." She pointed then across the room. "Dahnce with that Barnstone character."

"Pass."

"Dahnce with some of the bloody wives, then. Make their night."

No sooner had Lolly left than Kat McIntyre grabbed his arm to drag him out to the floor. "She's a real cutie, your fiancée," Kat said. "I'm happy for you."

Kat was a polished but predictable dancer. He supposed that people thought that about him in his day-to-day life, polished but predictable. His sister seemed especially disappointed in the realities of his existence. She even seemed to have doubts about his marrying Lolly. The song ended and another began, a fast one. He and Kat continued dancing. When he spotted Lise and Billy again, he understood that he wanted terribly to lead Lise to the parking lot and have sex with her in Billy's ugly Dart. He and Lolly would undoubtedly make love in his big, comfortable bed after this event was over, but the two acts barely seemed related—the furtive, urgent humping in the public dark and the slow caress beneath the dim of a nightlight. Both activities were swell, but they were hardly the same thing.

He and Lise had fucked on the beach, and he not only enjoyed it but *appreciated* that a woman might not mind sand on her butt in order to have sex by the ocean with the likes of him. But his fiancée was here now, and that time of his life was gone, and probably the beach was gone, too, he thought, washed away, a new layer of sand supplanting the old, much the way layers of flesh rotate themselves over the body. He was soon to be married, and by the time he took Lolly to that beach they would probably have children and middle-aged spreads, and the beach would be a plutonium mine, and the only women there would wear goggles and space suits and breathe through their mouths, including Lolly, his beautiful Lolly, and the government wouldn't let nursing mothers within five miles of the place. Not that he'd ever had sex with a nursing mother on the beach or, for that matter, anywhere else, and he'd never had sex of any kind in a mine, but still, who would want a plutonium mine where you used to have sex with a lovely young woman, the downy hair on her sacral dimples like mist on water, her young body eager to be handled? What did it make the two of them if not utterly alive? With Lise, he felt powerfully virile and handsome, as potent as a manhattan mixed by a bartender with a heavy hand and trying to impress a woman—maybe the same woman, small-chested and perfect in the ass, and so lovely (okay, not beautiful; Lise was not even pretty, but incredibly *lovely*) as to make him forget whatever was fucked up in his life, at least for the duration of the evening, her panties catching for an instant between her thighs as she pulled them down.

"Fuck your boss," she had said to him. They had been talking about his promotion. Lise was against it. She thought he should work with clients, finish his study, become a psychologist. He had tried to explain all that John Egri had done to make it possible for Candler to take over, but she had interrupted. "Do what's in your heart." Such a corny line, but she had delivered it without irony or—there she was again, in the black dress, her skin pale in this light, contrasting with the dress, her ass shaking for him and him alone. That ass was expertly aimed and sending its ineluctable messages. Did Billy suppose she was doing anything but using him?

"Hey," Kat said. A space had opened beneath the colored lights near the stage, and she wanted the maneuvering room. He followed her, knowing that now Lise would see him dance, and his ass would be (there could be no doubt) aimed at her and, yes, his ass would be speaking for his heart. Not that he was in love with Lise (that wasn't possible), but he was still occupied with her mind and heart and body. He wished his ass could articulate this precisely, but he knew it would merely be saying *Desirable me is aware of desirable you, here where I cannot have you and you cannot have me.* Or something like that. Something like that (why deny it?) times ten.

He did a triple spin, three full revolutions, and felt the incredible desire to lean forward and kiss Kat as a way to punctuate the sentence his body was conveying to the woman who was not his fiancée and who was dancing with his best friend.

He did not kiss the woman dancing with him, but his able, shifting feet were on fire.

Slow-dancing at the Phantom Limb, his arms wrapped around a gorgeous woman, high as a communications satellite, Billy Atlas was ready to marry Lise. He didn't know her last name, but he was ready to say *I do.* His divorce was final, and what the hey.

He hadn't had sex with her. This was their first date, and he couldn't help but notice the flickering glances in Jimmy's direction. Okay, so what? Lise had called *him*, hadn't she? She was here and in *his* arms (when the music was slow), and eventually, he had faith or wanted to believe or could at least imagine that she would want to be with him for the sake of him alone. Or not. He was a realist. He was thirty-three years old, and he'd had nonprofessional sex with only two women. One of them, twenty-five times; the other, just the once. He'd had a girlfriend in middle school for a month (hand-holding while they were walking around campus was the gist of their relationship), and since then (excluding the citizenship angle) nothing. The long ago girlfriend was named Paulina Peters, and his mother had told him that she lived in the San Diego area now, too. *Hope springs eternal,* he thought. Paulina had dumped him when she found out he ate only Cheerios and potato chips. That was his diet for years, with the occasional baked potato and a morning glass of orange juice. Other foods were disgusting to him, and he could not stand to put them to his mouth. Jimmy introduced him to pizza and insisted he eat a slice, and of course, he liked it, even though it was a Pizza Shack pie—the worst restaurant pizza in the country. Billy had eaten pizza almost exclusively for six months, and by the end of that period he refused to eat Pizza Shack or frozen pies, preferring gourmet pizzas. He taught Jimmy the difference between good pizza and bad. Years later, as an undergraduate at Northern Arizona University, Billy became a pizza chef. He genuinely knew pizza. It occurred to him that he could have gotten work again as a pizza chef, but the idea did not appeal to him. A step backward. He was now a man with health insurance, which had to be one of the sexiest things a guy could have these days.

Lise was a fantastic dancer. Most women were good dancers. He wasn't. He was still looking for exactly what it was that he was good at that mattered. Knowing pizza lengthened the list of foods he was willing to eat, and now he liked a lot of different foods; also it had provided gainful employment. But unless he wanted to spend the rest of his life smelling of oregano, it wasn't something that mattered beyond a single stage in his life. Not that being a good dancer particularly mattered, although it had gotten Jimmy laid at least a dozen times, and maybe, who knows, fifty or a hundred times. Maybe Billy had a lousy sense of what was going to matter.

For example, chess. Jimmy got a chess set from some dotty aunt of his when they were in high school, and he invited Billy to play and destroyed him. Billy didn't like getting destroyed, and it seemed like knowing chess was a good thing in which to invest himself. Chess almost certainly would matter. It was a measure of intelligence, wasn't it? There was no more challenging or sophisticated game, was there? Chess had legitimacy.

He read books and studied game histories. He joined the chess club. By the end of that same month, he was defeating Jimmy routinely, and by the conclusion of the school semester, he was the best player in the chess club. Within a year's time, he played in competitions at the state level. The next summer, his mother sent him to chess camp, where a nine-year-old boy from Ecuador beat him twenty-seven consecutive times, and Billy quit studying chess. He could still outmaneuver nine out of ten players, but what did it matter? He could have played the nine-year-old another million times and never won. That kid was now twenty-something and likely having regular sex with Arina Mikhaylova or some other supermodel but most likely one of the Russians. In Russia, chess mattered. Maybe in Ecuador, too, who knows?

How about this: he valued people. He was good at that. He was valuing Lise the whole drive over and he made her laugh when they smoked dope even though she hadn't gotten high, and he was valuing her now while they were dancing. He had picked her up in Jimmy's car.

"You trying to impress me?" Lise asked when she saw the Porsche.

"You mean this old thing?"

"I know it isn't yours," she said, "and it's a brainless car, anyway." She smiled at him, and he imagined kissing her and falling into her mouth and staying there, sleeping like hard candy on her tongue.

"I can't drive it either," he told her. "It's a stick. I stalled three times coming over. Jimmy's sister wanted my car 'cause it has a backseat."

Lise drove very competently. "Okay, I'm not endorsing the thing," she said, "but it is fun to drive." After a second, she added, "As long as you know how to shift and all." She asked him to tell her things about himself that she didn't know.

"That would be pretty much everything," he said. "You don't know anything about me."

"Something specific."

He told her about his chess successes and ultimate failure.

Afterward, she said, "I'm going to tell you something I never told James. You ready? I have trouble recognizing faces. It's a condition with a name and everything." The dysfunction was called prosopag-nosia, and she discovered only recently that she had it. "You tend to think your memory is messed up in general or that you're dumb in a very specific way, but it has to do with *locking in* on a face, which I just don't do. If I see somebody in a different context, or if maybe he's cut his hair or changed his shirt, I don't know him. It's not like I'm blind, but most people pick up on facial arrangement some way I don't get." The underlying topic—why she hadn't told Jimmy—took them all the way to Onyx Springs. Summarized: she was afraid he would think of her as damaged goods. She did not want to be in the same category as his clients.

Billy liked that conversation and in the basement of Danker, high on this Colombian pot that the utterly insane Vex brought, he told all his funny stories, the laugh always on him, but what diff did it make as long as she was laughing? Once they reached the bar, though, he ran out of material. He knew better than to go into detail about his marriage. He had discovered (the hard way) that discussing the truth about his arranged marriage, bimonthly sex, and eventual divorce was a turnoff for women—and even for men. The Hao brothers had seemed especially put off by it, and Violet hadn't even let him begin. Billy had known Violet forever, since he and Jimmy were eight. On the night she and Lolly arrived from London, Billy had waited up for them, taking advantage of the alone time to smoke dope on the patio. When Jimmy introduced him to Lolly, he said, "This is my buddy Billy. He's been smoking pot on the patio. Don't smoke on the patio, Billy. I'm a counselor and I can't have a bust on the premises. This is my fiancée, Lolly."

"Sorry," Billy said, "and nice to meet you."

"I'll smoke with you," Lolly said, "but not now. I only want to sleep now."

From just beyond the door, Violet said, "You're blocking the entrance."

Jimmy and Lolly apologetically moved out of the way. Violet set down her suitcase to give Billy a hug. "Jimmy said you'd be here." It was the kind of greeting he expected from her, the embrace combined with the noncommittal comment, a sort of intimate disdain.

He didn't much care to tell Lise about any of that. What did people talk about? Sometimes Billy felt he had a great deal to hide and very little to discuss. There was pizza, still. He had held that back. Also, he had once owned a collection of three hundred bluegrass record albums, and he was knowledgeable about its roots, the differences between bluegrass and folk or country or old-time music, the difference between bluegrass and Irish folk music, the subtle and not-so-subtle differences between progressive bluegrass and traditional bluegrass. He'd owned (before he sold it) a bootleg album of Bill Monroe playing with Earl Scruggs and Lester Flatt that Monroe and Scruggs had both signed. But he didn't listen to bluegrass anymore.

At the conclusion of a Prince cover done with a country beat, Lise said, "Let's sit." They made their way to the lobby. She wanted a vodka collins and Billy ordered himself a tap beer. He had a strange moment during which he thought the girl busing behind the bar was Karly Hopper. It wasn't, of course, and when she straightened, fingers inserted in beer glasses that she had swished in soapy water and rinsed in a gray sink of slightly less soapy water, he realized she looked nothing like Karly except for being fit and brown-haired. Could Karly bus tables or work behind a bar? She'd definitely get a shitload of tips, and maybe she'd let him drink for free.

Returning with the drinks, he realized he was going to have to resort to pizza episodes. His mind was otherwise blank. Lise seemed to be studying him as she sipped her vodka. She put her hand on his arm and asked him what he had done in Flagstaff to make his living.

"I was a pizza chef for a couple of years, and then I worked at a convenience store." He provided a few details about the U-TOTE-M chain of stores. He had worked at one store for the past ten years. "I guess I've been drifting."

"The same job for a decade doesn't sound like drifting," Lise said. "Sounds more like an anchor."

What he did not want to explain—what he did not think he could articulate—was the pleasure his job had given him. In some neighborhoods, a convenience store has a position of importance, given that everyone winds up there now and again. His role lent him authority. Not that people looked up to him so much as they recognized him, acknowledged his competence. He'd had a place in the community. People wondered why a guy like him was working at the U-TOTE-M, which made him think that the key to competence was finding something just below your level of ability. Too often it worked the other way around. He secretly suspected that this discovery would be in store for Jimmy if he got the job directing the center. Running a giant organization might be too much—or if he managed to be successful, it would come at the expense of something real in his personality: his sense of humor, maybe, or his ability to relax.

When the topic petered out, Lise asked him, "What do you want to do now?"

"Take you home with me," he said. Then added, "If you'll drive."

She studied him for a long moment before shrugging and taking his hand.

Violet had steered Lolly away from the young men, and now they were with a number of dreary women. "I'm getting tired." Violet spoke softly so only Lolly would hear.

"It's not late," Lolly said. She took Violet's hand. "You're grieving. It wears you out."

Yet another presumptuous comment. The truth: *she was relieved that her husband was dead.* Someone like Lolly could not conceive of the idea that Vi simply didn't want to talk about it. Lamentation seemed to be the national sport these days, but Vi would not become a player.

"We all like James," one of the women said. She wore cat's-eye glasses and had an oversized whirly hairdo, dyed an unnatural black. Violet hoped it was an intentionally ironic look. "He's such a gentleman, and without being so . . . without being ah . . ."

"Without being a *wimp*," another put in. This one was younger and drunker. "We get a lot of *wimps* in this line of work."

Lolly basked in the conversation, as if they were talking about some quality of her own. "What if I don't like gentlemen? What if I adore wimps?"

"It's gonna be your field day then," the drunker one said.

When Violet had told Jimmy, all those years ago, that she was going to marry her boss, he had said, "Arthur? I love Arthur." No hesitation, no crack about the difference in ages. Why oh why couldn't she show him the same generosity?

A middle-aged Asian woman whose surname, if Violet heard correctly, was How, asked for her impressions of California.

"I was expecting more stars," she said.

"Go to Santa Monica or Beverly Hills," one of them said. "I saw Lisa Kudrow in a boutique in Santa Monica looking at stockings."

"Celestial stars," Violet corrected. "I grew up in Arizona and the sky would fill with them. I was looking forward to seeing them again."

"The smog," said the Asian woman. "The ocean breezes it all up here."

"Pooh on the stars," Lolly said. "I want to meet the borderlines, the obsessive compulsives, the bipolars."

Violet could not help a tiny smile. Lolly could not tolerate the conversational orbit going beyond her gravitational pull. Thank god they had Billy's Dart. In the Porsche, she had to ride in a cubby space behind the seats like an oversized bag of laundry. The Dart was old and unhygienic but the backseat was at least designed for humans.

The women were trying to find a way to respond to Lolly's outburst. The one with the hair said, "You can't help meeting them now and again. If you see James for lunch, go early and wait in the anteroom. They'll trudge past."

"I want to get to know them," Lolly insisted. "What they feel and think and dream."

Was this why she had fallen for Jimmy, the stories he told about his patients? Perhaps she did need to meet them and be stripped of her romantic notions about damaged people. More likely, of course, she wanted to assert her own authority, the counseling certification she'd earned one summer. Her fingertip massage and blenderized flowers. *You're tooo hardon her.*

"I'm as compassionate as the next chucklehead," the blotto woman said, "but these people . . . they suck up your life."

"That's not how I'd put it," the older woman said. Her eyes, magnified by the glasses, zeroed in on Lolly. "But you do have to keep some distance. Many of them simply frighten me."

"Are they violent?" Lolly asked hopefully.

"If they have a history of violence, John won't let them in. He's scrupulous about that. It isn't that kind of fear."

"Afraid it'll rub off on you?" the drunken woman said.

"They're . . . *unsavory.*"

Patricia Barnstone spoke then. She was one of the counselors but James didn't seem to think much of her. He called her *the Barnstone,* as if she were an architectural feature. "You could volunteer," she said. "We need the most volunteers with the Minton House—that's the severely mentally impaired clients."

"John is phasing them out," the woman with the hair said.

"Candler doesn't work with them," Barnstone acknowledged, "but you could get a sense of the Center and what your boy does."

"That's a smashing idea," Lolly said.

"You look too young for Candler," Barnstone went on. "Aren't you worried about him sitting in some rocking chair while you want to boogie?"

Lolly laughed and explained that she and James were only seven years apart.

"Years?" Barnstone said. "Who's talking about years?" She flexed her shoulders and gestured with her hands. She took up a lot of space, Violet noted. The other women were backing off and slipping away. "Egri will tell you not to volunteer. He's afraid if you get your hands dirty—and you *will* get your hands dirty—you'll make Candler move to Europe or San Francisco or some other damn place, and then he won't have his fair-haired boy."

"I'm not afraid of getting my hands dirty," Lolly said.

Violet had to admit this was true of Lolly. "I'm only a little afraid of it," she said.

"It's settled then. You two staying with Candler? I'll call with the details."

"Do you know a young man named Mick Coury?" Violet asked. "He may be one of Jimmy's patients."

"*Jimmy.* I can't get used to that. Your brother can be *stiff.*" She twisted her head to include Lolly. "That's what I meant about being so much older than you. There's not a stiff bone in your body." She zeroed in on Violet again. "Mick Coury, nice kid. Lives off-campus with his mother and brother. His father used to have to commute fifty miles. They moved here so Mick could get treatment. A lot of people do that. Full residential is prohibitive for most families. Mick's father got an apartment in the city so he could skip the drive now and then. Then he found god—and probably some heavenly woman—and dumped his wife. Yeah, I know Mick. Drives an old Firebird. Not one of mine, but you get to know most of them, one way or another. If he could relax, which he can't, he might be a movie star. Such a pretty kid."

The How woman reappeared—Joan? Violet had met too many people to remember all their names. "I just wanted to say good night," she said. "I've called a cab. I've got a headache and I know my husband wants to keep playing as long as there's even one person on the dance floor." She rolled her eyes and smiled.

"It was so nice to meet you," Violet said.

"The body holds all of the daily karmic insults in the epithelial tissue." Lolly stepped near Joan as she spoke. "If you don't work them out, they sink down into the deeper tissues until they reach your organs, your brain being the most vulnerable of the organs, and you get a headache."

Violet instinctively scanned the room for exits.

"There's a pressure point here," Lolly said, pinching Joan at the base of the neck. Only Patricia Barnstone seemed to be watching, as far as Violet could tell. Thank god the room was dimly lit. "This touch is seeking your pain. You have to let it flow to this spot."

Violet stepped back, separating herself from the cosmic connection.

Lolly used her free hand to touch Joan How's forehead. "This completes the circuit." She moved the hand to the temples, stretching her palm over Joan's face. "Feel the flow of energy." Lolly held this pose for several seconds, which passed like minutes, and then dropped the hand to Joan How's chest. "Your heart is alive," Lolly said, and then she took her hands away. "How do you feel?"

"Weird," the woman said immediately. "Good, though. It made my legs weak." She smiled weakly. Perhaps she always smiled that way. "My cab is probably waiting."

Barnstone stepped in again. "Where'd you learn to do that?"

"I'm out of practice," Lolly said and launched into her history of fingertouch counseling, emphasizing the importance of practice.

Violet tried not to listen. Was there one meaningful thing in life that you could consciously practice? You rarely got to practice anything important, and yet you almost certainly would be tested, and you would not know the terms of the test until it had already transpired, and by then your evaluation would be unchangeable.

"It's all about positive and negative energy," Lolly was saying, "and flow. Everything depends on flow."

Stoned, Mick hid under Maura's bed at curfew as if armed men were coming at any moment to hunt for him. Maura dragged him out after bed check, and he called his mother to tell her he was sleeping over.

"Is that permitted?" she asked, and Mick assured her that everything was fine. "You sound like you're having fun," she said. "But is this a good idea?"

"Don't call Mr. James Candler," he said.

She assured him that she would not, and following a number of repeated assurances, the conversation dwindled and died.

Mick shut Maura's cell phone and tossed it onto the mattress. He was sitting on the bed and she was standing at the window. "Now what?" he said.

"I think this is the point where we take our clothes off and suck on each other."

Mick laughed hard enough that Maura laughed, too.

"You have any food?" he said. "I've got hungry feelings."

"Some things," she said. She had a minifridge with carrots, tomatoes, and celery cut into snacking lengths. "Barnstone has changed the way I eat. I'm like a health fiend now. I don't let myself have junk in the fridge. It's a good thing, too, 'cause if I had my typical crap, I'd eat like a pound of candy right now."

"A pound sounds good," Mick said. He bit into the celery. "The meds I'm on make some people gain weight, but not me. What I say, I say they steal my appetite. I had one once."

Maura wanted sex. Partly because she just wanted to, but mainly because she wanted Mick to get the idea that she could be his girl-friend, and that she'd be a lot better at it than the skinny ditz he was engaged to marry. Earlier in the week, while everyone else was gone for lunch, Vex had led her around the corner of the Old Farts Center, pushed her up against the block wall, and pulled down her pants. *What are you doing?* she hissed, and he said, *There's plenty of time.* His brain, he confided, kept better time than atomic watches. He said all this while he was pressed against her, and some part of her had liked it. Another part of her, though—her fist—had clobbered his skull. While he grabbed his head, Maura pulled up her pants and under-wear. The bulge in his jeans—his unzipped jeans—she also took in before scampering around the corner.

He reappeared saying, "Your unconscious messages are all the fuck crosswired. Like if I flip the headlamp of my Electra Glide and the fucking engine dies, that's you and your pussy."

She didn't know how to argue with that but demanded rolling papers and tobacco, which he obediently handed over, still ranting about her pussy and why persons unnamed should never hit anyone on the head. Vex wasn't even vaguely sexy but he was very *male*. Way more than Mick, and maleness had a definite draw. Maybe she had accidentally sent the grimy muckbrain scrambled signals. Girls were turned on by horses, but they didn't actually want to screw them, and this scrawny gorilla did tingle her parts, but between that tingle and the desire to actually drop drawers and mingle was a distance wide enough for a several semis to pass through.

A lot of men seemed to think that if you took the time to creatively insult them, you must want their penis plunging into your major ori-fices. This was not only annoying, it cramped her style. The fact that she was a virgin made it worse, like she had no platform to stand on, and so she had no choice but to take a bunch of shit from people, and now she was going to have to start wearing a belt. How had he gotten her pants and undies down so fast? Some men seemed to be born with very specific talents and even though they've had an electric beater shoved into their gray matter and the setting pushed from *blend* to *whip*, these profoundly male nutjobs still knew how to get a girl's pants and panties to her knees in one slick, two-second maneuver.

From that moment, she began plotting to get Mick into her dorm room and *granny-give-a-fuckall* (one of Vex's expressions) that he was engaged. She wanted to press up against him and pull his pants down. He was wearing cords.

"This is the best celery I've ever eaten," Mick said. "Why haven't I been eating celery every day? Why isn't it like chips and salsa, so you go to a restaurant and get a bowl of celery?"

"You're high," Maura said, "which makes you completely unreliable."

"I can still taste, can't I?" He remembered the waitress: *How does everything taste?*

"Yeah, but don't make decisions based on what you're tasting right now."

"Don't go buy ten pounds of celery?"

"I had chocolate milk one time when I was stoned, and the next week I complained to my parents about never having any chocolate milk in the house, and now my dad brings little cartons that fit in my fridge whenever they visit. I can't stand the viscous, smacky stuff."

Mick laughed at *smacky*. He smacked his lips. "I'm maybe going to pass out here soon."

"Pass away." She sat beside him on the bed. "Anything you do is okay with me."

"Really?"

She looked him in the eyes without laughing or smiling and said, "Anything you want."

"Thanks." His head tilted back and fell against the mattress. He reached beneath his back and withdrew the cell phone, which he placed on his stomach. Within seconds the celery stalks fell from his hand.

Maura touched his belt but did not undo it. She crawled on top of him, the phone a warm hard spot between them. She imagined pulling his pants down, taking his shirt off, running her hands over his body. Instead, she pushed him to one side and pulled the sheet from beneath him. She undressed in front of his shut eyes, then put on a T-shirt and lay next to him. She lifted his flaccid arm and put it over her.

Violet got Jimmy and Lolly in the car and on the road before four a.m.

"This whole thing," he said jubilantly, drunk and driving on the interstate, "the whole party started when I told them that you were coming here."

"No fooling?" Lolly asked. "The party was just for us?"

Violet, from the Dart's rear seat, wanted to point out that they'd known this all along.

"It appears that I brought you up maybe ten thousand times," Jimmy said. "It's so *nice*, isn't it?" He angled his head slightly to call into the backseat. "Isn't it *nice*, Sis? I've been here less time than any of the other counselors? Almost any. And this shindig for my girl? Nice?"

"Very generous," Violet agreed. "I wish you'd let me drive."

Jimmy nodded and spoke to his fiancée. "She has a point there, Loll. You and I are tanked, skewered."

"Off our trolley," she said.

He swerved into the exit lane and pulled up to the stop sign at the intersection. Violet and her brother traded places. The freeway was wide and empty, the sky wide and dark. The alcohol she had consumed was not enough to hinder her driving, and neither was it enough to make the dark world beautiful, but just another obstacle to get beyond.

"Patricia Barnstone thinks I could do fingertouch counseling at the Center," Lolly announced.

Violet knew the woman had said no such thing.

"That'd be something," Jimmy said. "Maybe Egri would approve. You must've danced ten times with him."

"Is my boy jealous?"

"Of Egri? I think not."

"That's good because I think he may have a crush on me."

Violet could not quite believe that even Lolly would say that. She looked for the radio.

"What right-blooded man wouldn't?"

"You're drunk, James Candler."

"I stand accused. Only I'm not standing."

They laughed. Violet drove. Perhaps a minute passed.

"You're a good sister," Jimmy said out of the blue.

"And a good friend," Lolly said. "Isn't she?"

"Please don't." She knew where this turn in the conversation would take them. Her brother thought they needed to talk about her husband's death. For a counselor, he had a capacity for complete insensitivity to the desires of others. His hand tapped her shoulder.

247

"I am so sorry about Arthur."

"Thank you, but—"

"No, honestly. I'm just . . . it's not fair."

"Yes, it is," Violet said, more forcefully than she intended. "Arthur had a good life, better than nine-tenths of the people born in this world. He lived well. Not as long as any of us would have liked, but we all die. Everyone dies. It's what living things ultimately do."

The car was quiet. Lolly slipped a hand back to him.

"I'm just sorry is all," Jimmy said.

"Thank you," Violet said.

"So," said Lolly, "which one of your patients do you fancy most?"

"We call them *clients*."

"Okay, which bloody client then?"

"I don't know. What do you mean? I don't like the ones who are hard to work with, I can tell you that. And I don't like the ones who are, I don't know, *tacky*."

"Tacky?" Violet said.

"Grungy? Not dirty exactly."

"Unsavory?" Lolly said.

"There you go. Just . . . there's this guy—a complete grown-up agewise, but he jerks off five, ten times a day. They all think it's this big success that he'll go into the john now and shut the door. He used to just whip it out. He's not high on my list, but he's in the workshop. He's not that bad, I guess, but I can't say I *fancy* him."

"She asked who you like," Violet said, "not who you don't like."

"Who's like a friend?" Lolly said. "Or would be your friend if you weren't his counselor?"

"None of them would be friends."

"Who do you look forward to seeing?" Violet said, trying to help.

"I'm not even supposed to talk about them."

"But you always do," Violet insisted.

"I don't know. The higher-functioning ones are more interesting."

"What about Mick?" Violet said.

"How do you know about Mick?"

Violet explained getting lost. "I expected one of your colleagues, but he was so young. Not that there seemed anything wrong with him."

"Adolescent onset of schizophrenia."

"A schizophrenic!" Lolly said to Violet. "No fair. You got a schizophrenic."

"It's pretty common in our circles," Jimmy said, seeming to sober up as he spoke. "We have a lot of high-functioning schizophrenics. Mick was an ordinary kid, and then he wasn't. He's sort of in love with another one of the clients, a damaged girl. I'm worried about him."

"Isn't love good for them?" Lolly asked.

"I can't talk about it, but he's a fragile kid."

"He didn't seem fragile," Violet said. "He was so courteous. He made jokes and he . . . well, he didn't seem like someone you had to worry about."

"We're always having to believe things that seem unlikely." He said something more that Violet could not hear, and then he said, "They don't like to take their meds. Schizophrenics, especially. It permits them to get by in the world, but it steals something from them."

"I can understand feeling that way," Violet said. She surreptitiously touched her face with her fingers to erase the tears. She must be exhausted. She hardly knew Mick Coury. Something had to be wrong with him, so why did this diagnosis bring on tears?

"There was a basketball player, an all-pro NBA star," Jimmy said, "and he was great, would tear up the defense, and then after the game he would go in and tear up the locker room. Couldn't help it. So he's making, I don't know, a million dollars an hour, and he's able to get the best help, the perfect medication, and sure enough he can function without the destructive behavior, but guess what? He's not *quite* the same player. In fact, he goes from being all-pro to not quite good enough to play at all.

"That won't do. They try changing his dose. Lower it and he can play, but his life's out of control. Raise it high enough to help, and—you have to keep in mind that those guys in the NBA are all great. The difference between the top and the bottom is a half step here, a second of anticipation there. Raise his meds, and he washes out."

"So what happened?" Lolly asked.

"He's still playing. Got suspended early on this season for going after a fan who was harassing him."

"They don't give him his medication so he can play a game for them?" Violet said. "That's obscene."

"I'm sure it was his decision. Think about it. Your choices are being a hero athlete and millionaire, or just some guy."

"We should have Mick over for dinner," Lolly said. "He'd like that, wouldn't he?"

Jimmy sighed. "There was this one client when I first got here. Smart, high-functioning, lively guy. I liked him, and I didn't know anybody. He was walking home—he lived independently, an interesting person. Anyway, I gave him a lift. We got to talking and decided to have dinner together later in the week. No big deal, meet at a steakhouse and talk.

"What do you think happens? He tells everyone that we're pals, implying I like him more than the others. Which was true. I did like him more, but you can't have your clients thinking that way. They all became needy as hell—and hungry, like I was supposed to go out with all of them. I canceled the dinner we'd planned and traded him to another counselor. It was a dumb mistake, and I haven't repeated it."

Violet was disconcerted by the story. Shouldn't he have taken them all out to eat? Didn't he dismiss this person simply for his own convenience?

Lolly spoke to Violet to fill the silence. "That Egri character practically guaranteed that James would get the position, that he'll be the super of the whole place."

"He was loaded," James said. "There are two other finalists. Just announced this morning. Clay Hao is one. He was in the band. The other is this psychologist who got an article published in some important journal. Got her an interview, but no way they're hiring a psychologist as administrator."

Violet said, "Who's the girl Billy was with?"

Jimmy grunted something unintelligible.

"I've talked to Billy every day since we arrived, and he hasn't said a word about her," Lolly put in. "He's told me all about the people at his workshop but nothing about this woman. He certainly seemed happy to be with her."

"I'll say," James said.

"I can't recall Billy ever having a girlfriend," Violet said. "He's such a lummox with women. I assume he must be less of a lummox otherwise."

"He's always a lummox," James said, "but it's worse with women on the scene."

"I thought she was cute," Lolly insisted.

"If you go for that type," Jimmy said.

This struck Violet as a peculiar statement, but Lolly had a different reaction. She crawled over the seat and into the back, her bare foot tapping the side of Violet's head.

"I want to kiss you," Lolly said.

Violet concentrated on the road and the sky. There was a blanket of stars now in the expanse between Onyx Springs and the coast. They burned millions of miles away, consuming themselves. It was the least she could do to acknowledge their beauty.

Candler was not surprised to see that Billy had parked the Porsche not in the garage but at the curb. He hadn't bothered with the cover. The light in Billy's bedroom was off, and Candler decided against barging in. Instead, he snatched the spare key from the hook in the kitchen.

No sooner did he start the Porsche than he noticed the purse on the passenger seat—a billfold on a cord. Lise kept her identification and cash in it. This would give her an excuse to call Billy again. Perhaps she even calculated that James would find it and take it to her. He pulled free the driver's license to look at her face. If he had only the photo to judge by, he would have thought her plain. There was the attractiveness that any fit body carried for the duration of its youth, but the real woman had more, something about the way her body was an expression of who she was, how some aspect of her self animated her body. What did you call that part that shone through and made her face not ordinary but lovely? *Her personality?* Such a flimsy word, worn down by overuse until it was nothing but a transparency. *Her character?* Better, if old-fashioned, but what did he know of her character, really? Did he genuinely believe he could intuit her character from the time that they'd spent together? *Her soul?* That was the word he wanted, all right, except he didn't believe in souls. Nevertheless, it was the precise word he was looking for. Her soul animated her otherwise ordinary face and made it lovely.

The clicker for the garage door was on the sun visor, and Candler had shown it to Billy. He wondered why he hadn't used it. *Unless,* he thought, as he clicked the device, a complicated feeling seeping into him, *unless Billy hadn't been driving.* Billy didn't handle a stick very well. Candler engaged the ignition, shifted gears, the vehicle moving slowly forward, while his thoughts attempted to back away. Was it possible that Lise was in his house, lying in Billy's bed, possibly even lying beneath Billy? He dropped the keys twice getting out of the car.

He found Lolly and his sister in the kitchen making tea. Why would anyone want tea at four in the morning? It seemed to him that he had been in the garage a long time, and he had expected them to be in bed, at least in their pajamas. But here they were in the kitchen, muddling around in their rumpled party dresses.

"Billy up?" he asked.

"Someone's in the loo," Lolly replied. "Tea?"

"I guess." He leaned against the opening to the hall, which provided a view of the bathroom door.

"I know what you're doing," Lolly said.

In the moment that followed, Candler felt the guilt and shameful culpability over his affair with Lise that he had managed to skip earlier, and it turned him solid, a statue. He felt like a grotesque figure in an Italian frieze, the single humpbacked, multimouthed creature lingering among the innocents. How could they fail to recognize his misshapen, monstrous self?

"You can wait till the morning to tell him he's supposed to leave your precious car in the garage and not out in the elements." She laughed. To Violet, she said, "Men are so predictable."

Candler felt the terrible urge to laugh with her. He held it back, his face coloring and seeming to collapse inward. What had he done? What had he been thinking? Any moment now, the curtain would pull back and they would see him for what he was. The bathroom door opened and a woman stepped out. She wore one of Billy's shirts. Her legs were bare. There was water on the bathroom floor. She eyed him steadily. Lise. *His* Lise. Her eyes had no color in the dim hall, only depth, and such depth, one could build a fortress with that kind of space.

Lolly and Violet turned at the sound of the door, but only James could see her walk down the hall, her white thighs, bare feet. She disappeared into Billy's room.

"See if he wants tea," Violet said to James.

"It wasn't him," he said softly.

Violet and Lolly exchanged a look. They poked their heads through the door, but she was gone.

"Good for Billy," Lolly said.

"Oh," said Violet, pointing. "The commode's misbehaving again."

James nodded, his throat too tightly constricted to permit a reply.

Lise had told herself that the best thing was to let him go. Instead, she got hold of Billy Atlas. She went to the dance party and saw that the flesh-and-blood fiancée was much like her photograph. She reminded Lise of a stripper who had called herself Minx and dressed in short plaid skirts and regular white cotton panties—never the frills or thongs the other girls wore. My, how thrilled the johns were when those panties came off! As if, even in a strip club, they could not see through the charade. How could she hope for James to imagine that his sweet girl from London who called herself Lolly, like the sucker, was anything but as advertised?

She had lain beside Billy Atlas listening for the others to arrive. "No sex," she had told him. "We can lie together. Snooze together. That's it." He agreed readily. Maybe he was even relieved, which might have made him seem pathetic if he hadn't said, "As long as we can cuddle." It was a line that on some other night, in some other house, might have won her over. She was hardly a prude, after all, and far from a virgin. But when she and James made love that first time, she was no longer a former prostitute, she had never been one.

When she heard the car park at the curb, she slipped into the bathroom and waited until she was sure that James would be out there, that he would know and be in the hall looking for her. She flushed the toilet and ran water in the sink, as if to wash her hands. The toilet leaked at its base. *No handyman, that one,* she thought, as she pushed open the door and stepped into the dim hall to let him see her.

What she was doing now she didn't know or couldn't bring herself to say. It was no longer merely a pastime. She recalled again the night she first drove to the Corners, coasting soundlessly by this very house—a house designed to look both southwestern and ostentatious, the stucco painted a light shade of sand, as if to pass for adobe, but no one would actually mistake it for adobe, the walls too perpendicular, the corners too sharp, the bloated garage too incongruous, the color too pale—an off-white shade that one clothing manufacturer called *tusk*.

She had eaten that night in a Corners diner, thinking about the awful house—not that it affected her opinion of Candler. Rather she was trying to think if there was a term for the way the builder had cast a nod at traditional southwestern construction without trying to pass it off as genuine. The house did not look southwestern but it *indicated* southwestern style. Television comedies were like that, she thought, not actually funny but indicative of humor. She paid her bill and motored by the house again. There was a light in the front room now. He was in there, just across a stretch of recently mowed grass. She could follow the red paving stones to his door.

Instead, she had a drink in a Corners bar, maraschino cherries bleeding exuberantly into her drink, before heading down his street once more, passing slowly, treading water, stars appearing in her windshield as well as in her chest, stars of apprehension, anticipation, trepidation, and glee.

So many things had happened since that night, but not the right things, or not enough of the right things. She was here in the ugly house but in the wrong bed. *Be careful what you wish for.* She propped her head up to stare at the man sleeping beside her. He was sweet. He was kind. He wasn't handsome, but he was okay. Those people in the basement smoking pot thought the world of him. She could choose him, and he would marry her. He would be thrilled to spend the rest of his life with her. He would never stray into another woman's arms. He would love her as she had never been loved. She touched his hair, which was stiff with dried sweat. James Candler was a better dancer than Billy but less likely to be a faithful husband. His relationship with her was proof of that. James was quicker and more handsome, but he was not as naturally kind and he would never be as devoted. The heart was a tyrant, like a child demanding ice cream instead of broccoli and throwing a fit to get its way. She lowered her head carefully and lightly kissed Billy's forehead, his salty skin. A perfectly fine man, she thought, and not at all for me.

Karly could not find the remote and got up to turn off the television. The windows in the room were like water you shouldn't drink, which meant it was morning almost. Something was wrong with the phone, which she held to her ear. It didn't even make the *bong* sound, and she couldn't call anyone, not her mother, not her sister, not even Mr. Billy Atlas, who said to call him plain Billy, and he wrote down his phone number on square pieces of paper and gave each person in the workshop a square. He had slipped her square in the ID folder that she wore on a chain around her neck. "So you'll always have it with you," he said. Now she always had it with her.

She stepped carefully around the clutter on the floor and made her way to the bedroom. Beetle Man wasn't coming back. She could tell by how dirty the place was. Did she ever go get the wheelbarrow? It belonged to Mr. and Mrs. Hoeksema who lived next door and liked to swim in their swimming pool without any clothes, which Karly didn't do even when Mr. Hoeksema said it was okay, he would go inside. Her mom said when in doubt keep your clothes on. She had her clothes on now. Her pants didn't smell very good, and the sweater was hot until she turned up the a.c., which she did by turning the number *down*. Down was up. That was so funny.

She smiled and went into the bathroom, which was on the way to the bedroom, to look at her smile in the mirror over the bathroom sink. She looked just like she thought she would look. That was what people liked about her, how she looked. And it was the same. Why wasn't Beetle Man coming back? What he said and what he meant by what he said were different, like that game he couldn't teach her, where she was not supposed to say a whole list of words to make him guess a word like *Oz*, and she couldn't say *wizard* or *Toto* or *Dorothy* or *good witch* or *tin man*, and what in the world was left while sand was running out of the little tipper? "You could've said, 'Not in Kansas no more,'" he told her, "or whatever, it don't matter. Do another one." This time he didn't even turn over the sand tipper, and the card said *rain check* and it took a long while for her to say, "Put your hand out the window," and then they both played solitaire and now he wasn't coming back.

Her desktop computer was still making light on her desk by her bed. It was supposed to screensave, but sometimes it didn't screensave. Her screensaver was jungle animals. Her favorite jungle animal was the meerkat like in *Lion King* and also in the San Diego Zoo, where she had seen all the jungle animals on her screensaver. It wasn't Beetle

Man who took her to the zoo, but her mom and sister when they visited last time. She missed her mom and sister, and her father, who was dead and used to tell stories to her when it was bedtime about all the mountains he would cross to be with her. They were hard mountains, but he always made it.

Earlier that night, on the internet, she had taken the *If you were a Muppet what Muppet would you be?* quiz, and she was Elmo, which was the best one to be unless you were Kermit or Big Bird. Before that, she took the *Friendly Clouds–Unfriendly Clouds* personality test and scored 80 percent, which was good and promised fair skies, and she did the *Do Aquarians Have More Fun?* and it said that she did have more fun. Her ranch on Saturn was growing corn as tall as tall buildings, and as soon as they sprouted corn on the cob there were only two more levels before she was an honorary Saturn citizen, which would give her a golden hoe for her satchel. She used to wear a golden ring on her finger so people would think she was married, but it was plastic and the golden wore off. She was so tired, so very tired, but sleepy was different from tired, and the house was scaring her by having no one else in it for so many days now and getting so dark.

She clicked the computer screen button to make it go off. She pulled her ID folder necklace over her head and changed into her pajamas. Not the pajamas that Beetle Man gave her because they were uncomfortable on her bottom, but the ones that her sister gave her that had Josie and the Pussycats playing guitars. Beetle Man said her life was too complicated for him anymore and he didn't like men coming over to hit him, which she had thought he was making a joke. Jokes were hard to get, but she liked them. His joke was about her life. That was what he said, *her complicated life.* What was funny about her life? She didn't like being alone in her house all the time, which wasn't so very funny.

What does the all alone girl in her house say?

Wash my clothes, please, and the sheets.

The phone isn't working even a little bit.

Some of the sounds are so frightening to me.

She had another phone right next to her bed, and she wouldn't even have to get out of bed to call someone. Her mom and sister didn't like calls during sleeping hours, but would Billy mind? She liked him because he was always nice to her, but the phone beside the bed didn't work either. Rhine was always nice to her, too, and Alonso, too, but Rhine went to bed at ten o'clock and Alonso didn't talk on the phone very good, and the phone didn't work, anyway.

She could call Mick at any time of the whole night, but he always wanted to talk about marrying him. He could drive, but he wasn't a grown-up, and you could only marry a grown-up. Everyone knew you married a grown-up. One you liked. She only liked Beetle Man part of the time, but he was good at telling her which things to do and reminding her of all those things she kept forgetting. He wasn't coming back, and Mick wasn't a grown-up, and Mr. James Candler owned a house with bad trees and when she wore a skirt, he looked at her legs even though he tried not to look at her legs. But her skirts were all dirty.

What was she wanting to say on the phone? Not just *hello*. Not just *hey*. Not just *checking in*. She picked up the phone and pretended. "Hi, Billy, it's Karly from the sheltered workshop. You told us to call you Billy and not Mr. Billy Atlas. How are you tonight, Billy? You gave me your number on a square of paper and the phone works so I called you."

What would he say to her?

Hi, Karly. I'm so happy you called me on the telephone. That is why I gave you the square of paper, so you would call me on the telephone.

"Here I am calling you," she said. "It's not just to say hello, Billy Atlas. I'm feeling very . . . *poured out*. If like the orange juice is empty and you've already swished water in it and drunk that, which I did yesterday. The grocery is too far, except for the Sonic, and I lost Mr. and Mrs. Hoeksema's wheelbarrow when Beetle Man drove away forever. I like orange juice in the morning and at night, but my mom says just mornings."

What would he say to that?

I will get you a new wheelbarrow.

"Why doesn't my phone work?" she asked him. "Why did Beetle Man not come back? Where is the TV clicker? Can you show me one more time how the washing machine works? What mountains would people like my dad go over to see people like me? Why is it so hard for me to pick up everything on the floor when I am all alone in the house? Why is everybody liking the way I look so much? Why is being nice to everyone you meet dangerous my mother says? Why is everything so wrong when I do it?" She remembered the other joke she had written down, but she didn't know where to find it. She wanted to tell Billy

Atlas the joke but she didn't want to put the phone down. "Why does the woman and man—they're married. Why does the husband and the wife take the umbrella in bed?" She waited, laughing. The phone made no sound, like he couldn't think of the answer to the joke. She couldn't think of it either. "It was something really funny," she said, laughing harder. "And I left my real umbrella someplace," she said. "I lose things."

When she was through laughing, she said, "Good-bye, Billy. See you Monday." She put the phone on the phone holder. The whole room was the color of water you shouldn't drink. Wasn't that so funny? In a while, it would be morning, and she would sleep. In almost no time at all.

If you could see time, she thought, it would look just like this.

7

Violet found Billy Atlas barefoot at the kitchen table, fresh socks in his lap, eating homemade salsa—his specialty, she recalled—from a bowl, like soup. His face was pale, his natty hair standing up on the back of his big head. She tried at that moment to like Billy Atlas, but the best she could manage was a vague fondness, much the way one feels about a bad dog that has nonetheless been in the family for years. He looked up hopefully at her, spoon in his mouth, but then his face fell.

"Oh, Billy," she said. "Why don't you get yourself a life?"

"I've been thinking the same thing." After a moment, he added, "Good morning."

That his girl from the night before was gone, he didn't need to say. The hangdog look said it all. He likely had a bedroom disorder, a deep psychological wound that would not permit normal relations with a woman. He had always been a mess. She didn't understand his friendship with Jimmy, which was deep itself, with a long history. For that reason alone, she should value at least the fact of Billy Atlas, but the same thing—the fact of him—made it hard to do. She fixed a pot of coffee and declined a second offer of salsa.

"It's good on toast," he insisted, but her refusal was firm.

"I remember when you ate almost nothing but cereal and potatoes," she said. "What happened to your woman friend?"

"Nothing," he said. "I just don't know where she is. I woke up and the bed was empty. I mean, *I* was in it but she wasn't. She might have to work today. I guess she took a cab instead of waking me. That's thoughtful if you think about it."

"Then why are you down in the dumps?"

"This isn't the dumps," he said. "This is only a neighborhood or two away from more-or-less content. A warehouse district, maybe, but not too far from home."

"Where's Jimmy?"

"Taking her home, I imagine. Or maybe he's still asleep. She lives in Ocean Beach, which would be a helluva taxi tab. The thing is, I sort of woke up when she got out of bed, but I thought she was peeing, you know? I didn't rouse myself. I thought it was better to stay under."

"You thought it was better?"

"I get very shy, sometimes," he said, "especially—"

Violet changed the subject. "How did you meet?"

His eyes darted around the room as if following a hornet, and Violet understood that he was about to lie to her.

"She had a flat and I changed her tire."

"How chivalrous, you and your lug wrench. What does she drive?"

"A car."

She flashed on the rental that she and Arthur had picked up in Chicago—this was on their odd, lovely honeymoon—a tiny red thing, like a fire ant, and her father had called it *hideous*. Her father was an artist, and the car offended him. Violet was not going to let Billy off the hook. "Was it a big car?"

The eyes again, flying around. Perhaps this meant he was a basically honest person, she thought, this complete inability to lie persuasively.

"A Dodge Dart," he said at last. "That was the key to the whole hooking up." He smiled, showing his too-big teeth. Billy had been the first boy of James's group to have a car, but it was that homely Dodge Dart, old even then, the same miserable, stinking car she was driving the night before, lost in Onyx Springs. What would her father think of that car?

"That was lucky," Violet said. "You must know everything about Darts."

"I can change a flat. The thing is, what I was going to say before . . ." He lowered his voice. "You think a woman in bed with you expects sex?"

Violet poured the remainder of her coffee into the sink. "I'm going to shower."

"But do you think—"

"Yes, Billy. There might be exceptions, I suppose, but if she spends the night in your bed, probably so."

He nodded sadly. "I thought so, but I didn't know how to make the first move. Then after a while she was asleep. Or acting asleep. And then I was asleep, acting part of the time myself, but sleeping, too."

"Touch her hair or her cheek," Violet said and blushed. "Did you kiss her?"

He eyed the socks in his lap. "We talked some. She said she just wanted to sleep, but cuddling was okay. I cuddled, but I guess she—"

"Good," Violet said. "That's good. I'm going to bathe."

"She asked about you, actually. Wanted to know what you're like."

Violet inhaled sharply. She comprehended with a sudden certainty that this woman was Jimmy's girl. She couldn't guess at the complications, but she understood the woman did not love Billy Atlas, and Billy knew it.

"I don't want to know how you described me," she said.

"It was all good things."

She knew this would be true. Billy was not one to put down others, or even to genuinely see their bad parts. He *was* like a dog—a good dog, at that: house trained and utterly devoted, in possession of a repertoire of simple tricks.

"If everything you said about me was good," Violet said, softening, "then you didn't give her the straight story."

Billy laughed, shaking his head. "You're maybe the best person I know," he said, and in the same breath continued, "Do you think if I sent her flowers, it would be too much?"

Violet was touched by the offhand compliment. Yet she wanted to correct him, reveal all her flaws, tell him how, at the end, she had wanted her husband to die. What would he think of her then? Instead of speaking, she placed her hand delicately on his shoulder.

He angled his head up at her. "You're thinking flowers is too much after just one date?"

"I think you should save your money." She patted the shoulder, ready to leave the kitchen but his shoulder was sticky. "Have you been eating honey with your salsa?"

"Oops," he said.

She stepped to the kitchen sink, thinking—for no good reason that she could see—of the day she first caught on that something was wrong with her husband. He already knew, of course, had the diagnosis, the prognosis, had read stories about the course of the disease and what it did to the family and friends, the toll it took. He had decided to hide the fact of it for as long as he could, pretending some days to be stiff from an imagined workout, or claiming he was getting absent-minded and a mental lapse had caused his clumsiness.

One morning in their kitchen—she loved that kitchen and how it filled with early light—she caught his reflection in the window, saw him lower his head to slurp coffee from the cup like a cat dropping its head to a water bowl. "What is it exactly that's wrong with you?" she asked. She chastised herself later for the sentence, as it pretended to know—to have known—and she was only just making the discovery.

He straightened up. She could see as much in the window's reflection, but she did not turn around, instinctively knowing not to take the full brunt of it face to face.

"I should have known I couldn't hide it from you."

"How bad?"

He took a deep breath in through his nostrils, which made a whistle. "Love, as bad as we might be able to imagine."

She turned then and in the turning she metamorphosed into the wife of an invalid, and even now, as she adjusted the water in the sink to wash her hands, she had not completely stepped away from that role. Arthur was buried in Tiverton, his childhood home, but she was still nursemaid, the grieving wife, only now the object of her attentions was less cooperative than ever, and her hands quaked with idleness, quaked with obligations she could no longer keep.

"Good morning, sinners," Lolly said, stretching in the kitchen doorway, her hands above her head, the top to her modest white pajamas rising to expose a strip of bare flesh. The lovelorn Billy seemed to appreciate that glint of skin. What a dopey smile.

"Where's Jimmy?" Violet asked.

"Snoozing," Lolly said. "He had a terrible time getting off to sleep last night. He kept waking me without really waking me, all toss and turn. Normally I'd have Florence Nightingaled him, but I was just too knackered."

"Scientists have proven," Billy began, but the sound of the front door opening stifled him. They all held themselves still and listened. The door closed. Someone approached.

The young woman was in the same attractive black dress she had worn the night before, carrying a cardboard tray of disposable coffee cups, a plastic bag dangling from her wrist. "It took me forever at that place," she said and smiled doubtfully. "I'm Lise."

In the flurry of introductions and the awkward shuffling about that followed, Violet backed away from the table and watched. It should have made her hopelessly uncomfortable to have guessed that Lise was her brother's lover and then to see her here chatting with her brother's fiancée, but perhaps her character was irretrievably flawed: she rather enjoyed it.

Lolly decided that the appropriate topic for conversation was the magnificence of Billy Atlas, intuiting perhaps that the hapless lout needed all the help he could get. The women sat on either side of Billy, and he politely pushed his morning salsa bowl to the middle of the table. He draped his arm around the back of Lise's chair. She unconsciously leaned forward, away from his claim, putting her elbows on the table.

"You are so lucky," Lolly was saying. "Billy's such an angel."

Vague abstractions, Violet thought, *they come in so handy.*

"Are you English?" Lise asked suspiciously, and Violet took a liking to her.

"Oh, heavens no," Lolly said, "but after living there, I can't seem to shed the accent. I suppose I'll pick up the California *twang* if I stay here long enough."

If only her cell phone worked in this country, Violet thought, she would make a video. There should be some record. Lise had taken some trouble with her hair, and it looked much as it had the night before. Lolly had also put in effort with her hair, which was beautifully disarrayed, the type of frowsy morning look that turned men into slaves. All that was missing was her sleeping brother. She lifted the water handle and switched on the garbage disposal, which, like everything else in this house, was a cheap model that made a fantastic amount of noise.

"You'll wake Jimmy," Lolly said.

Violet took her time cutting off the grinder. "I wasn't thinking, was I?"

She had missed some of the conversation. Billy was telling a story. Violet realized with a start that he was talking about her mother. "She had me pose with my underwear on—I was a tighty-whities guy back then," he said. "But the painting showed me nude. A twelve-year-old in the raw, sitting in a kitchen chair, a ladderback chair. I know that 'cause that's the title of the painting: *Ladderback Boy.*"

Violet had never heard this story. She crossed the room and took a place at the table.

"I was holding a cat in my lap, but you could tell I was in the raw, only I hadn't been. Hadn't had a cat, either. She added the cat and subtracted the undies. And, *man*, the grief I got from my parents. *Those Candlers are not respectable people. What filth are they exposing you to?*" Billy laughed and then deadpanned, "My people are a simple people."

Violet knew the painting. It was one of her favorites of her mother's, but she had never made Billy to be the naked boy. More surprising, though, was how his parents thought of her family. Her parents were artists and professors, and all the children in the neighborhood liked to gather at the Candler house—including Billy to a greater degree than any other. That Billy's parents looked down on her family was shocking.

She realized the others were staring at her. Evidently, she was making a face. "That painting, I was just trying to remember. Yes, it's in the Houston Museum of Fine Arts. They put together a traveling show of Mother's work a couple of years ago—maybe ten years ago—and they acquired three or four of her pieces. That was one of them."

"I'm a museum piece," Billy said proudly. "It's about time."

He might have gotten a laugh but Jimmy had entered in his pin-striped pj's, stepping on the punch line. He did not do a double take, but he widened his eyes and offered a clumsy smile.

"This is my brother Jimmy," Violet said gleefully. Her cheeks hurt from the spread of her lips. "Jimmy, this is Billy's girlfriend, Lise."

Lise stood. They shook hands. If Violet had harbored any doubts, the handshake eradicated them—Jimmy's eyes seeking the ceiling, the floor; Lise's sly, regretful smile. They were lovers. She was forcing the issue. And Jimmy boy, clearly, was feeling the pressure.

"I think I'm too hungover to talk," he said. "Pretend I'm an inanimate object."

Violet handed him the remaining cup from the cardboard tray. "Lise ran out for coffee and bagels."

Jimmy smiled a thanks to Lise and took a sip. "I need to nuke this," he said, meaning, presumably, the coffee.

Lise wanted to flee. She had not intended to make James suffer. She had not meant to make him angry. What had she meant to do? She could not lay hands on that. They had moved to the living room, everyone in sleeping gear but her, feet on the coffee table, she and Billy and Lolly on the couch, Violet in a kitchen chair, and James—trying to hide his smoldering anger by feigning a hangover—in the La-Z-Boy. Above them, that awful pretend piece of art, a glass nest designed by someone who'd never seen a bird. Why in the world had he bought this travesty of a house? His hand covered his eyes. She hadn't wanted to leave without seeing him, that was all. She wasn't by nature cruel. James's sister asked her a question.

"I work at a clothing store, a fancy boutique in La Jolla. This dress came from there. I'll be paying for months to—"

"It's smashing on you," Lolly said. "How did you meet our Billy?"

"I changed her tire," Billy said quickly.

"Before he worked at the sheltered workshop," James put in, "Billy parked cars in San Diego."

"I understand you drive a Dart," Violet said.

After a second's pause, Lise said, "I drive a Rio. A Kia Rio. It wasn't a Dart," she said, firmly, glaring at Billy. "You're deluded."

"I thought it was a Dart," he said happily.

"Did he force you then?" James asked. "Saved you on the highway and then forced you to go out with him? Emotional blackmail?"

"Hey, not so rough," Billy said. "Take it easy on Mr. Atlas."

"I went out with Bill—"

"Sounds fishy is all I'm saying."

"James, you're being an absolute punter."

"I like him." Lise touched Billy's shoulder and then ran her hand through his hair: a rodent's nest. "He's kind and cute, and he drives a reasonable car. I couldn't believe that thing you borrowed last night. Where did find such a pretentious piece of—"

Violet's laughter inadvertently cut her off.

"It's my car," James said. "I tell everyone it was a mistake. Don't I? Violet?"

"An enormous mistake, looks like," Lise insisted.

"I'm rather fond of it," Lolly said. "You boys should take Billy's Dart to work. I'd look very dashing in that car."

"Is this house like a commune?" Lise asked. "It's big enough to be a commune, and you have this convenient barn room."

"They call it the grand room," Lolly said.

"The house was a mistake, too. Okay? And it's *great* room, not that it is, but that's what they call it."

"You're quite the Mr. Grouchy today," Lolly said. "Serves you right for drinking so much and dancing with every woman in the bar."

"He didn't dance with me," Violet said.

"Or me," said Lise.

"I saw you and Billy on the dance floor," James said. "You make a lovely couple."

"Oh, Lise," Lolly said, "we do have to teach your boyfriend some steps."

"Whoa now," Billy said. "I know a lot of steps—the, ah, bob and weave, the bob and lash, the, ah, bob and bob."

"To bob is not to dance," Lolly said.

"To bob is mortal," Lise said, "to actually know a few steps, divine."

"You're a great dancer," Billy said.

"Thank you," Lise and Lolly said simultaneously. They might have laughed, but neither did, which made it embarrassing—though not to either of them, evidently. Violet was embarrassed for them both.

"You're a polished dancer," Lise said to James. "Did you take lessons?"

He offered a modest shrug.

"He used to pick up birds that way," Lolly said.

"She means *chicks*," Billy said.

"Were you terribly successful?" Lise asked.

"Now and again. You never know, though, who it is you've met."

"What do you mean?" asked Lolly, and at the same moment Lise asked, "What do you mean by *that*?"

"The character of a person is impossible to judge from her dancing."

"His or hers," Lise said. "The same is true, I would imagine, for men."

"He's always telling me to be a more confident dancer," Billy said. "I want to take you two up on the lessons." He said this to both Lise and Lolly, but neither acknowledged him.

"So do you," Lise said, and then corrected herself, "*did* you—did you just take them home and screw them?"

Lolly covered her mouth with her hand and tittered. "Do tell, James."

When Jimmy didn't immediately reply, Violet said, "It's time for me to get a shower. It's been lovely meeting you, Lise. I hope Billy will have you over again."

Lise stood to shake her hand.

"Yeah," James said. "I'd just take 'em home and fuck 'em, but that's all in the past now, the deep, dark, dim, distant past."

"It bloody better be."

"Can you take me home?" Lise asked Billy.

"Not in my car," James said.

"That's a relief," Lise said.

"Just gotta get some shoes," Billy said. "And pants."

"Would you mind terribly if I took the first shower?" Lolly asked Violet, who had failed to make her getaway. "It's just this hair. I ought to whack it all off." She looked to James for a protest but he was staring resolutely at the wall.

"Go ahead," Violet said. "I may lie down for another few minutes."

In a matter of seconds, Lolly departed to shower, Violet to lie down, and Billy Atlas to dress, which left Lise Ray alone with James Candler.

"We just slept," she said softly, and her sentence was followed by the vibration of water pipes. "He was happy just to sleep beside me."

James made an uncertain gesture with his hand. "I was certainly surprised to see you last night."

"I wanted to get a look at her."

He seemed to accept that. He didn't offer a full nod but his head jiggled. Lise understood that she was a ridiculous figure, a spurned woman trying to measure the meaning of a man's waggling noggin. Amazing how long it had taken for that insight to reach her: this affair was a joke, and she was the butt of it. She felt a deep stab of self-hatred and looked away from him, saying, "She's pretty. She seems nice."

"She's beautiful," he said softly. "She's wonderful."

The disconnect became palpable: this man was nothing but a shadow of the man Lise had met in Los Angeles, the man whose life she had worked daily for years to imagine. This man was petty and capable of cruelty. He was arrogant and he drank too much. He loved another woman and treated her, as well as Lise, dishonestly. She felt this break between the first James Candler and the second in her chest, but not as if her heart were breaking, more like the way a hiker who has ascended a ridge only to discover yet another ridge beyond it feels disappointment and resignation, along with a powerful announcement of fatigue. This particular hiker, though, was not tempted to turn back; if anything, casting away that initial image of the man had lightened her pack.

"I'm not going to say anything to anyone," she told him. "If that's worrying you—I would never do that."

"You shouldn't be here."

"I know that. You don't have to tell me that."

"Evidently, I do."

"Don't be a prick."

He said nothing for the longest time, and then he said, "Sorry."

"I thought I could disappear from your life."

"You going to see Billy again?"

"He sort of proposed to me on the drive home. I don't think I can just dump him."

"When I saw you last night, I . . ."

"Sorry. I'm sorry. It was—"

"I was thrilled," he said. He had spoken too loudly, and now he whispered, "It was thrilling. I wanted to take you to the parking lot and . . ."

Inexplicably, she began to cry. She tried to hide it but there was no use. One of the hall doors opened, and she said quickly, "I won't sleep with you while she's living here."

"All right. That's fair."

"What's fair?" Billy Atlas asked.

"Nothing is," Lise said. "Nothing, nothing, nothing."

Driving Lise to Ocean Beach took Billy thirty minutes. That Lise fell asleep on the drive was a relief, as he had run out of conversation and didn't want to ruin a perfect morning. At her apartment, she gave him a kiss on the cheek but did not invite him in. Nonetheless, he was elated on the return drive and disappointed to find the house empty.

Lolly had left him a note:

> *Billy!*
> *If you're not too zonked after all the rumpus with your girl, get*
> *your arse to the Blue Willow for some food and a few rounds*

*with Vi & James & me! Who knew you were on the pull all
this time! Give us the lowdown. Your girl is lovely!*
Lolly

The meaning of the note was mostly discernible (rumpus?) and
the tone was friendly, but he had decided to send Lise flowers. It
would take time to pick a florist from the yellow pages and to get
up the nerve to make the call. (He knew from experience that roses
could backfire.) He didn't much feel like drinking, anyway, and talking about Lise in front of Jimmy could be iffy.

He got out the phone book to begin the deliberations, confident
that he'd order flowers and confident, too, that it would take him
twenty minutes to convince himself to make the call.

After he got off the phone with the florist, he dialed Lise, reaching her voicemail.

"Hey," he said, "I've thought about you all day—since getting
back from dropping you off, I mean. It's only been an hour, holy cow.
Anyway, what I'm saying is, *you're not here*, which is a bummer. That
reminds me how Lolly says *bum* for butt, and how you've got such
a nice one. Nice bum. And if the doorbell rings, answer it. I won't
say why, but it won't be me. Had a great time just talking to you at
the house and on our drive, the part where you were awake. And the
cuddling last night. And, well . . . got to do some important work,
so . . . Enjoy the rest of the weekend. This is Billy. Atlas. The guy you
spent the night with. 'Bye for now."

He would like to revise the message, especially the *bum* part, but
it could all use a red pencil. Once he had written out everything he
meant to leave on a woman's machine, and he called and recited it all
without realizing that he had gotten the actual person. "Have you had
a stroke or something?" she asked.

He wished he did have some important work to do. On weekends
he missed the workshop and the workshop gang. The job had exactly
the right element of demand and reward, and his flock was an interesting bunch of misfits, like those army movies. All it took was a brave
sergeant and they became a troop or outfit or whatever it was men
became, ready to conquer the world, or at least some Nazis.

Thinking about this, he recalled the stories he had them write.
He hadn't read them. He came up with the idea of their writing stories

while he was riding home with Jimmy one evening. Jimmy was prais-
ing Billy's work and trashing the previous supervisor. "One day the
electricity went out at the facility and to keep them busy, Crews made
them wash his truck." Jimmy laughed and shook his head, but it set
Billy to wondering. What would he do if the electricity shut off?

He made a list of possible no-electricity activities. He had already
started special projects for them—making change with Karly; teaching Rhine chess, and when that didn't work, checkers; teaching Karly
how to use a washing machine; smoking a joint with Mick; showing
Alonso some tasteful nude photos from a safe soft-core site; giving
Vex an ANGER RUINS JOY T-shirt; and teaching Karly what he remembered of the foxtrot from his aborted Dance 101. That class was
a bad memory. When he finally got to dance with the woman he was
attracted to, she said, "With you it's more like the *hippo*trot," and while
he had laughed at the time, he never returned to the class.

He needed something the whole group could do. Ultimately, writing a story topped the list. Counseling, as he understood it from his
own brief experience with it in college, was mostly telling stories on
yourself. Billy had seen a mental health counselor at the university
after having sex with Dlu while she was still Jimmy's live-in girlfriend.
"I loved it," he told the young woman, whose great square glasses made
her seem remote, and the room was so dim she melted into the panel-
ing, and it seemed like he was talking to one of those mounted heads,
like a deer or a moose, but a human mounted head, who nodded now
and again and took notes. "It was slow," he said, meaning sex with
Dlu. "She wouldn't let me do anything fast, and while I was kissing
her . . . her *parts*, I . . . You need background here, about my sexual . . .
attempts. If success in bed is making your partner satisfied and making
yourself satisfied, then my batting average would be precisely zero.
Partly, granted, because I never had an unpaid partner before, but . . .
I'm getting off the subject. What I mean to say is, I got a satisfactory
erection, solid and sensitive and at the ready, which, in my history,
anyway, is rarer than you might think . . ."

Sex with Dlu: she initiated it, of course, one weekend when Jimmy
drove home because his sister was visiting. Why hadn't Dlu gone with
him? She didn't like Violet. Billy never understood why. The relationships of women had too many secret panels and trapdoors for Billy
to analyze. In any case, Dlu invited him over to eat the remains of a

pot roast that hadn't come off. Jimmy had cooked the roast the night before, his turn to make dinner, and he didn't let it cook long enough. Billy saved the evening by making a pizza from stuff he found in the cupboards. He couldn't remember all the ingredients, but capers was one and raisins another. Dlu had let the roast cook another few hours and she didn't want to eat alone. That was important because later, halfway through dinner, she touched her napkin to her mouth and said, *How do you manage all those meals alone?*

At this point, just when he finally got to the meat, so to speak, of his story, the wall-mount said, "That's all for today," and sure enough the hour was up. Why hadn't he ever gone back to her? Counseling was free at the university, and Billy had never been short on time, but he didn't go back. *It wasn't a pity fuck,* he wanted to say. Dlu loved him. Not the same way she loved Jimmy, but it was still love.

His briefcase, which he bought at Goodwill for three dollars and had only required two short strips of black tape, was in the kitchen, beside the table. He had to put it on the kitchen table every night so he'd see it in the morning when he swilled his coffee; otherwise, he'd forget it. Tactics for getting by—it took a lot of them to keep him from screwing up. Someone—probably Violet—had moved his briefcase to the corner. She was reluctant to appreciate other people's tactics because she didn't need any. She sailed through daily life as if it took no concentration to manage all the requirements of food and bath and so on. Not that she knew what the hell to do with herself since her husband died. Billy had never met him. He counted this as one of the big regrets in his life.

The briefcase held very little but the papers, which were crinkled and wadded up now, among the remnants of several lunches. Why did he continue to bring bananas when he never ate them? He flattened the sheets of paper and spread them out on his bed, leaving his door open in case Lolly or Violet passed by and he could tell them about the work he was doing. Of course, they weren't home. He wondered how often he did this. How often did he orchestrate his actions to accommodate contingencies that were not in play? He guessed the answer was *all the time*, and even now, even after thinking about it, he didn't want to shut the door, and the way he displayed the stories and even the way he leaned over to read without lifting the pages from the bedspread was a performance for an imaginary audience.

Rhine's paper had so many erasures, the paper was see-through in several places.

Once upon a time. The boy had one mother and one father. The boy had one brother and one sister. The boy and the one father and the one mother and the one brother and the one sister all lived together in one house. Each person had a bedroom each. The mother and father shared a bedroom, but each of the other ones had one bedroom each.

That was as far as Rhine got.

Karly's handwriting was large and looping, but her story was short.

Once pond a time frogs and bees and in the water things. Swimming.

Billy liked this one. *Once pond a time* sounded like poetry. He needed to go to Karly's house to do her laundry. The washing machine in the utility room at the senior citizens facility was a top load and Karly's, according to her pantomime, was a front load, and it was too confusing to her—and to him—to make it clear what she needed to do.

"Boys and girls are different," Karly said to him the day he was trying to teach her how to use the washer.

"Boy howdy," Billy replied.

"Boys do whatever you want them to," she explained. She smiled at him and shook her head to make her hair swing.

Billy had to quit thinking about her or he would never get through the stories. The girl broke his heart.

Alonso's paper featured no words but only circles, fairly neat ones, in three rows, like a stack of firewood seen from the side.

OOOOOOOOOO
OOOOOOOOOO
OOOOOOOOOO

That was Alonso, all right. All logs and no flame.

Mick's story:

Once upon a time in the land of Yuma, Arizona, when the boy was in high school, and he was fine back then, and he was happy it seemed like all the time, he went to a beach with his friends. They slept on the beach, which was long and made of sand, which is just

rocks that the ocean has taken a million years to soften, and there
were three girls and just two boys, and they weren't boyfriend and
girlfriend and the numbers didn't match up, and that made it easier
because they could just be friendly, and late at night when for some
reason they woke up, the boy is saying he was going to swim and he
took off all his clothes right there—how could he be the person who
did that? He didn't know how, but back then, he took his off, and the
others did theirs, too. It was five not dressed people in the water, and
in the water they swam, and back on the sand they ate cheese and
honey sandwiches with no clothes on and they slept with no clothes
on, and later on, back in Yuma, after he was sick, one of the girls
that had been there came every day to see him for a while, and one
night she said, "You have to get better." She said, "That was the best
night of my life." And if only

It stopped there, and Billy thought it was a pretty good story, given the naked girls and everything. He had driven through Yuma once, but all he could remember were gas stations, fast-food places, and the heat, but he knew there was a prison, an old-west prison where desperadoes were sent. He made a mental note to ask Mick about it, and maybe he would rent that old cowboy movie *3:10 to Yuma* and they could watch it together.

Maura had turned Little Red Riding Hood into moderately effective porn. She might have a future writing the stuff. Not for the movies. He was pretty sure porn movies didn't waste money on writers. It took him three seconds to imagine a script:

The plumber arrives.
Housewife happens to be wearing thong when she opens door.
Plumber: "You got a plumbing problem?"
Housewife: "What big tools you have!"

The movies were just a stall until the clothes came off, but there was an overlooked market of porn *readers*, people turned on more by reading about sex than by seeing video. Billy counted himself in this group. His favorite type of story involved surprise. An unsuspecting man would see a female friend, and this guy would say just the right thing, and the woman would . . . He had to quit thinking about this, too. Reading such stories made him horny, but thinking about them made him sad. He could never write that kind of story, but maybe it was Maura's particular gift.

The final story belonged to Vex. It was full of words he had crossed out but could still be read.

They went into the ~~woods~~ forest ~~together~~. The trees were tall. The shadows ~~of the trees~~ were deep and long. ~~Stickers~~ ~~Small plants~~ Undergrowth scratched at their ankles. They ~~trudged~~ hiked until they reached a ~~meadow~~ clearing filled with grass. There was a puddle at the center of the clearing. They took off their clothes. ~~When they were naked, they held each other.~~

Another thing came out of the forest. It was a tall man in dark clothes. He told them not to run. When he reached them, he put a hand on each neck. He choked them until they passed out. He raped them and urinated on their clothing. He went back into the forest.

~~He~~ The boy came to first. He looked at the girl. She was on the grass. She was naked. She was unconscious. ~~He He He~~ What he did next is unclear.

Then they got dressed in their ~~bad~~ ~~ugly~~ ~~stinking~~ foul smelling clothing. They went back into the forest. They held hands. The plants tore at their ~~smelly~~ ~~scented~~ fragrant clothing. Smelling that way, no predator approached them. The path was not easy to follow in the ~~night~~ dark. They were in the forest ~~forever~~ for a long time. They are in there still. The stench of their clothes keeps them alive.

Billy read the story twice before grabbing his keys from the kitchen hook. He was going to drive to Onyx Springs and find Vex. Billy had his address, a halfway house near the railroad tracks. He could call the van driver for directions. Billy was afraid of what he might find. But that was his job, wasn't it? To know the people in the workshop? To keep them safe?

Being with his fiancée and his sister at the new restaurant in Liberty Corners, Candler decided, was a lot like being the referee in a boxing match.

No, that wasn't right. Boxers *know* they're fighting each other. A boxing match is an acknowledged hostile engagement, while the conflict between these two women was pointedly unacknowledged. For that matter, with boxers, there was nothing personal in their violence.

Each merely agreed to act as if he had reason to pummel the other's head and body; while the clash in the Blue Willow was, he was certain, deeply personal, not to mention psychologically submerged, emotionally indirect, and perversely cheery. It was nothing at all like a boxing match, and yet he was very much stuck between them, like a referee. Where the holy fuck was Billy when he needed him? It couldn't take more than an hour to drop off Lise and return. Unless he had lingered at her apartment. Candler didn't want to consider that possibility. He thought about purchasing boxing gloves. Violet and Lolly could go a few rounds, and he and Billy could go a few more, and then maybe they would all be fine together. Boxing suddenly seemed the epitome of civilized sophistication and diplomacy.

"What is this noise they're playing?" asked Violet, smiling grumpily. She had to be perfectly aware of the enormous retro jukebox and the fact that Lolly had punched in the preferences.

"Oh, you have to love this," replied Lolly, showing maybe a thousand teeth. She undoubtedly recalled that Violet disliked rock and roll, especially the screaming variety. "I only picked songs from your generation," Lolly continued gaily, though she could hardly be ignorant of the fact that "Communication Breakdown" was released at least fifteen years before Violet entered high school.

"Let's all order, shall we?" Candler said, unnaturally cheery himself. "Billy, that rascal, may be gone all afternoon. We may never see Billy again."

"I'm so happy that there's a new place to eat in the Corners," Lolly said.

"There's not one piddling thing on the menu that looks appetizing," Violet replied.

"Hamburgers are a safe bet, I bet," Candler said. "Yum. Yum. Yum."

"These fluorescent lights give our skin a green tint," Violet said. "Luckily for you, your hair looks good green."

"Thank you!" Lolly said. "Fluorescent lighting *is* green, you know, peachier for the environment. I was thinking we could make the house greener if we put in a few fluorescent bulbs, and do we have to flush every time? If it's *yellow, be mellow,* that kind of thing?"

"Yes, indeed, a burger for me," Candler said. "*Ham*burger. America's—"

"*Mellow* is one of those words that makes me . . ." Violet's head seemed to have developed a tremor.

"Unmellow," Lolly offered and laughed. "Mellow makes you unmellow."

"I'm going to have cheese on my burger," Candler said brightly. "Sharp cheddar." He pointed to the menu in his hand. "They let you choose what cheese."

"Daddy would disapprove," Violet said—a sentence like a lifeline, separate from the feminine tussle, and Candler yanked on it.

"That's right," he said. "I'd forgotten that." To Lolly, he added, "Our father objected to cheeseburgers."

"Still does, I'm sure," Violet said. "He hates how people put cheese on everything. It's a point of honor with him." She smiled ever so slightly.

"And burgers are cheaper without cheese," Candler put in, "but he did seem to be philosophically opposed."

"I can't wait to meet him," Lolly said.

"He loved Arthur," Candler said, recalling the first time that their father met Arthur. James had been there to witness the encounter.

Violet nodded but clearly did not want to talk about her late husband. "I guess I'll have a burger, too," she said. "If there's nothing else. No cheese for me."

A sweet respite of silence followed while they scrutinized their menus again.

James had not only attended his sister's wedding, roughly ten years earlier, he had also joined the newlyweds on their honeymoon—for the second part of it, anyway. Their mother and father had divorced a few weeks before Vi's wedding, and their mother's decision to fly over the Atlantic for the wedding necessitated their father's decision not to come. He claimed to have pneumonia, but James and Violet were not fooled.

Their mother was not much fun in London, and would hardly engage with Arthur, who was approximately her age. After a day of this, during an interval when Arthur had left the apartment on a business errand, Violet burst out, "I'm not marrying *Dad*," and James had the urge to flee down the stairs and run after Arthur. "He's *nothing* like Dad. Besides, I never dated any other older men, and I hardly dated Arthur. I worked with him for years before—"

276

"No details, please," her mother said. "I like Arthur fine, but it will be easier from a distance. My own affairs . . . The wound is too recent." Her lip quivered but she did not fully lose her composure. After another moment, she added, "She's not even pretty, you know? It's, I don't know, *insulting.* To be left for a girl who isn't even attractive, and she's no goddamned painter. He just wanted a young body. That's all. What am I supposed to . . . just a young body. Young flesh. She modeled for him, and, well, it's so tawdry, and he's nearly forty years older, and I am aware that you and Arthur aren't the same thing, but forgive me, I cannot help my feelings right now, and you'll just have to put up with me."

"All right, I'll put up with you," Violet said, and she did. She kept their honeymoon plans—which included a week in the U.S.—secret from her. They chose Chicago because Frederick Candler had moved to nearby Kentucky. Following a few days in the Drake Hotel in downtown Chicago, they flew to Paducah, Kentucky, from which they would drive to the tiny river town of Wickliffe and on out to the farmhouse that Frederick Candler had purchased. Violet had asked Jimmy to meet her in Paducah, and in a drunken moment at the reception, he agreed to be there.

Candler hadn't wanted to dip into his savings again, after flying to London, and he drove to Paducah from Flagstaff. Dlu was supposed to have come with him, but she was annoyed not to have been invited to the wedding. "I'm not welcome in London but I'm supposed to come to a farmhouse in Kentucky to see your father and his concubine?" Billy volunteered to take her place and share the driving, but Violet nixed that. "I want Arthur to have a *good* impression of us," she had explained.

Jimmy drove his Corolla from northern Arizona to western Kentucky alone, in a single ill-advised twenty-four-hour nonstop trek. He was sprawled across a row of seats in the Barkley Regional Airport, profoundly asleep and dreaming of the white lines on the highway, when their flight arrived.

"You need a bath," Violet said, waking him. "Couldn't you have bathed, at least?"

The Corolla wouldn't start, and they had to rent a car. Jimmy nodded off in the backseat, his head against the suitcases that would not fit in the trunk, on the drive to Wickliffe, but he roused himself when they took the county road to the farmhouse. Their father had purchased a farm of more than one hundred acres. Land in Kentucky was cheap, he had explained to Jimmy over the phone. "A hundred of the richest acres this side of the Valley Nile."

Jimmy caught the reference. "Okay, Big Daddy. See you soon."

But his father had not let it drop. "Is Skipper coming?"

"Sister-woman does not want Billy there."

"Ah, Billy. Skipper and Gooper rolled into one."

It wasn't just the farm that had their father playing Big Daddy, Jimmy reasoned, but also Violet's strange decision to visit him on her honeymoon. She was afraid their father would die without ever meeting her husband. The pretend bout of pneumonia had worried her, even though she had known it was just an excuse not to come to the wedding. The irony—the ugly, bitter, awful irony—was that their father was still alive, and Violet's husband was dead and gone.

Frederick Lansing Candler was sixty-eight the spring day that Jimmy, Violet, and Arthur arrived at the farmhouse, but he might have been mistaken for fifty-five if he would have condescended to dyeing his hair. He had grown portly—not fat, neither Jimmy nor Violet could ever have attributed that adjective to him had he weighed a ton. On the day they arrived, as they trundled up the driveway, he was watering a flower bed with a hose, wearing overalls, which Violet could not help but comment on—"What an affectation," she said. It was not a working farm but an old house with a screened-in porch that wrapped around three sides where her father and his girlfriend set up their easels. Their father bent slightly to peer into the car as it motored up the gravel drive. When he recognized Violet in the front seat, he threw his arms open. His hair and beard were long and unkempt, and the overalls seemed silly, but the gesture—spreading his long arms as if he might lift off—pleased her so much that she tossed herself forward against the constraint of the shoulder belt and cried, "Daddy!"

Candler counted that moment as one of his sweetest memories.

"What an awful car," her father said when Violet climbed from the rental and ran to him. "I could paint that car, it's so hideous."

Jimmy had followed right behind her, but Arthur took his time getting out, giving them a moment together. This small gesture defined one of the things that made Arthur who he was—a type of consideration about which men of Jimmy's generation had no clue. Jimmy loved his father's embrace, the residual smell of paint, even the tang on his breath left over from his morning chewing tobacco. Jimmy had been upset with his father about the divorce, but he had a different take on it than their mother. The family had been falling apart for a long while. Wrapped in his father's arms, he could muster no anger.

"You're not so old," their father greeted Arthur. "May made you out to be ancient. I damn near rented a wheelchair for you."

Jimmy hoped his sister didn't remember that line. Some ironies in one's life could simply never be appreciated.

They expected the girlfriend to be homely but she was nothing of the kind. Sally MacLean possessed a narrow waist and large breasts, and while her face was not conventionally attractive—her wide mouth nearly equaled the span of her eyes—she had a friendly, laconic manner and a soft, imperturbable voice. What Violet did not like about her (she would confess this to Jimmy while they were strolling the grounds that evening) was the scrutiny the woman inspired. Violet caught herself looking for flaws, stories of an unhappy childhood, wondering why this young woman had chosen their aging father. She hated herself for doing it, as it was precisely what their mother had done in London.

Jimmy liked Sally immediately. She was his age and friendly, shy but also pleased that they had come. She seemed to make their father happy. What else did you need to like someone?

The second night in Kentucky, without Violet having asked—Jimmy hadn't even thought about asking—Sally said, "I was in a fog, you know? What to do and why to bother? Fred is answer enough. I feel grounded. The questions are still there, but they don't much matter." She shrugged and looked out to the porch where Frederick and Arthur—the grown-ups—were sitting in kitchen chairs, drinking and chatting. "Maybe we'll get ten good years. Possibly more." She revealed what they already had guessed: Violet's father had not been ill. That was a story to satisfy May. He had not come to his daughter's wedding because he and Sally had married on the same day. "It's not a coincidence," she told Violet. "Your wedding pushed things to a head."

Sally was twenty-three, a Capricorn. She painted miniature canvases, no larger than her hand. She dropped out of the fine arts program when Frederick was forced to retire. "It was screwing me that got him axed." She smiled, an embarrassed acknowledgment of pleasure. It was the first time she stretched that wide mouth to reveal its barricade of teeth, which transformed her face, and made her quite attractive.

"I understand your wanting to know," Sally said, speaking to his sister, but then expanding to include him, "and I appreciate that you don't judge." After a moment, she said, "There's something I'd like to know. It's about your brother."

Of course, Jimmy thought, the endless mystery of Pook.

"He killed himself," Violet said. "I suppose you know that much."

She nodded. "I have the facts but not what really happened, you know?"

Did anyone ever know what really happened? Jimmy knew more than the facts, but he could not say what really happened. His sister, though, had an answer.

"What happened is, it destroyed our family," she said. "It turned out that Pook was the glue that held us together." She offered a sad smile. "Who would ever have guessed?"

Jimmy said nothing, but he had known as much from the beginning, long before Pook died. Pook had been the secret part of them that made them whole.

Ten years later, and May Candler still did not know that Violet and Arthur had come to the U.S. on their honeymoon. Candler suspected that if he made the effort to look up Dlu, she still would not have forgiven him for not taking her to London. And the Corolla never ran again. He'd had it towed to a car lot and traded it in, along with the remainder of his savings, for a Toyota pickup, which he drove back across the country, taking three days, sleeping in the cab at rest stops. He drove the truck through graduate school and up until he heard about the Boxster. He missed that truck. Sometimes, more often than he liked to admit, he missed Dlu. And he missed his family and how they'd once been a single group, not always happy, but always always always bound together.

"You have to like this one," Lolly was saying. A new song began on the jukebox. "It makes me think of us." She reached past James and took Violet's hand: Aretha Franklin, "Bridge over Troubled Water."

Except to mouth the word *us,* Violet said nothing.

The halfway house was nothing more than an old Victorian on the wrong side of the freeway, painted mustard yellow, inside and out. What had Billy expected, a lobby and rec room? A list on the wall provided room numbers for the occupants. It was full of cross-outs and scribbles to indicate the current dwellers. Henry Veeks lived on the third floor, room 301.

The place reminded him of an apartment he and Jimmy had shared in Flagstaff. It, too, was an old house, with beaverboard partitions to create extra rooms, full of guys who wore kerchiefs and women with hair to their waists, people who played their music constantly and burned incense that smelled exactly like an angel food cake tossed into a campfire, which Billy had done accidentally one time. It became obvious they had to move after Dlu spent the night a few times. "This is officially a hellhole," she said after something raucous upstairs—likely sex but possibly dancing or a fight—had shaken the walls and a fluff of black insulation fell into her bowl of chowder.

On the positive side, Billy twice saw Dlu naked in that terrible apartment. To get to the bathroom, you had to go through Billy's narrow bedroom, and the door didn't want to stay shut. The first time was just a glimpse, but the second time he lay on the bed and watched as she dried herself after a shower. She wrapped her hair in a towel and stared into the mirror over the sink to put on makeup, bending in ways that made her butt flat and unattractive (a lesson in why not to look at sex scenes in Hollywood movies because they only show perfect angles, which ruin you for a real person). At one point, mascara from the tiny brush fell on her, and she made a sweeping motion to wipe it away. That just killed him. God, he loved that woman.

He wondered if any of the others at the workshop lived in such dumps. He had been to Alonso's and met his parents. "Onyx Rehab has been a godsend for our boy," Mrs. Duran told Billy and insisted that he take home a slice of ginger cake. Such nice people. He had gone there to deliver some comic books from his own stash that had been riding in the trunk of the Dart since he left Flagstaff. His plan was to read one to Alonso each day that he went until noon before shanking his baloney pony in the john. So far Billy had read two issues of *The Incredible Hulk* and one *Aquaman*—three successful days in one week.

He climbed a flight of yellow stairs to a dusty second floor, the only sound of life a humming that might have been a novice harmonica player or a refrigerator that needed balancing. He couldn't find another flight of steps. An aluminum ladder at the end of the hall finally clued him in. He did not care for ladders, having never counted among his talents the gift of *balance*, either the literal or figurative type. Above the ladder, as flat as the ceiling, an attic door had the numerals 301 scrawled upon it. Billy had to ascend four rungs to tap on the door.

Vex's voice called out: "Who is it?"

"Billy Atlas."

That got no response.

"Billy Atlas from the sheltered workshop. Your supervisor."

"What do you want?"

"I read your story."

"'Bout time."

"I want to talk to you about it."

The attic door swung down from a metal hinge. He had to duck, and the ladder teetered.

Vex scowled through the opening. "Don't fall," he said. "If you knock the ladder over, I can't get out."

Billy planted his hands on either side of the opening and pulled himself up. *I'm doing this,* he thought. *I'm climbing high on a ladder. To visit a psychopath in his dim attic room. Why am I doing this?* The attic was a low-slung garret, all one room, too short for standing upright. The narrow windows were covered with aluminum foil.

"I prefer artificial light," Vex said. He was wearing the ANGER RUINS JOY T-shirt. "The sun is the last thing I'd try to control, except to keep it out. You got a problem with that?"

In one corner was a toilet and a bathroom sink. The porcelain sink was maybe six inches above the floor, and the bottom of the toilet was set below floor level, on a subfloor of some kind. A shelf beside it was crammed with canned goods, a microwave, and a roll of toilet tissue. A minifridge stood beside the shelf. The room had garish carpeting that looked like it had come out of a Taco Bell. Several mismatched lamps, all heavily muted by their shades, offered fettered light. On the floor, beside a low table, lay an ax, the blade a bright red, the handle made of pale polished wood, like a great and gently curving bone.

"You don't have to like the place," Vex said, "but at least shut your gaping mouth."

Billy did as he was told. He was bent over awkwardly and holding his head up, like certain long-necked, humpbacked ogres. Vex had the advantage on his knees. Billy gave it a go. "Much better," he said, rolling his neck. "Quite the place you've got here."

"Did the plumbing myself."

"I might have guessed that."

"And the electrical, drywall. You got to sit to pee. Otherwise, it's no hardship."

Billy nodded quickly, a quacking sort of nod. The lamps inhabited the room like sullen prisoners, which made the light seem trapped and reluctant.

"You want knee pads?" Vex asked.

"I'm okay."

"I'm in the middle of something," Vex said. "Not quite the middle. The premiddle."

At the far end of the room a tarp was spread over the floor. The tarp was covered with mechanical pieces, a bicycle chain, and a flat shaft of some kind.

"A hobby?" Billy asked. "I used to collect bluegrass albums."

"You come here to buy dope? I don't have any to share. My connection dried up, not entirely dried up but he's no longer . . . *moist*."

"I'm not here for that."

"My story then?" Vex asked. "Am I in trouble?"

"Your story scared the holy shit out of me."

"That's what fairy tales are supposed to do."

The room was hot and stuffy, and Billy's nostrils were reluctant to carry the requisite oxygen to the familiar destinations. "I came to talk to you face to face, man to man, like," he said, wishing he could take off his shirt. "I came to ask if you're a danger to others or me."

"Yes, *kimosabe*, I'm a danger," Vex said, "and don't you ever forget it. I won't hurt anybody, though. I'm just dangerous. There's a difference, like potential energy and the actual pistons cranking."

"Can I sit somewhere?"

Vex knee-walked to a low table. Billy followed and seated himself on a plaid cushion. The guy was less scary walking on his knees.

"Beer? Soda pop? Water?" Vex said. "The water tastes funny. I don't get a lot of company. Fucking unannounced visitors."

"Beer sounds good. It's kinda hot in here."

Vex knee-strode to the minifridge, flipping a switch along the way. A window unit hummed to life, and the cool breeze changed everything. The place immediately began to grow on Billy. There was the charm of the miniature about it, and the rent had to be minuscule.

"I had a room downstairs," Vex said. "It was noisy and expensive. Except for the workshop or some other job you guys give me, I have no income whatsoever. Not a cent. My old man is tapped out, and my former employers won't let me on the premises." He handed Billy a can of Miller Lite.

"Have you ever hurt anybody?" Billy asked. "'Cause your file doesn't say if you've ever hurt anybody."

"Depends on what you mean by *hurt*. You ever hurt anybody?"

Billy thought as he popped open the can. "Not counting disappointing my parents, or letting down a landlord, I *tried* a couple of times to hurt people, especially this one girl, by snubbing her, but no luck."

"Turns out I may be luckier than you." Vex had a beer of his own and drank from it. "What of it?"

"I don't want anyone in the workshop hurt because if you're like a lunatic or something."

"I'm *some*thing, I guess. Not a lunatic, exactly. What is a lunatic exactly?"

"He hurts people. Like with a gun or a knife or his hands or his feet or that ax over there."

"What about rape?"

"That definitely qualifies."

"I've never raped anyone, but I was accused of it."

"Is there a story there?"

"No story. Except when a guy came after me with a tire iron and another time this guy swung a shovel and once when these two guys wanted to cut my balls off with a weed whacker, I've never hurt a living person. Dead people, sure. We hurt the dead every minute we're alive. They depend on us to correct their mistakes, the dumb dead sons a bitches."

"A weed whacker, really?"

"They were sick motherfuckers who treated that weed whacker like shit. You have to mix in oil with the gasoline. That kind of two-cycle internal combustion job needs it."

Billy drank his beer thoughtfully. "May I ask why they and the shovel and tire-iron guys were so eager to bash you up?"

"Conflicts."

"Such as?"

"I ate a candy bar out of the fridge downstairs, and yeah it wasn't mine, but you take a shovel to the head of somebody who ate your York mint?"

"Not likely." Billy didn't like mints. "Okay, check off the shovel. The tire iron?"

"I might possibly have kicked the jack when he was changing a flat. Humor. A joke that didn't quite take. His leg wasn't crushed or he couldn't've run after me."

Billy nodded resignedly. "My jokes often zip right over people's heads."

"Anyone get pissed about it?"

"In high school. Wit's a big problem in high school. What about the weed whackers?"

"I fucked their sister. She was young."

"How young?"

"I don't know. Twenty-four."

"That's not so young."

"I'm twenty-*six*. And I knew I was pushing my luck. The family kept her sheltered. She'd never even had her picture taken."

"I don't think—"

"And she was pregnant. Pretty big in the gullet."

"This was consensual sex?"

"No, from behind. Like I said, her gut was like this." He made the traditional watermelon gesture with his hands.

"But the sex was her idea, your idea, came up out of the blue, what?"

"You kidding? She didn't want to fuck. My idea."

"This is where we get into sticky territory. If she didn't want to do it, then how did it come about that you two fucked?"

"We had a bet. Whether I could put my whole fist in my mouth, which I can. I kept telling her I could, but she didn't believe me."

"And if you'd lost?"

"She got to chop off my nuts, but I knew I was gonna win."

"Still."

"Thing is, we have a history. I used to be married to a friend of her sister's, back when I was a welder. You read my file?"

"You were in an accident."

"Somebody says *welding accident* and people expect you to be burnt and have those white blotchy scars, like the other person inside you is trying to surface, but I cut a pole too deep and the fucking thing bent and *bam*, I'm dead. Out of it, anyway. Coma for a while, then I wind up the fucker you see now."

"You were different before."

"So they fucking tell me endlessly. What do I care? I ain't gone to hurt you. Not gone to hurt your gerbils, either. I halfway like them. I fixed the assembly machine, didn't I?"

"You did that?"

"Took it apart, put it back together. You know what a blind flange is? Yours was cracked to shit. I stole the part. That's what I wasn't supposed to tell you. Let's make like I didn't say that. Also, I broke into the senior citizen joint to do the work. Wasn't going to tell you that, either."

Billy drank from his beer. He was moderately terrified that this guy might take the ax and chop his head off. Also, if he kept drinking beer he'd have to pee, which was almost equally troubling. "Thanks for, ah, fixing my flange."

"Blind flange. You're welcome. What about my story?"

"It's good and all." He pulled the folded pages from his pocket. "But a little dark, don't you think?"

"Gingerbread man gets eaten alive," Vex said. "Hansel and Gretel get cooked in a pot. Beanstalk Jack gets a fucking giant after his ass, smelling blood. What fairy tale isn't dark?"

"Valid point," Billy acknowledged. "It's partly the rape thing. Not too many rapes in fairy tales, and since you've got this accusation against you. But you say it was a bet."

"That was a whole nother thing. Separate incident."

"I'm confused."

"People tell me I am, too." He took a long swallow and crushed the can. "Okay, I guess I forced her, but she was my *wife*, and after I got hit on the head, she treated me different. We were in bed, see, and we didn't hardly have any clothes on, and I wanted my wife back."

Billy had spent hundreds of nights in bed with Pilar wanting to have sex with her. He felt for Vex, but Billy would never force himself on anyone.

"It wasn't a crime in an alley," Vex said. "Not like I pushed her up against a wall and pulled her pants down till she smacked me in the head. More like I rolled on top of her. She didn't push me off or scream or nothing, and I thought if we just did it once, she'd see how I was still . . . Ah fuck, sometimes I get desires I'm not proud of. So what do you do? You make yourself live in a high place no one comes to. You concentrate at work like nothing else exists." He covered his mouth as he sighed. "She dropped the charges when I agreed to her divorce business. Maybe that was the plan all along. I haven't had nothing to do with any woman since then."

"What about smoke breaks with Maura?"

"I wouldn't never hurt Maura. No more than you'd hurt that Karly."

"I'm not going to hurt anybody," Billy said.

"Especially not Karly, right? Maybe once I did tug on Maura pants. I wasn't going to tell you that 'cause she didn't like it. She hit me, but then she borrowed my papers and rolled herself a smoke. We talked about head injury and humping and she wasn't even upset."

"You can't tug at Maura's pants in the workshop," Billy said. "And only elsewhere if she wants you to."

"I thought she wanted me to. You ever thought someone wanted you to, but she didn't?"

Billy could only sigh and nod. He indicated the manuscript. "How 'bout you read it to me."

"Out loud? For fuck's sake. Give it to me."

A few lines into the story, Vex burst into tears. "Get *out* of here. I ought to take your fucking head off for making me do this." He thrust his head at Billy, his face a furious red, but Billy was no longer afraid of him.

"I want to hear the rest of the story."

"There wasn't no welding accident, all right? I *fabricated* that. Get it? I was a metal fabricator, so it's funny, trust me."

"Then what happened to make you this way?"

He shrugged. "I guess I did get bumped on the noggin, but barely enough to knock me out. The coma was only sorta real. The definite story, see, is I just like being this way."

"Then why are you at the Center?"

"Ah, fuck me, I guess I'd like to be a *little* different."

This seemed a lot like therapy, Billy realized, which he probably wasn't supposed to do for a few months yet.

"That chain saw belongs to Bob Whitman." Vex pointed at the pile of parts on the tarp. "That ax had a broke handle. I fixed it. It's Bob Whitman's ax. Bob Whitman is my counselor. I fix things for him. We pretend it's therapy so he doesn't have to pay me much."

"I can't fix anything," Billy said. "I can mop up after a toilet runs over, but I can't fix it."

"I'll fix it for you. There's nothing made by man I can't fix."

"How about a salad? Can you fix a salad?"

"Fuck no, you got me there." He laughed reluctantly. "You and Maura. Make the laughter come out of me. You ever looked at clouds and realized how they're like garbage?"

Billy shook his head. "I'll drink one more beer if there's a curtain for the toilet."

Vex shrugged. "I got a blindfold."

The bag of groceries was getting heavier, Karly thought. It couldn't really get heavier, so maybe it was because she was lost and wearing two different shoes. One shoe was the sneaker she always wore but the other one was her slipper with pink on it. So she was wearing just one different shoe, and the other was the same. Where its partner was, she didn't know, or how they got separated and lost from each other, and now she was lost from her house.

The problem was, she got too hungry and walked to the store that Beetle Man used to drive her to and bought one bag of groceries with the money from her spending money, which she kept in her pocketbook, which she finally found in the kitchen, and she only had to put a few things back. The cashier had helped her figure out which ones to put back. She was a very nice cashier, who had gray in her hair and a pale and shaky face, and she was so funny! She wore her glasses for her eyes *in her hair!* And she called everybody *honey.*

She said, "Haven't seen you since I don't know when, honey."

And "How you keeping yourself?"

And "Happens to everybody. No skin off my nose."

And "We got all the time in the world."

And "You might oughta put in for some detergent. Jeans're gettin' kinda ripe."

All of the popcorn bags went back and the chocolate-covered things and the candy and the Coke drinks and the marshmallows and then she had enough money without using her emergency money. An emergency was when you're in the hospital or if there was police.

Then she saw the cashier again when she was in the parking lot and the cashier was yelling at the boy with the sparkly car.

"I know 'zactly who you are and who you ain't, and you ain't nobody this girl needs to talk to nor get a ride from."

The boy had offered her a ride from the store to her home, and Karly had said, "Only to the corner," but the cashier said she shouldn't ride in his car at all.

"You forget I've seen your driver's license, Joshua McDowell. I 'member faces and names, and specially when they bounce checks and stuff tallboys down their pants. I 'member you very well, Joshua McDowell, and don't you forget it. If this girl has any trouble at all, the police is gonna be hearin' your name, too."

The she said something very funny because it was loud. "You hear me?"

Karly promised not to take any rides from the boy or anyone, which she would never do anyway except because the car had sparkly paint and seemed like it could be an exception. The boy said nasty words and drove off, and she must have gone the wrong way because when she followed the arrows she had drawn on her hand it got dark and she wasn't home yet and she was sweaty and some dogs barking at each other wouldn't stop. If she had a microwave, she could eat the pot pie. She was hungry and tired and the new boy in the workshop yelled a lot and had a funny name he called himself. She just thought of that for no reason.

She had seen every kind of flower on this walk—red, yellow,

purple, and blue. It was still Sunday. Her mother was on a trip far away where her cell phone didn't work, and now Karly's phone didn't work. "I'm going with a man," she had told Karly when their phones still worked. "You haven't met him, but you will. He's a nice man. You'll like him." Karly could email her mother if she was home and wasn't lost and her computer was on and the email worked. "They're so doing it," Karly's sister had said when it was her time on the phone. "Mom is all bouncy and absurd. She was singing some absurd commercial in the kitchen this morning. And he's such a baggo, you won't believe it. Dad is no doubt crying in his grave." And there were some other things she said, back when the phones . . . Karly felt funny all at once and took a big breath and got a spinny feeling in her stomach and head. She bumped into a fence.

Being lost gave her a lot of time to think, but the bag was too heavy, and she set it down, and she tried to figure out a plan but she didn't know what to do and she was so sweaty and she was so really tired, too, she realized, and the one slipper was ruined and when she started walking again, a man's voice called out from behind her.

"You forgot your bag, young lady," the man's voice said. He was an old man with a white beard and dark-brown skin. He was on the other side of the fence she had bumped into, and Karly was on the different side.

"It's too heavy," she said. "It wasn't at first, but now it is. Isn't that so funny?"

"Where you going?"

"Home."

"Where's that?"

She didn't know how to answer, but she pointed in the direction she was walking.

"Hardly any homes out that way, less you live in the salvage yard."

Salve-itch-yard. What a word. It meant something. But she didn't think she lived there.

"You want to use my telephone?" he asked. His eyebrows moved a lot. Roly-polies. "I can bring it out here to you, if you like."

"Who should I call?" Karly asked.

"You got me there, but it's dark and there must be someone. Isn't there someone?"

"Of course, silly," she said. "There are a lot of someones."

He opened the gate to his yard and picked up her bag. "I'll get you the phone." He directed her to a folding chair with flat cushions. Whoever heard of cushions on an outside chair? She laughed. It felt so good to sit down.

The man with the yard and the gate and the dark skin and the white hair walked funny. Like he had a flat tire. She could hear him inside talking to another person. Then a woman came out. She was in pants and carried a glass of water that she gave to Karly.

"Goodness," she said. "You're red as a beet. Are you homeless?"

Karly smiled and drank the water, wondering what kind of beat she meant and if she was homeless and where had the man gone and who could she call if he came out with a phone.

"I'm Karly," she said.

The woman said her name, which Karly didn't hear right because she had started drinking the water again. It was the best water! The woman wasn't as old as the man and maybe was just a girl, like Karly. Then she remembered her ID folder, which was hanging around her neck, inside her shirt, and inside it was the square piece of paper with the phone number that belonged to Billy Atlas.

"I have someone to call right here," she said, her hand over her heart.

"When you think about it," Billy said, "our bodies are lousy machines. You have to lubricate them all the time. I must drink six glasses of water—or beer or whatever—every day, and if you had to lubricate some machine that often, like, I don't know, name a machine."

Karly smiled at him and handed over her key.

"Like the assembly machine at the sheltered workshop." Billy took the key from her. "If you had to oil it or whatever six times a day, even Vex wouldn't be able to keep it running."

Karly nodded. "Everybody knows that," she said softly.

He had been in Vex's attic apartment when she called, and it had only taken a few minutes to get to the Newsomes' house, the family that had taken her in and given her water and a sandwich and rubbed aloe on her face and arms and the back of her neck. "She's out of it," the youngest Newsome had said, a black woman roughly Karly's age. Billy had not offered any explanation for Karly's confusion except dehydration. "You're very kind," he said. He felt mature speaking that sentence, and he repeated it. "You're all very kind." His washing machine lessons hadn't taken and her clothes stank. He made a mental note to study different kinds of washing machines for future reference.

And then the door to her house opened on a disarray that made him freeze on the threshold. Not that he was exactly Mr. Clean-and-Uncluttered himself, but the piles of things on the living room carpet unnerved him—dirty clothes and dirty dishes mixed together, three separate mounds of garbage, magazines splayed over the garbage, unopened mail in a corner, wrappers from fast food partially concealing her toothbrush and soap.

"Are you all alone here?" He had the funny notion that someone had made her do this.

"No," she said and smiled. "You're here."

"Okay," he said. "Do you know where the trash can is?"

"Don't be silly," she said and led him into the kitchen.

The white plastic container was under the sink and empty. Billy pulled it out and asked why she hadn't used it.

"It doesn't have a bag," she said.

He nodded. Someone had told her not to use it without a liner.

"We're going to make a shopping list," he said. "Show me around."

It wasn't that she didn't know how to wash dishes or take out the garbage, he discovered, but between knowing and doing there was some impediment, a step she couldn't take. Billy was no stranger to this condition. Sometimes people needed direction, someone to tell you things, to guide you around. He had known that his English papers were due, but he had never done them until the last minute, even after flunking English twice. He had spent ten years working at a convenience store for no good reason that he could see now, and that whole time he had told himself that the work was not permanent. One girl had to say *dead-end job,* or he might still be working there.

In each room, he encountered new calamity, including, in Karly's bedroom, a big heap of dirt—black dirt that had to have been shoveled in.

"This is kind of unusual," he said.

"Isn't that funny?" Karly said, but she wasn't sure and something besides her usual ebullience showed through.

"Doesn't matter," he said. "When I was a pizza guy, I had such a pile of pizza boxes in my room that I turned it into a project. You know? I wanted to pile them up until they were as tall as me."

"The boxes were tall?"

"Yeah," Billy said. "I stacked them up until they were as tall as me."

"This tall," she said, touching the top of his head.

"I called it the pizza man sculpture, but no one thought it was funny or even vaguely interesting."

"Were you sad?" she asked, and Billy had a sudden desire to kiss her.

"I laughed it off." He knelt to keep himself from touching her. "This is a lot of dirt."

"If you put a seed in dirt," she said, "it's supposed to grow."

Once pond a time frogs and bees and in the water things. Swimming.

"That buzzing is the dryer," Billy said. "You have clothes."

After the first load of clothing was clean and dry, Karly showered while Billy continued cleaning. He found watermelon seeds in the dirt and softening rind on the floor of the bedroom closet. He recalled one time, years ago, when he was a boy in Tucson and Pook had walked home with him from the Candler house. Billy needed to shower and put on clean clothes, and then they'd walk back. Having Pook along would keep his mother from corralling him and saying he had to spend a night at home. When he got out of the bath and dressed, he couldn't find Pook. "Did he go home?" he asked his mother, knowing he hadn't. Pook wasn't one to abandon a friend. His mother leapt into a rant, how difficult her life was, how Billy was no damn help bringing such creatures into her house. She wasn't a bad person, Billy knew, but she was afraid of Pook and that led her to say mean things. Billy backed out of the kitchen and looked in his room. He found Pook sitting on the closet floor, having carefully pushed Billy's shoes aside.

"What are you doing in there?" Billy asked.

"Noticing," Pook had said.

Billy was on his knees in Karly's bedroom closet with a sponge when he heard the shower end and Karly step into the room. He could tell by the sound of her step that she was barefoot and by the dripping sound that she was still wet. He was afraid to turn his head, afraid that she wasn't dressed, that she had stepped out of the shower into her room, and here he was on the floor of her closet like some perv waiting to get a peek. And he *did* want to look at her, which meant that he really was a perv *(big effing surprise),* but he didn't look. The sponge was blue and bubbled with soap.

He said, "Are you decent?"

Karly laughed and said, "Don't be silly."

PART FOUR Noticing

The gods too are fond of a joke.
—ARISTOTLE

8

Barnstone paused in the kitchen doorway to examine Andujar seated on the piano bench, hands over the keyboard, fingers a millimeter above the ivories. He was dark-skinned, born in Honduras but raised in California, a former client of Barnstone's, and now? What was he now? He was her *roommate*, she supposed, but he had his own room—her *housemate*. He slept in her bed, though, and sometimes they had sex. He was her *lover.* That was misleading, as well. He was thirty-two and she, fifty-eight. She loved him but it was the love of a mother for a difficult and damaged son. The sex was like therapy for him.

Mercy, that sounded like rationalization, even to herself.

His hands remained suspended over the keys. He waited. For what? What went through his head in such moments? He had written songs before his breakdown, but he could no longer read music and did not play anything recognizable. He composed *racket,* or so it had sounded to her until his playing woke her one night, and she realized she had been listening to it in her sleep. She heard it then as strange music arranged by association with the other keys. It would be like writing according to the order of the alphabet, so that *neck* and *head* would have nothing to do with each other, but *neck* and *nook* would be related.

She was expecting guests—Candler's fiancée and sister, as well as Maura Wood and Mick Coury. Candler had talked his women out of volunteering, claiming a conflict of interest. A load of shit, but when Violet called with the news there was nothing to do but invite them over. They wanted to get to know some of the clients. Good for them. And screw Candler. Like every other professional at the Center, he had turned against her when he heard that Andujar was living with her. She clung to the belief that she'd had a good working relationship with them all before the disclosure.

In reality, the breach between Barnstone and the other counselors had always been wider than she imagined. She was as ambitious as any of them, but her ambition was tempered by a sense of humility and personal ethics that she thought everyone must possess, but which was in reality so specific to her character that to others she seemed inexplicable. If she was forced to name this overriding characteristic, she'd have called it *integrity*. It was why she had to include lyrics in her songs that kept them off the radio, why she would never adopt the prevailing rock fashion onstage or in the music. Never mind that her early bands played music that appealed primarily to the head-banging set. It might have been bad music, but she had believed in it. The belief was complex and artful, even if the compositions had been trite and simplistic.

This same internal code forced her to take in Adam Herring when his funding ran out. He was a child and would have been on the street. A harmless, damaged boy, who needed the summer to finish his high school equivalency. Roommates for a couple of months was the plan, but he was late applying to colleges and how could she throw him out? She taught him to cook easy dishes, keep a checkbook, mow the lawn, do the simple repairs that made one *handy*. When he left for San Diego State, she felt good about his chances. And he was succeeding. His grades were not good, but he had what could pass for a normal life. Maybe it was a C- sort of life, but that was a passing grade.

The second roomer was a more complicated case. She might have *used* the idea of integrity to give herself permission to house him. Andujar moved in while Adam was still there, which meant he had to sleep on the couch, until one night he climbed into her bed and slept beside her. His full name was Joseph Andujar Freeman. No one knew they were lovers. No one but Adam Herring, who was busy in San Diego keeping his head above water.

Andujar was born in Tegucigalpa but sold to a couple from Chicago who could not get pregnant. *All right,* she conceded to her internal inquisitor, her love for Andujar was not like a mother's for a son. No one would approve of their sleeping in the same bed, although everyone would acknowledge that physical closeness was good for him. They shared a mattress. She had made over Adam Herring's room for him, but Andujar preferred to sleep beside her. After this had gone on for a while, one night he plopped his erection against her hip. It both put her off and turned her on. They had sex once every three or four months. Did she desire to see him live independently? To see him move away? Her feelings were so profoundly confused that she aggressively worked to make him independent to appease that dictator within her, that sense of integrity that created labor and held her back, that kept her honest and encouraged others to find her inscrutable.

Some of the Onyx Rehab crowd might have accused her of sleeping with Andujar if not for their flawed conception of her. They assumed she was lesbian. She was single, had never married or borne children, and she did not dress in an especially feminine manner. She never dated anyone at the facility, and the years of wailing away in smoky bars left her with a gravelly voice. She knew of this misconception and had been tempted to correct it, but that seemed to imply she saw something wrong with being lesbian. She made a conscious decision to not correct them. How else to avoid slipping into the same slough of prejudice? And so it was her integrity that let her keep a damaged boy in her bed without creating scandal or getting herself fired. If Egri discovered the truth and she was forced to resign, what would that be but another breakdown on a big highway? It could prove to be as lucky as the first accident.

The doorbell rang. Mick and Maura appeared on the stoop, visible through the side window, a half hour early. Andujar rose from the piano bench, and she gave him time to disappear down the hall. "Come on in," she called.

The door partially opened, and Maura's face appeared. "Will you tell this freak we can just waltz in?"

"Waltz. That's an order."

Mick Coury slipped through the door without opening it more than a few inches. Maura followed, throwing the door wide.

"You can see why we can't ever have Rhine over," Maura said as they entered. She spoke as if the house was hers, which pleased Barnstone.

"He'd have to straighten the cushions," Mick said, "shake out the afghan, vacuum the rug. Are those albums in alphabetical order?"

"Hey, kids," Barnstone said from the kitchen entry. "Want something to drink?"

Mick hesitated, froze, his expression that of a criminal caught in the act.

"What have you got?" Maura asked.

"Nothing for me, thanks," Mick said.

"Oh god, I know you're thirsty." Maura charged past Barnstone to the refrigerator.

"It's my fault we're early," Mick said, taking in the kitchen with his nervous eyes.

Barnstone imagined how the kitchen must seem to him—crowded with things, the big appliances not matching and slightly askew from the walls. For a kid like this, the room would embody anxiety.

Maura spoke with her head inside the refrigerator. "Don't apologize for that. I was so grateful to get away. They let me go with Mr. Reliable here 'cause you put in some kinda word?"

"Is that how you think of yourself?" Barnstone asked the boy. "Mr. Reliable?"

He offered a shy smile, which made him quite beautiful. "Not exactly those words."

"What words then?"

"Mr. Goomball," Maura called, coming out of the refrigerator with soft drinks.

Mick laughed. "I was thinking more like *Mr. Cool.*" He laughed harder and put his hand in his hair, tugging at the ends.

"Who else is coming?" Maura asked. "Andujar?"

"Of course," Barnstone said. "Well, probably. He may or may not make an appearance. And the two women—Violet and Lolly." She cast about for oven mitts and pulled a cast iron pan from the oven. She set it on the counter, a pot holder serving as coaster. She handed Mick a grill fork and a carving knife. "We're having sandwiches," she said. "You're doing the slicing."

"This is serrated," he told her.

Barnstone merely waited. Patience was important with kids like this one. He stared at the blade for thirty seconds before plunging the fork and knife into the roast. He was perfectly capable. Violet and Lolly had asked specifically to speak to Mick. She wondered if one of them had a crush on this kid. She lit a cigarette and offered one to Maura. "Smoke?" she asked Mick.

"No, thanks." He was sawing the meat. "I used to smoke. Before I got sick. Not a lot. At parties. In my car. Or when I was with friends. Certain friends. Most of my friends. Maybe a pack a week. I tried to stop but couldn't. Urges. For some reason, don't have the urges now."

"What did you have?" Barnstone asked.

"Marlboros, when I bought them."

"I mean what illness did you have. A pulmonary thing?"

"My illness. What put me in the Center."

"It's got a name, Mick," Maura said. "You might as well say it."

"I don't like to say it."

"It's called monkey-headedness," Maura said, "and you've got it bad."

Mick offered a happy, relieved laugh.

Barnstone had heard a lot about this boy from Maura. He hated the word *schizophrenia* and would not speak it. Maybe that was healthy, resisting the marker written on his file, branded on his forehead. And maybe it wasn't healthy, a denial of his trouble. If she knew him a little better, she might be able to say which. And she might not. What *was* clear, though, was that he liked cutting meat. He was getting a kick out of it. Several slices of roast beef lay flat next to the remaining hunk, as if the first had tripped and caused a pileup.

"That should be plenty," Barnstone told him.

Mick put the utensils in the sink, which was full of dirty dishes. He began rolling his sleeves.

"The profession tosses around a lot of labels," Barnstone said. "They're useful, but they can encourage circular reasoning and they often cause pain. Most things are like that. Take this roast, for instance." She leaned over the counter and inhaled the odor. "Good for my taste buds and bad for my thighs." She slapped her thighs. "Christ, I've got to get dressed. Are you going to do the dishes?"

He paused in his sleeve rolling, eyes zipping about, trying to figure out his own intentions. "It looks like it," he said.

He was struggling, she understood. The boy probably never willingly took his meds. She would only mention it if he was really in trouble. This was how they learned what they needed.

"You're a saint," she told him.

"Saint Brown Nose," Maura said.

Who could blame him for wanting to be on his toes? Barnstone had never been a heavy drug user, unlike many in the rock world. Perhaps if she'd ever had the luxury of success, she might have felt she could indulge. She could not judge this boy, who was kind and handsome and intelligent, and whom, Barnstone was increasingly certain, Maura loved. She wondered whether Andujar would join them or spend the whole evening in his room. She was in the same position with him as Maura was with Mick. If Andujar were well, he would not be with a woman almost thirty years his senior. It meant she had to do all she could to make him well, or she'd become one of the self-serving ones who fed on the illness of others. Did Maura understand this? Was this something they could talk about?

In her bedroom, Barnstone discovered Andujar standing in the corner he liked, a lit joint in his mouth. He was not beautiful like Mick Coury but he had an aura of masculinity that Mick lacked. She knew it was a facade and yet she liked the facade. He bent down and blew smoke through the screened window. "I thought you were at the park." She had heard him leave while she was in the kitchen. He liked to walk down to the fountain and through the town park.

Andujar nodded. "There and back. Got a little feeling edgy."

The window screen was bent, and she understood that he had climbed in through it, which was why she had not heard him return. The flimsy aluminum frame was cockeyed from his comings and goings. It would never again be truly straight.

"Our guests have begun to arrive," she said.

"I know Mick. He goes way back."

"And you've met Maura."

"I've met Maura."

"All right then. Put that out and let me change clothes."

"I'll wait in my room."

"All right then."

But Andujar didn't move. She would have to change in front of him. She didn't much care for showing off her body in daylight, but it was a silly concern. Andujar would not be affected one way or the other. Perhaps that was why she didn't want to do it.

Violet spent the morning cleaning Billy's Dart. He promised to let her use it for the Barnstone excursion, and it was distressingly filthy. She found a rather amazing array of items beneath and between the seats, including several partial baggies of pot. The usual detritus—pens, coins, dollar bills, keys, ragged road maps—she put in an empty flower-pot by the front door. The drugs—she found unidentifiable pills, as well—she threw away. But what was she supposed to do with the Astral Personal Vibrator? It was the size of a ballpoint pen and looked unused. There was an enormous pacifier, too large for a baby's mouth; a pair of joke eyeglasses that permitted the wearer to see behind him; bread crusts from perhaps a dozen white-bread sandwiches; three dirty and chipped coffee cups, one of which was shaped like a woman's breast; earplugs; nose clips; a blindfold; an eye patch; filthy earphones; a Lumberjacks baseball cap; a crud-encrusted stuffed animal of indeterminate species; parking tickets dating back nine years; cracked CD cases; two paperback novels; used tissues; unused tampons; a Polaroid of a woman's bare thighs and knees; and a pair of coffee-stained (she hoped) boxer shorts decorated with clocks. There were perhaps thirty lists, written on the backs of envelopes or scraps of paper—grocery lists, to-do lists, book lists, lists of names, lists of places, lists of mysterious words that made no sense to her—each in Billy's awkward hand.

Violet found the letter written by Billy's wife saying that she was leaving him, a brief, nicely written letter, explaining that she had adequately mastered English to pass a citizenship exam, and she no longer needed to be married to him. Didn't he want this? Didn't he feel obliged to hold on to the important documents of his life? She might have dragged Billy out to go through the things, but a dark, slender man had arrived on a motorcycle to visit him. Except for Lise, this was the only visitor of Billy's she had seen. And Lise, as Violet might have predicted, had never returned for a second visit.

The Dart's tank was empty, of course. She took a break to drive to a gas station and fill it. With Billy riding to work with James, the Dart was available every day. She wanted to drive to the ocean, but didn't yet feel comfortable negotiating San Diego traffic. She needed a few less-ambitious journeys first. She had thought Lolly might help her clean, but Lolly had discovered a gym nearby that was open on Sundays, and she went there to exercise. The car took fifty dollars of gas.

Shortly after she got back to the house, a silver car pulled up. Violet was trying to decide what to do with a string of packaged condoms, linked like sausages, that she had found wedged in the crack of the passenger seat. A door to the silver car opened and Lolly climbed out, her gymwear made of shiny stretch material. A man had driven her home from the gym, a handsome man whose eyes took her in the way a hungry mouth devours a biscuit.

"Cheerio then," Lolly called to him, and Violet cringed. The man said something in a low tone before driving off.

"Made a new friend?" Violet asked.

"I was about to ask you the same thing," she said, eyeing the condoms.

"You wouldn't believe the rubbish in this car."

"I wish I'd stayed and helped instead of going to the gym," Lolly said. "I'm dreadfully sorry to dump it all on you. And it was a waste. The men in there just wouldn't leave me alone."

"You'll be happy to hear then that I'm not even close to finished."

"If only I weren't so knackered from the workout Rudy gave me. That was Rudy who brought me home. He's a personal trainer. He's been showing me what his workouts could do for me. Free sample. Obviously, he just wants in my knickers, but why not get the freebie?"

Billy emerged from the house with a bundle over his shoulder—a bedsheet, held by the corners, clothing stuffed inside. Shirt sleeves flapped free of the bundle. The thin dark man was with him. He walked directly past her without speaking, mounted his motorcycle, and sped away. Billy opened the Dart's trunk and shoved in the clothing.

"Looks like I'll be riding with you to Onyx Springs," he said.

"Who was that?"

"A guy I know. He fixed the hall toilet, the ceiling kitchen fan, and the lock on the back door. Was here an hour and a half. I gave him twenty-five bucks. That's fair, isn't it?" It took him three tries to get the trunk to close around the bundle. "Thought it'd be a good parting gift, fixing the stuff Jimmy'll never fix."

"Parting gift?" she asked. "What are you doing?"

"Getting a life," he said. "You told me I ought to. I got a place in Onyx Springs. Just confirmed it on the phone—a neighbor's phone. The place doesn't have a phone right now. It's way cheap. Shorter drive to work. I've been here long enough, don't you think?"

"Yes," she said, but too forcefully and his face fell. "I mean . . . I'm happy for you."

"I'll let you know how it goes, and you can let me know how yours goes."

"My what?" Violet asked.

"Your attempt to get a life." He headed back to the house for another load, but he paused at the door. "Thanks for cleaning out the car. I've been meaning to do that for like fifteen years."

Maura carefully poured gravy from the pot into a soup bowl—a gravy boat was not the kind of thing Barnstone would own. Maura had eaten Barnstone's roast a few times, and this was her standard job. The roast was okay but it was obvious Barnstone wasn't much of a cook. Maura ran a wooden spoon through the gravy, tasted it, and added salt. Adding salt was the sum of her talent with spices.

Mick finished the dishes. The blade had cut through the meat, and he himself made it happen. Hardly miraculous work, but he couldn't remember the last time anyone offered him a knife. "Should you be doing that?" he asked.

"Loosen," Maura commanded, shaking her behind as an example. "We need music."

Mick followed her into the living room. He had not skipped his meds but had taken a two-thirds dose at bedtime instead of in the morning. He did not believe he might tip over into the irrational. Now and then he balanced it perfectly. But there was no system. He would need his regular dose tomorrow, and the day after he might not need any. He liked imagining the day that he would need nothing and would return to the world as it had been before. The simplicity of it, the basic clarity of existence, would once more belong to him. There were times when it was so near that he brushed up against it—a warm transparency. If he could lean down and position his arm just right, he should be able to nab it. Like at the door, he had heard Barnstone calling "Come on in," yet the tone of the voice was crumbly, which could indicate that she meant the opposite, like how people would say *fuck you* while they were laughing, or how the same word from different mouths had distinct meanings, and the sunlight on the stoop merely emphasized the shadows, and the shadows made the whole house seem ready to fall. These things meant something. Even the disarray inside the house, the scatter of magazines and throw pillows, a guitar lying on the floor; they seemed to him not signs of a comfortable life but the *ruins* of an orderly life. This world, his world, was the ruins of the life he'd had before. Yet he could sense that other world lingering within the archaeological site, rooting for him, waiting until he could knock his head through the curtains.

"She listens to awful stuff," Maura said, "but I left some of my CDs here."

He asked, "Do you know a song that has a sewing machine in it?"

"Imogen Heap," Maura said without looking up from the CDs. "Or maybe it's Regina Spektor. I don't have any of their stuff here."

"I drove to this beach one time. My car was full of people." He told her about taking friends from Yuma to Mexico, a remote beach so vacant that it seemed like a landscape out of a dream. They had stayed the night, three girls, Mick, and another guy. The girls were all supposed to be spending the night at each other's houses.

"A nice trick," Maura interrupted to say, "and not as hard to pull off as you might think."

Mick could not imagine trying to pull it off now. "I wasn't pretending. I just told my parents that I was going to be out all night."

"They let you do that?"

He shrugged and continued. They built a campfire. The girls were in the choir and sang songs. One of the songs had a sewing machine in it. Late in the night, they went skinny-dipping, and still later the ocean suddenly became a source of light. They all witnessed it. There was a full moon, and when they went to the water's edge to investigate, they saw that the whole beach was glimmering. It was covered with tiny silver fish. "Grunion," Mick said. "I didn't know the name for them at the time, but they're grunion. They mate on the shore."

"You were the kind of boy who went off with a bunch of girls and stayed out all night?"

Thinking about it now, he wondered at the confidence he'd had, the ability to feel wonder, to let himself become part of an unknowable world.

"When I take my meds before bed," he said, "I have dreams that are just pictures."

"You want Arcade Fire?"

Luckily, she waved a CD case at him. "Sure," he said.

"What do you mean pictures?"

"Like a movie screen of things."

"A landscape."

"More like a toolshed. Or medicine cabinet. Or kitchen cupboard."

"You dream a cupboard? What happens to the cupboard?"

"There's just a cupboard or one time a desk. The dashboard of a car. I'm not in the dream in any way."

"There's nobody?"

"Just this image—not like a photograph. It's real enough. Like someone could reach up and take something, but there's never anyone there to do it."

"That's a really lousy dream," Maura said. "If you were Barnstone's boy, she'd take you off that shit. She took me off everything but iron and an antidepressant."

"I need it some, for another week or two. But if I take it every day, I get . . . *flat*."

"I've seen you like that. You're like a zombie."

"Maybe I never told you, but when I got sick, I was in my room watching *Night of the Living Dead.*' "

"You should sue."

"I didn't become a zombie. It's the meds that do that."

"What did you do?"

"I started writing down all the lyrics to the movie."

"It's not *lyrics*."

"I wrote page after page, I couldn't keep up, and for some reason it wasn't okay to pause the DVD. When the movie was finally over— it makes a movie long, believe me, to write the whole time. When it was over, I couldn't read what I had written. It looked like it was that Japanese picture writing."

"I think it's called calligraphy."

"I thought maybe I just couldn't read my handwriting, so I picked up one of my textbooks. The writing looked like English but the words kept coming loose and sliding up to the next sentence, and they got jumbled. I remember one thing I was trying to . . . something like . . . *The Paleolithic bony mass conforms to expectations.* I kept thinking that was the key to everything, and I copied it down and watched it change into Japanese as I wrote it. My hand would form a letter but it would come out a picture word."

"That's a weird breakdown."

Mick listened to music without speaking, a love song, though not a very happy one. Why was love so depressing? Karly was avoiding him. For instance, why wasn't he with her today? He should be upset with her, but how he felt about Karly was like a thin raincoat he had to wear inside out. Try putting *that* into words that would mean something to somebody. He was grateful to Karly, even for snubbing him. The way the dog that's been spanked still wants in the owner's lap? More like the blind man who trips over his guide dog and falls onto broken glass, but while his eyes are full of shards, he can see color where before there was only the black. Is that something a person could speak?

There was one time his father picked Mick up after a session with his psychologist, this nice woman who wore dresses that were like suits, which seemed to Mick like banners she waved to prove she was qualified for her job. The day was cool and his father had the heat in the car on high. He probably meant to be respectful and show interest in his son by picking him up with the heat on high and then saying, "My therapist knows your therapist." There, coming out the door, her professional flag bearing the pressures of her body, was Mick's psychologist, walking in those stiff psychologist shoes along the hard, cold sidewalk. His father's therapist was a marriage counselor, and Mick imagined the two therapists talking and his dad's counselor saying, *If you can just get that boy to straighten up, this marriage will be fine.*

Now, if he tried to say how he was grateful to Karly, and how his new way of seeing made him want to say *thank you* to her (if she would only let him near), Maura would likely only get enough of it to feel bad, which was how Mick had felt with his father. The problem with complicated feelings (were there any other kind?) was that the small part you could put into words was never enough to take the listener all the way to the end. If he could be like a dog or an elephant or the bird that flies low and hungry over the ocean thinking only *fish, fish, fish,* then he would have no trouble explaining, and Maura would hear him and shrug and start on some other topic. But he wasn't that dog, that elephant, that ravenous bird. And wasn't *ravenous* a word to mean *full of the raven?* Could there be a seabird full of the raven?

Maybe he should have taken a scribbling bit of his meds this morning, he thought. Just licked the pill.

Candler was to meet John Egri at a bar in La Jolla. "If I'm not there when you arrive," Egri had said over the phone, "sit your butt down and wait for me. Don't tell anyone what you're doing."

"Is all this intrigue necessary?" Candler asked.

"I don't know," Egri replied. "I don't think our phones are tapped— though I'm calling you from a pay phone just to be safe."

"What are you talking about?"

"I'm pretty sure I'm being followed. Sounds ridiculous, I know, but you be careful going down there. Make sure no one is on your tail."

Candler felt idiotic doing it, but he took elaborate precautions, driving north on Liberty Highway and stopping on a deserted stretch, studying the cars that passed him, doubling back to look for parked cars, and then heading north again. He took a county road west to the coast, where he drove south into La Jolla. Vigilant today, but the night before, he had told Lolly that he was secretly meeting with Egri about the promotion.

"I feel weird about the whole thing," he told her.

"We're going to need the money." She had been over his finances. Without the promotion, they would be pinched until she got a job—and it'd have to be a decent job, as she would need a car. The conversation took place in bed with the lights off. "I spent a big part of my life trying to believe that money doesn't matter much," she went on, "but I was lying to myself. I *like* money, and so does everybody. People who say otherwise are liars or pretending."

She began a story about her days as a schoolteacher in New Jersey. This was after she had given up eking out a living from fingertouch but before she left for London. "It was a suffocating job," she told him. To survive it, she colored her hair every Friday after school. "Dyed it the black of plastic cooking utensils." She filled her piercings with rings and studs, and spent entire weekends in New York, sleeping on a friend's floor or in some man's bed. She interrupted the story to say, "I hope this doesn't upset you."

"I like hearing about your sordid history."

"*Wanker.* I'm trying to tell you something important."

"I'm listening," he said. "Hear me listening?" On one of their last dates in London, she had shown him the tiny scars from her piercings, which (except for the earlobes) had all closed. She produced a photograph. He did not recognize her: Lolly slouched on the asphalt of a city street in full regalia—eyebrow toothpicks, lip and nose studs, a hoopsnake ring dangling from her nostrils, a half dozen earrings to the right, and three more to the left. Her bare midriff revealed a tattoo: an octopus, its arms arranged in a V. Even her jeans had holes. "No piercings in the tongue, nips, or snatch," she had said, "so don't get too aroused." She'd had the tattoo removed but it was still visible, though indistinct. The first time Candler noticed it, he'd thought it was a birthmark. "That's the shadow of my former self," she had said.

"Those weekends felt like the *real* me," she told him, "while that mousy second-grade teacher was the impostor I was forced to play. I was pretty good with the kids, but I couldn't find a path. It was all *what now, what now* from one moment to the next, like I didn't know how to be that person. I'd be all sixes and sevens until Friday arrived." Then one winter weekend in New York, her friend with the apartment asked if she wanted to sell small quantities of cocaine in Jersey. "Just to your pals," she assured Lolly. Her friend needed to sell enough to cover her expenses, and the implication was clear: Lolly had snorted her share of the woman's stash.

"That threw a spanner in the works," Lolly said. "I decided I didn't like my impostor life *or* my real life."

"So you moved to London."

"London was part of it. The key was understanding that I needed a new costume." The piercings and hair, the tattoos and clothing had given her definition. "A role to play, and I was good at it." All she needed to do was redefine herself in some equally definite but more desirable way, a role that would permit her to make a respectable life for herself. "That's the story of my birth, this Lolly you claim to love. She doesn't do drugs except maybe a puff of pot. She doesn't take it up the ass— not even for you, lover—and she isn't ashamed of wanting money. I've gotten very good at this *me,* and now that I've met you, I never need to dye my hair and don that mask again. All the gaps in my face are closing up."

"You don't have to act with me."

"Oh yes I do."

"The glasses you wore at the publishing house?"

"Just plain glass, and only required on the job, but yes, part of the costume, and the hair, the clothes, the stockings. I had quite the bed-room routine worked up until you nixed it."

"Your accent?"

A long pause ensued and Candler was readying an apology before she said, "Bollocks."

"I'm sorry, I . . ."

"No, you're right. I wanted a new way of talking, and don't ask me to let it go. The whole thing falls apart without it. You'd need the king's horses." After a moment, he felt her hand on his hip and she said, "When Vi first showed me your picture and talked about you— she adores you, you know—I decided to make a play for you. What I hadn't planned on was falling arse over elbow for you. Now I've fessed up. You're engaged to a mirage."

"Always wanted to be engaged to a mirage."

"I know it's a contradiction—telling you all this, trying to be honest, but still wearing the toupee, so to speak."

"It's *bloody* okay with me," Candler said. "Everybody's fucking bald. But about this taking it up the ass thing . . ."

"On our twentieth anniversary," she said. "You can start crossing the days off the calendar."

They had held each other until Candler's arm fell asleep. Lolly was conked out by that time, and he'd had to extricate himself carefully. Now she was with his sister at the Barnstone's *bonding* or something, and he was playing Sam Spade. He parked in a La Jolla garage and continued the charade, meandering through shops and leaving through back doors, stopping in a Kinko's to study the street from behind a partition, and when he was certain that he was not being followed, strolling by the boutique where Lise worked, wondering if she was inside.

It had made for an enjoyable if silly morning, all that make-believe skullduggery. Their rendezvous point was the Crow's Nest, an upscale bar and grill. Egri was seated in a booth by himself, dressed in marine gear—short-sleeved shirt, khaki shorts, deck shoes. Candler sat across from him in the booth, and Egri lifted from the bench a floppy green hat to display it.

"I used to have a sailing cap," he said, "but now I'm reduced to this thing."

"You actually think the gargoyles are following you?" Candler asked.

Egri pursed his lips and eyed the ceiling. His journey to the Crow's Nest had been even more elaborate than Candler's. He had rented a catamaran and sailed it to a nearby pier where he called for a cab. "It was reasonable on my part to assume as much, but I know now I was wrong. I found out precisely ten minutes ago. My wife hired a detective." He lifted a stein of beer from the bench and drank from it, returning it to the bench beside him. "The sad thing is, I've never fooled around on Cheryl. Not one affair. Oh, I smooched a woman at a party, felt some bouncy cheeks in the back room, things like that, but Mr. Ralph has kept to his zippered quarters."

"What does she think is going on?"

He shook his head slightly. "Not here to talk about my merry-go-round." His eyes lifted to the approaching waitress. "Order something, then I'll give you the inside dope on the carousel that matters."

Candler ordered a BLT and a beer without looking at the menu.

"The important thing is that I still have the board's trust." He drank again from the stein before describing the two interviews for the directorship that had already taken place. On Tuesday, Ava Greene, the psychologist, impressed everyone during her presentation and the Q and A session, but over lunch Egri casually asked her about the attention her article on systematic empathy was garnering. She responded enthusiastically, as if it were a friendly question. Egri's follow-up included mention of the UCLA Department of Psychology. Greene faltered before admitting that she had applied for a position there. "I was encouraged to apply," she said. "It's unlikely that I'll be offered the job or even be interviewed."

"The funny part?" Egri laughed. "There is no job at UCLA, and if there were they wouldn't be taking applications in the *summer*. I had an acquaintance of mine rig up an email account, and I sent her a phony job description, a glowing review of her article. You want people to do something stupid, flatter them."

Candler still did not understand.

"The hiring committee will listen when I say we don't want a director who's flirting with the universities for jobs. Her goose is roasting in wine sauce."

Clay Hao's interview had taken place Thursday, and he came off exactly as Egri predicted: competent, thoughtful, and dull. "He suggested we target clients who have just begun showing signs of trouble. He had statistics at the ready to show they had a higher success rate. But the therapy he's pushing is called *mindfulness*, which I found easy enough to mock with the board. Had to be careful with the Hao Dog, though. Didn't want to tip my hand."

"What is it about Hao that puts you off?" Candler asked. "He's the most qualified of us."

"Hao's not suited for the job," Egri said, "and we lose our best counselor in the deal. He has no understanding of politics, not in any real sense. You, you've got a feel for it. You've got the initiative, besides, and when you walk your balls got a swing to them. That's gonna be important. Not *mindfulness*, Christ. That's just therapy crap."

Candler's interview was Tuesday. He would spend all day with the committee. His presentation would be on the successes of his existing innovations—the evaluation hub and the sheltered workshop. Egri coached him to offer no new projects, and to emphasize the importance of stability. They ran through the questions to expect. "They're making a point of asking the identical questions of each of you," Egri said, "so you're set."

"You know," Candler said, "I've been studying mindfulness, too."

"You think I care? Just keep your gob shut about it. Wheeling and dealing is the job. For example, technically the entire board votes on the hire, but the personnel committee makes the recommendation, and it'll almost certainly be followed. Are you listening? I'm teaching you how to manage things after I'm gone. I'm on *all* the committees, and I encourage the board to divvy up the duties. Divide and conquer. I'm the only one who has all the information and I pack the committees with ringers; ergo, I'm the one who always wins."

They ate their sandwiches. The conversation veered to the presidential election, the wretched Padres, the economy, the brunette with her legs crossed at the bar.

"I love women," Egri said, "but I also need men, camaraderie, the occasional poker game, sports outing, trip to a titty bar. That's what the detective's going to discover. Not that I'm unfaithful to Cheryl, but that I'm a fucking man with a man's predilections. I used to like sailing, but now I have to pretend to sail in order to meet with a friend and shoot the shit. Pathetic, no?"

Candler drank his beer to avoid replying.

"We're close to the wire. You interview Tuesday, the committee meets Wednesday, and the board makes its decision Thursday or Friday. If I have my way, you'll come in and sign your contract Friday afternoon. You hip to all this?" He didn't give Candler time to answer but grabbed his floppy hat and twirled it on his finger. "There'll be a few things I'll want you to throw my way once you're in power. I'll be asking favors."

"What favors?"

"Friendly favors, nothing close to what I've gone through on your behalf."

Candler sighed. "Have you wondered, have you even considered that maybe I'm not the right person for this job?"

"You're the *only* person for the job," Egri said. "This lunch, of course, never happened. You make sure, during the interview, to re-member all you don't know."

Candler assured him that he would.

"I can't quite believe she hired a detective. Used her private credit card to do it. Still doesn't know that I have all her passwords. Trust is the basis of a good marriage." A smile flickered across his face. "Found the charge on my smartphone just before you got here. What's with your sister, anyway? Pretty enough in a foundling way. Not my par-ticular taste, but plenty of men at the Limb were eager to chat her up. She wouldn't give them a nod."

"Her husband died," Candler said. "It hasn't been long."

"I guess you told me that." He lifted the stein from the bench. "The ocean calls. I have to get sunburned or the whole charade will convince no one."

"Why do you keep your beer mug on the bench?"

"Deniability," Egri said, emptying the stein before grabbing his floppy hat. He left without saying good-bye.

The advice Barnstone offered as she went to answer the door was *Be yourself*. For Mick, this command had a specific meaning: he had been right in cheating on his medication.

"I *like* being myself," he said, feeling a sudden infusion of joy. Then he added, "She's always telling me about you."

Barnstone paused at the door to make a face he could not read, and she said something unintelligible, not words but a kind of grind-ing noise. Then Violet and Lolly were inside—as if time had skipped forward—and he was shaking their hands, his wide grin making his face ache, their dry hands in his hand, feminine hands in his hand, skin to skin.

"I'm sorry we're late," Violet Candler was saying. "I'm so stupid with directions, I could get turned around in a coffin."

Mick lit up. *Turned around in a coffin*. He laughed. *Turned around in a coffin*. Then it was already later and he was sitting and Maura was complaining, "I'm on the there-are-a-million-things-that-aren't-cheese diet." Barnstone had set a platter of cheese and crackers on the table, time jumping onward again, skipping like an old thirty-three-and-a-third. "*You* put me on the diet," Maura accused. "Got any chips?"

"Besides the one on your shoulder," Mick put in.

Barnstone laughed. To Maura she said, "I see why you like this one."

"I told you he's funny," she said.

The Candler girls smiled at him with their eyes and the skin around their eyes.

"I just let the chips fall where they may," he said.

"Are you going to make puns all night?" Maura asked.

"You can chip in too," he said, "even if it's just a microchip. Or a chipmunk. Chipped tooth. Chip N Dale. Chip shot. Chipper. The big chips. Time to chip out. *I got chipped!*"

They were all laughing.

"Everything is chip shape," he said.

"Chipped beef?" Lolly said.

"Chipworthy," Maura offered.

"The Starchip Enterprise," Mick said. "I chip you not."

"Stop now," Barnstone said, and remarkably, he did. He could almost see kindness radiate from Barnstone's person, and he would trust that, not his impressions, which, after all, often got him into trouble. His desire to believe in her was what he had to trust, not the hammering of emotional strings that comments like *stop now* set off. He let those go, let them slide beneath his consideration, like a lifeguard watching a sea of swimmers drown: against his natural impulses he stayed in his elevated seat. A wooden seat, likely. The sea air would weather it. Watch for splinters.

They ate in the living room, plates in their hands, conversation awkward. Mick felt his immense pleasure slipping, sliding, defoliating until Violet Candler mentioned how truly awful the Calamari Cowboys were, and Lolly put in that all the songs were thirty years old, and Mick understood they were laughing at the expense of Mr. Clay Hao and his band, which Mick found enjoyable, joy-making, joyous, joy-us, joy-them, *rat-a-tat-tat* to the happy strings that lined his belly. And Ms. Patricia Barnstone revealed that she had played in a series of rock bands when she was young, which was so *wild*, and she told a story about an epileptic drummer having a seizure onstage, a funny story, which meant they were laughing about someone's disability, and that was *wicked* funny.

When the comfort returned, it returned doublefold, and Mick heard himself talking to the women, *the Candler girls*, sister and fiancée of Mr. James Candler, who had never once spoken to Mick as Ms. Patricia Barnstone had spoken to him all day. Not that Mick had lost respect for his counselor, just that there was something big jelly about Barnstone and also the big jelly laughter . . . no no no, he didn't want to lose it. He took a breath and held it, pulled his attention back to the moment. The sister, who'd been so nice to him when she was lost (her movement in that parking lot, the fluidity of the night around her body's moving parts, and her smile, the grimace that made her ugly and proved her beauty—should he warn the others about that smile?), she was right here, in this room, saying how much she liked California in a way that made it clear she was bored. What *was* boredom? It was all he could do to keep up with his thoughts, except when he was medicated and then he could not think quickly enough to be bored. Maybe this comfort could turn to boredom, a nice kind, like listening to a favorite song over and over. "What do *you* think of it here?" the Lolly one was suddenly, fervently saying, addressing either Mick or Maura, hard to tell. "James tells me about the Center, but he only has the perspective of the counselor."

"It's a zoo," Maura said. "It's helped me, but it's still a zoo. I just happen to be in the best part. Mick and I have the nicest cages."

He expected Barnstone to admonish her, but she was sly-eyed and ready to laugh. "It's not really a zoo," he put in, "though Maura *is* an anteater." *Snooting up the ants,* he thought to say, but let it play only in his head. *Snozzing up the nosy* . . . He pulled himself back, like yanking a string that straightens a puppet, a marionette, the proper puppy puppet, *ruff, ruff,* the rough edges of the assembly machine at the sheltered—listen! Listen to Maura's mouth.

"Hah," she said flatly.

"More like a factory," Mick said, "pretty good factory, where the workers—let's say it's a car factory—where they're trying to convince the cars to build themselves. *Build yourselves, you cars you.* Like an Audi or Nissan factory. Ford. Caddyshack. And there are all of these parts on the conveyor belt, and the counselors, here's Mr. James saying *The fender bone's connected to the chassis bone,* and we chassis types are trying to lure the fender over—here fender, fender—but it's harder than he sounds." He bursts into laughter and the others follow. *Good good good,* like a river good. But watch it now, watch it now. Slip and you'll drown. River's deep. River's wide. Swim, little buddy.

All of a sudden it was later, maybe seconds later, maybe minutes later, the conversation accelerating again, Candler girls asking
questions, Maura shooting something at him and Mick slapping it
back over the net. She explained the hierarchy of the dorms, that the
psychologists—*see-cologists?* Shouldn't it be *see-cologist?* Or *sigh-cologist?*
Psycho-ologist? She was still talking, that Maura, and he joined in about
the workshop, about Rhine, Vex, Alonso, skipping over Karly, each
knowing, without saying a word, to pass her by, like their brains were
one brain hovering in the room, a flying saucer brain, and Maura yanking on his arm and in his ear the wet lisping whisper of one friend to
another, Maura *lispering:* "Thlow down, monkeyhead," and remarkably, again, he did it, the whole carnival ride giving up the spin, slowing, *thlowing,* simmering down.

He told a story about a girl who was in the sheltered workshop
before Maura started, how she wore more and more makeup until one
day she got on the van with her entire face covered in lipstick. "Crews
just let her work. Hup two three four. During the lunch thing . . . the
lunch *stop,* I asked her why she painted her face with lipstick, and
she said *I'm swallowing myself.*" Saying it made him see her in one of the
women there, the woman Lolly sitting right there, covered with lipstick, hair to chin. "I'm swallowing myself," the girl had said to him,
and later she said something else. What'd she say later?

There was a lot of silence in the room, like the noise in his brain
had maybe exploded and this was the after. "She scared me," he said.
"She's still around still, not in the workshop." Later she said what to
him? Don't repeat it, whatever it turns out to be. She said what? Don't
repeat it. She said, "I want inside me again." And later yet: "Don't you
want it, too? To be inside yourself?" Should he tell the others or swallow the words?

"I love that story," Lolly said. "This is just what we wanted, isn't
it?" she asked Violet, who merely smiled and then spoke to Mick.

"It's lovely to get to know you, Mick. You saved me that night."
She told the story of getting lost and meeting him, making herself out
to be a birdbrain and Mick to be kind and generous and valiant. He
wanted to tell everyone that it was Violet who had been kind, but Lolly
burst in again.

"I can't understand why James wouldn't tell me all this. He's so
closemouthed about it." She stopped abruptly, staring. Andujar stood

just beyond the hallway. Maura called to him by name. Barnstone introduced him to the women. He nodded at them but did not speak. He took a chair slightly removed from their circle and nibbled on a single cracker for the longest time. He wore a green baseball cap, a long-sleeved shirt, and dark pants. The cap did not go with the nice clothes and called attention to itself, as if it were a necessary anomaly, covering a patchwork of hair, or the scars of recent surgery, or gears and the mechanics of a machine, or there could be a bird under that hat pulling a worm that is part of his brain.

"It's all so much clearer to me now," Lolly said, the lipstick gone from her platypus. *Her platypus?* Her platelets? Her puss! A mouth was a puss in some of those black-and-white movies! *You got the kinda puss a guy just wants to smack.* Mick kept his laughter inside like a bright light. He could surf this wave all the way to shore.

"Keep in mind," Barnstone said, "these two are maybe the smartest, liveliest—well, lively without being merely disruptive—folks of everyone at the Center."

"Including the staff, I gather," Violet said.

"No one on the staff scores too high on the *lively and interesting* scale, do you think? With certain exceptions, of course." She batted her eyes dramatically for a laugh.

Braying from the vicinity of the kitchen caused their heads to turn. Beyond the sliding glass door someone was splashing in the hot tub while another person looked on.

"Holy fuck," Maura said. "It's Mr. Shrimpy."

"Oh," Barnstone said, glancing at her watch, "that's Cecil and his cousin. I told them they could use the tub. They're two hours early, damn them. I'd introduce you, but it might give his shit of a cousin a way to slip free."

"Cecil Fresnay," Mick said. "Like Wednesday only Fresnay. Used to shelter in the workshop with us."

"He was fricking horrible at it," Maura said. "He did like one box a week."

"I've known Cecil since he was a baby," Barnstone said. "His parents were my clients. They're both mentally retarded, but Cecil is *not* retarded—or challenged or impaired or whatever term you want to use—and we need to determine what his problems are, but there's no money for it. Candler put him in the workshop as a favor."

Violet made herself stand. She told the others that she wanted to meet Cecil, and when Lolly started to rise, Violet added, "Let's don't overwhelm him." She had to get out of that room. She liked Patricia Barnstone well enough, and the kids were sweet, but she was weary to the core of Lolly's interrogation of them.

When she stepped through the sliding door, Cecil quit splashing and the cousin gave her a furtive, hopeful look. "Don't for a minute think that you can leave," she said. She introduced herself but didn't linger, strolling to the limit of the yard—a well-kept lawn with catalpa trees. She found a spot in the shade, ready to depart and yet without any interest in being home.

The cousin, she noted, held a cell phone to his nose. She considered borrowing it and calling Billy Atlas to come rescue her. The tree trunk felt good against her back. She tried to imagine what exactly she was going to do with herself, but Cecil made whale sounds, which rendered concentration impossible. Instead, she recalled an afternoon lunch in London with Arthur and an Irish author of short stories. This was in her early days at the publishing house, long before she and Arthur were an item. He was merely her boss, and it was her job to arrange the luncheon. She surprised him by asking if she could come along. The author was one of her favorite writers.

They ate at a brightly lit bistro near the author's hotel. Arthur was reissuing three of the man's early books that had been out of print for years with the hope of luring him away from his much bigger publishing house. Violet was delighted that the great man looked exactly like his jacket photo, and she was pleased, too, by his manners and by his charming brogue, but the conversation was tedious. "I should have warned you," Arthur said afterward. "Meeting a writer is always a letdown. They're never as interesting as their work. If they were, then they would have failed their books. They write to be better than themselves."

She felt the same peculiar deflation now. Mick and Maura were not boring but they were hardly the fascinating creatures she desired. The desire was voyeuristic and childish, but she had enough character to admit that she had come to this house because of it—not to teach Lolly a lesson or anything else she might have told herself.

From the hot tub came an announcement. "Trees have people in them," Cecil Fresnay said. "It's how they get arms." He raised his own pale limbs to demonstrate.

Billy Atlas was impressed with the cleanliness of his car and unembarrassed at the things Violet had found in there, including the vibrator, which he'd bought as a present for Dlu, way back when Jimmy was first dating her, and then hadn't given to her when he realized it was a bad idea. What had tipped him off? He couldn't remember. Dlu: Jimmy was an imbecile not to marry the woman. When he ditched her, he cut her out of both their lives. Before leaving for Onyx Springs, Billy put all the debris Violet removed from the car in grocery bags and fitted them in the backseat, and he insisted that he ride back there. It was his stuff; no one else should have to sit by it. One day he'd sort it all out, the stuff that was junk, the stuff that was history.

He didn't know his way around, but Onyx Springs wasn't a big city and the freeway divided it neatly in two. If he approached the freeway he knew he was going the wrong direction, and within minutes of leaving Violet and Lolly at Patricia Barnstone's, he was approaching the freeway. He pulled into a convenience store. He needed a city map.

The Buy-N-Go was neat but poorly stocked. The guy behind the counter didn't greet him when he entered, and the last mopping had left streaks on the green concrete floor. The clerk had a goatee, which made it hard to tell for sure, but he appeared to be scowling. *Excuse me for keeping you employed,* Billy thought. He was pretty sure that several of his workshoppers could do this work, and maybe that could become his specialty: training them to be convenience store clerks. There was room in the senior citizen's cafeteria for another work center. He'd need a cash register, some shelves, and a bunch of things to sell. They could fake the cooler.

He grabbed a diet root beer and a city map. He didn't like diet sodas, but he was serious about his exercise regime. So far he'd lost half a pound, and even that depended on what time of day he stepped on the scale. Still, it was something. And now he was getting his own place. Well, not his *own*, exactly, but he was leaving Jimmy's soap opera before it exploded. Not that soap operas literally exploded, but Jimmy's was going to. Billy didn't like to think ill of his best friend, but Jimmy couldn't stand to see Billy have Lise, and now he was trying to have his cake and eat it, too. Though, really, what else could you do with a cake?

"That it?" the bearded clerk asked.

"What's Buy-N-Go pay these days?"

The man snorted. "Minimum wage to start, and then if you work your ass off for a few years, they'll give you minimum wage plus fifteen cents. Place sucks. I'm just doing it till my probation is cleared, then I'm fucking outta here. That's eleven fifty-nine."

"For a map and a root beer?"

"I don't make the prices."

"Can I just look at the map and put it back?"

The clerk sneered. "Whatever. You want the drink?"

"Not really."

"If you're not buying anything, take a hike. What? This look like a fucking library?"

"I used to work in a convenience store. For like a decade in Flagstaff."

"That supposed to make us brothers or something?"

"I just know you can let me look at the map if you want to."

"Flagstaff is my least favorite city in the entire country. I got arrested in Flagstaff for *sleeping*. Can you believe that?"

"I slept there all the time and never got arrested."

"Count yourself lucky and get outta my store."

Billy left. That guy could use his training course for sure. Billy pulled back onto the street, heading away from the freeway. Could he actually think himself lucky? He was giving up free rent and Jimmy's soap opera for another place with free rent and maybe his own soap opera. It was time he had his own, wasn't it? He didn't want to get too optimistic about it, but why not him? It might be a complicated way to live, but at least he was needed, and hey, everybody else had stuff in their lives. *Get yourself a life,* Violet said to him, and okay he was doing it. He should have said to her, *Doctor, heal your own life.* He hadn't because her husband was dead. Billy wished he had met him, some old British guy, and their mom—Violet and Jimmy's mom—hadn't approved of him. Billy was still friends with their mom. Sometime soon he'd call her and tell her how her kids were doing.

He passed a tire store and a hardware store and a couple of vacant buildings. He was nowhere near the place, but as long as he was driving away from the freeway he was headed in the right direction. That was worth something, no? To be headed in the right direction? He'd just look for trees. He had been there once before, but nothing on this street looked familiar, and he had not bothered to notice the name of the street where Karly lived. She needed someone to help her get by. Most people were like that, except for Violet Candler and a few like her, those insanely competent people who seemed to carry around a whole world inside themselves, and they hardly needed anybody. Billy felt again regret for never having met her husband, one of the few who had made his way inside Violet's shell.

Jimmy was not like his sister. He might be as bad as Karly. Her mess maybe looked worse, but it had taken the two of them only a few hours to put her house in order. She had enjoyed the work, singing songs and laughing. Billy liked it, too. Not that he had a sudden passion for washing dishes or vacuuming rugs, but he liked showing her where to find the liners in the grocery store, how to change the vacuum bags, how much soap to squirt into the sink. "Why'd you wrap the soap and your toothbrush in an Arby's wrapper?" he asked her. Her face pinched in concentration. She said, "I thought if there was a trip I was taking I'd need them."

He would find her house. The neighborhood had giant trees, like sentries or lookout towers or lighthouses. Things so tall and obvious, you'd have to be blind not to find your way.

Candler pretended to be shopping, ducking the attention of the other salesgirl until Lise could free herself. The shop had once been someone's home, and the store owners had taken pains to make it elegant. Faux elegance was big business in the country, he thought. If only he'd gotten in on the ground floor of that industry.

"Is anyone helping you?" Lise asked him.

"I'm just looking," he said. "Could use some guidance, though."

She moved him by increments to a back room, where he tried to kiss her but she placed a hand on his chest. "What are you doing here?"

"I was in the neighborhood," he said, which was true, but he understood that she would think he was lying. He decided to let her give him credit for having come all this way to see her.

"I thought so," she said. "I saw you walk by earlier."

"I had a meeting," he said, disappointed that she saw through his honesty. Or had she failed to see through his honesty? "My life is an insane mess at the moment."

"You want me to try something on for you? Otherwise, I can't stay back here too long."

"I can't buy anything."

"I know that."

"I just couldn't imagine coming all the way down here and not seeing you. Can you take a break?"

She shook her head. "What's your problem?"

"Work. Colleagues. Home. I don't know, what's my problem?"

"You don't know who you are," she said. "You've forgotten. Maybe you never knew."

"And you do?"

"I have an idea, but it's looking like maybe I was misled. Hoodwinked, you might say."

"This is not what I need right now."

"Is that my job? To wait around till you show up and then provide whatever it is you need?"

"I didn't mean it that way. Why are you so upset?"

"I promised to disappear, and I didn't," she said. "Now it's up to you. Be here or vanish. If you want to be here, I'm for it. Otherwise, I need to sell some clothing."

"It's just, this meeting, you know, I'm being told that the promotion—"

"I don't want to hear about it."

"Don't you want to hear what's happened?"

"Tell your fiancée. I'm not doing it anymore. It's too aggravating." She took a paisley dress from a rack and displayed it over her body for him. "This is made from Italian wool. It's handmade. Someone cared to make it perfect. It took a lot of effort."

"Can't we skip the drama and just . . ."

"I'd like to tell you that Lolly is a creep or something, but I can't judge her. She's probably fine or could be fine. If you want to be with her, be with her. If you have doubts, then . . . then, well, make up your fucking mind."

She shoved the dress at him and stalked off, leaving him among the aisles of elegant clothing. He returned the dress to the rack. Its price tag indicated that it was marked down to $890. He felt a powerful urge to wipe his nose on it.

"I haven't been there," Mick was saying when Violet returned from the yard. Patricia Barnstone was in the bathroom, but nothing else had changed. "To any beach. It was the old me that went there."

"I know that beach," Andujar said. "Sand, water, people in sand, people in water."

Violet poured herself another glass of wine—a mediocre merlot. She filled it to the brim. She had borrowed a cell phone from Cecil's cousin and sent Billy a text saying they were ready to go and to please come get them immediately.

"Do you know how to get there?" Lolly asked.

"The freeway," Andujar explained.

"Is it as beautiful as Mick says?"

Andujar nodded. "Sand, water, some of those birds they got."

"That's the place," Mick said.

Maura and Lolly laughed, but Mick didn't. He hadn't meant to be funny, Violet understood, but his face softened. He didn't mind their laughter. A pretty kid and so eager to be friendly. It was easy to see the little boy's face residing in the young man's, a face that would have been very easy to love. Jimmy had told her that schizophrenia just happens. No one knows why. Teenage boys were especially vulnerable. She tried to imagine what the boy's mother had gone through, her perfect boy suddenly incoherent and lost. Impossible.

"I can draw a map," Andujar said. He walked quickly to the hallway and was gone.

"Does he live here?" Lolly asked.

Maura nodded. "Barnstone takes in strays."

"I have a car," Mick said. "When I drove, back when I was him, the road from Yuma took him—me—over the mountains and right through Onyx Springs. I could do it again, couldn't I?"

"You'll take us to the beach?" Lolly said. "That's so nice of you."

"Yes," Mick said. "I can."

"Oh," Violet said, "that's all right. James will take us, sooner or later."

"I want to go," Maura said. "I could maybe go if you guys went."

"Go where?" Barnstone asked from the hall.

Lolly explained in excited terms that they were all going to the beach.

Barnstone made a face. "I suspect that you'd have to have an official from the Center—"

"Like you, *duh*," Maura said.

"—and an email from your parents giving it the thumbs-up."

"Then it's settled," Maura said. "We'll go. You want to go, don't you, Andujar?" She yelled this in the direction of his room, but he was standing in the hall, just beyond their ability to see him, listening.

"Yes, yes, sure," he said, without showing himself. "But I'm not sure."

"We wouldn't all fit in the car," Barnstone noted. "I'm not certain all of us want to go." She looked down the hall at Andujar.

"Not so much," he said. He returned, carrying a pencil and a sheet of white paper.

"Are there any quiet beaches?" Lolly asked. "James makes them sound like outdoor meat markets."

"Mick knows a secluded beach," Maura said.

Mick nodded, afraid now to speak, his mind tumbling, running, time sputtering about, now and later all the same. The beach in Mexico where the grunion ran. He could find it, he was positive. He would never find it, and he was positive of that, too. But it had to be there, didn't it? He had changed, but the coastline would be the same. The world hadn't turned upside down, no matter that it felt that way.

Maura suddenly blurted out, "I think it's crazy that you're marrying Karly."

"Are you engaged?" Lolly asked. "I'm engaged, you know."

Violet started coughing and set down her wine too hard, sloshing it over the rim.

Mick retrieved a sponge from the kitchen, moving so quickly that he was in the kitchen while he was still on the couch, the same sponge he had used to wash the dishes—there was a pile of plates and utensils he had missed! No, new dishes, what they'd eaten from, soap like thoughts bubbling in his fist, and purple bubbles where the wine had been, and somehow he was back in the living room.

"I'm so sorry," Violet said softly as he cleaned up the spill.

"You can't stain that table," Barnstone said. "It's already the color of mud."

In the kitchen again, alone, the sponge in the sink and a wine bottle already to his mouth before his hand could grasp the neck. Four times he lifted the bottle. He counted. Slowing himself. Four long gulps, which finished off the bottle. He set it down with such care that the noise was no more than a tick, like a fingernail against the wooden rail of a flight of stairs, which led up to another level. Hadn't he always known there was another level?

Maura had sneaked in behind him, taking his elbow, and again her mouth to his ear. "I shouldn't have said anything about Karly," she said and apologized. His mind slowing again. Losing steam. That mad steam. He was okay, after all. Wasn't he? Okay? Back into the living room they went. The energy of the conversation dissipated, and the braying of Cecil Fresnay made a brief appearance, almost visible, like a ghost. The Candler girls began the shuffling-about business that anticipates departure, but Lolly had another question for Mick.

"If I were a counselor?" Mick said.

"This should be interesting," Maura put in.

"Who or what am I dealing with?"

"How about with you yourself," Maura said. "You're the client you have to deal with, and your mom has called you to say, *My Mickey didn't take his meds this weekend.*"

Mick nodded, suddenly serious, heavy, the chair squeaking with his weight. "I'd want to ask him why—and really find out—why he didn't want to take his medicine. Like what was going on in his life. What did the drugs do to him besides what they were supposed to do?"

"You'd want him to really talk to you," Lolly said.

"How is this different," Violet asked, "from what Jimmy would do? Jimmy is your—James, I mean. James is your counselor, isn't he?"

"Mr. James Candler is my counselor," Mick said, his mind now as clear as glass. "He sent someone, a nice person, to give me a note, reminding me that I need meds. He tries to understand, and I try to be understandable."

"And once you hear him," Barnstone said, "then what do you do?"

Maura leapt in. "You don't dope them up," she said, and proceeded to rail against the overuse of medication.

326

Mick thought of a dozen different answers to Barnstone's question, and then a hundred answers, and he knew he was letting the illness get in his head again. But really, if he could answer this question, would he even need Mr. James Candler?

Maura had a thesis about letting people be whoever they really were, that they shouldn't be forced to adhere to society's norms if they didn't share those norms. She had a convert's fervor and a good argument, so long as no one scratched beneath its shiny surface. Not only Barnstone but Violet, too, could see that this was about Mick and her desire to love him, to treasure him as he was. The medications did not, in Maura's mind, serve to restore him to his former self. She had never known that Mick and did not want to believe in his previous existence. This was the only Mick she knew, and it was plenty. She quoted a line from a book Barnstone had recently given her, altered to fit her own obsessions. "Medicated schizophrenics are all alike," she said. "Each unmedicated schizophrenic is his own person." She paused for a dramatic second before adding, "So in conclusion," hamming it up precisely because it meant so much to her, "people have to be free to be exactly who they are."

"What if they don't want to be who they are?" Lolly said. "What if they're not anyone?"

"Everybody's somebody," Mick said. "Even if he can't remember being the somebody he is, he's still him even when he isn't."

"But what if," Lolly began but she shook her head. "Maura's right, of course." She joined in the harangue, one of those general and insubstantial and never more than half-articulated tirades that serve to unite people in a general fury against *them*.

Violet took a stab at changing the subject by asking Andujar whether he worked at the Center.

"Hmm," Andujar replied.

"Andujar is a graduate of the Center, staying with me until he can manage a place of his own," Barnstone said. "He works, has a couple of jobs actually. He can tell you about them, maybe, or maybe he's feeling shy. He keeps the house in running order. Plays the piano. Your basic Jeffersonian man."

"Jimmy had that nickname," Violet said and blanched. The nickname was one Dlu had given him, and it wasn't quite *Jeffersonian Man* but *Renaissance Boy*. There was no way not to tell it now. "He was good at a lot of things, but they were all *boy* things, dancing and basketball and making up stories . . . I mean, he's not like that now." Before the subject could switch to her brother—something she knew he would hate—she said to Andujar, "I wondered who played the piano." He had seated himself on the bench, his hands inches above the keys.

Andujar did not respond. It was Mick who spoke. "I'd give him another chance." He had all this time been thinking of what he would do if he were counselor to himself.

"Won't Jimmy do that, too?" Violet asked.

Mick nodded. He didn't want to try to explain that the chances he got from Mr. James Candler were always chances to become the person Mr. James Candler wanted him to become. Not that it was all that different from the person Mick wanted to become, but what was a person but this small difference and that one? Like if you were kind or too kind, quick or too quick. Thoughts flooded him again, and he knew he had to let them go, let them wash away. It was just his mind.

"Jimmy became a counselor because of our brother," Violet said. "At least, that's what I believe."

"Pook," Lolly put in. "James will hardly talk about him."

"Our parents are both artists," Violet said, "and they didn't believe in . . . well, they never had Pook examined or studied. There was something wrong with him, but he wasn't so very different from other people. Awkward and—I don't know how to put it. Gruff, I suppose. Jimmy has told me that he might have been autistic."

"High-functioning autism," Barnstone said. "Most people call it Asperger's now. Usually means that the boy—it's almost exclusively males who are given this diagnosis—the boy is bright, especially in math, for some reason, but socially inadequate. Blunt and self-centered. Often, they don't care to be touched. Sound like him?"

"Not exactly. Partly, maybe. He loved animals," Violet said. "And he painted. He was quite a gifted painter. My parents thought art would be his redemption." She told them the story of Pook's paintings and the opening in New York, but she did not describe the way he died.

"I've seen one of them," Mick said. "It's in Mr. James Candler's office. It's got a man you can see through."

Violet shook her head. "That doesn't sound like one of Pook's."

"And behind him is a wall with pieces of paper."

Violet touched her fingers to her lips. *Pook's room.* Could there be a painting of Pook's she had not seen?

"James never told me the whole story of his brother," Lolly said. She could not hide the distress in her voice. "What happened to Pook's paintings? Do you have any of them? Are they valuable?"

"Unless this painting in his office is one of Pook's," Violet said, "I'm afraid they're all gone. I wish we had at least a few. I think my mother may have one, but I'm not sure." Her mother owned a painting, but Violet did not believe it was actually the work of Pook. Following his suicide, his paintings were in demand, and her father sold all that had not been in the show. Once they were gone, her father began painting them himself. He sold a few of them before his friend, the art dealer in Phoenix, figured out what he was doing.

This story had come to Violet from her mother, who'd been so upset with her husband that she briefly left him. "The funny thing," her mother said, "was that they were not as good as Pook's. The craftsmanship was far superior, but the paintings . . ." She frowned and shook her head. This conversation had taken place in London, on the eve of Violet's wedding. "Now I wish I'd never gone back to him," her mother had said. After a moment, she added, "Poor, poor Pook."

Violet was not willing to reveal this final chapter of family scandal to these strangers. She had surprised herself by talking about Pook. She wanted to go to Jimmy's office and look at the painting. Pook's real name was Paul. His middle name was Knowles, their mother's maiden name. Somehow, Paul Knowles became Pook. Poor, poor Pook. What Violet actually believed was slightly different from what she had said: Jimmy became a counselor to *understand* Pook. Perhaps he thought he could spare other families the sorrow that had damaged theirs. No one could know the real reason, not even Jimmy, but some things are compelling because they touch on one's history in secret ways.

When Barnstone stood to gather the dinner plates, Violet leapt up to help her. They were in the kitchen when the doorbell sounded.

Maura yanked open the door. Mr. James Candler stood on Barnstone's stoop. He smiled at her. "Hi, Maura." He introduced himself. "Do you remember me?" People evidently liked his smile because he knew to offer it. "How do you like William Atlas at the sheltered workshop? He doing okay?"

She shook the hand he offered. "Big improvement over Crews," she said. "But no one calls him *William*."

Candler laughed. "No, I guess no one would."

She had to admit that he had a swanky smile. "You want to come in or something?"

"Could you tell Ms. Barnstone that I'm here to pick up my sister and fiancée?"

"I can hear you," Lolly called. "What are you doing here?"

"Hello, guys, sorry to interrupt the session."

"It isn't a session," Lolly said. "Why would you call it a session?"

Mick could almost hear a lid clamp down over the afternoon. He felt vaguely accused. He needed to breathe and count, but he didn't want these people to see him counting.

"Well, hello, Mr. Coury," Mr. James Candler said, the lilt in his voice slight but there, a lilt that meant he felt less friendly than he was acting.

Mick nodded hello, but Mr. James Candler had already turned his attention to Andujar, and he was not entirely successful at hiding his surprise and disapproval.

"I'm James Candler," he said. "Do you remember me, sir?" He paused for a moment, but nowhere near long enough for the shy man to respond. "Just the four of you?" he said to Lolly. "Isn't there supervision going on?"

"We're just talking," Lolly said. "We had lunch. Violet and Patricia are in the kitchen."

"I thought you weren't going to be volunteering."

"We're not."

"Volunteers aren't supposed to be left unsupervised for the first three weeks."

Lolly colored. "We came here to have lunch with Patricia and her friends."

Candler stepped across the room to the kitchen. Violet and the Barnstone had their heads through the sliding glass door and were talking to a person in a hot tub. Candler rapped on the glass. The women pulled their heads in.

His sister looked relieved. "I'm surprised to see *you* here," she said.

"Came to get you. Hi, Barnstone."

"'Lo, Candler."

"Billy called from his new place to say he was unpacking and wondered if I could pick you guys up."

From behind him, Lolly spoke. "Did he say to come now?"

"I thought that's what he meant." He offered a shrug. He hadn't expected this gathering—or this greeting. "I thought I was doing Billy and the two of you a favor."

"I texted Billy." Violet set her wineglass on the kitchen counter. "I didn't mean for him to quit packing or to call you. This is awkward. I'm sorry, Patricia."

Barnstone rocked her head. "No biggie."

"Mick says you have one of your brother's paintings in your office," Lolly said.

The group migrated to the living room, waiting for Candler to reply.

"You could have a sandwich," Mick said. He had enjoyed the conversation too much. It made him bold. His mind was racing, but he spoke carefully. "We have some sliced roast beef left over. Perfectly sliced rose beef."

The smile Mr. James Candler flashed was unmistakable—not one of gratitude but of comic disbelief. "I'll see you tomorrow, hombre." He turned to his sister. "It's Pook's, but it's never been catalogued. There's a story behind it. I'll tell you on the drive." With that, he fled, holding the screen door for the women. "Sorry for the misunderstanding," he called.

"Don't think too badly of us," Violet said.

"I'm so bloody embarrassed," Lolly added.

"We'll do it again," Barnstone offered.

They stepped through the portal and the screen door slapped shut, but they paused on the stoop. Lolly faced them through the screen, her mouth opened to speak. Finally, she addressed Andujar. "Maybe next time we'll hear you play."

"Okay," he said and shifted around on the bench in preparation.

"Oh," Lolly said. Violet's head appeared beside her through the screen, and then Candler's head, above them.

Andujar played, both hands in the lower keys, more a thunder than a tune.

"This is one of his own compositions," Barnstone said, and then whispered through the screen, "It's very short."

The piano rumbled and then his right hand shot out and touched a single high key, without interrupting the rumble, which seemed then to coalesce around this single note. It reminded Mick of something basic in the world, something more elemental even than the thunder it initially called to mind. Again the hand shot out for a single note and returned.

Cecil Fresnay, in the hot tub, stood up, naked, his quite adult genitalia swinging with the rocking of his head. The final high note was hit and held while the rumbling ceased. The man in the tub slapped at the water in delight, making his whale sound.

"Thank you," Violet said.

Andujar kept his eyes on the floor, but nodded to her as he stood and slipped his hand through the door to hand her a wadded sheet of paper from his pocket. Then he fled the room. The Candler girls likewise fled.

"Well," Barnstone said. "I think the day is complete."

In the Porsche, from her grocery compartment, Violet thought she might be watching them tear apart their love. The idea that they might shred their bonds did not much bother her, but having to witness their boorishness did. If she turned her head, she didn't have to watch them, but there was no way not to hear. She and Arthur had rarely fought, at least not with heated language and loud voices. Once, in a restaurant, after a young man they knew had openly flirted with Violet, Arthur said, "I'm not entirely acquainted with the finer details of American manners, but in this country, when a married woman wishes to behave seductively with a random man, she is encouraged not to do it in the presence of her husband."

Violet denied being flirtatious. "I was merely being polite."

"I'd appreciate it if you'd be less polite in the future."

"I will not. I did nothing wrong."

That was the extent of the argument—the verbal part of it, anyway. They ate in silence, and Arthur buttered a roll so fiercely that the knife cut it in half. On their way to the tube, he took her arm and said, "I suppose I'll have to get used to the attentions offered you by men half my age." She put her arm around his waist, and the argument was over.

Violet twisted around to save her aching back and they pulled her into their personal storm.

"Aren't we?" Lolly demanded of her.

"I wasn't listen—"

"I've told James that you and I accepted Mick's invitation to go to the beach, and we're damn sure going."

"You can't go with Mick," Candler said.

"I would very much like to see you make an attempt to stop us."

"I'll take you to the beach."

"You may or you may not, but you don't have the power to tell me what to do with my time."

"Mick is my client. I *can* tell *him* what to do. That is my job, telling him what to do."

"Is that so? I thought your job was to help people like Mick, but if you think his spending an afternoon with me and your sister would be such a corrupting influence, then I suppose you'd only be doing your job in advising him to avoid bad influences."

"Don't be an ass," he said. "You act like this is me being controlling, when—"

"*My job is telling people what to do.* You don't think that's controlling?"

"That's not what I meant and you know it. Violet, you understand what's wrong with this, don't you?"

"I'd rather you didn't drag me into the middle here."

"I am a health professional, and I have to make certain that my relationship with my clients is a professional one."

"Then by all means you should not come with us. Not that we invited you."

They passed a big truck, and its windy bellow silenced them.

Violet understood they were not obliterating their relationship after all. They were tearing away the initial illusions each had about the other with the underlying belief that this violence would permit them to rebuild afresh—like people taking apart the pieces of a puzzle before beginning the real work of assembly. (Human behavior is no simple matter, and the unfolding of a single act can paper a house. This book is that house.)

How men and women lived together was never rational, Violet decided. The walls in James's miserable house were hollow, and she heard James and Lolly having sex all the time. Oddly enough, she didn't mind it. She did not enjoy it, but it didn't bother her as much as she thought it might. A man and a woman about to take the leap of marriage ought to pitch their bodies against one another as often as possible. If Lolly had insisted that they wait to marry before having intercourse, they would already be husband and wife. The promise of Lolly's body was too much for any healthy young man to resist, but perhaps repetition would reveal its limits.

She had not asked him to see the painting because she didn't want to go with Lolly, who would want to know what it might sell for. Or she would gush about it, say how much she loved it, no matter what. Violet would get Jimmy to explain some time when they were alone. Right now, she needed to think about her own life. Arthur's publishing house had sold for a nice profit, and she'd made out well on the flat. He'd had decent life insurance, and the retirement plan he'd put in place for himself was now hers. She wasn't a wealthy woman, but neither did she need to work. She could not imagine herself dating men, but the frequency of sexual relations taking place about her had forced her to imagine having sex. She suspected that if the extra man in the house were someone at all presentable she might have slipped off one night to his room for erotic exercise. This was not and would never be a possibility with Billy Atlas. She would troll the bars like a harlot before she'd have anything carnal to do with him.

Arthur, like any man, had had his little preferences. He liked to have sex outside the bedroom. The couch was a natural favorite, but he also liked to bend her over some piece of furniture or have her lie on her back on the kitchen table. In his eyes, she was youthful and beautiful. He saw no imperfections in her body and no signs of aging. He had children from an early marriage, and he did not want children with her. She accepted that—or she had until near the end when she had tried to get pregnant. Erections were not governed by muscle and he could still get them to the day that he died, and she would crawl on top of him—in the bed or in his wheelchair, or sometimes she would have a nurse help her position him on the couch. But she had never gotten pregnant, and she guessed that she had waited too long to try.

Her brother would have children. With Lolly or some other

woman. She examined his troubled face. She liked the idea that he would one day become a papa.

Candler, for his part, regretted the argument and blamed himself. Why had he rushed off to get them? Had he assumed he'd be rescuing them from the tedium of the Barnstone? And why hadn't he taken them to the beach? This stupid mess was his own fault. It was just such a wearying thought, the traffic, the crowd—what was it Lise called them? *Body nazis.* He imagined Barnstone's motley bunch among the beach crowd, Andujar Freeman and Cecil Fresnay, Mutt and Jeff of the mentally ill. He began laughing.

"I didn't know you find my plans and ambitions funny," Lolly said.

"I was thinking about that scene at the Barnstone's. The naked manchild on the patio and that buffalo playing the piano."

"I thought we were talking about my trip—mine and Violet's—to the ocean."

"You've made it clear that you know more about the well-being of my clients than I do, so fine, go to the beach with Mick and the gang. By that time this other stuff will be over."

"You mean your interview?" Lolly asked.

"Barnstone is good at managing chaos," he continued, "which is more or less what we teach our clients to do—how to manage their chaos."

"I guess it *was* a funny scene," she admitted.

From the back boot came laughter. Violet covered her mouth but could not contain it. Lolly joined in, and then James. And the animosity slipped away.

"Mick described a vacant beach that he used to go to before he became ill," Violet said. "That's what I'd like. Someplace without people."

"On the weekend, every inch of the beach is packed," James said. "I suppose there could be some secluded place, but Mick . . . It's your decision. What do I know? As long as it's after Friday afternoon, you two do whatever you want."

Violet said, "I haven't decided whether I'm going."

"Oh, you must!" said Lolly.

James turned his head and eyed his sister. "Don't let her tell you what to do now."

Lolly slapped his shoulder and laughed again.

"You'll need to have someone from the Center with you. If the Barnstone can't go, nab someone else. Otherwise, the trip could be misconstrued as an official but unsupervised function, and that creates a bad situation for me. Especially right now. I absolutely cannot be party to it."

"I wouldn't want to jeopardize your promotion," Lolly said.

Candler whipped around, ready to battle again, but he realized the statement was in earnest. He put his hand on her knee and she covered it with her hand.

"But I absolutely *am* going to the beach with my friends," Lolly said. It had the tone of an addendum. "So that's settled?"

When Jimmy turned to Lolly and nodded, his chin rubbed against Violet's shoulder.

"The Barnstone strikes again," he said softly.

Lolly unbelted herself to kiss Jimmy, and Violet tried to move her head, but the blond swath of hair swatted her cheek. The car was an abomination, and she understood that she was ready to go home, her real home. Let these two make their stupid mistakes without her, she wanted to go home—if only she had one.

After they exited the freeway, just a few miles from Jimmy's house, Violet thought of the wad of paper Andujar had pressed into her hand. She casually stuck her fingers in her purse to be sure it was there, but she waited until the car was in the garage, and the lovers had disappeared into the bedroom. In her room, she flattened the paper over the mattress, running her hand repeatedly over the crinkled paper. The single word *MAP* was printed on one side. She turned the sheet over. A pencil mark made a flat line for about an inch, and then it angled down to the right.

Beach

PART FIVE
Chaos in the Hacky Sack

To forget one's purpose is the commonest form of stupidity.
—FRIEDRICH NIETZSCHE

9

Candler had not been to many bars in Onyx Springs, and he had never even heard of the Fish Out of Water Saloon, a dive in what had obviously once been a fast-food restaurant, complete with a drive-through. The new management had filmed the glass, changed the lighting, and piped in marimba music. Though it was noon, the room was so dark that there was a two-dollar cover charge for the penlights they handed out at the door. "You get your money back when you leave," the girl at the door said, "as long as you return the light." Her teeth glowed green in the reflected light. "Or some people leave the two dollars as a tip."

"I'm meeting someone," he said. "Am I supposed to just shine my light in every face till I find him?"

"Is it Billy you're looking for?"

"How'd you know?"

"He told me his friend would be coming." She motioned with her hand. "Follow me."

Candler could have made his way minus the light and the guide, but he could not have made out the faces without stopping at each table to peer. Fast-food booths still lined the walls. An inflatable shark hung from the ceiling, lit from within by a blue bulb. Billy had moved out on Sunday and Candler hadn't spoken with him since he left. It was only Wednesday, but it felt funny, and Candler decided to respond to the lunch invitation that Billy had left on his machine.

His guide shone her light on a booth and then in Candler's face. "You're right here," she said.

Candler thanked her. Billy sat alone in a corner booth. The hostess and Billy exchanged a few words and she left to get them a pitcher of beer.

"I can't drink beer," Candler said. "I have to get back to work. So do you."

"I asked for a personal day to move in," Billy said. "Drinking at noon is about as personal as I know how to be."

"This is a weird place," Candler said.

"I didn't actually get the personal day," Billy went on, "'cause I haven't worked at the Center for three months yet. I'm just taking a personal lunch."

"Everything all right at the workshop?"

He might have nodded. "Best job I've ever had. I usually go out to lunch with the crew. They're good company."

"Nice of you to make the sacrifice to see me. I can't quite get over this place."

"Used to be a Long John Silver's," Billy said. "I like it. I know when we were in college we'd've loved it, which I remind myself whenever I get bored here. Also, it's in walking distance from my new place."

"I would never have guessed such a bar existed in Onyx Springs."

"There's fajitas. Pot stickers. Pita sandwiches. Junk food from around the world."

"It's good to see you, if I could see you."

"You can see me." Billy set his miniflash on the table, angling the ray to provide some illumination. Billy's face was ghostly in the strange light.

"Let me get something out of the way. Did you move out because of Lise?"

"No way." Billy smiled, his teeth glowing purple. "She was just using me to get you back. And I had fun being used. So . . . no hard feelings."

This exchange permitted Candler to say that he had been seeing her on the sly, that he was obsessed with her, and he didn't know what to do about it.

"Why don't you marry her instead of Lolly?" Billy said.

"I love Lolly."

"Then why don't you quit seeing Lise?"

"I think about her all the time."

"We're back to number one. Either choose Lise or quit thinking about her. If you're thinking about marrying Lolly while you're obsessed with Lise, well, I'm no expert, and I've had less than perfect luck with women, but I think that makes you a *prick*. You need to pick one and stick with her. It's not actually complicated."

A waitress wearing eyeglasses with tiny headlights in them appeared with a pitcher of beer and frosted mugs. She took their lunch orders and filled the mugs before leaving. Her platform heels lit up as she walked, like kids' sneakers.

"I'm not sleeping with Lise," Candler said.

"That must mean she won't let you," Billy replied. "That's not the same as being true to Lolly."

"At lunch, I guess it was Monday, Lise told me about going with her mother on a special trip to St. Louis to buy clothes when she was about to start high school, and—you know that kind of story. It took some twists and turns, and they bought a lot of expensive stuff the family could not afford, and worse, it was all her mom's taste and Lise knew she would never wear it."

"Yeah," Billy said, nodding, "*conversation*, sometimes it's no fun."

"That's the thing," Candler insisted. "It was a *good* story. Or I liked it anyway, and I came here thinking I'd tell you about it, but then I realized it's just some mom-daughter shopping-bonding story that you wouldn't have any interest in hearing."

"Go ahead and tell me. Give me the long version, if you want. I'll listen." He switched off his light. "At least, it'll seem like I'm listening."

"I liked the story because of the way Lise told it, or just because it was her telling it, or . . . Fuck, Billy, I'm losing my mind."

"No you're not." He flicked his penlight back on. "The interview go okay?"

Candler had spent Tuesday with the personnel committee, chatting and answering questions, hearing one official spiel or another, answering more questions. His presentation to the board had taken no more than an hour. *If you could change one thing about the Center,* a gargoyle asked, *what would it be?*

"If you mean magically change something, then I'd have an anonymous donor provide us with enough money to fund everyone who needs treatment. That's not likely going to happen, but I do understand that fund-raising is a crucial component of the director's job." Candler had smiled then, and they all smiled back. It was a slick answer they knew was prepared in advance and signified nothing, but they nonetheless treated it as if it were genuine.

While he explained all of this to Billy, their pita sandwiches arrived in webbed plastic bowls. The bowls glowed in the dark. Candler said, "They seemed to like me. From what Egri says I maybe didn't hit it out of the park, but a solid ground rule double."

"Once this stuff is settled, you'll feel better," Billy said. "The job, the women, the various hoops and ceremonies they're putting you through. When at least some of this stuff is over, we'll have a real conversation. I've got plenty of things to tell you. Big things, small things, all kinds of things. *Important* things. And a few questions. Like, am I going to be your best man?"

"Who else?"

"For either babe?"

"I'm marrying Lolly, and you're my best man." They ate for a while in silence. The glowing shark turned its head in their direction. Except for its luminescent blue eyes, it was a realistic-looking shark. "If I get the promotion," Candler said, "I'll take her to Hawaii for the honeymoon. I've always wanted to go to Hawaii. If I don't get the promotion, I don't know where we'll go, maybe Tijuana. I could almost afford Tijuana."

"I'm not going to date Lise," Billy said, "no matter who you marry. Just so you know."

"Thank you."

"I wish you could've been my best man," Billy said, "but it was all of a sudden, and you didn't even live in Flagstaff anymore."

"I understand. Not a problem."

"Any time I get married, I'd prefer for you to be my best man," Billy said, "whether you actually do it or not. If I get married ten times, it's you times ten, even if you're never around."

"You should eat something."

"And if you do something that pisses me off, I'll forgive you. No matter what."

"Are we talking about Lise?"

"Just talking. Friends forgive each other, is what I'm saying. Even if one does something he knows will piss off the other. He must have a good reason, so he gets forgiven."

"We *are* talking about Lise."

Billy may have shrugged. Some dim movement of his neck and shoulders seemed to have occurred. Candler was reminded of talking in bed, those darkened conversations that anticipate sleep. A waitress down the aisle appeared in the halo of her penlight and seemed to be looking right at him. The penlight flicked off and he realized that he had not been imagining Lolly or Lise in his personal dark, but Dlu.

He took another drink and understood that his plastic mug was empty again. Three beers on a workday lunch. Why on earth was he thinking about Dlu?

"You could go to Tucson," Billy said, "honeymoonwise, as long as it's not a summer wedding. Tucson's cheap and you could see your mom. Does the best man go on the honeymoon?"

"Not traditionally."

"I might, though, if you go to Tucson. I could stay with your mom."

"You could stay with *your* mom."

"Of course. Sure. Your mom's a better cook, though, and she likes me better."

"Which of them would you pick?"

"My mom or your mom?"

"Lolly or Lise."

"If I were you and not me, then ; . . uh, I'd marry either one of them," he said, "and I don't want to pick one 'cause if you wind up with the other one, then I'm the idiot who tried to prevent it, and if you choose the one I like, any time you have a fight you'll blame your good old bud Billy for your troubles."

"What a load of shit. I'm asking you as a friend for help."

"Lolly is technically prettier, but they're both plenty good enough looking."

"Let's get beyond the surface."

"Okay, the deep stuff. Lolly is sexier, but Lise is plenty sexy."

"That's not the deep stuff."

"You mean like, what? Personality?"

"Personality and deeper."

"Like heart and soul?"

"Yeah, who would Springsteen tell me to marry?"

Billy finished his beer and used one of the penlights to check his watch. "All I can say is that night at Petco Park? It was like the best time I've had in maybe ten years."

"That *was* fun," Candler agreed. "But haven't you had sex in the past ten years?"

"It was way more fun than sex. C'mon. *Baseball*, your best friend, a bottle of scotch, a bucket of beer, and Lise was pretty nice that night. Really nice. And we almost got that foul ball. If it'd bounced our way instead of the wrong way, we'd've nabbed it. Look at it like this: who do you turn to when you need to talk?"

"You."

"Yeah, well, you and I are already married, so the question is, which one of them is most like me?" He poured the last of the pitcher into the two glasses.

"You are *no* fucking help."

"Eeny, meeny, miny, moe?"

"You'd marry Lise? Is that what you're telling me? 'Cause she got us Padres tickets? That's the deciding factor?"

"You could stay single."

"That's good advice. That may be the first good advice you've ever given me."

"I've given you a ton of good advice. Who told you to lay off teasing that goon Parsons?"

"That was seventh grade."

"Eighth. And I'm not telling you not to get married. I love being married. Quit thinking so much is what you should do. Use this." He reached over the table and patted Candler's chest.

"Use my rib cage?"

"The ticker in the cage." Billy gulped down the last of his beer. "I've got to go. I've got to be there when my gang gets back."

"When am I going to see your place?"

"I'm studying how to make phylo-topped Moroccan chicken stew. It's harder than it looks. The first try was not so impressive. Cumin is a dangerous spice when used in large quantities. But I'm working on it. Then I'll have you and Violet and Lolly and/or Lise over for Moroccan chicken stew. Really, I can't see entertaining until you drop one or more girl from the menu. For that matter, the thought of cooking for your sister terrifies me."

"She wouldn't come, anyway."

"Thanks for lunch," Billy said, standing.

"Who says I'm paying?" Candler asked, but Billy merely stepped away from the table and shut off his penlight.

Rainyday phoned him to say that Mick, his one o'clock appointment, was in. "By the way," she said, "the scrambling over the corpses has begun."

"What are you talking about?" Candler asked. He was cleaning his desk with a Clorox-laden towelette, wishing he was better prepared for his afternoon. He didn't feel drunk so much as sleepy, but he had no idea what she was referring to.

"Your clients," she said. "They'll have to be divvied up once you're the head muckety-muck. Patricia has asked for Mick. Seeing him here reminded me."

It took him a moment to turn *Patricia* into *the Barnstone*. Of course, she'd ask for Mick. The phrase *she wanted him in her clutches* came to mind but that was ridiculous. The request annoyed him, but there was no argument to make against it. She was a good counselor, and she already had a relationship with Mick.

"Hey-ey, anybody there?" Rainyday said. "You don't have any objection, do you?"

"Let me think about it." He hung up the phone and took in a big breath, which made him yawn. He recalled one of the exercises that Clay Hao had taught him. *Look at your client as he or she walks into your room as if you'd never seen the person before. See who's actually there, rather than what you expect to see.*

The door swung open. Candler saw a young man of average height and slight build with incisive green eyes, a surprisingly handsome if uncertain face. Candler took a moment to place the uncertainty, which was not that of a person opening the door on what might be a tiger, but of a person wary of looking into a mirror, afraid to see who he might be today. Mick Coury was a good kid, but he did not know it because he could not lay hands on who he was. He walked through life with the distraught manner of someone fretting over imminent catastrophe, and he understood that the source of the devastation was from within. He was not paranoid, did not think the world conspired against him, but understood that his mind conspired against itself. "Come in, Mick. Have a seat. Give me a second to look at your file." Those stabbing green eyes! How had he never noticed them before? Lustrous and tragic and belonging to a child. He was not a child, but those eyes. They were not an adult's eyes.

"I don't like that word *relationship*," Lise had told him. When was that? The last night they spent together? The night before Lolly arrived? "We're lovers," she had said. "Temporary lovers. At least we're honest about it. A lot of people keep their eyes shut to avoid looking at their connections with other people. They pretend and lie and blind themselves." Lise and Lolly; Lolly and Lise. *That night at Petco Park? It was like the best time I've had in maybe ten years.* And last night, after dinner, he and Lolly had excused themselves and slipped off to bed. He heard his cell ring while they were making love. He was having a humiliating time, his penis as soft and floppy as a puppy's ear, which had made Lolly high strung. She tried to joke about it but she was too upset to be funny and couldn't smile even when Candler forced himself to laugh. She decided instead to become extra sexy, which quickly turned preposterous, and Candler made her stop. He pulled her close and ran his hands over her body. After a few moments, he got hard—partway there, anyway—and she offered her warm hands to hurry him along. It was while she was helping him thus that his cell rang. He had the urge to answer, thinking it was Lise, and this stray, suspect, disloyal thought coincided with the thickening of his cock. The sex, once they got going, was fine, and Lolly seemed to feel that they had crossed some bridge.

"Established couples know how to handle these things," she said, and she wasn't trying to be funny.

Still naked and in bed, Candler dialed his voicemail. The message was from Karly's mother. "I was in Europe when you phoned. Karly should have told you about my trip, but we both know she can be a bit unreliable." It took him a moment to recall why he'd called Mrs. Hopper—the evidence that Karly was living alone. He assumed that had been taken care of. She had come to her last counseling session in clean clothing, and Billy Atlas no longer noted anything in his reports. He missed part of the message. ". . . to reach Karly, but her phone was cut off. I got hold of a neighbor today, and she told Karly to call. I just finished talking to her, and I can see that you worked out a solution. I'm grateful for that, even though, well, I have to keep making adjustments, don't I? She is a full-grown woman, and . . . I'm going on and on. I'll call your office next week." He had no idea what she meant by *solution,* but he guessed Karly was once more living with the trucker. Probably, her mother had not known about him before.

"Very solid performance at the workshop, Mick," he said, as if he had been examining the file. He had to question the boy about his relationship with Karly Hopper. He should have done it days ago, weeks ago. Had his reluctance to do with the promotion? Had he worried about making waves? He didn't want to leave this task for the Barnstone. "So . . . tell me what's going on with you and Karly."

Mick blinked in the slow manner associated with the taking of his medication.

"We're getting married," he said.

"I'm surprised to hear that. Have you set a date?"

"Am I supposed to? Do you need that?"

Candler told him that he didn't require the date. "Have you met Karly's family yet? Have you discussed this with your parents?"

Mick took a long time to reply. His eyes wandered the room while his mouth remained set to speak. "I asked my parents if what I've got is something that can be passed to children. They said no. That's as close as I've come. Marriage is . . . big news. My mother still thinks of me as her son. Her little son, I mean. It's the way they are. I don't want to hurt or surprise them."

"There's an interest inventory I'd like you to take." He buzzed Rainyday and asked for the new behavioral profile. It would require Mick to answer one hundred multiple-choice questions, which should keep him busy, Candler reasoned, until he could get the van driver to fetch Karly Hopper. Mick would not believe anything that did not come directly from her. Sooner or later, he had to understand that Karly had no intention of marrying him and better for it to be supervised than for Mick to stumble upon it. (It did not occur to Candler that he had not met or even spoken with Lolly's family. He had not told his parents that he was engaged—though he imagined that his sister had. Everything had happened quickly, the world—that intensely vivid world—zooming by.) "This is a test you can't flunk," he told Mick, smiling and spreading the booklet out on the desk. "It measures your interests, your likes. It'll let us know what keeps you tuned in. Maybe give us a clue about what makes you happy."

Mick nodded seriously. "That's something I'd like to know."

Because he had skipped or skimmed his meds too many days in a row, Maura had suggested that Mick shave one of his pills and snort it up his nose. It had been a dumb move, Mick decided now. He felt both sluggish and confused, the worst of both worlds. Yet he liked the test Mr. James Candler had given him. It was designed to figure out what, of all the things in the world, he liked most, which meant it was mainly about Karly. It didn't surprise him then when she walked through the office door, as if his heartfelt answers had conjured her.

Mr. James Candler trailed her in, smiling and talking with her. He was carrying a chair, which he situated next to Mick. Karly sat in it and smiled at him.

"Hi, Mick." She was always excited to see him. "We're both here, aren't we?"

Mick was delighted by her arrival, and the room, too, brightened. He didn't speak, though, as if his words were still caught up in the test sheet that lay on the desk.

Candler took his seat, studying the way the two interacted. Such broad, delighted smiles. Mick seemed to expect her arrival. She didn't seem surprised to see him, either. They both looked happy and unsurprised. Mick took her hand and she looked at their hands and *god*, what a smile she had. Such beautiful creatures. A stranger gazing in would find it impossible to believe there could be anything seriously wrong with them.

Karly's clothes were clean. Someone was helping her through the day, and if it was the truck driver—or some other man—Mick needed to know. As much as Candler hated to spoil this moment, Mick had to know.

"I wonder if we could talk about your plans together," Candler said.

"That test," Mick said, glancing at the white sheet on the desk, "it'll show we should be married, won't it? It's just what we need. *Evidence*."

"I can't talk about the profile until I score it," Candler said, "and no test can tell you whether you should marry one person or another." He shifted his gaze to Karly. He asked her to talk about her plans.

"Me?" she said, and he had to ask again. "Plans are what you make with them." Her manner today was an imitation of the smiling, flip manner of a television actress.

Candler cut to the chase. "Have you spoken with Mick about your recent living arrangements?"

The puff of exasperation lifted her bangs, and then she smiled and wagged her head: she didn't understand the question.

"Have you told Mick that for a while there you were living with a man? That perhaps you're once again living with him?"

Mick dropped her hand and slowly got up. He raised his arm and extended it, pointing at Candler as the final part of the gesture. "You're saying things without looking at the test, without thinking about our marriage."

"I understand this upsets you. Let's stay calm. Take your seat again." He waited until Mick seated himself. "I *am* thinking about your happiness. I want to make cert—"

"We love each other," Mick said. He sounded utterly calm now, though his arms were shaking. He took Karly's hand once more.

"I just . . . I want to be sure that the two of you are speaking, you know, *openly* before you make major plans."

"This isn't fair," Karly said. "I don't have to marry anyone I don't want to. And even if I want to, I don't have to."

"Okay," said Candler. "But let's get this out of the way: who lives in your house with you?"

"I don't get what you mean," she said.

"Do you live with your parents?"

She shrugged, smiled, winced. She ran through her brief emotional repertoire.

Candler repeated the question.

"I'm twenty," she said.

"One," Mick interjected. "You're twenty-one."

"I'm twenty-one," she said. "I don't have to live with my parents."

Mick nodded in agreement, but Candler could see his face clouding. There was no way out of this conversation now. Better to get to the heart of the matter. "Don't you live with someone, Karly? A man? Don't you have Mick drop you off and pick you up at the end of the block to keep your relationship a secret?"

She opened her mouth a few times to speak but didn't say anything. Then she adopted a new tack. "Everyone knows *that*. I told Mick all about *that*." She waved a flaccid, dismissive hand, as if Candler's questions were humorous. "We just don't want the others talking— that's what he says and me, too. And he can make pizza without even calling the pizza guys, and when we folded sheets together, he was on that end and I was on the other end, and it was so fun."

Mick kept his eyes on Mr. James Candler and his hand in Karly's grip, but he became aware of the air—the breathing air—how it was different in this office from the hallway and the lobby, how the air at the Center was different from the air at the workshop. Mr. James

Candler was gazing at him, the air around them taking on light. He was waiting for Mick to speak. "We're get-getting married," he said, the lucid swimming light shooting past him in the unsullied nothing like tiny incandescent fish.

"Oh," Karly said, "I can't do that. I'm already married. Don't be silly. Mick's so silly."

The air altered its disposition, thickening and deepening, less air than sound, less sound than vibration, and Mick was expected to breathe this? He stared through it all at Karly, nodding now, he realized, as if this were news he had expected.

The other one, Mr. James, was speaking. "I don't think you mean literally married, but you're living together and sleeping together and . . ." His voice kept on until it was Karly's voice. "I already told you that a hundred times," she said. "It doesn't mean I won't eat your fried chicken or anything."

"I'm sorry, Mick," Candler said, and the scene locked back into place, his counselor leaning toward him, Karly's hand no longer in his own. Voices like traffic now, without words but moving sensibly about, meaningless but sensible. Mick climbed back into his senses much the way a pilot—that pilot in his brother's video game—returns to the cockpit of the malfunctioning plane that had almost crashed, having no confidence that the mechanics repaired the craft, but having no other choice but to strap himself in or give up the heavens altogether.

"I thought you needed to know," Mr. Counselor was saying.

"I can change all of this," Mick said. "But not like this. Not in this way."

"You made him cry, Mr. James Candler." Karly put her arms around Mick and held him close. "Mick is always nice to me."

He was crying? How could he be crying and not know it? The counselor was suddenly standing, impossibly tall, blocking the light. "Karly, if you'll come with me, I'll show you a fun activity I'd like you to do."

"Wow," she said, smiling. "Good-bye, Mick."

The door made its noise. He heard a car somewhere far away abruptly quicken, like a drowning boy breaking the liquid membrane and sucking air. And in this moment, a particle of time within the drama of his ongoing breakdown, his body recalled its sure locomotion, felt the confident way that he slapped the clutch and slammed the gearshift. Like a bubble of air in a river of blood, he had a moment when he recalled who he was, and then it passed, and the thick obscurity that filled the office swept his recollection out of the room, and he understood that he had never wondered who he was back then, back when he was the person he really was. If he had tried to understand himself back then, he would have lost his mind. Or at least his confidence. At this moment, sanity seemed to him like the ultimate distraction, the best of all dodges, the safe, self-righteous way to keep from recognizing the abyss within, the deep, vast, endless black nothing of being alive and having no purpose but the measly things rationality might invent.

From his knees, he watched a crowd of figures in the near distance, their shapes muted by the light, but they seemed to move purposefully, like a posse, a green posse, just beyond the desk, and then they were inside him, moving within the parts of his body that were neither organ nor bone, not blood and not skin, the unnameable regions of the soul where love and anger and beauty and fear took turns ruining his sanity. They were leaves, these forms, waxy leaves on a city of trees just within and just beyond the domestic glass.

Among the gloom-laden currents appeared a human face, bloated by the belching upheaval of air: Mr. James Candler, pretending not to be himself by slipping his face long, a stretching that was not fatigue but something richer, like the beginning of a beautifully awful story. Mr. James Candler was in a door frame, air and light sweeping out, and Mick's lungs were empty, and he understood that madness was water and he could not swim in it and could not drown. And then he had the upsetting impression that Mr. James Candler's mouth was filled with a huge viscous eye, and when he spoke, the words stared unrelentingly at him, his head the cliff from which the sadness waterfalls down.

No, not sadness, *words*. He said something to Mick.

Mick replied, "I'm feeling like no driver can straighten out this curve."

Candler had set Karly up on the assembly station. He had meant to do that anyway, to see if her speed had increased since she had been working in the sheltered workshop, but now he just needed her out of his office. He had not expected to find Mick on the floor. "Mick," he said, but the boy didn't look up. Candler sank to the floor and put his hands on Mick's shoulders. "Mick, what are you doing? You're kneeling."

The boy looked in Candler's eyes several seconds before speaking. "If I'm on my knees, I must be praying."

"I'm going to call your mother," Candler said. "I want you to sit in this chair, okay?"

Mick nodded and let himself be lifted and situated in the chair. The liquid air swept in around him. It buoyed him and held him down. Held him up and held him down. He could breathe but he was drowning.

Lise waited for the woman to emerge from the dressing room. Waiting seemed to be the main activity of her life. She had finally quit believing that her life could return to its previous routine. She had not been fully aware just how many of her daily habits had been tied to her interest in James Candler. He had been the center post in the construction of her daily affairs—or rather, her *idea* of him had been the post. The actual him couldn't hold up an umbrella.

"Are you sure this is a ten?" the woman called from the dressing room. She was one of Lise's regulars.

"It's made in Italy," she called back. "The size is an approximation." This was a lie that the woman would recognize as a kind of politeness. The truth was that the woman had a size ten body with a size twelve butt. Some size tens would sheath that bottom to great advantage, and others would make her look like a beanbag.

"It's tight around my ass," the woman said.

No kidding. "Let's take a look."

"I have a lifelong history of dresses not fitting. I tend to prefer loose-fitting clothing."

"Now and then you might find a piece of apparel that emphasizes your bottom in a way that—" The door to the dressing room opened and the woman stepped out. She was tall and otherwise thin, with fussy hair that must have cost her a fortune to keep exactly that fussy.

The dress was perfect.

"My god," the woman said, "it directs the attention, doesn't it?"

"Your boyfriend is going to love it," Lise said.

The woman frowned. "My hope is that he sees me and eats his fucking heart out."

352

"Trouble?"

"He needs his fucking *space*. The lamest line in the history of lame lines." She crossed her arms and continued frowning into the mirror. "I halfway thought he might be dating you."

Lise remembered him then, a twenties-something surfer boy in flip-flops who had accompanied the woman the last time she was in the store. He was probably five years younger than Lise and at least a few years younger than this woman. Lise would sooner date a walrus. She would sooner date an Amish minister who would neither watch television nor drive a car, a blind monk who spoke an unintelligible language.

"Not my type," she said.

"So he *did* hit on you?"

"If you mean the young man who was with you the last time you were—"

"Ted Kooperman, but he goes by Tiko. It's his beach name. He's the kind of cruddy adult child who has a beach name."

"I've only seen him when he was here with you," Lise said, "and I wouldn't give him the time of day."

The woman gave the lovely shelf of her buttocks a final look and turned from the mirror. "Why not? I mean, what's wrong with him?"

"Besides what you just said?"

"I'm pissed at him, but he *is* cute. Why wouldn't you—"

"He's too young. Too aware of his appearance, and I don't go in for the surfer thing. Not to my taste. He looks like he's never read a book in his life. He also struck me as arrogant—that young-man arrogance that some women are drawn to, but I don't care for it. He dresses—"

"Okay. Okay," the woman said. "Not your type. That's all you needed to say."

"If you don't take that dress," Lise said, "you're crazy. Or blind."

"I'm taking it, for Christ sakes. What's gotten into you?"

"I may be a little tense."

"You could use a surfer dude or two," the woman said, turning her back. "Even when it's some lousy quickie, it lets you know you're still, you know . . ."

"Desirable?" Lise said, at the same moment the woman said, "Alive."

"I went three years without sex," Lise said. "It was the most alive I'd felt in my life."

The woman faced her again. For several seconds, neither spoke. Then she said, "Do you have this in a light gray?"

"It's one of a kind."

"I'm sorry I said that about, you know, needing to get laid. It's a stupid thing to say. I was just pissed. And Tiko is a turd, a completely worthless floating turd. I'm attracted to the worst sort of men. I can *see* myself doing it, and I still go ahead. I pretend. I imagine he will be different when I know they're all the fucking same. When I was in college, there was this sweet boy who sat near me in Spanish, and I think he loved me, but he wouldn't make the first move. I hated him for that. In my head, I was all *Be a man or you can't be with me.* But really, I liked him the way he was, you know? If I'd given him any encouragement . . ."

"Men and women," Lise said sadly, as if citing a natural catastrophe.

"I'll take the dress. It'll attract more of the type of swine I seem to need."

"There are nice men in the world," Lise said, "who would also appreciate the way you look in that dress."

"Name a couple." She gave her fussy hair a serious shake. "You want to get a drink sometime? Maybe go out and meet some of these decent men together?"

Without hesitating an instant, Lise said, "Not a good idea."

Sometimes what draws two people together is that they're going through the same door, and the bumping of their hips seems not merely the product of limited space but divine intervention. Which is to say: tears filled the woman's eyes, and she turned to touch her fingers to her face. Lise could not quite believe the response.

"I'll just wear the dress," the woman said. "Ring it up."

"No man would look my way," Lise said, "if we were out together."

"Hah."

"I just don't do that. Look, I'm hung up on this particular guy. Have been for years. And he's engaged to someone else. I tell him off one day and have lunch with him the next. He means something to me that I can't even name, and I spend every hour of the day waiting to see if he'll choose me over her when I know there is no chance. None. But I can't let it go."

"I get it." The woman nodded and turned away. "You're more fucked up than me."

"Way more," Lise agreed.

"But you also don't like me."

"Not especially. Not outside the store. We have nothing in common."

"Okay, fine. I'm changing." She charged into the changing room and slammed the door shut. "We should be allies, you know?" she called out. "This is why we go with fucked-up men, because we treat each other like garbage."

And later, in her subcompact car, driving to the Ocean Beach apartment that she shared with a friend, it occurred to Lise that Whispers and Lies was nothing more than another stop along the road to the person she would eventually become, no different from Bare Barracudas or Amoeba Records. And this *Lise* who seemed to her so genuine was perhaps no more solid or real than Beth Wray. *The girl who had escaped the many-headed monsters discovered that the conjurer could not go on saving her indefinitely, and that her paradise was not an exotic outpost but more like an intergalactic bus stop, and those who did not keep moving turned to stone.*

Stopped at a traffic light, she cut off the air conditioner and lowered her window. Accordion music poured from one of the cars nearby, that Mexican polka music—lively and intense. Whoever was listening to that music, she thought, must know precisely who she is.

After Karly went back to the sheltered workshop, Candler sat with Mick in his office and waited for Mrs. Coury to appear.

"I've canceled my appointments, Mick. We can talk as much as you like."

"All right," Mick said, "then none, please." He was not crying any longer but his face was red and blotched.

"We don't have to talk about Karly," Candler said. "Your mom said it would take a while for her to get here. Where does she work? I can't seem to recall."

"She works." Mick nodded. "For money."

"Doesn't she do something with the school district?"

"She does something." He ran his hands through his hair, one hand, the other.

"I'm so sorry this turned out this way," Candler said.

"Me, too," Mick said, and then he took his head in his hands. "I'm sad," he said. "My feelings make me this way."

After a long while, Rainyday appeared in the doorway to Candler's office. "Your mom's here," she said to the boy, and she offered her hand.

Mick stared at the hand and stood. He thanked Candler and followed Rainyday into the hall. Candler thought to go out to see Mrs. Coury, but they had spoken on the phone and he didn't know what else to tell her. "He's having trouble with the news that Karly is living with a man," Candler had said. "He's taking it hard."

Candler stood by the window and jotted a few notes in Mick's file. He tried to determine why things had gone so badly. Through the window, in the lot at the edge of the grounds, Mrs. Coury walked her son to their silver car. She put her arm around him and either whispered to him or kissed him, Candler could not tell. Beyond those two, past the bordering fence, wind moved over the avocado orchard in a consecutive shudder, like the trained men with rifles in military exhibitions. After the wind fled the orchard, there remained the two-eyed tractor staring back at him. "What?" Candler said aloud. "What did I do wrong?"

"You didn't go home," Rainyday replied. She was standing behind him in the doorway. "And now, even though you canceled your appointments, there's someone here to see you."

"Send her in."

"She's a him," Rainyday said. "Will I get a raise when you're the boss?"

"Send him in, please," Candler said.

"And my husband needs a job. And I want a new desk. My desk is too weensy."

"I'll get him myself," he said.

"Mick'll be okay," she said as he swept past her. "Somebody's always breaking down."

There was only one person in the waiting room, a scrawny man sitting on the floor with his back against one of the chairs. He looked like a high school kid, and Candler tried to imagine who it might be, but he could not concentrate. When the kid saw Candler approaching, he stood. It was Guillermo Mendez, the War Vet.

"You're surprised as shit to see me," he said.

"I didn't recognize you in civilian clothing."

Mendez looked down at his T-shirt and jeans. "Temporary," he said. "I'm still in the Nasty but your report did something. I'm not going back to the desert. Not yet anyway. Army agreed to have its own headwashers do a scrub to see if you're full of shit or not." He let his head loll—a shrug. "Fucking guy will probably say I ought to spend the rest of my life in Baghdad, but he can't see me for another three weeks. Which gives me, well, *three weeks*. I've got light duty, and I wanted to let you know they may be calling you to talk, and I wanted to say thanks."

"You don't owe me any gratitude," Candler said.

"Sure I do." He offered his hand and Candler shook it.

"All right, then," Mendez said. "You got work."

"The truth is . . ." He wasn't sure he ought to say it. He glanced about the room, but they were alone. "The truth is, I didn't want to write the report the way you needed me to. But I told someone about you, and she . . . Telling her was a breach of confidential—"

"I don't give a damn about confidentiality bullshit."

"Maybe not, but I should. And the hell with it, I was only telling her about you to get in her pants." He looked again to be sure no one else had heard. He lowered his voice. "I was making my job sound important and I was making myself sound compassionate. I hadn't written the report yet, but I pretended that I'd gone to bat for you."

Mendez pursed his lips. "Did it work?"

"You mean—"

"You fuck her?"

It was Candler's turn to shrug.

"Can't begrudge that, then."

"I started seeing more of her, and when it came time to write your report, I don't know, I couldn't make up my mind what to do, so I decided to be the person I was pretending to be."

"In the desert, it's the same deal," Mendez said. "You're always scared as shit and playacting. Then comes the rock and roll, and all you can do is go on pretending."

"That's kind of cynical, isn't it?"

Mendez made a face. "I hadn't planned on spending all day here. I just wanted to say thanks and give you a heads-up 'bout the phone call. Look, you remember that girl I told you about, middle name Iris?"

Candler could not remember but he nodded anyway.

"That's the same way I knew I must be in love, 'cause I was a better person when I was around her." He sighed. "I don't give a rat's ass why you did it. You did it, and that means I'm here and not in the desert." He turned and ambled to the door.

Candler stared at his hands for a moment. He should go home, he thought, or maybe for a walk, a walk in sunlight, and then he was in the stairwell going down, bursting into the lobby as Mendez, who had taken the elevator, pushed the door to the outside. Candler did not speak to him, kept his head down. He could not imagine wrestling with the car's wretched cover in front of the War Vet, but he had not come for the car. He had gone down the stairs to take a walk, his appointments canceled, a sunny day. He veered onto one of the white sidewalks that angled across the grass. A walk, a stroll. He did not know where he was going until he reached the rock wall and stared over it. The tractor was not where he expected to find it. He walked a few steps to his right and went on tiptoes to look again. No tractor. He tried to identify landmarks. He tested several spots, but he could not find the tractor. How was that possible?

Rainyday was standing at the entrance to the Hahn Building. She had the jacket to his suit draped over one arm. "See something out there?" she asked but did not wait for a reply. "I wasn't sure you had your keys."

Candler's watch told him that the day was spent. Time had slipped away or jumped ahead. Everyone but Rainyday had gone home. "I have my keys," he said. "But thanks for checking."

"Someone around here has to have a brain."

He put on his jacket and walked with her to the parking lot.

"I'll be making something fast and dirty tonight," she said, "but you're welcome to join us for whatever it turns out to be. We have beer. My husband always has beer. We're keeping several national breweries in business."

Candler declined, thanking her again.

"If we get real fancy," she said, "we'll order pizza. Everybody likes pizza."

This time he merely smiled and waved before going to his car and tugging at its cover. He took his time, folding it carefully. He was grateful today for the task.

The thought did not fully form itself until he was behind the wheel, the engine humming softly. Karly had said that the man with whom she lived had folded sheets with her. He knew how to make a pizza. No fucking way that was the trucker. Yet someone lived with her.

The drive to Lantana Avenue would take only a handful of minutes. On the way, he passed the Fish Out of Water Saloon. A line of people stood outside the door. Happy hour, he thought. Happy hour in a blackened room.

Maura saw no good reason for the requirement of letter writing, but she trusted Barnstone and didn't want to lose the few privileges she possessed. She sat at a lunch table trying to explain to her big sister why she liked the looks of the Onyx Rehab cafeteria, which was gray and white in alternating horizontal lines. The chairs were padded and movable, half of them the same shade of gray as the wall, and the other half, the same white. The colors made her think of the ocean, a fact that made no sense, but it was true, and letters didn't have to make sense.

Dinner was over, but she stayed in the cafeteria to avoid Rhine, who was pursuing her. He lived off-campus and had no access to the cafeteria and the place was probably expensive, as they advertised the fresh, organic quality of the chow. She had seated herself with some of the Danker girls to listen to their general unhappiness, their attacks on their counselors, their parents. Silence was hardly her thing, but she was in the mood to be quiet. It was a celebratory silence, and the last thing she wanted was to have it cut short by Bellamy Buttfuck Rhine.

Mick had gone to his counseling session after lunch, as he always did, and he did not return. Instead, Karly was called out to join him. She came back after an hour or so, but Mick never made it back. Billy Atlas took a call in the office and spoke on the phone for a long time.

"What did they say about him?" Maura asked. "What's wrong?"

"Don't you worry," Billy told her, taking Mick's place in the assembly line, "I'll cover his losses." He was nowhere near as fast as Mick, but Maura liked that he was helping out. It meant that he expected Mick back.

"What happened?" She took Billy's arm and shook it. "What's wrong with Mick?"

Billy displayed his huge teeth, a wacky wide grin, and she knew he would give her the goods. He was the kind of man for whom secrets were a burden. Her father was like that, and she decided she would always like Billy Atlas. Whatever benefit of the doubt she had to grant him, she would. Even if he didn't come through with what happened to Mick, she wouldn't be upset with Billy. At the same time, she remained confident he would spill his guts.

As for Billy, he had never been able to say no to a woman. "See, Mick and Karly were talking to Jimmy, and I guess Mick didn't like what he heard, and kinda lost it."

Maura was not the only one listening. Rhine asked, "What did he lose, Mr. Billy Atlas?"

"It's just Billy," he said and shrugged. "Mr. Atlas, that's my dad."

"Mr. Billy Atlas," Alonso said.

"Mick flipped out, happens to everybody."

"Who is Jimmy?" Rhine persisted.

"Jimmy Candler is Mick's guy," Billy said. "His counselor."

"Mr. James Candler," Alonso said.

"What happened in there?" Maura demanded, but Karly was examining a spider box in that way she had and didn't seem to hear. Maura whisked past Billy and yanked Karly by the arm. "What happened to Mick?" she demanded and everybody but Vex stopped folding boxes.

"Let's not start jerking people's arms," Billy said.

"Mick's my friend," Karly said.

"What did you do to him?"

"We met with Mr. James Candler," she said. "I did a test and Mick did a test in the office. It made him cry. It's sad to see people cry."

"There was a misunderstanding," Billy said. "We need to all get back to work."

"They're *not* getting married!" Maura said. "Karly, Karly, *Karly!*"

Karly looked up, startled.

"Did you tell them you're not getting married? That you and Mick are not getting married?"

Karly smiled. "Everybody knows that," she said. "If anybody asks, I'm not married at all, right, Billy?"

"Let's just get back to work," he said.

Maura plowed through ninety-three boxes in the final hour of the day, the fastest she had ever worked. Mick and Karly were *kaput*, she told herself, her fingers like tiny, independent creatures that knew just what to do with the cardboard, as if they were making nests, saving up pantyhose for the winter.

Rhine must have understood the same thing, must have seen that Karly was now open season, not that the dickface had a ghost of a chance. Maybe she, Maura, didn't have a chance with Mick, either. Maybe she was as flaky and hopeless as Rhine, both of them pining after people who were out of their league. She didn't want to think about that. She wanted to be happy with the news. Inexplicably, the report had the opposite effect on Rhine. He became frustrated with the boxes, tearing two of them, which earned him a demerit: tear two boxes and you had to forfeit one that you'd packed. Rhine's face turned the red of ripe tomatoes, and he said, "Something is really bothering me."

"Let's say I tore that one," Billy Atlas put in. "No point in losing any credit, right? Power to the people. Support the workingman."

When it was time to leave, Rhine tried to pull Maura aside. "I have to tell you what I'm feeling, Maura. Maura, I have to share something, Maura."

Maura leaned down to him. He smelled bad. She had never noticed that about him before. He stank like milk that had turned. The guy gave her the creeps. She was *not* like him. *Nothing* like him. "I already know what you're feeling," she said, "and here's my broadcast for the day: we're not the same, me and you. Hear me? I'm not like you."

"I have to share something, Maura," he went on, but she turned from him and zipped out to the parking lot where she boarded the van.

Rhine followed her. He rode his scooter to the workshop and was not permitted in the van, but he tapped on her window. He had to reach up to do it, and when Maura gazed down at him there was something about the part of his hair, the perfect part, the joint of flesh visible beneath it, that almost made her relent, but her desire to separate herself from the diminutive burp was greater. She moved to the other side of the van. When he raced around to that side, she returned to her original seat. He did not give up, and she continued switching places until the van pulled away, leaving Rhine sweating in the parking lot gravel.

During dinner, she spotted him again, circling the cafeteria, plastering his face to the glass. She lowered her head, ate her soup and celery and carrot sticks, pleased to witness his distress from a safe distance. He waited at the door for her, which was why she took a pen and pad of stationery from her purse, and she remained in the cafeteria to write her big sister.

> *This guy wants to think we're in the same boat, that we're bound together by some shared experience, but we're not in even the tiniest way alike, and yet he's been pursuing me all day and night, wanting to talk, to commiserate.*

She was exaggerating, but why not? She might as well make it interesting. She wanted to call him a *buttface sheepherder*, that was the term that sprang to her profane mind, but Barnstone forbade nasty language in the letters.

> *This guy, of all the witless creepy people at this home for the witless and creepy, bugs me the most, and the idea that we have something in common is repulsive to me, sort of like when you went to the prom and there was another girl wearing the identical dress, which was bad enough, but it had to be that Darlene girl you hated? That's how this guy wanting to share his stinking thoughts makes me feel.*

She wanted to tell her sister something else, something she couldn't write, something she might not be able to put into words. It had taken her a month to admit it: leaving the dorm—sneaking out to Alonso's—had been a mistake. Could she explain how this simple statement, which must be obvious to everyone else, shocked her? Sneaking out had shown bad judgment, had taught her that she was still a dumb-fuck. *You have to be honest with yourself,* Barnstone had said. *Not hypercritical and not rationalizing, but genuinely honest. Otherwise, you're playing yourself for a chump.* She couldn't tell her sister this without acknowledging her illicit acts, and such an admission would make its way back to the Center—her fucking mother would see to it—and dump her back in Cagin Dorm with its crazy precautions and no chance of continuing at the sheltered workshop, of seeing Mick. She couldn't tell anyone but herself. Okay, okay: *maybe there were reasons for the rules.* She took a deep breath and shook her head, as if in amazement.

When she was sure the coast was clear, she went to her dorm, setting a fast pace, making it safely. No sign of the nitwit. She dropped off the letter at the front desk, where the Sinatra guy smiled and noted it in some file. "Consider it mailed," he said. Such a friendly man. His name tag read *Castro*. No first name. Castro whose daughter sang "Summer Wind," Castro who listened to the same crap song a thousand times so he and his daughter could harmonize. "Thanks," she said to him, showing all her teeth and patting his hand on the desk.

She went to her room and did her exercises. She showered and put on the pajamas her mother had sent her. They were white with tiny blue flowers, but what Maura liked about them was their size: they were far too big. Her mother had no idea, thought she was still piggly-wiggly. She didn't have Mick's home number or she might have called him. It was probably better to wait out the weekend, though, give him time to get through the worst of it. Instead, she called Billy Atlas. He had given out his cell number to everyone.

"Hey, Maura," he said, almost as if he was expecting her call. "Zup?"

She told him she wanted to know more about Mick.

"People in my position can't talk about clients."

"He's my friend. Be human." She wheedled another thirty or so seconds, ending with: "I thought you were cool. Don't be like this."

"You keep a secret?" He confirmed that Mick was under the impression that Karly was going to marry him. Karly had misunderstood.

"Bullshit," Maura said. "A blind dog could have seen how Mick felt about her. She dumped him for somebody."

"Well," Billy said. "It could be that she's living with someone. She needs living help."

"Girls like her always have guys hanging around."

"Girls like her are usually living with or married to some architect or rugby player," Billy said, "or going out with some lawyer in New York or some guy whose old man owns Hawaii or something. But Karly—"

"Fuck a duck," Maura replied. "He's better off without her."

Billy Atlas started telling her the story about having a vision while on peyote, but she cut him off and told him about dating Skinner and how one time they took acid and rode around town all night in a city bus. "We were convinced that we'd got on the wrong bus and it had taken us to some city we didn't know. Nothing looked familiar."

"Cool," Billy Atlas said, and then he said, "Someone's at the door. Gotta go."

Maura sat on her bed, wondering what to do next. She thought about going downstairs to watch television or talk to some of the girls, but she'd have to get dressed and pretend to care about their lives. She decided to read instead, but the words kept moving around on the page. Mick was not marrying Karly, and even the printed words on anonymous sheets of paper could not be held in check.

This time when he parked on Lantana Avenue, he did not hide. He had not caused an accident on the way over. Though he stumbled on the curb, he went directly to Karly's door.

Billy Atlas answered the door in a white T-shirt, boxer shorts, and white socks, his cell phone in his hand. He opened the door only an inch until he recognized Candler, and then he threw it open. "Jimmy!" He displayed all of his too-big teeth. "Come on in."

"What are you doing here?" Candler asked. He eyed the boxers. "What have you done?"

Billy lifted his hand to display a gold band. "I've gotten married."

Candler could not speak.

Billy turned his head to call out, "Darlin'? You dressed?"

Candler backed carefully to the edge of the porch.

"Don't be upset," Billy said. "We wanted you at the wedding, but it was a spur of the moment thing. I almost told you about it at lunch, but you've got too much on your plate right now, and until last night Karly and I hadn't even told our parents. We were on the phone till eleven. I think we'll have a big party or something in the fall."

Candler said nothing.

Karly appeared in jeans and a bra. "It's Mr. James Candler," she said. "Hi, Mr. James Candler." She looked down at her bare feet. "I should put on more clothes."

Billy agreed and she laughed as she trotted down the hallway. He turned back, smiling. "We were just getting cleaned up to go out to eat. Want to join us? Karly makes me shower after work. She has a charming way of suggesting it. She says, 'Billy Atlas, you smell funny.'" He laughed. "I don't wear the ring at work. Don't worry. We're keeping it all on the down low."

"She's mentally impaired," Candler said, "and you're her workshop supervisor."

Billy nodded seriously. "That's why it's gotta be hush-hush. I figure by the fall, Karly will be on at the factory, and we can tell everyone."

"She has an impairment."

"It doesn't bother me." Billy shrugged happily. "I mean, it's not like she's completely out of it, just slow on the uptake. And she's beautiful, you know? I mean, *god*."

"She loves you? You love her?" His fists clenched. He wanted to punch Billy. He wanted to punch his best friend in the face.

"My first wife didn't even pretend to love me, but I didn't want her to leave. I mean, you only live once and all that. I'm not exactly a spring chicken, and if I waited for the perfect girl, I might be alone for the rest of my life."

"Goddamn it, Billy, she's *mentally retarded*."

"But she's a U.S. citizen." He shrugged again. "Six of one, half dozen of the other."

"I got you that job. Doesn't that mean anything? You're here fucking one of my clients."

Billy winced. "Well, not yet. I mean, we've only been married since Monday, and I didn't want to rush it."

"You're married but not sleeping with her?"

"I've been sleeping on the carpet, beside the bed. It's what I thought she needed."

"That makes no sense."

"Does to me. Not that I'm not planning—*we're* planning—to have sex, kids, the whole bit, but we're both hesitant to . . . It's just, what's the rush? We have our whole lives to do it."

Candler dropped his head. He had not shined his shoes this morning. He recalled the trucker stashing the toothpick in his hair and then retrieving it, sticking it back in his mouth.

"It's *love*," Billy said. "It is—all I know of love, anyway. I don't know what you and Lolly have. Or you and Lise. Whichever turns out to be the real thing. I only know this. It's what I've got. And I'm happy. Can't you be happy for me?"

"No," he said. "If this gets out, you'll be fired."

"Who's gonna tell?"

"And if I'm the director? And I *know* . . . Do you see the position you put me in?"

"I didn't mean to. Stuff happens, Jimmy." Billy was still smiling. He scratched under his arm, waggling his head. "We're happy."

"I should turn you in."

"We're going next month to L.A. so I can meet her family."

Candler turned and walked to his car.

"My mom cried when I told her," Billy said. "She and Dad can't wait to visit."

Candler just shook his head.

"It's love," Billy insisted. He left the porch, running in his socks and boxers to the car. "Karly said she loves me 'cause I'm always nice to her. All these years of being nice to girls, and finally I find one who likes it."

Candler paused at the car. The shiny red roof of the Porsche separated them. He was close to screaming something.

Billy kept talking. "I came over the first time just to help her out, you know? Wash her clothes, vacuum. Put in deadbolts. The place was such a mess, and the guy who used to help her had just up and left. And what the hell, Jimmy, if you need to turn us in, I don't mind. I love the job and all, but I know you've got responsibilities. I mean, I knew you'd be pissed, but I hoped you might be happy for me even if you were pissed, but what the hey? Fire me. I'll go back to pizzas or there's a Buy-N-Go in town that could use a good man. Just don't ask me to leave her."

Candler only stared.

"I can *talk* to her," Billy said. "We talk. We listen. I tell her things. She tells me things. It's good. And this house is paid for. I can take care of her. And she . . . she's . . ."

"Just because she's good-looking," Candler said, "doesn't mean—"

"She's *kind*," Billy said. "Her first impulse is always kindness."

Candler opened the car door. He counted his breaths to calm himself.

"Good-bye, Mr. James Candler." Karly had on a shirt now but she was still barefoot, and she stepped into the yard, crossing it to join Billy. "You look so good in that car," she called.

Billy put his arm around her. He kissed the top of her head.

The drive to the Center passed unnoticed. He must have steered, must have stopped at signs and watched for pedestrians, but somehow he did not notice the drive. The parking lot was almost empty. He stumbled getting out of the car, falling to one knee. *If I'm on my knees, I must be praying.* Fucking Billy. That fucking idiot. Candler used his key to enter the building. From his office window, he spotted the tractor. It had not moved, but somehow it could only be seen from above. He sat on his desk and looked up the number for the chairman of the board. He got an answering machine.

"It's James Candler calling. I know you're making the decision today or tomorrow. I'm withdrawing my application for director. Clay Hao is more experienced and better qualified. He's a better person for the job."

Afraid to say anything else, he hung up.

The knock on the door caused Maura to look at the clock. It was probably one of the girls on this floor, locked out of her own room, or maybe it was Castro, coming with news. Maura imagined what info he might have to give her at this time of the night—an ill parent, sibling hit by a car. It couldn't be good news. The tapping was rapid but not hard. She opened the door only a crack. She liked wearing the oversized pajamas, but she didn't like people to see her in them.

No one was there. Yet she heard a voice whispering her name.

On his hands and knees, just outside her door, was Bellamy Rhine, and he didn't look good, his narrow face sweating and red, an awful contortion straining his features.

"What're you doing here?"

"I'm very *worried*," he whispered.

"Of all people, *you*, breaking the rules, going to get us both in trouble. I would've guessed a thousand names of who might be at my door at midnight before I guessed *you*."

"I'm very worried and I need to talk to you." He was still whispering, still on his knees. "It's eleven thirty-seven," he added.

"I would've guessed Bush and Schwarzenegger and Amy Winehouse before I guessed *you*. Don't you understand I don't want to talk to you? I am *nothing* like you. I don't give a flying fuck about you and Karly. Why aren't you slobbering and sweating at *her* doorstep?"

"I'm here to get your help," he said and he wiped tears from his face. Real ones. "I'm very worried about Mick."

"Mick?" She opened the door, and Rhine poured himself through. "How did you get up here? Is Mick downstairs?"

"This is a very nice apartment, Maura," he said, getting to his feet. "Very nicely appointed." He nodded his tiny head in rhythm with his speech. "I'm afraid Mick is in a hurtful state because Karly has chosen me over him, and when I was afraid Karly had chosen him over me, I was in a very hurtful state, and I think we need to see that Mick is all right."

"Karly's living with a dude, is what I hear."

Rhine started making her bed. He was shaking his head so hard sweat was flying. "Karly and I are going to be married, and we have to worry about *Mick*. I do not, *cannot* believe it's possible that there is, living in Karly's house, any . . ." He shook his head harder while he searched for a word.

"Dude," Maura offered.

". . . *dude* living with her." He fiercely tucked the bed corners, and Maura realized he was going to lose his shit. That he had long ago lost it.

"You're right," she said. "Just teasing. You know me. Sorry."

"Apology accepted, Maura, but teasing isn't nice when there is so much . . ." He took a breath and another and another. His lips moved. He was counting. She let him finish, and he did seem calmer.

"How'd you get up here?"

"I could be in a great deal of trouble," he agreed, nodding. "I asked the dorm attendant, and he would not let me go up the elevator but some people outside started yelling at each other, and he left to talk to them before I could ask about the stairs." He took another deep breath. "I tried to go to bed tonight, but I kept thinking that Mick might do something bad." He was nodding. "Sometimes people do bad things to themselves."

There were reasons for the rules, she reminded herself. *It had been a mistake to sneak out of her dorm.* Not more than another second passed before she replied. "Okay, I believe you. Let's get on your scooter and go to Mick's."

"I can't *find* his house," he said, tucking in the top sheet, fluffing the pillow. "I've never been there, and wherever I turn, it's the wrong way. I was looking, looking, and it's a *cycle*."

"I have a city map," she said.

"Can you read it?"

"You're trembling, Rhine."

"I'm *very* worried."

"Close your eyes," she said. "I'm getting dressed."

In a matter of minutes, they were in the basement. Maura pushed Rhine through the window before climbing through herself. They would get caught, and she would be grounded or worse, but she didn't have any choice. Rhine's fear had rubbed off on her.

She climbed onto the scooter and wrapped her arms around Rhine's ribs, yelling directions in his ear, which he repeated over and over. He was an annoying clod, and if this was a wild goose chase, she would make endless fun of his trembling. Maybe. Maybe she liked having an excuse to go to Mick's house anyway. She had never been there, never met his mom or brother. They had become exotic creatures in her imagination, these people who lived with Mick, who shared his genes. Besides, she liked having the wind in her hair again. If this meant she was still sick, she'd have to learn to live with it.

"Turn left on the next street," she said.

"Turn left on the next street. Turn left on the next street. Here? Turn left here?"

"Yes, for fuck's sake."

"I'm turning left, Maura. Here we go left."

There was no traffic to speak of, and she had to admit that Rhine was pretty good with the scooter. How late was it? It couldn't be much past midnight.

"Do I go straight, Maura? Maura, do I go straight?"

"Or what? Go in circles? Yes, straight. This is his street."

"This is his street," Rhine said. "This is his street."

"It's going to be on this side," she said, tapping his right arm. "We're almost there."

"I'm not going to cry, Maura," he said, his tears blown back onto her face. "Maura, I'm not—"

"Pull over. Here."

"Here? Right here?"

The house was two-story but narrow, as if built to fit between the trees on either side of it—spooky trees with black leaves as big as boxing gloves. All the windows were dark except for one around the side and upstairs. Mick's bedroom was upstairs; she knew that much from talking to him. She had made a plan on the ride over, and she followed it now without thinking. She ran to the door and rang the bell, pounded on the door, rang the bell again.

"No!" Rhine called. "You'll be rude!"

"Mrs. Coury!" Maura yelled, pounding and ringing. "Mick!"

Lights and noise came from the house, a rumble of movement, and the door flew open. It was Mick and it wasn't Mick, just awakened, a T-shirt and pajama bottoms, his lovely bare face. "What? What is it?" And then calmer: "You're Mick's friends." The brother. The little brother. He was fifteen.

"We're here . . ." she began. "You're Craig, right? We need to see . . ."

A woman in a robe appeared behind the boy, her face probing the dim room.

"We're very worried," Rhine called. He had put his helmet in the empty spot beneath the seat of his cycle, which had made him slower getting to the door. "Hello, Craig Coury. Hello, Mrs. Coury. It's Rhine. I'm very worried about Mick. Maura and I both are very worried. This is Maura Wood."

Only then did it dawn on the Courys that Mick alone had not responded to the ruckus. Mrs. Coury—her name was Genevieve and she was forty-two years old—turned and ran up the stairs.

10

"Death—or near death—whatever this turns out to be, it makes me want to fuck," John Egri told James Candler. They were sitting apart from the others in the waiting area and speaking softly. There were eight altogether at two a.m. waiting for news about Mick Coury. Candler was surprised by their number and surprised, too, by their clothing, the asinine T-shirts and cartoon-laden pajamas, the terry-cloth slippers and other inappropriate garments (Bellamy Rhine wore a motorcycle helmet), and the casual manner they assumed, how they chatted and mixed powdered cream into their coffee while they waited, Bellamy Rhine asleep on the couch, his knees bent, his socks the color of bubble gum, his helmeted head in the lap of Maura Wood, and another boy in Batman pajamas—Mick's brother, evidently—playing a handheld electronic game, and how no one cried or collapsed when the ER doctor told them the boy was alive but not out of the woods. "Not just fuck, but procreate," Egri continued. "Spread some seed. You counter death with life, I say. Not that I'm going to wake Cheryl up by climbing onto her Mount Olympus, but I feel the urge, you know." He eyed Genevieve Coury meaningfully.

Candler did not know what Egri meant and did not catch the ogling. He had been at home, on the couch with his laptop when the call from Mick's mother came. He had declined Lolly's invitation for a private viewing of her new bathing suit, her new nightie, and god knows what else she had bought. *Some work to finish up,* he'd told her, and when she asked, he said, yes, it had to do with the promotion.

She left him alone then and Violet was already in bed, which permitted Candler to get online and advertise the Porsche on craigs-list. *Must sell,* he had written. *Tyvek cover included.* Within the hour, he had a dozen responses. Another decisive act, he told himself. That he had dropped out of the competition for the job—his first decisive act—he had told no one. He felt a powerful urgency to take action on all the tattered, flapping things in his life, and there was no shortage.

The car would soon be history. Next? What would be the next decisive act?

He would move out of his house.

He could not possibly ask Lolly, who had come all the way from London, to find an apartment. She could stay as long as she wanted. Bob Whitman had a cabin in the Laguna Mountains that Candler had used when his place was being fumigated. Maybe he could camp there again. Or maybe he would take a room in one of the old motels in Onyx Springs. Or a hotel in San Diego with a view of the ocean.

Was he serious?

Yes, he would move out of the house. He did not intend to break it off with Lolly, necessarily—probably but not necessarily. But they shouldn't live together. They had rushed things. He was still tangled up with Lise. There was another decisive act to undertake: he had to tell Lolly about Lise.

That would be part one. Part two: he had to quit seeing one or the other.

Or both. He had let himself believe that he had to choose between the two women. Was that the issue? Whatever it was he was going through, he was not required to choose one of these two women. He could cut it off with both. He could go back to his carefree bachelor ways.

Though it was harder to imagine his life without Lise. Had he cheated on the Mendez report merely to impress her? He had already told her the story. Whatever impression there was to make had been made. To keep from lying to her? Given the amount of subterfuge in his life recently, he was unwilling to accuse himself of a wanton bout of honesty. Then why? Because the kid shouldn't have to go back to war? Because Candler wanted to be able to sleep at night?

The phone rang, and Candler answered it.

"This is not your fault," Genevieve Coury said, and in the minutes and hours that followed (and in the months and years that would follow) Candler was (and always would be) grateful to her for that greeting.

"I think I'm responsible for this," he told Egri. He started to explain but Egri cut him off.

"Get all of this self-flagellation out of your system tonight," he said. "You don't want any of that muck floating around. Not that the board members would hold you responsible, and they might even like that you're such a bullshit martyr, but it could make it hard to immediately put the crown on your balloon. Follow my drift?"

"We shouldn't be talking about that stuff now," Candler said, imagining for a moment how Egri would respond when he found out Candler had withdrawn. "That boy almost died."

"*Almost died* is nothing," Egri replied. "Like *almost pregnant* or *almost indicted.*"

"He's a good kid, and he might still die."

"So what if he's a good kid?" Egri demanded. "If he was a bastard you wouldn't care whether he lived or died?"

Candler had no reply. He recalled something he had discovered a couple of days earlier—that his sister believed it was Pook who had knocked out her front teeth by swinging a baseball bat. "It was something like a blessing," she had said to Candler. Her teeth were crooked but as long as their slant caused no real trouble, their parents couldn't see any reason to have them corrected. But the injury required braces, and when they came off, she was suddenly attractive. "It made me distrust personal beauty," she explained. "And I never would have been drawn to Arthur otherwise."

"I thought I'd knocked your teeth out," he insisted.

"That's not the way I remember it," she had said.

Billy had been there, tossing a pretend curveball, and their mother had thereafter banished them both from the house. No, it was he who had done the damage—and provided the unexpected benefit. Why was he thinking about his sister's teeth in this awful hospital corridor?

Egri tapped his arm. Mrs. Coury stood just inches from them. Her hands blossomed at her waist as she spoke. "He's going to make it," she said. "They're still concerned, but I can tell. I've been through this before. He's going to make it. He's going to be his old self."

"Thank goodness, madam," Egri said softly.

Candler could not speak, knowing that *old self* meant the boy he knew and not his old old self, the boy who would never consider taking his life. Candler did not feel he could put much faith in the woman's pronouncement. She was telling them what she needed to believe. She was cheating death, or trying to, denying its proximity. When he had lived with Dlu, one of her many ethical obsessions concerned grocery bags. She had hated them and collected canvas bags and insisted the checkout clerks use them. This was a common practice now, but Dlu had been ahead of the curve. Candler had dutifully kept a stash of canvas bags in his truck, but he inevitably forgot them until his goods were being scanned, until the clerk actually said the words *paper or plastic*. He recalled lugging the plastic bags to his car and repacking the items in the canvas bags. How many times had he done that? *Keeping the peace*, he'd thought at the time. *Staying out of harm's way*. Or just *cheating*. Pretending to be better than he was. *In the desert, it's the same deal*, Mendez had said. They were just boys pretending to be soldiers and dying in the process.

Candler understood then what he had long worked to ignore: *he should have married Dlu*. He had rightly determined that it would have been a difficult marriage, and the strain would have made him unhappy. But at this moment, in a flash of insight he would regret, he understood that happiness was maybe not the most important thing after all, and that if human life was capable of even the smallest moments of exaltation, they might require work and, for one such as himself, a partner who was willing to embrace such work and by her own example encourage it was invaluable.

How the holy fuck did people know what to do with their lives? Candler gave them tests to help them see where their interests lay, but shouldn't they know what interested them? Shouldn't that be one of the things in life that was absolutely obvious? The constraints of work—he couldn't leave that out. They had to work for a living, spend their waking days laboring, and that work might be more bearable if it related to their interests, their passions, and it ought to be work that made use of their talents and did not make demands on their intelligence or physical abilities to which they were not equal. That's where the evaluator came in, juggling all those factors, weighing them in his palms, and then discerning a pattern. *If you pursue your passion for XYZ, you'll be happy*. Or at least you'll have a shot at happiness, but should happiness be the goal? Everyone wanted the happy ending, but there had to be more important things in this world than happiness. *Can't you be happy for us?*

Mrs. Coury patted his shoulder before moving to the next group.

"Moses and Mary, would Mr. Ralph like to go spelunking with her." Egri gripped Candler's arm, shook it slightly. "Don't make any more blunders, and leave the rest to me."

Blunders, Candler thought. How were the living supposed to avoid them? Egri stepped over to Genevieve Coury and spoke softly to her. They embraced, and he stared over her shoulder at Candler. *Blunders*. Egri had just unwittingly blamed this on him, Candler realized. His cell phone vibrated, a text message. Candler waited until Egri had been swallowed by the elevator doors before looking. It was from Lolly: *I'm up*.

He texted back: *No news*.

Then he distanced himself from the others and phoned Lise. "He's unconscious, but they don't seem concerned about that." He was standing down the hall from the waiting area, his cheek up against a window. "I don't know why they're not concerned. It seems like being unconscious should worry the hell out of us."

"I'll make coffee if you want to talk. So I can stay awake, I mean. I don't expect you to drive all the way down here, but we can talk on the phone."

"I'm exhausted," he said, "but I don't want to leave just yet. I'm too tired to talk." But they did talk. "If that boy dies," Candler said a dozen times without ever completing the sentence. "I thought I was helping by making him face the truth, but maybe that's a crock. I should have kept my mouth shut."

This would be James Candler's final conversation with Lise Ray, the last time he would hear her voice. In the days to come, he would tell Lolly about his decision to move out, how she could stay as long as she liked in the house, and then he would drive to Ocean Beach, the Porsche sold by then to a San Francisco buyer who would pick it up the coming weekend—his last drive in that awful car. The housing crash that would make his stucco barn worth less than what he owed had announced itself, as well, and politicians were scrambling before the election to come up with a response. Candler could not foresee all that was to come, but he did understand that he would walk away from that drafty monstrosity. He parked on the street in Ocean Beach, outside her building, eyeing overfilled trash cans joined by a pair of giant cardboard boxes. The boxes, damp with dew, held more trash.

Someone is moving, he thought.

The note was tacked to the door, a folded sheet of paper bearing his name. He pulled it loose, unfolded it.

Dear James,

I used to be a stripper in Los Angeles. I was arrested at a party for having coke and turning tricks. My probation required me to see a counselor, and it turned out to be you. At that time, I called myself Beth Wray. I had enormous tits and my hair was bleached. Remember me at all? I suppose I'll always wonder. We had one session before you moved away. I'm not going to try to explain why—I'll leave that for you to figure out—but what you said that morning changed the terms of my life. Also, I fell for you.

I suppose my behavior of the past few months could be called stalking. I don't like that term, and I don't think you'll use it even after you read this note, but that's up to you. I guess I thought you could continue to guide me. I'm not certain I was wrong about that, and I'm quite certain that I love you. It may have started out as some kind of illusion (*transference* is the fancy term you types use; I've read some books), but I've seen through that for a while now.

I've also come to understand that you're not the key to the remainder of my life. Whatever else I may be, I'm not a coward. I'm moving on. I've quit my job. I've quit you. I know if you choose to, you'll be able to find me. I'm asking you now not to do that. I hope you have a good life.

With good wishes and no regrets,
Elizabeth Ray

The note would be the final push that would usher him along to the next phase of his life, but he would not see it for a few days yet. He held the phone to his ear, his cheek against the cool hospital windowpane, and listened.

"There was one time," Lise said, "somebody asked me—demanded—to explain what in my life had put me in the situation I was in. I don't want to go into details, but I was in a bad place. At first I gave him the usual baloney, but he wouldn't bite, just kept smiling and shaking his head. I spent a long time trying to figure it out."

"What did you come up with?" Candler asked.

"I had made compromises," she said. "Not like you can have the bathroom first on Mondays and Wednesdays, and I'll take Tuesdays and Thursdays. That other type of compromise, when you let some part of yourself be dented or tarnished or sold because it's easier than protecting it, or because everyone else is doing it, or—I'd tell myself it was temporary and meant nothing. Just until I got my bearings, but that's like sticking your head in a river and saying *It's just until I can get a full breath of air.*"

The quality of Candler's attention changed, and he propped an elbow against the glass, his head in his palm. "Was this a therapist who asked you to—"

"Not a therapist. It was a friend . . . my . . . it was my dad, actually. He and my mom were worried about me."

"What does your dad do for a living?" Candler asked.

"He's an electrical contractor. My mom works for the phone company."

"What part of yourself . . . I don't know how to ask the question."

"What had I compromised?"

"If you want to tell me."

"I've wanted to tell you for a while now."

"Sorry, I'll shut up."

"I don't have a name for it. But it's the central part. Like . . . like downtown, you know? The part of me that's all me. I can change other things and still be me, but this part I can't change. I have to stick with it."

Neither spoke for several seconds. Candler was sleepy and grateful to her. "You love your father," he said.

"I love the man who made me see I was hurting myself."

"I'm sorry I don't know him," he said.

The night had been a lark until she saw Mick's inert body, at which point a shudder passed through her, and she understood that this unmoving body was her life, and it might be revived or it might be extinguished.

Fortunately, Mick's mother gave her something to do. "Get clean pajamas from his dresser, the top left-hand drawer." She cradled her son's head in her arms. Craig, the brother, was downstairs calling the hospital. Rhine was in the hallway, crying. Mick had wet himself, and his mother wanted clean pajamas. She knew how long the ambulance would take. There was time to change him. Maura helped. "He's still breathing," his mother said, and then she offered her hand. "I'm Genevieve."

Maura pronounced her own name. She added, "I love your son."

"I know that, hon," Genevieve replied. "Get me a wet washcloth."

He had taken all his medications, all those pills that had been accumulating because he wanted to be sharp. They bathed him with the washcloth and awkwardly worked the pajamas over his damp legs as the sirens approached, and it was not until the ambulance took Mick and his mother away that Maura burst into tears, which permitted Rhine to finally quit his moaning and comfort her. "Don't cry, Maura," he said. "Don't cry." He said the same thing over and over and over until she finally quit crying.

Policemen came. They drove Maura, Rhine, and Craig to the hospital, the three of them in one long bench seat behind a wire screen, as if they were criminals, and she had a wild thought that she should tell these cops about Bert and Ernie in the pickup truck, but the thought immediately embarrassed her. One of the policemen said, "It's a beautiful night, otherwise," but nothing else from the ride stuck with her.

Then came the waiting, just the three of them at first in a room the color of pumpkins, that same orange and a green trim like the vine. Was that how fashionable people decided what colors went together and what colors clashed? Did they rely on the natural world? Fucking farms and plants? People arrived and joined their waiting—Mick's mother emerged from the room where they were trying to save him, and then Mick's father and his girlfriend, who wasn't wearing a bra, sat with them, and then Mr. John Egri showed up, in jeans, and he shook their hands and said something to Maura too low for her too hear.

"What did you say?" she asked, her voice like an explosion in the room.

John Egri smiled and repeated, "Hang in there."

Rhine fell asleep, wearing his helmet so he wouldn't lose it. He put his big, plastic-covered head in her lap, and she let him.

This wasn't the first time Mick had tried to kill himself, and the Courys knew how to behave. Mrs. Coury said encouraging things to everyone. Mr. Coury and his girlfriend did a lot of praying. When a nurse summoned the parents through the swinging doors, the girlfriend flipped open her phone and called someone. Who would she be calling, Maura wondered. Did she have a friend she could ring in the middle of the night? Was she close to her parents? When Mr. and Mrs. Coury returned, accompanied by a nurse or doctor—a dark-skinned woman with bulges beneath her eyes—a moment of mayhem followed. Mr. Coury and the girlfriend dropped to their knees, holding hands and praying in loud voices. Mrs. Coury ran to her other son and took him in her arms.

"What?" Maura said.

The dark-skinned woman answered. "He's alive. So far. Vitals better. Not out of the woods, but there's reason for hope." Her mouth made an uncertain gesture. "We've done everything we can do."

Mr. Coury spoke from his knees, addressing Maura. "A miracle has taken place, young lady. They said those drugs were powerful enough to kill a bull. I heard them. An Andalusian bull. But God, with the help of these fine people and their amazing machinery, God—"

"It's still touch and go," the dark-skinned woman said. "I have been very clear with you."

"Join us," Mr. Coury said and offered Maura his hand. "Join us in thanks."

"Pass," she said, and Mr. Coury seemed to see her then for the first time—her weary eyes, the skin around them darkened, bloody paths through the whites. A tear shuttled over Maura's cheek to her lip and the hiding tongue, like a predator, slipped from its cave to trap it, savor it, make it disappear.

"There's a reason Christ is called the *savior*," Mr. Coury said to her. "Do you have a better explanation? The doctor here cannot explain it. Do you know why our son has been spared?"

Maura nodded. She slapped the sleeping boy's helmet. "'Cause this freak spazzed out."

Mr. Coury merely stared, his mouth falling open, and Maura shut her eyes, wishing she actually could pray without making it into a joke. She needed something to do. She had missed the arrival of Mr. James Candler and was surprised to see him sitting along the wall with everyone else. He wore a suit and tie, a black suit, which upset her, as it seemed like he'd come to hear that Mick was dead. Rhine's father showed up later, and he did not stay long. Rhine's father was tall and normal looking, and he gently woke his son. "I can carry you," he offered but Rhine declined. He flipped up his plastic visor to talk to people. "Good-bye, Mr. James Candler," he began. Despite his sleepiness, he said good-bye to each of Mick's people. When he came to Maura, he started to hug her but chickened out.

Maura wrapped her arms around him. "Good night, you retard," she said.

When she was alone again, she felt she had to be honest with herself. She could not avoid the truth. When she'd heard that Mick might be okay, she had felt enormous relief but also—she couldn't deny it—a letdown. A shameful, niggling sense of disappointment. It bothered her so much that she went to the nurse's station and called Patricia Barnstone.

"I'm downstairs," Barnstone said. "They won't tell me what floor or where to go."

Maura took the elevator down. Barnstone was all the way across the room. She sat alone in the sad and ugly room, her back against the dark, gigantic windows. The shirt she wore was too large, a shapeless disguise, and when she shifted in the chair she seemed to be shrinking, disappearing into the fabric. Her short hair was standing on end. She looked like just anybody you might see in a hospital and not very much like the woman Maura knew. Maura ran to her anyway. Barnstone opened her arms to catch her.

"Candler called me," she said. "He told me you were here."

"When I saw Mick," Maura began but she didn't know how to explain, even to Barnstone, what she felt, how the whole world teetered over a big black nothing.

"It's no joke, is it, being a living thing?" Barnstone's coarse voice filled one ear. "One little pissy moment, and you can throw it all away."

"I had no idea," Maura said. She cried for a long time before she was able to say, "I can't believe I did this to my parents." And in that moment, she forgave her family everything, all their failings, real and imagined.

Candler remained in the hospital after the others were gone. Even Mick's father had left. Candler was not sure why he stayed. He found an odd comfort in the waiting area, his hands buried in his suit pockets. He had talked with Lise on the phone for a long time, until he could tell she was nodding off. Her drowsy voice reminded him of the sounds she made during sex, interrogative exclamations that climbed a ladder as she neared climax. "Up, up, uut, uph, up," she'd say, her voice distant, higher in pitch than normal, the tone more curious than excited, her eyes closed, and—almost like platforms along the climb— she would add a quick half-whispered sentence: "No, I knew that," the tone of the words falling, her eyes still closed, the climb up up up beginning again, and when she reached the top, the sentence repeated, "No, I knew that. I knew that." The first time she spoke it during inter-course, Candler thought she was addressing him, commenting on his performance, indicating an error in execution, but she wasn't speak-ing to anyone.

"What happens to you when we make love?" he asked her.

"The nerve endings in my clitoris are stimulated," she replied.

Lolly also spoke during sex. She was an energetic and uninhib-ited lover, and the first night Candler went to her London flat, he discovered that she owned an array of citrus-scented oils and color-ful candles, several drawers of lacy undergarments, and recordings of instrumental music from remote parts of the world. Those first nights in her tiny bedroom had been exhausting. There was an unreal quality about them, the choreography switching by the minute from *National Geographic* forays to *Satyricon* outtakes, and he thought per-haps she was too artistic for him, but the next day at the publishing house he would find her in those black-rimmed glasses and business tweeds negotiating a contract with an agent or amortizing authors' advances, and a weight would sink into his balls and he would want to take her on the desk. After three nights in her bedroom, he insisted on going to a hotel. Free of the papaya incense and thrumming sitars, dressed still in a three-piece suit, the skirt almost reaching her ankles, Lolly seemed unsure what was expected of her. "Just be yourself," Candler said, and they watched *The Graduate* on television and made love in the semidark of the old room, the sound of traffic and the vague odor of mold their only accompaniment.

"You want it plain?" she asked him.

"Scout's honor," he replied.

"You're an odd duck," she said.

In that hotel room, Lolly said things like, "Yes. Yes. Do it to me.

Fuck me, big boy. Harder." It was a routine, but he did not mind it, perhaps got a kick out of it. But one day in Violet's flat, on the narrow bed where Candler was supposed to be sleeping, Lolly lost herself in the act, and what she said then was "That's good," muttered softly, almost to herself, "That's it. That's the ticket. On the money. That's money."

What complicated organisms were women, with their complex systems of desires and needs. Men wanted to love and loved to fuck. They wanted bright houses and big soft beds. Women had to have worlds within worlds, and that was part of their attraction, he understood, the desire to attach one's self to something larger.

He did not yet know that he would never make love to Lolly or Lise again, and yet the tone of nostalgia in his sleepy considerations was unmistakable. The waiting room was empty, only Candler in his suit, thinking about sex to keep from thinking about his mistakes. *If I'm on my knees, I must be praying.* He had made a mess of things. *No, I knew that.* He had gone too fast, and Mick Coury might die. *That's money. You win.* He could not go on like this. *This is not your fault.* He had to—

"He's still unconscious." It was Mrs. Coury, her kind, lovely face just inches from his. "It's nice of you to have waited, but you should go home to your wife."

"My lover," he said. Then he made a stuttering correction. "I'm not, we're not—"

She seated herself on the couch beside him, taking his arm in an intimate way. "Did you talk to my husband?" she asked.

Candler said that he had. Tom Coury had thanked Candler for coming, *for providing your professional care for my dear boy.* Tom and Genevieve Coury behaved genially together, an air of exhaustion and camaraderie about them that suggested the connections they shared were more permanent than the divorce.

"And his girlfriend?" she asked. "Did you talk to her?"

"Not much," Candler said. "Just a handshake."

Tom Coury and the girlfriend had knelt on the carpet in the middle of the hallway, nurses sidestepping them, and held hands to pray for Mick's recovery, loudly at first, and then softer, a mumbled entreaty, audible to Candler in terms of syntax, that deep dyspeptic motor that funneled human sound. Thinking about it, he felt a new wave of sleepiness wash over him.

"Do you know how many times our son has tried to kill himself?"

Candler made an uncertain gesture with his head. "Several times."

"This is the ninth," she said. "The ninth that we know of. The first two times, Tom never left my side. By the third, well. It's hard to describe, but you learn to hold something back, to wait and see."

"Mick does so well most of the time," Candler said apologetically.

She patted the arm she was holding and laid her head against his shoulder. "He loses perspective," she said. "He can't remember the people who love him. All he can see is the immediate problem, and it seems to him that his death would solve it."

Suicides tended to believe their death would affect no one who knew them, except perhaps to improve the quality of those lives. And couldn't that be true? Wasn't it necessarily true that some people were nothing but a burden on the world? Had that applied to his brother? Candler could see how Pook might have thought himself nothing but a burden—except that Pook's consciousness did not work in a fashion that would ever produce such a thought. No, Pook had seen the cumulative result of his art, and he could not go on. It wasn't even that the art mattered to him, which meant it had to be what the art revealed. What had he seen in all those images of himself staring back? What would any man see if he could, by his own lights, create a mirror that genuinely reflected who he was? Could any of us endure it?

Mrs. Coury was silent, clutching his arm, her body warm against his shoulder, and Candler felt himself ease back into the dense yet softened regions of consciousness where memory and fantasy resided. He slipped into a dream of his life, of this moment in the hospital, and in the dream the woman holding his arm was speaking. She told him that her husband had met his girlfriend during something they called Prayer Circle, and Candler immediately heard the man praying . . . *my son, struck down by madness . . . I beg of you please to release my boy's chains.*

Candler opened his eyes to the orange indent in the hospital hallway that everyone called *the waiting room*, but it was not a separate room, and the woman beside him was again speaking, softly speaking, the light from the ceiling an unnatural white like bleached teeth, and what was she saying now, this sad and lovely woman in a Neil Young T-shirt, her hair smelling of apples, and who had already forgiven him, what was she saying? He listened and slept, his drowsiness and his attentiveness holding hands as the praying couple had done from their knees.

Genevieve Coury was resigned not to the death of her son but to the frequency with which he would approach it. If he actually died, she would be as shocked and devastated as any parent losing a child, but she had learned that the agony of apprehension was not an obligation she had to keep. She and Tom sold their home in Yuma, abandoned their friends and jobs, moved away from family, and then her marriage, too, was sacrificed to the wrathful god of schizophrenia. She would not surrender her second son to redeem the first, but except for this, she held nothing back and had no regrets. She missed her husband, but the man she loved no longer seemed to exist. He had to glorify their sacrifices by bringing god into the picture, and she could not entirely forgive him for that. Candler heard her and did not hear her, unsure what was real and what was dream, and it did not yet end.

It was Genevieve, he understood, who had thought to grab Craig's Game Boy and take it to the hospital. It was she who offered her bedroom to her ex-husband and his girlfriend for the night, reminding them that Craig had school in the morning and to set an alarm. It would be she who slept for what was left of this night in the chair beside Mick's bed. It would be she who wrote letters to Rhine and Maura, thanking them for saving—or trying to save—her boy's fragile life. And it would be she, standing beside her son's grave at some point in the future, who would have a clean conscience, who would know she had done everything she could to save him. And it would be she who'd be nonetheless inconsolable. Candler heard her and slept, nodding at the right moments, touching the hand that clutched his arm at the elbow. He wanted to thank her for the way she had greeted him on the phone, but he had been stripped of language and could only listen to the dream of this woman's life.

When she rattled the arm she held, he saw his brother standing over them, his brother's big closed face, his brother's strong grip, and behind him were those paintings lining the walls as they had in the New York gallery. When he opened his eyes, the woman next to him was speaking. "Mick used to make amazing buildings out of his plastic bricks," she was saying. She lifted her head from Candler's shoulder, slipping to the edge of the upholstered couch. "He was the most wonderful child and obsessed with those plastic bricks." She released Candler's arm and stood. "He'd say, *Mom, I've built you a castle.*"

Candler nodded. "I understand," he said. "I understand what you're telling me. I'll leave you two alone."

Her smile was beatific, and he believed he could love her. He could give up Lolly and Lise and love this woman, adopt her tragic son, and this became part of the waking dream, and by the time a clattering cart pushed by an orderly brought him fully awake, Genevieve Coury was gone, the dream was gone, and Candler was alone.

People encounter death in vastly dissimilar ways. Some see a light in an otherwise dark universe, and they move toward that light or flee from it. Some see the faces of the people they love, and they are filled with joy. Others see the dead they betrayed and belittled scuffling along a narrow corridor, forming a line. For many, though, there is only a slow cessation, which is a source both of despair and of relief. And for everyone, there comes a time when consciousness of every kind evaporates, and the thing that we have thought of as our soul trembles and vanishes, not like a flame, but like the memory of a flame, and it cannot be relit.

This was not the first time Mick Coury had died. Twice among his attempts to kill himself his heart had stopped and he had been revived. And his illness, when it descended—that, too, had been a kind of death. A limited kind of death. There were degrees of death, just as there were degrees of darkness, degrees of love, degrees of knowing. Mick had died a number of times before this night, and he was dead now. His father was born again, and he was dead again. If his body had been capable of laughter, he would have laughed.

He wanted to be revived. He hoped it would happen. This seemed like a contradictory desire, as he could have declined to kill himself and then he would not need reviving. But *revival* and *survival* were not the same thing. *It's like a reset button with you,* his brother Craig had said after one of Mick's attempts. *You come to all better, straightened out, feeling good.* Mick had nodded and said, *Maybe I should do it more often.* His brother had thrown back his head and laughed.

In death, there is no schizophrenia, and Mick felt his pain at losing Karly with a degree of irony. He understood that she was mentally impaired. He understood that her mind, but not her soul, was diminished, and if he still felt love for her, it was mingled with the understanding that he would be better suited with someone more intellectually compelling for a life partner. If only he had a life . . . and if he could carry over this ruthless sanity into it.

It was cold, being dead, not icy but there was a chill, and the light was not a friendly light, and whatever was going on about him registered as shoves or mechanical noises, like the grating of enormous gears. He would miss light. He would miss the magic of human light.

Human light? *What the fuck?*

He filled with his old old self, and what a glorious feeling to be straight and wickedly handsome and horny and if only he could get the fuck up and out of this place, out into the vivid-ass world out there.

His stomach hurt, which meant he might be brought back. Or it might mean that the pain of dissolution had begun. Each of his organs would fail and fail painfully. Death is not unconsciousness. He would feel it all. The pain of the pieces giving up, giving out, life easing along into the ether.

The guy he had been once upon a time, back in Yuma, the guy he felt once again fully inhabit his body, that guy would have gone about this Karly business differently. He would've wanted to get her out of her clothes and onto her back. That guy would have wanted to *get some.* A ripple of desire moved through his body. But the body could not follow it up.

If he was going to stay dead this time, he had plenty of regrets. Like the beach. He wished to hell he could have gone back to that beach, ripped off his clothes, and strode over the sand like a goddamn god. Gods did what they wanted, took whatever and whomever they pleased. He would have bent Karly over the hood of his Firebird and taken her, and afterward he would have spanked her bare bottom, and he would have walked naked into the sea.

And then what?

PART SIX Phantom Limb

I paint flowers so they will not die.
—FRIDA KAHLO

11

Same Man stands over the body of the boy who killed himself. The body looks just like Same Man. People are watching. They are barely out of the frame, watching.

Someone says,

> WHY DIDN'T YOU
> SAVE HIM,
> SAME MAN?

Same Man does not have the power to disappear. The hospital room is bright. The dead boy just lies there. Same Man stares out of the frame, as if waiting for directions.

Someone says,

> YOU WERE GOING
> TOO FAST,
> SAME MAN.

Same Man closes his eyes but the people watching do not disappear. He cannot see them, but they are there. His closed eyes look like smooth clamshells.

In the next frame, Same Man's eyes are squeezed tightly shut, like tiny pursed mouths. There are drops of sweat on Same Man's forehead.

Same Man's face fills the whole panel. Sweat runs down his jaw. His eyes are pinched.

The next frame is dark. This is what Same Man sees with his eyes closed. It is not all black. There is the boy who killed himself. You can almost make him out in the dark.

More dim frames follow, each with more patchy light. The boy becomes clearer. He is no longer on the hospital bed. He is kneeling. He looks just like Same Man.

He says,

IF I'M ON MY KNEES,
I MUST BE PRAYING.

The image in the frame is so close that only the crease in the bridge of Same Man's nose and the indentations that are the corners of his shut eyes are visible. The crease looks like a black bridge connecting the sockets.

AS LONG AS
SAME MAN
CONCENTRATES
THE BOY IS ALIVE.

A doctor in a white lab coat stands in the bright room beside Same Man, who has his eyes hard shut. The doctor wears a headband that holds a metallic mirror, which is cocked over one eye. A hole in the mirror reveals the doctor's eye. He holds a needle and thread. The mirror obscures his face, but the careful reader can tell he looks just like Same Man.

In the next panel: nothing but Same Man's shut eyes, the stitches like the hide of a baseball.

The final frame is dim with dark patches. The boy is rising from his knees. He is almost standing. He looks just like Same Man.

RECALCULATING.

12

The window of Mick Coury's bedroom is illuminated. It is not especially late, but the remainder of the house is dark.

Genevieve Coury is asleep, on top of the covers, wearing the gray
sweatpants and Neil Young T-shirt that she changed into after arriving home. She hadn't meant to fall asleep, just wished to rest her eyes
for one moment, one moment, one . . . A dreamless sleep, or almost
so, only a vague sense of churning inhabits her mind, a churning
that may be the ocean, that may be the rhythm of her heart, that
may capture the convolutions of her complicated life. Stray, disloyal
thoughts attempt to stand up to the churning—*Did I turn off the lights
downstairs? I haven't made Craig's lunch for tomorrow. I should check on
Mick one last time before going down for the count.* The churning swallows
up the unhappy lines and they disappear beneath the beating waves.
She sleeps.

Craig is awake in his room, the lights off, music playing on his
computer. He reclines on the bed, wearing only his underpants, head
propped up by a tumble of pillows, texting with a girl who is at a slum-
ber party, and all the girls there, she writes to him, want to know what
he's wearing, why he doesn't let his hair grow out again like he did in
eighth grade, and if he thinks Lady Gaga is a tramp ha ha. The tiny
cloud of light created by his cell phone haloes his head.

Across the narrow hall, in his bright tidy room, Mick Coury
stands beside his faithful bed, holding pills in his hand, the meds that
have failed to help him, failed to repair him, failed to mend his broken
mind. They make a mound on his palm. He intends to swallow the
handful and end his confusing misery once and for all. He intends to
wash the handful down with the glass of water on his nightstand. He
intends to eat the meds and then lie on his bed, his hands clasped at
his waist or behind his head—the only decision he will have to make
after he takes the pills is what to do with his hands. He has been
through this before. The key to killing yourself is to make up your
mind and then quit thinking. The key to killing yourself is to make up

your mind and follow through. He has made up his mind, his woeful, muddled, worthless, pain-ridden mind that the drugs failed to restore and now he will neutralize, will rub out, will do in, will murder himself. Mind-murdering drugs.

It's a melodramatic business, is suicide.

Q: What are the pills?
A: Thorazine.

Q: Why isn't he taking one of the new generation of antipsychotics?
A: Client developed a facial tic with one drug and experienced sleeplessness with another. With Thorazine he seems especially fortunate, as he has not gained weight or shown any signs of nervous system disorders. Thorazine is the best available drug for him.

Q: Why hasn't the Center's psychologist lowered his dosage to permit him to find the precise balance he needs?
A: Client's dosage has been adjusted up or down five times in three years. The psychologist has been responsive to the client's self-reports. What appears to be the perfect dosage from external observation—confirmed by his counselor and sheltered workshop supervisor—nonetheless seems to the client to steal from him his mental quickness and lower his intelligence. Client's subjective analysis and the contrary professional reports leave the psychologist with the following dilemma: should she permit her client to be a little slow or a little irrational? Few therapists would choose the latter.

Q: Why hasn't the psychologist made an appearance in these pages?
A: The psychologist adds nothing new to the story, and the narrative is quite long enough as it is, don't you think? She is neither culpable in any manner nor particularly interesting as a character. She is happily married with two well-adjusted children. She reads Regency romances and subscribes to two journals on antique furniture. She scrapbooks.

Q: Given Mick's history, why hasn't his mother controlled his access to the medication?

A: She has done exactly that. The pills in the client's hand are the ones that he has pretended to take, the pills that accumulated from the client skipping days in order to be fresh, bright, alert, at the ready. While it is a consequential pile, it is not reasonable to expect his mother to have insisted on watching each pill traverse his throat, or to suggest that a more diligent parent would have searched his room and discovered the cache of untaken pills. Any reasonable observer would offer an extremely positive assessment of the client's mother regarding care for her son—or, for that matter, in terms of any aspect of her life. She is an exemplary human.

Q: How can you know all of this?

A: Psychology is a science, and the practice of this science follows certain time-tested traditions. The experienced practitioner combines objective observation and subjective intuition with the principles, practices, and traditions of the science to create a holistic approach to every individual.

Q: Which can be boiled down to?

A: My brain told me.

Mick's heart hurts more than he can bear. He is hot and sweating. He has blocked off the floor vents by covering each with T-shirts and stacking books on top. He's not sure now why he did that, but the room is hot and his skin glistens. He has put on his best pajamas, the striped ones that his father gave him. He believes his father will understand what Mick is saying by wearing these pajamas, but he doesn't want to think himself about what they mean—*forgiveness* or something along those lines. He clicks off the overhead light and stands in the middle of the darkened room, still holding the pills in his palm. Moonlight enters and carries off the darkness—not all of it, a partial expulsion, the room dark and light at the same time. Sweat from his forehead gathers on the bridge of his nose, trickles down to the tip, and just as he raises his hand to stuff his mouth with Thorazine, a drop of sweat falls from his nose to the jumble of pills.

This gives him pause. From his brother's room comes the sound of a satellite radio station played through the speakers of a laptop. It's the seventies channel, and the song is one that was recorded long before Mick was born—approximately seventeen years before. Yet he has a history with the song dating back to the other side of the mountain, to when he was that other boy. It is a simple history: he *hated* the song. It played at a wedding he attended, a shotgun wedding of classmates, the girl just beginning to show beneath her off-white dress, the boy with a barbed-wire tattoo circling his neck, and from a gunmetal gray ghetto blaster came the recording of the woman's voice, all syrup: *We've only just begun* . . .

Mick doesn't merely recall disliking the song, he actively hates the song in the moment, as it pours under and around and through his door and rises up to his ears. *What a sentimental piece of Nutrasweetened garbage! Of all the songs* . . . He can't see himself dying to this hateful tune, which means he'll have to wait a few minutes and hope for Creedence Clearwater or David Bowie or . . . what is the best seventies music to die to, anyway? Styx? He supposes he could ask his brother to change the station, but to what? And if . . . and if . . . and if he hates this awful song, isn't that evidence that he's getting better? More like his old self, all opinionated about tunes?

It's not too late to change his mind. He can still go to the beach. They set a tentative date for the trip—this coming Saturday. He can still attempt to make the journey to the ocean and lead the others on an adventure. *I've got an itch for adventure*—who had said that to him. Karly? No, it was Maura. His friend Maura. He could do that much for her, couldn't he? With his free hand, he flips on the overhead light, which erases the moonlight and the residual darkness, both at once.

He steps from his room to the hall, the sound of the dreadful song rising in volume: *white lace and promises, a kiss for luck and we're on our way* . . . No one is in the bathroom. He locks the door behind him. He bends to drop the pills into the toilet without making a big splash. He pisses on them, which is so pleasurable that he imagines pissing every day on his meds. He flushes. The pills chase one another in a circle and dive into the opening, vanishing, vanishing, gone.

Mick does not attempt to kill himself after all. He is dead in the hospital morgue and he is not dead, returning now to his room, the repugnant Carpenters song giving way to "The First Time Ever I Saw

Your Face." *Why do people like '70s music?* he wonders, covering his ears. He shuts the door to his room to muffle the sound of the song. It feels terribly selfish to him, this decision to continue living. And possibly incompetent. Rude. He is ashamed and crawls into bed. Spiraling through his regret and remorse and self-hatred is a thought: *The beach.* Other thoughts trail it. *I can find the beach. I can be somebody's guide for a change.* This swirl of thoughts forces the others out of the frame, and he drifts off into sleep.

Readers encounter the impossible in vastly dissimilar ways. Some throw the goddamn book across the room and curse the author by name. Others imagine the snide comments they'll post on a book review website. Still others keep the faith, shaken yet willing to continue. But every reader wants the impossible acts addressed: a big brother's sudden and permanent and utterly inexplicable disappearance—how is *that* possible? A son's baffling descent into madness? A husband who one day cannot lift his coffee cup? A woman who discovers she has put a price tag on some part of her soul? A young man who finds himself in uniform and firing a lethal weapon at other human beings? Or a tiny swimming mishap in the neighbor's pool—a few seconds too many beneath the surface—and the child's ability to function in the world is forever diminished? And now a boy who died has also not died? Every sane person has to find every day some manner of accommodating the impossible, some way of covering up for the failures of the rational world. This might actually be a reasonable definition of *sanity.*

The lead car in the beach caravan is Mick Coury's Firebird, which he has washed and waxed. He spends an hour vacuuming the interior to ensure that his passengers will be comfortable. As things turn out, Maura Wood is his only passenger, sitting in the Firebird's bucket seat in her sunglasses, a man's white shirt, and cutoff jeans. Underneath, she wears a black one-piece bathing suit that has a tiny skirt. Mick is fully dressed, including his brown loafers and a long-sleeved striped shirt. He is much more concerned with the drive than with the swim, and he dresses as he imagines a successful driver would outfit himself, including a tie until his brother tells him the tie is overboard. His swim trunks, a towel, a second towel, and sunscreen are in a cloth bag in the trunk, along with two boogie boards and a huge cooler packed with sodas, sandwiches, and ice.

Barnstone and Andujar drive one of the Center's vans. Barnstone drives for the first leg, wearing dark shorts and a white blouse, arriving at James Candler's house in the Corners at nine twenty a.m. to pick up Lolly and Violet. She is relieved to discover that Candler is not at home, and she no longer feels obliged to drive. She turns the wheel over to Andujar, who is utterly competent behind the wheel despite his many and significant mental problems. He wears a white T-shirt, Lakers shorts, and sandals. He will not drive unless he has another person in the front alongside him, but otherwise his disorder does not show itself.

Violet's bathing suit is a flowery one-piece, six years old, and was not terribly fashionable when it was new. She and Arthur went to the south of France, which was the only time she wore it. She regrets not trying it on before the trip, as it is tighter than she expects. She prefers the idea that it has shrunk to the obvious alternative. Over it, she wears a smart terrycloth beach dress, which she is fairly certain she will not remove. Her flip-flops are newly purchased at the grocery around the corner. Lolly wears a diaphanous beach dress over a black thong bikini. Her sandals have heels and elaborate wraps of string that climb her legs. If being *stunning* means that the men cannot move their eyes from her naked behind as if a hammer has been applied to the back of their heads, then she is stunning.

The third car in the short parade is a Dodge Dart, with Alonso Duran, Bellamy Rhine, and Vex in the backseat, Billy Atlas behind the wheel, and Karly Atlas née Hopper in the seat beside him. No one in any of the vehicles knows that Billy and Karly are husband and wife, except for Billy. Even Karly does not fully understand since she did not wear a white dress to the justice of the peace, which creates a tiny doubt in her mind. On this day, she wears a white bikini beneath a yellow halter top and short green skirt. It is not a modest bathing suit but tame compared to Lolly's gear. Billy's trunks advertise Corona beer, and he wears a white short-sleeved shirt, unbuttoned. They have forgotten shoes and towels, but Billy has packed a cooler full of beer and a dozen burritos wrapped in tin foil from the taco stand near the sheltered workshop.

Alonso's mother dresses him in beach sandals, loose trunks, and an oversized Padres shirt, clothing that will permit him to masturbate without disrobing. Rhine wears a swimsuit ordered from a special website for sun-sensitive people. It is long-sleeved and has leggings that reach his ankles. It is one piece and basketball orange, except for the trunks, which show a blue sky filled with white clouds. Rhine cannot wear flip-flops due to the unhappy post that separates the big toe from the remainder. He opts for black rubber boots. Vex wears jeans, motorcycle boots, and the butt-faced elk T-shirt. He has only agreed to come in case there is a breakdown on the road and repairs are needed. His tools are in the trunk.

Barnstone has described the outing as a personal expedition, which means she has to pay for the gas herself but permits her to avoid the Center's guidelines for field trips. There is no way she could have gotten permission for an official trip to the beach, and yet she cannot understand a facility near the ocean that allows no provision for such excursions. It makes no damn sense. She naps while Andujar drives, and she does not understand they are crossing into Mexico until Mick and Maura are already on the other side and there is nothing to do but follow.

A bright morning at the adobe house in Tucson. Jimmy is ten, and Pook stands at the door to Jimmy's room holding a milk carton. He fills the entire doorway. Light in his hair. Larger than any mere man. Pook holds the milk carton at his waist and with both hands. He holds the carton as one might hold a camera with a waist-level viewfinder. He carries it as one might carry a trophy or a severed head or the ashes of the beloved. He carries it as one might carry a fishbowl filled with water, a single goldfish swimming uncertainly in the waves.

Jimmy is making his bed. He has to make his bed each morning before he can go outside to play. *Rules.* His mother's rules. Billy would already be waiting on the porch. The Dog would be panting beside Billy on the couch. The multitude of cats would be awake by now and greedily ignoring the human world. But it all has to wait while Jimmy makes his bed. The sheets are white. Sunlight from the open window lights the sheets as they float over the mattress, as if in slow motion they float down—and the thousand dust motes in that slash of sunlight, like a glimpse into another universe.

Pook enters the room slowly, awkwardly. Pook enters the room hesitantly, clumsily. Pook enters Jimmy's room with the ponderous movements of a deep-sea creature clodding about the shore. He bends his head apologetically, now clutching the milk carton to his chest as he makes his way to the bed. He sets the silo upright in the center of the ivory plane and shoves his hands in his pockets: a milk carton on a single bed covered with a white sheet. The carton casts a long shadow on the bed, longer than the carton is tall. The shadow dips over the side and touches the floor.

Jimmy tosses his pillow so that it sails over the milk carton. It lands crookedly, partly against the headboard, a relaxed pose, as if it is a living thing and sitting up. His mother might paint that pillow, Jimmy thinks, the way it landed, how it seems to express its personality in its pose. Not his father, though. It is not his father's kind of painting. The empty milk carton rocks with movement of the mattress, the vibrations from the falling pillow turning it slightly, but it does not fall over. Jimmy bends closer. It's just a milk carton, the local dairy, red lettering on the white, waxy carton. Whole Milk. Pasteurized. Homogenized. Vitamin D.

Jimmy says, "Is there something you want to show me?"

Pook frees a hand from his pocket and points. Dirt rims the nail of the pointing finger.

Jimmy Candler crooks himself even more to examine the milk carton. He puts his hands on his knees and lowers his head. He hunkers like an umpire behind home plate. He hunkers and stares. On the back of the milk carton is the picture of a child. This child disappeared from a Florida trailer park several years earlier, a tiny boy wearing a shirt with sea horses and dolphins. (Two years later Pook will paint this shirt from memory, but it will no longer be a shirt. It will become wallpaper in what has to be a room, the sea horses transformed into unreal chess pieces, the dolphins with wings like mythological creatures, a great wall of repeated images, such perfect mistakes that they all but erase the cheap shirt worn by the vanished boy.)

Pook's dirty fingernail scratches at the waxed photograph. His voice is a gurgling whisper. He says, "Idn't that me?"

When the three vehicles finally park and turn off their engines, Mick experiences immense relief. In order to drive at a reasonable speed he had to skip his meds, of course, and yet he has found the ocean and it's a perfect day, a perfect stretch of shore. Though it's true that the sand seems to vibrate as it kneels beneath the uncontrolled fury of the waves. And the curl of the beach, slithering out of view, reminds him of other disappearing things, like the thread of a thought or a dream that vanishes when you turn over in bed. And for several moments the entire landscape ticks like a clock—or like hot automotive engines in the oceanic breeze. Oh, he seriously doubts that this is the spot he went to before, where the grunion turned the coast silver, but he has gotten them to a deserted beach, and that pleases him.

They set up camp, unpacking and erecting Rhine's elaborate screened tent, which requires of everyone thirty minutes of earnest, stake-driving labor. After the tent is eventually upright and secure, Vex yells, "I'm taking my boots off, goddamn it." Barnstone reclines in the shade of the tent, while Rhine, who looks like an exotic sea creature with great orange limbs, walks to the edge of the water but does not go in. Violet and Maura stay in the shallows with him, Violet encouraging him to wade up to his knees and Maura mocking his ocean wear. Billy Atlas, beer in hand, and Karly, who looks surprisingly skinny in her white bikini, make their way through the water. Billy moves his arms rhythmically, and Mick understands that he is demonstrating to Karly how to swim. (What Mick feels for Karly is less attached to her now. It is like his love for his father, which has not diminished in size or intensity, but no longer applies in quite the same way to the man. One day his feelings for Karly and for his father will be entirely free of them, he believes, ribboning through people and objects in the world, turning them bright and golden. For now, he tries not to pay too much attention to Karly.) Vex shadows Billy and Karly, walking along the edge of the water in his jeans and long-sleeved shirt, yelling things that no one can hear. Andujar kneels at water's edge to feel the wet between his fingers, as if to check that it's really there.

Which leaves Mick and Lolly to swim out and then float back in on the short boards he found in the garage from the old days when he loved bodyboarding. It all comes back to him, the mechanics of it, as well as the timing, the knowledge of which waves to ride and which to let pass. Lolly is new to it all and follows his lead. They practice on a few low waves before he leads her to deeper water. They lie on their boards, the rolls of water lifting and lowering them, and it is impossible not to think about the size of the ocean, how inconsequential they are, tiny specks that cannot even stay afloat without Styrofoam planks. Lolly's thong shows off her beautifully rounded cheeks, and though she occasionally flicks at the bit of material attached to the center cord, it seems determined to display her ass.

Seeing her bottom—pretty much all of it—seems like an astounding thing, and at the same time, the ocean thinks so little of them, Mick feels that his head is clearing. Or it may just be the water in his ears. He laughs out loud, and Lolly turns to look at him, her wet hair flat and pushed back, and there is about her face a quality of the rodent (one of the nicer rodents, Mick quickly amends, not a rat but a pleasant ferret, perhaps) and yet when she smiles and asks him why he's laughing, the teeth, that white screen hidden behind those plush lips, eradicates the image of the rodent, and he cannot respond to her because there rises behind them a wall of water and it is time to stroke and kick, and he indicates as much to her, and the great body of water expresses with this single wave the heightened spirits of all mankind, Mick thinks, as they ride up the curl and fly weightless in the crest, side by side, and Lolly is calling out happily, and then she is pulled under while Mick rises higher still in the ocean's gaping mouth. He crashes, too, at the end, scraping his chest against the sandy shore, but he is on his feet quickly, steadying himself against the incoming rush of water. He yanks the wristband that tethers the board to him and sends it whirling in the direction of the beach. Only then does he notice that the others are no longer there—the elaborate tent and parked cars, the crowd of people in the shallows. Some current has taken Lolly and him away, and there is no time to think about it.

He calls Lolly's name, a silly gesture in the face of the ocean's ability to swallow sound. She has not come up. He wades out, looking for her mop of blond hair, but he sees instead the board pop free of the water, fly for a moment, and then splash down, its tether attached to nothing. And too far out. It means that the wave has driven her down, has pummeled her down, has hammered her into the ocean's unforgiving floor.

He swims. His body takes over. Thoughts leave him. He is no longer thinking too fast or too slow, and here at long last is the secret: to quit thinking altogether. He swims. His body knows just how far, and as he prepares to dive, he sees a flailing hand and adjusts his submersion, moving to his right, grasping the hand, and the woman comes with it, coughed up and coughing, his arm around her waist, sliding over her bare chest—she has lost the top of her bathing suit, which would have certainly undone every trace of clarity for him at any other time, but he does not consider her breasts, just holds to her slick body and swims with a single arm toward shore. She coughs seawater into his hair, and then, while he still swims with her, she vomits into the ocean, which carries it off and away from them. A wave sends them under and when they bob up immediately after, she throws her arms around his neck and clutches him fiercely, which makes it impossible to swim with anything but his legs, which he discovers are powerful, frogging out and back, and the ocean itself—mercurial in its desires—helps them along now, and when he sends down a tentative foot, his big toe touches bottom and then the ball of the foot and then he is walking, with this blond creature still draped about his neck, and a wave hits their backs and sends them sprawling, one on top of the other. He is up quickly and she, slowly, her bikini bottoms low on her thighs—the ocean is denuding her—and she makes no effort to pull them up, a dark chimney of hair at the fork of her legs. He takes her hand, but she will not settle for it, and he lifts her into his arms and carries her to dry land, where they both lie exhausted in the sun-baked sand.

The full extent of his fatigue hits him when his head touches the warm sand, and in a few moments he is asleep, a blessed dreamless sleep, and when he wakes she is tugging down his trunks. She crawls on top of him, kissing his mouth, offering her breasts, and then he is inside her and she is rocking over him, and again his body has not forgotten and knows what to do.

When they are through—*rutting* is the word that leaps into his head—she lies beside him and says, "You saved my life."

He isn't so sure. She was near the surface when he reached her, and the next wave would have tossed her again in the direction of shore. He tells her as much, and the words come out just as he wishes for them to. Maybe it is the body's relief after sex or it is his enormous fatigue, but his mind cannot race. He lies still and lets the sensation flood through him, the sensation of clarity. This is it, he tells himself, this is the way he was, his former self at long last. Exhaustion permits him to settle into it, exhaustion slows his thoughts, weights him with sanity, which if he does not move, does not let himself be distracted by the naked woman, he can hold onto, and this leads his sensible mind to understand that sanity, too, is a prison.

Lolly doesn't accept his argument. "You saved me," she insists. "I would have drowned. I'd be dead. Can you imagine?"

She has been imagining, he understands, and it has turned her on, being naked and alive and almost dead on a warm beach and a perfect day in a foreign country with a handsome and damaged young man. Sex is called for to complete the picture, and he is merely that completion, the handy, penis-endowed hero, and he feels suddenly that he understands her well, too well, as if she is a window and so easy to look through that he can barely concentrate on her actual self, her naked self, leaning over him now, with the frizzing hair and maybe beautiful but maybe ferretlike face, and his tenuous hold on his former way of being slips away.

He is sunburned and he doesn't like her hand on his thigh. Where are Maura and the others? He will have to watch the waves and determine which way it was that they drifted, and almost immediately upon gazing at the water, he spots Lolly's bikini top, stranded on the beach by the fleeing tide. He rescues it and hands it to her, then retrieves his trunks. He runs out to rinse off the sand. When he returns, she is dressed in her tiny clothes, some gray marks on her abdomen, like ghostly fingers, and he has a moment to think that maybe she had an abortion, and then he points in the direction from which, he is pretty sure, they came.

Before Lolly and Mick return and Lolly's story of nearly drowning dominates the conversation, Violet lies on a towel talking to Patricia Barnstone. She has brought a guitar, which Violet quite passionately hopes she will not play. While the others amuse themselves in the water, they exchange histories, the basic premises of their lives, and then they revisit them to include the crucial details.

"I like my life," Barnstone says. "I've been alone a lot of it, but that's permitted me to do things I never would've done otherwise. I don't claim it's any better than the traditional route, but it's all mine."

"My husband, at the end, could not speak," Violet says, "could not turn his head. You're going to think I'm awful, but at the end, I wanted . . ." She doesn't finish.

"I don't think you're awful," Barnstone says.

"I had a dream about Arthur." Violet was once again on the porch of the Congregation of Holy Waters Museum, perched on the swing at twilight, when something brushed against her leg and simultaneously she smelled his breath, the particular odor of Arthur's breath, not a pleasant smell but so specifically him. And there he was, slouched behind the swing, his hands in the pockets of his worn corduroys. This image of him was so real that her sleeping self believed in him, understood that the illness and death had not been permanent after all. She smiled at the folly of the misunderstanding—of course Arthur was alive—and made room for him on the swing. He nuzzled her neck, which chafed her skin. He needed a shave. When he spoke, the voice was precisely Arthur's. He told her how much he liked American television. Violet didn't respond to the comment, saying instead, "Are you happy with me?" She understood what she was asking of him—she wanted him to say that she had treated him well while he was dying, that she was sufficient to the chore of giving him up. "The comedies specially," he replied, "that comedienne who pretends she's happy all the time—what a talent!" Violet doesn't describe the dream in any detail, only how real it seemed and how her dead husband would only speak of television. "He hardly ever watched television," Violet tells Barnstone.

The sound of the ocean covers their silence, and they douse themselves anew in coconut-smelling lotion. Violet had looked for Barnstone when she visited Jimmy's office. That was three days past, the same day that her brother moved out of the house in the Corners. She has not seen him since the office visit, and they haven't spoken. There was no mistaking the painting. Her big brother stared out at her, his body merely an outline, those scraps of paper behind him, as they had hung in his room—except in the painting they had days of the week scrawled on them, abbreviated and misspelled. Why would he add the days of the week? She wondered but she could not guess. For Pook, as far as she had ever been able to tell, every day was the same as the next. There is no way to explain any of this to Patricia Barnstone. Violet doesn't even understand it herself. She closes her eyes and listens to the waves.

After a lengthy silence, Barnstone says, "What do you think of your brother withdrawing?"

Her eyes open. "What do you mean?"

"Taking his name out of the hat. He had the job sewn up. That's what it looked like to the rest of us."

"To become director?" Violet asks. "He withdrew?"

"I'm sorry. I'm speaking out of turn."

"I can't believe it." She sits up abruptly. "My god." When Jimmy left the house, he told Lolly and Violet to stay. He needed to do some thinking, he explained. Lolly—and Violet, too—assumed that he was getting cold feet. Violet can't say that she has missed him, exactly. The house is so much quieter without him, and Lolly is almost bearable if there is no man around.

Barnstone's revelation provides a new slant on her brother's departure. Perhaps he is ashamed. Violet knows enough about his finances to understand that he cannot continue his manner of living without the promotion. He may be humiliated, as well he should be. It's a national disease, living beyond one's means.

"He hasn't been to work the past few days," Barnstone says. "I assumed you knew."

Violet says, "He hasn't told Lolly."

"Maybe he wanted to wait until after this outing," Barnstone says. "Spare her or something like that. I shouldn't have said anything."

"Arthur tried to keep his illness from me. I suppose he did for a while. I'd give anything to go back to then, back to not knowing."

"He leave you a pretty bundle?"

"Some. Enough. It's not the same as a life," Violet says. "The truth is, I don't know what to do with myself."

"What do you like?"

"I'm not sure. I don't like people." She is so surprised by the statement that she has to pause. "I don't mean that. I just mean I don't like— don't want a job dealing with people."

"Your brother's got a bunch of tests you could take," Barnstone says. "They examine your personal preferences, your talents, let you know what you might enjoy doing. I could get photocopies for you. Not supposed to, but that's just not the sort of rule I respect."

"That might be a smart thing to do."

"You want to hear a song?" She grabs the guitar by the neck.

"No," Violet says. "I'd rather not."

"You're a frank one."

"I don't like rock music. It made me something of an outcast when I was young—and now, too, for that matter."

Barnstone laughs. "It's childish, I guess, but it has a lot of vitality. Maybe that's why you don't like it."

"I'm sorry if I offended you."

"I'm not offended."

"You seem to think Jimmy despises you. He doesn't despise you."

"Oh? He's fond of *the Barnstone?* I'm not saying your brother is a bad man, but I'm a woman approaching sixty, not in the least attractive or useful to him. I don't mother him, and I don't kowtow. He just doesn't see the point of me."

"That's severe, don't you think?"

"Maybe. But he's a young man, driven by all the things that make young men go—young women, for starters, and their own sense of themselves. Mercy, I grew up in rock and roll. Give a young man an audience, and he'll tell you every thought that ever entered his head. Give him a typewriter, and he'll crank out several hundred pages. He'll provide you every thought that's dawdled in his head, and revise everything he ever did wrong. And here's the most confusing part of it all—I love the company of young men. That kid Mick is a doll, Bellamy Rhine at his core is a sweet boy, and Billy Atlas, a wonderful kid."

"Billy's hardly a kid. He's thirty-three, same as Jimmy. They went to school together. Friends since elementary school."

"That surprises me."

"It surprises me and I've known them both forever. It's a piece of my brother's life that makes no sense to me."

"My, you're a hard case."

"You're one to talk."

Barnstone laughs again. "Can't argue with that."

It's good that Jimmy has stepped away from the directorship, Violet decides. Otherwise he'd eventually have to fire someone like Barnstone, who considers making trouble a matter of honor. And, of course, there's Billy, who will certainly have to be dismissed one day soon. Before going out into the water, he revealed that a newly designed spider box arrived at the sheltered workshop, and the packets of hose did not fit in them. Instead of calling the factory for direction, he had the crew cram the packets into the boxes. Billy told the story as if it were funny. "Had to cover the losses coming and going," he said. "I guess I didn't *have* to, but I figured I oughta." He paid the factory for the ruined product and reimbursed his crew for their lost wages. He found it all terribly funny. He and Karly are out there now, together, waist deep in the water. God knows what their relationship is, but it can't be appropriate. Someone will have to terminate him, and thank god it isn't going to be Jimmy.

Alonso makes a happy bellow. Vex is in the waves now, too, in his pants and shirt, up to his belt with Billy Atlas—Karly on one side of Billy and Vex on the other. Both have their arms over Billy's shoulders.

"Jimmy's not going to marry her," Violet says, as if Lolly is among the splashing group. She takes a moment to look for Lolly and Mick out in the deep water, which makes her picture Lolly's bathing suit. The ridiculous string bikini didn't surprise Violet, but she was astonished at the faded tattoo on Lolly's abdomen—a Medusa with snakes for hair and aimed downward, pointing (or gaping) at Lolly's privates. The tattoo doesn't fit with Violet's conception of Lolly, but her attitude about the woman has too much momentum to be easily altered. "I can see this breakup coming like trains approaching on the same track."

"If you ask me," Barnstone replies, "she shouldn't marry *him*."

"What is it with you and Jimmy?"

"He's reckless. He plows ahead without worrying about the people in his wake. I'm not talking about me, necessarily."

"Then why this animosity toward him?"

"He's such a poster boy for the other side, an opportunist. And the way he's going about it, there'll be bodies on the side of the road."

"But if he has withdrawn from the job . . ."

Barnstone sighs. "That changes things, sure. I suppose. Unless it's a ploy."

Violet doesn't like these accusations against her brother, but she can't pretend she hasn't had similar thoughts. "He asked Lolly to marry him after they'd spent two weeks together," she says, "so I suppose I can guess what you mean."

"And if you're right, now he's going to toss her aside."

"Did you notice that tattoo she has? What does it look like to you?"

"Like a poor erasure."

"But what was it originally?"

"A spider, obviously."

"It's not obviously anything."

"A black widow with the red hourglass and everything. Your Jimmy boy can tell you after they're married."

"You think he'll go through with it?"

"Why are you so obsessed with your brother's wedding plans?"

"I introduced them—not in any romantic way, just . . . I thought the tattoo was a mythological creature."

"I have a tattoo on my ass," Barnstone admits. "Got it back in the days when only bikers and hard rockers had them."

"What is it?"

"A lawn chair."

Violet bursts out laughing.

"I had a band called the Lawn Chairs. I was dead certain we were going to be superstars." She reaches again for the guitar. "Don't scream. I'll keep it short. It's one of my old songs."

"I don't like rock and roll."

"I know. You'll hate this." She plays a few very low chords and then begins strumming fiercely. The lyrics are about the war, the ma-chine, the *man*, and pollution. Her voice is an expressive, deep-throated grumble. The song ends before it becomes completely unbearable.

"Well," says Violet.

"I was a headbanger for a long while. And good at it. Good at a crappy thing, but still good, you know?"

"Yes," Violet says, "that was splendidly awful."

"Thank you. Any crappy things you're good at?"

"I cared for my husband while he was dying. That's a pretty crappy thing, but I don't know that I was all that good at it."

"I bet you were just fine."

"There were a few times near the end . . . this particular day that we were in the van, going to get him a new chair—a new electric wheelchair, quite the apparatus. The old one kept breaking down and we were in a van with a lift in the back." *I still think he's handsome,* Lolly had said one day near the end. The memory strikes her so suddenly that Violet cannot continue speaking. She and Lolly were searching a medical supply store for a head immobilizer that would not restrict Arthur's vision, and Lolly said, *I still think he's handsome.* Violet turned on her fiercely. *No, god, stop it!* The muscles in Arthur's face could not keep the corners of his mouth from drooping. His eyes had retreated into the sockets like a lizard's. *Don't patronize me. I'll leave you here, god-damn you.*

"Go ahead," Barnstone said, "you were in the van, going to get a new chair."

"Sorry," Violet said. "There was this Irish nurse, a man named Denny." Arthur's favorite nurse because he brought him beer and poured it down his belly tube. He would hold Arthur on the bed so that he could make love to Violet. "Denny was driving the van, which left me to watch Arthur, riding with him in the back. At some point his breathing tube rattled loose, and I didn't notice. Arthur turned his eyes up to me and moved his eyebrows. His head was strapped to a brace. By that time, he could not speak or lift a hand. And he was suffocating while I held his hand, that awful flaccid hand." No, she realizes, there had been no strap on his head. Lolly had found a head immobilizer. She had gone out on her own and purchased it for him.

"Violet?" Barnstone says.

"Honestly, I don't know how anyone put up with me while that was going on."

"Tell me the rest of the story."

"I sort of screamed when I realized the tube was loose. I cried out and I was on my knees trying to get it back in. Denny pulled over, and while I was fumbling, he came charging into the back and got it in place, got him breathing again. Arthur never quite lost consciousness, but I almost killed him." She takes a moment to control her own breathing. "Denny reconnected him to his laptop. A wire attached to his eyebrow—he could still move his brows. He typed a message." It was so arduous to type anything, but he wrote to her. "Four words: *like going to moon.*"

"I don't understand."

"It was thrilling. That's what he was telling me. To almost die." For a moment, she can see that face sinking in on itself, the mischie-vous eyes, those articulate brows. She had not wanted him to die. She so desperately had not wanted him to die. No matter how ruined his body, she had not wanted to lose him. Why is it so impossibly difficult to admit this to herself? Whatever scrap of him remained, she had not wanted to lose.

Barnstone offers her a spare towel. "You miss him."

"I used to. All the time, I used to." She misses him, she under-

408

stands, with all her heart. She cannot engage other people for missing him. She cannot stand being with people who are not him. She opens her mouth to say the next thing, but Lolly and Mick are approaching the tent, weaving in the sand, and Lolly tells them over and over how Mick rescued her.

Your type is always being rescued, Violet thinks to say but keeps to herself. *Let's not pretend it's news.*

While the others listen to Lolly's tale, she finds herself thinking about Tucson—not, at long last, about either of her brothers or her parents or her late husband, but about the desert. Perhaps what she missed about the U.S. has more to do with landscape than with family or personal history. She couldn't see that until now. Her grief and other people's business have camouflaged her desires. What is that word? There's a specific word for when it storms in the desert and the dry arroyos will temporarily reclaim their purpose, rushing to fill the scorched banks, emptying into a desert basin. A *bolson.* The temporary lake is called a bolson, and it may hold a slice of rainwater a mile wide but only an inch deep, a watery mask that will vanish the first hot day.

"I thought I'd pegged out," Lolly is saying.

Violet supposes that *pegged out* means *passed out* or *drowned* or *died*— some idiotic Briticism the woman has appropriated. For a moment, she can see the computer screen of Arthur's computer: *You re tooo hardon her.* Perhaps what he meant was that she should learn to overlook the woman's (many many many) faults. For better and for worse, Lolly is the person who helped her get through Arthur's demise.

Violet closes her eyes and what she sees is the painting in Jimmy's office, Pook's painting, and as she drifts toward sleep she understands that it is not a self-portrait but a painting of Jimmy, Pook's vision of his brother. She cannot explain this insight but she believes it. There's something about the way the figure stands, and the way the mouth . . . how the slightest bit of sly pleasure . . . and something more: Jimmy is Pook plus the intervention of time, time visible within him, those days of the week encapsulated by his transparent body. Perhaps that is what was wrong with Pook, that he could not embrace time. Can that be a disability?

Violet keeps her eyes shut. She wishes to look at each of his paintings again, study them and identify the figures. She has to tell Jimmy. Perhaps later, they will tell their parents. Pook was painting the family

409

all along. These thoughts come to her without remorse or pain but with a sense of relief that is remarkably similar to happiness. She is over her brother's death, she realizes, which leads her to understand the next thing: one day she will be over Arthur's death. This thought is hard to take, as she thought she was already over it.

Violet takes a long breath and opens her eyes. Lolly has planted herself on the towel where Barnstone had lain. Violet puts her arm around Lolly's sun-warmed shoulders. "I'm glad you're safe," she says. And later that afternoon, when the two are again lying together, having moved out of the sun and into the tent, the animosity Violet feels for Lolly finally evaporates. She feels a connection with Lolly she cannot name. (Let us name it for her: they are women unfairly abandoned by men who made promises.) Speaking softly, almost a whisper, Violet says, "You should come to Tucson with me."

Without a moment's hesitation, Lolly says, "All right." After a few seconds, she adds, "James can find me there as easily as anywhere."

Violet lets that go. "That tattoo on your abdomen," she says. "What is it?"

Lolly replies, "It's the shadow of my former self."

The power of the ocean to soothe and restore is not simply myth. Billy Atlas feels alive and brave and happy. He glops sunscreen over his sunburned shoulders as he walks along the beach. "You ought to put some of this on," he says.

Vex shakes his head. "They make it out of what? Chemicals they find in glass and hard metals, that's what. How else to give the sun the bounce?"

"You're turning into a fire truck," Billy says.

"I've always been a fire truck," Vex replies.

They walk along the edge of the water. The others are eating, but Billy's exercise regimen requires him to hike and not to overeat. Also, he had three burritos on the drive down. He holds a cold beer in one hand, with four more linked together by their plastic collars in the other. He and Vex will get in some exercise while Karly and the others eat and nap and sculpt things in the sand. Karly has a talent for sculpting. She is especially good with mashed potatoes. She has a lot of surprising talents, like how she remembers everybody's name, how she knew the way back to Onyx Springs when they took a drive in the mountains, how even in getting lost or having a flat tire there is something funny. She has taught Billy a morning routine that he finds especially useful. They stand together outside, their toes aligned on the edge of the concrete stoop, and check themselves out—shoes, socks, pants, the works. Twice, Billy realized that he forgot his belt and once Karly made him change his shoes. He'd put on his red-and-gray sneakers with white tube socks, and Karly said, "You can't wear those, Billy. That's silly."

Billy stared. "What's wrong with them?"

"They're really really really ugly," Karly said seriously. "They're fuzzy."

Billy pursed his lips and nodded. "This is exactly the kind of advice I need on a daily basis." He kissed her then, and they both went inside to fit themselves up with what they lacked.

Sex is still not a big part of the marital picture, but they have broken the ice on two occasions. Once in bed, with only partial success, and once in the shower, a rousing victory. In bed, Karly made a few comments that inadvertently led to complications. "Don't you have to get big first?" she asked, right as Billy was about to enter her, and later, at another crucial moment, she said, "Is it in?"

"The first time is always practice," he said afterward, and she laughed, saying, "Everybody knows that."

The shower was a different story. Billy was in there to wash the stink off after work, and she joined him. They soaped each other, and there was a moment while she worked up the suds in his hair with one hand that she freed the other hand to grasp the shampoo by taking the washcloth she was holding between her teeth, the cloth hanging from her mouth, lengthening as it saturated. *Jesus, that washcloth.* They made love standing up and laughing. And afterward, still in the shower, arms around her, Billy found himself crying. A day to be remembered forever: Billy Atlas crying with gratitude or from sheer happiness.

"The problem with beer in cans," Vex says, staring at his Budweiser, "is the motherfucking cans. You can't wait to crush the bastards."

"Anyone ever suggest that you've got anger issues?"

"Almost everybody. 'Cept the ones too chicken-bait to talk."

"And? What do you think?"

"I think I kicked their fucking asses."

"You haven't kicked everyone's butt."

"I can't fuck up everybody that deserves it," he says defensively. "I'm only one person."

It is obvious to Billy that Vex should not be in the sheltered workshop or, for that matter, in the same zip code as the workshop. Vex has slipped through the famous cracks, and Billy suspects that either Bob Whitman's counseling report or the evaluation Jimmy did should have eliminated the nutball. But neither Bob's report nor Jimmy's evaluation has been handed over, and Billy is pretty sure they'll never arrive. Bob seems to have an endless number of tools and small appliances that need repair. And Jimmy? Billy understands what the rest of them refuse to see: Jimmy Candler is gone.

Vex drops his can in the sand and stomps on it. Billy gives his own a shake: half a beer to go. Vex leaps with both feet to drive the smashed can into the sand. He has on socks but not shoes, and the toe ends flop as he pounds the can. He picks up the flattened aluminum and slips it into the back pocket of his soaked jeans.

Billy hands him another beer. "You don't get violent when you drink, do you? Just curious."

"Not that you would notice."

"'Cause if you get violent," Billy says, "somebody will get hurt, and I like all these people. Including me."

"It'd be better if there was one person, just one person, it was okay to hurt."

"I guess that's true. I don't know, though. Who'd volunteer for such work?"

"Doesn't seem like too much to ask. There's a fuckload of people in the world."

"Life's hard," Billy agrees, "but also surprising."

"How can you know if you've got surprises coming?"

"You can't," Billy says, "but I guarantee you do."

"You're fucking with my head."

Earlier, standing beside Rhine's tent, watching Lolly and Violet sleep within it while the others gathered around the castle or person or possibly bear that Karly was sculpting, Billy tried to tell Barnstone that Jimmy wasn't coming back. She turned to engage him, but across a stretch of sand Andujar was opening the van door and climbing in. "I have to lower some windows," she told Billy, and then there was no one to tell. Jimmy is not coming back to the Center, not coming back to Lolly, not going back to Lise, and not likely returning to his house. Billy guesses that he's in a hotel somewhere, trying to make up his mind what to do. He hopes it isn't a high-rise hotel, though he doesn't think Jimmy will jump out a window like his brother. He isn't the right sort of person to kill himself.

What sort of person is he then? If anyone should know, it's Billy.

Vex is talking now about Bob Whitman's rototiller, which has 392 pieces, if you count every screw and washer. Billy realizes that he'll need to find new things for Vex to take apart after Whitman retires. Otherwise, the guy is liable to throttle somebody. While Billy considers what all he might offer—Karly's dishwasher, the lousy air conditioner on Karly's roof, the Dart—it occurs to him that Jimmy is out there somewhere doing the same thing: taking his life apart in order to put it back together. If Pook were alive, Billy reasons, he would live with Jimmy, and Jimmy wouldn't be a counselor but whatever he's genuinely cut out to be. Maybe he would have written comic books—or some kind of books—that Pook would have illustrated. Who but Billy knows this? Billy doesn't have a PhD or even a skill, besides pizza cook, but about this subject he is the supreme expert. No one knows as much about Jimmy Candler as Billy, including, most obviously, Jimmy himself.

"See that?" Vex points at the ocean. "I'm slowing that wave down just with my mind."

It does look slower than the other waves. "You think that bonk on the head gave you superpowers?"

"Anybody can do it, but I'm the only one makes the effort."

"I used to think if I went to pee during a key moment in a baseball game I was watching on TV that my team would suffer."

"That's fucking stupid," Vex says. "Mind waves can't go through television. You can't digitize mind waves. That's dumb as fuck."

"I'm feeling nostalgic," Billy admits. "Happy and nostalgic at the same time."

"Must be getting your dick wet every night. It depletes the chemicals in your brain to come so much. What you think is happiness is just holes in the gray matter. Why you think stupid fucks are so happy all the time?"

"You must be an effing genius then."

"If I knew how to want the right things," Vex says, "I'd want them.

Anyone would. But even if you *know* the right things, which nobody does, it doesn't mean you fucking want them, even if you *want* to want them."

"That sounds like a pop song," Billy says. *"I want to want you, baby."*

Vex stoops to pick up a chipped white shell. "You ever thought how clouds look like garbage?" He tosses the shell like a Frisbee.

"You've asked me that a million times. I can't see it. It makes no sense to me whatsoever."

"Garbage without all the fucking friction. So it floats. *Friction* ought to be a four-letter word."

"Why don't you say *friction* instead of *fuck* or *shit* or *motherfucking?* People would immediately like you more."

Vex finishes his beer, drops the can into the sand, and stomps on it, leaps on it. He picks up the flattened can and sticks it in his back pocket. "Just like that? People will like me?"

"No, not really, but you could still try it."

"Shut the friction up," he says. "Friction your mother. I've got crazy bullfriction in my head." Tears appear in his eyes. "It's okay, I guess."

A cloud moves in front of the sun, and both men lift their heads to admire it. The evening of the shower sex, Billy and Karly ate hamburgers and watched a dumb movie on television that made both of them laugh. When they went to bed, he did not want to sleep. He wanted to hold tight to his happiness. Not many days would be like this one, he thought, and he did not want to let it slip away just yet. At the same time, he understood that happiness was only one thing that this marriage would permit him to claim, and the other things might be complicated and difficult and contradictory. But happiness was what he could claim that evening, and he gripped the sheet in his fists as if to hold on to it. Today, strolling along the beach, he feels the same. Who knew such pleasure was available to a person? The cloud moves off the sun, and the men resume walking.

"It's like this," Vex says, "I take things apart and I put them back together."

"That's the late-breaking news?" Billy laughs. "I'd sorta noticed that already. The question is, why do you do it? What does it teach you?"

"Everything 'cept the magic," Vex says. "What, you know, puts spark into the world."

Billy considers this for several steps. "That's still a lot to know. If you know all that, then you must have some guess about the spark."

Vex shakes his head. "It's like a deaf motherfucker inventing drums."

"You should join me on my exercise program."

"The last thing I need to lose is fucking weight."

"Friction weight."

"Sorry."

"It'll give you something to do besides take stuff apart."

Vex sighs. "I'm not going to hurt anyone today. Quit worrying. I haven't hurt anyone for a long time. Like weeks."

Billy pats him on the back. They're just the same, he and Vex. Not that Billy is the slightest bit violent and his own head doesn't have a crazy fireball bouncing around in it, but there's something between them that's the same. He likes knowing that. He finishes his beer and drops the can on the beach at Vex's feet.

He says, "Be my guest."

If Mick Coury dies in the Onyx Springs hospital, Candler is in a hotel room, on the twelfth floor, standing on a balcony that overlooks the ocean. If Mick Coury pisses on the pills instead of swallowing them, Candler is in the Laguna Mountains, at Bob Whitman's cabin, on the screened porch, one hand raised to a roof beam. He's drinking from the same bottle of scotch either way. The rail around the balcony is wrought iron and reaches midthigh. A sliding glass door is open to its full length, letting the wind off the water sweep past him and into the room. It is a wet, warm wind. Conifers tower over the cabin, and a chipmunk scrambles under the porch. The sound of what might be a mountain stream infiltrates his ears. The sun is sinking. Candler stares at the ocean and smells the pines.

Bob Whitman's Jeep ascends the gravel drive. It is still light, but Bob has his headlights on. The Jeep turns in the narrow lane and makes a precise maneuver to back around Candler's rental car and up to the porch. Lashed to the bumper is a rectangular gray container. Candler sets down his coffee cup of scotch. He has spent three nights on the mountain, and it's Saturday afternoon. The cabin has electricity and running water, but no phone, internet, or television. His cell phone gets no reception. There is an old radio, and he has listened to the Padres bungle leads, drop fly balls, get thrown out at home. Down a slender path from the porch, in a narrow depression, lies a miniature lake, a blue lozenge surrounded by trees. Candler thought he might fish, but he hasn't touched the pole or tackle box. Each day, he has taken a book to the lakeside, settled in the shade, and read, books that he found in Bob Whitman's cabin, war novels, detective stories, and now a science fiction epic called *Ramshackle*, about the conceivable future, survival after the world has fallen apart and then fallen down, a lively, messy book, full of characters. And he has reread the note that Lise tacked to her front door. He uses it to mark his place, reads it each day before opening the book. He remembers the girl in L.A. to whom the note refers, the bleached blonde, the stripper, the novice prostitute, but he cannot make her into Lise. The transformation seems to him more than cosmetic, as if the molecules of her body were altered.

Deer have approached the cabin to nibble the grass; fish have made circles on the lake's surface, flipping their silver bodies joyously into the air; a hawk has coasted serenely overhead; and the chipmunks that live under the porch have skittered and scrambled about aimlessly; but Bob Whitman is the first human Candler has seen in three days.

"How's it going?" Bob asks. Candler helps him unload the container—a trash barrel with snap locks for the lid. The barrel has to go back and forth each time anyone visits the cabin. "Otherwise you get bears," Bob explains. He tells a story Candler has heard before about arriving to find a big black bear stretched out on the porch, a battered trash barrel spilled across the plank floor. "Scared him off with the car horn," Bob says, "or I don't know what I'd've done."

Traffic in the street below sounds almost composed, like the impossible piano music of Joseph Andujar Freeman, like the impossible portraits of Candler's big brother, like all the impossible things that haunt the living. Candler has cut himself off from everyone he loves, but he is not about to jump. He has no intention of jumping. And yet he cannot help but imagine Pook standing on a similar balcony, and he understands that his brother did not jump. *Jump* is the wrong word. He would have thrown one leg over and then the other, seated himself on the rail, perhaps for a long time, resting there, *noticing*, and then he would have let himself slide off; perhaps he would have taken one step. But he did not jump. This is not something Candler can know definitively, and yet he does.

A pelican skims the surface of the ocean, the sun sinking behind it. The dying light is the purple of a dead boy's exhausted flesh, and the skimming bird, in that crazy light, seeks fish foolish enough to swim near the surface. A shout comes from the street or beach, exultant or angry, male or female, from this distance it is impossible to tell. This is his third night in the hotel. Except to step onto the balcony, he has not set foot outside his room. He is getting to know the staff. He has read and reread the note that Lise left him, but he has not listened to the messages on his phone. Most seem to be from John Egri, but not all of them. He does not want to listen to them, but he wonders who sent them. Clay Hao has called, as has Kat McIntyre, but they may have called and hung up. If the call goes to voicemail, is that a missed call or a received call? He resolves the mystery by erasing all the messages and turning the phone off. On the day he arrived, he read one email before packing away his laptop. Genevieve Coury emailed to say the service would be private and she knows he will understand.

"I just got the window unit repaired," Bob Whitman tells him, opening the Jeep's rear hatch. "This time of year, you need the a.c. during the day and a sweater at night." He and Candler carry the unit to the back of the cabin. Candler has not walked to this side of the cabin, and he is surprised by a wide, green yard with a reclining chair. The grass is mildly overgrown. There's likely a mower here somewhere, he thinks. They remove the screen and set the unit in place. Wings on either side of the device close the gaps.

"I appreciate this," Candler says, meaning the cabin, the a.c., the trash barrel, Bob's trek up the mountain.

Bob sidles up to him and pats him gently on the back. "Solitude," Bob says. "Sometimes it's the only cure for what ails us."

What does ail him? He has withdrawn from the promotion. He has moved out of his house and away from his fiancée. He has sold his car. He has inadvertently helped his best friend bed a client. He has run Lise out of California. He messed up the conversation between Mick and Karly, causing Mick to have a breakdown. But Mick seems to be better. It is Mick, after all, leading the others to the ocean. They should be there by now. They may even be on their way home.

"I brought you a few supplies," Bob says, retracing his steps around the house and to the Jeep. He lifts a cooler from the rear seat and hauls it to the porch—a metal cooler with dents in the side. "If you decide to fish," Bob tells him, "you can set this right in the lake. Stay cold forever." Inside the dinged metal box: sandwich meat, a loaf of bread, shards of lettuce, cherry tomatoes, cheddar cheese, Dijon mustard, dill pickles, hamburger patties, several bottles of beer. "And the kitchen cupboard ought to be full of canned goods," Bob continues, gesturing to the door. "Soup and corn and whatall. I hope you've helped yourself to whatever you need." He unfolds chairs from a slanting rack against the wall. "Sit down and have a beer with me," he says, "and then I'll leave you to your business."

Candler leans back in the folding chair, rocks back until the front legs rise from the porch. He takes in a deep breath of the fresh mountain air. He has not seen a bear up here, but a bear has watched him. It watches him now, from the forest, standing on all fours. What the bear sees through the porch screen are the blurred forms of two humans. The screen makes them mysterious. Their voices remind him of moving water.

Candler is not exactly pleased to have Bob Whitman dawdle on the porch, but what does it matter? So what if he is forced to spend time with someone who is not at all important to him—a minor player in his life? The man has done him a favor. Several favors. The small-time players in our lives often wind up mattering more than any one of us can possibly predict.

Someone is at the door. Tapping professionally at the door. Room service. Candler hasn't eaten. Pook's painting is propped against the minibar, and Candler has to step around it, Candler's brother's limpid body *(mon, two, wen, thrus, fry)*. The painting stares out at the ocean, at the pelican, at the purple light. Candler opens the door on a man in a red jacket, white shirt, black pants. He holds a silver tray on one shoulder. A new face, the weekend crew. *Welcome to my humble abode,* Candler thinks. He says, "You can put it on the bed."

"Motherfucker," the man replies and follows Candler in. He sets the tray on the bed.

Candler is not deaf. He has heard the man but thinks he must have misunderstood. He reconciles the line by recalling that he has been drinking. More than he realized, evidently, as now he's hearing things. "The tip is added in," he says, "right?" He knows the tip is included. He has eaten nothing but room service since arriving.

"What the hell are you doing here?" the man asks.

Candler examines him then. His bland, pale, bumpy face is like a sack filled with miniature doughnuts. It's Les Crews. Candler blinks and refocuses to be certain: Les Crews who once ran the sheltered workshop.

"I'll be damned," Candler says. "I wondered what became of you."

"Bob Whitman fired me," he says. "I got this job a few days after. Sorry 'bout messing up. I owed you for that job, and I let you down."

"You don't have to explain anything to me," Bob Whitman says, snapping open a bottle and passing it to Candler. It's a big bottle. Bob is in no hurry to depart. "This is the only beer I drink these days," he goes on, levering another bottle cap, which bounces against the plank floor of the porch. The bottle opener is part of his key ring, and he deposits it in his pants pocket. His pants have enormous pockets outlined with discontinuous yellow thread. In the sci-fi novel Candler is reading, keys play a big part, and key rings are talismanic objects. Everything electronic has been replaced with mechanical parts. Even spaceships have no computers and must be run by the manipulation of levers and pulleys and cranks that swirl around the pilots, requiring a constant dance to stay afloat. Everything has changed since the collapse.

"You bring a sweater?" Bob asks. "Coat? Has it been brisk at night?" He points with the beer bottle to a stack of wood and what looks to be a new red ax at the far end of the porch. "Build a fire if you want. You won't really need it, but a fire can be comforting."

"Don't worry about me," Candler says. "I'm fine." The beer complicates his mouth, a cold stew of flavors. He swallows and examines the bottle.

"It's a double IPA made up in Sonoma." Bob savors a sip and shakes his head in appreciation. "Let me just say, I don't blame you for dropping out of the race," he says, imagining this prying so subtle as to defy recognition. "And don't feel you have to talk about it."

"You never owed me," Candler says.

"Like hell I didn't," Crews responds. "It's just that I needed money and took a second job, which was fine till I started cheating on the workshop. I shouldn't've done that. It's just that my girlfriend was pregnant, and I wanted to show her something. You get me? Wanted to put some cash in the bank. Wanted her to move in with me and start thinking that I could be a permanent solution."

It takes this conversation for Candler to recall that he recommended Crews for the job. Before he moved from Onyx Springs to the Corners, Candler played basketball every Sunday morning with a group of guys, and Les Crews was one of them. That Sunday game seems like something out of the distant past, played outside on a concrete court, and Les Crews with a decent set shot—easy to block but effective if he could get it off. He had been looking for a job just as Candler got approval for the sheltered workshop.

"I'm not the most easy guy to be with, I've been told," Crews is saying, "but she liked me some. I liked her. It's just that it takes money to make a family."

"Want a beer?" Candler asks, indicating the bottle on the tray that Crews himself delivered. "Or I've got a bottle of pretty good scotch."

"None of the hard stuff for me," Bob Whitman replies. "I used to enjoy a good whiskey, but I've got too many miles on the old pumper. I stick to beer." He takes another swallow. "You think Clay'll do a good job, then?"

"Why wouldn't he?" Candler asks. "Look, Bob, I don't have a good reason for withdrawing. I can tell you're interested, but I just decided . . . I don't know. It's not what I want to do. I could use the money, and there are plenty of things to like about being in charge, but it's not what I intended to do when I picked this line of work. I was in a PhD program—"

"That weekend program," Bob says.

"It's a legitimate program," Candler says patiently, "a really *good* program, actually. I'll re-enroll. If all goes well, I'll be a psychologist in a few years' time. That's more in line with my plans. I never wanted to be an administrator. I just didn't have the sense to say no to it."

"I understand completely," Bob says. "Leadership takes something out of you. All that stress. The decision making. The weight of the world on your shoulders. The part I wouldn't like is fund-raising. I don't think Clay will care for that part of it, either." He lifts the bottle again but before it touches his lips, he says, "Is John Egri angry with you?"

Candler sighs. "I imagine that he's furious. I haven't returned his calls. Or even listened to them. Fortunately, my cell phone doesn't work up here."

Bob nods. "What about that fiancée of yours? Lovely girl, by the way."

"After I got fired, she picked this guy who installs cable over me," Crews says. "I told her it's a bad job 'cause everything'll be wireless in another hour or two, but how can I talk now? What am I now but some guy in a red jacket running errands a child could do—toting trays and picking up laundry and parking cars. Some people put their shoes out to be polished."

Candler takes a beer from the tray and hands it to him.

"I shouldn't," Crews says, sitting on the bed as he accepts the beer. "I know you've got a house out on Liberty Highway. What's got you holed up here?"

"Something happened," Candler says.

"I guessed that much."

"I got distracted by one thing and another, and a boy who was under my care, he killed himself."

"Wasn't Mick Coury, was it?" Crews drinks from the bottle of beer.

"How'd you know that?"

He swallows and shrugs. "That retarded girl give him the bounce?" Candler nods, and Crews continues. "You shouldn't blame yourself too much. You weren't cutting lawns on the side. Blame me. I should've told you weeks ago that he was gonna be in for a tough fall."

"I worked it out anyway," Candler says, "but I didn't handle the whole business very well, and it cost Mick his life."

"I can't figure it that way." Crews takes another long drink and the bottle is empty. He holds the bottle at eye level and shakes it. "The kid's got some loose wires and something's going to cause a short sooner or later. That Karly is heating up his wires something fierce, and so, okay, he shorts out. It's not her fault and it's definitely not yours. It's the wiring."

"Everything's on hold at the moment," Candler explains.

"She wanted you to take the promotion," Bob Whitman says, "didn't she?"

"She may have, but she'd support whatev . . . Aw hell, Bob, do we have to talk about this?"

"No, of course not," Bob says, "though it might be the best thing for you. Here's what I think, the success of a marriage—or any romantic bond—is two parts mystical and three parts practical. The mystical, that's what everybody thinks about, the magical sense of attraction, sex, and all that locomotion. But the practical—making a living, sharing duties around the house, talking over troubles—that's the heart and soul of a marriage."

"Well," Candler says. "Okay." He upends the beer bottle and takes a long chug. He is desperate now to drive Bob Whitman away. He considers inventing lies about his sex life with Lolly—dark, disturbing episodes that would make Bob worry for his cabin and hurry home to tell his wife. The beer is delicious.

"Not that there's any reason you should listen to me," Bob says, "except that I've been happily married forty-two years. Longer than you've been alive, I daresay."

"I've been unfair to Lolly," Candler says, "and coming up here is another chapter of it, I'm sure. But I had to take bold steps. My life was . . . I don't know. It was . . ."

"Spinning out of control?"

"Another way to look at it," Crews says, "you and me, we've been fucked over lately by various shit. But we're stronger than Mick. We're not about to kill ourselves. We're men and we'll tough it out. We'll maybe break some furniture and move to a different neighborhood and sit in the dark doing nothing for hours and hours until finally we think it's maybe possible to sleep, but we're not going to kill ourselves. You got to be strong—ah, fuck, I'm not *strong*, but you know . . . not *too* weak. *Durable.* Or something like that. And Mick wasn't. I'm sorry he's dead and all, but it's like—"

"My big brother killed himself when I was twelve."

"Ah, Jesus, that makes it hard on you then. Fuck."

"I keep thinking about him."

"But you had to know, going into counseling, that there were going to be fucked-up kids thinking about slashing their arms or hanging themselves like nine thoughts out of ten. Why'd you go in for a job that sooner or later pretty much guarantees to put you in this hotel room, drinking like a fish? Seems to me if my brother kills himself, then I do *anything* other than counseling, you get me?"

Candler drinks his beer.

"Another way to look at it, see, there's all this stuff coming out now about 9/11 and how the whole attack never should have happened, how the government should've been able to stop it," Crews says. "What they never talk about is that during the Clinton years these bastard terrorists were trying the same shit, and he stopped them. Just barely, and luck was involved, from what I've read, but my point is, he gets no recognition. A bomb *doesn't* go off—that doesn't make you a hero."

"I can't see where you're going with this," Candler says.

"You've had a ton of guys under your care who didn't kill themselves, but you give yourself no credit. Eventually some Mick's going to come along and do himself in, and as far as you can see, your record is 0-1, 'cause how do you know how many kids you've saved?"

"You're saying I set myself up for failure?"

"I could say the same shit about myself and this girl, this crazy girl I can't quit thinking about. Why her? Why her when I know it's going to be complicated as all get-out? The world is full of women, so why go for a difficult one? And if I hadn't tried to squeeze in those yards while I was supposed to be at the workshop, my son or daughter would still be in the womb. Instead, I lose my job and she gets an abortion. Feels like a mortal mistake." He tilts the bottle to let the remains dribble on his tongue. "You get me?"

"Don't burn your bridges," Bob says. "That's my advice."

"I'll keep that in mind," Candler replies.

Bob finishes his beer and as he stands, he slips the bottle into the giant pocket, where it bulges obscenely. "Make yourself at home now," he says, as if Candler hasn't already been there for three days. *"Mi casa es su casa.* I may even send up another care package for you."

"No need to do that," Candler says quickly. He thanks Bob continuously on the walk to the Jeep, leaving no opening for further stories or commentary. He veers onto the path that will take him to the lake. He passes within a few feet of the bear, the bear that has been watching him, a black bear, an adult male, a little over three hundred pounds. The bear is curious. Curiosity in bears, as in humans, is not doled out equally. This is an especially curious bear, rising again to his hind legs as the man approaches, ready to adopt a threatening posture, but the man does not see him, does not smell him, does not hear him breathing. How can such a creature survive?

Candler makes the short hike to the lake, the color of the water deepening as light flees the sky. The people who populate his life are passing through him—there's no other way to put this, as he is not thinking about them in words or images, and yet some quality of them inhabits him. It is an uncomfortable feeling, but he has come down to the lake to experience it. Strange sounds skim the water. Candler believes there is something he does not understand, to which he has been blind, of which he has been ignorant, something large and meaningful for which he has no name. The sounds are not coming from the water. Candler pivots as a black bear ambles past him, within arm's length. The bear pauses at the lake to drink, turns to take a final look at Candler, and then trots round the water's edge to some indefinable spot, where it steps into the underbrush and disappears into the trees.

"I keep going over that day I got fired," Crews says. "I keep imagining that I didn't go off, that I just stayed there and did my job." He shakes his head. "I better get back before I fuck *this* job up. You got to sign for this."

Candler writes in a ridiculous tip.

"You don't have to do that," Crews says, "though I can use the dough. Thanks."

"Take care of yourself," Candler says.

"If there's ever anything I can do for you, James, you get hold of me and consider it done."

"Good luck with the girl."

He squints and his head dips, as if he's been slapped. "She's gone. Might as well be dead. I'll never see her again." After a second's pause, he says, "You paint that?"

Candler shakes his head. "My brother."

"The dead one?"

Candler nods.

"It's got a quality to it," Crews says, and then he's out the door.

Candler settles on the bed. His steak is overcooked but otherwise good. He finishes the last of the beer and pours the remainder of the scotch into the tub. The drain is shut, and he has to reach in and lift it. He rinses his fingers and sits again on the bed to scroll through the channels. There is nothing on television he wants to see. He goes to the balcony: the traffic, the sun under the water now but the sky still light, the air cooling. How long does he stand there? Thousands of people cross below—people on foot, people in cars, people on the boardwalk, people barefoot on the sand. Headlights and yellow windows, and on

424

the beach, the flare of a single lighter. Candler is thinking, though it doesn't feel like thinking. He stands at the rail while the world goes dark. Until there's a knock on the door once again, and Candler goes to it.

Lolly stands on the plank porch. She's wearing jeans and a plaid shirt. Her skin is pink from the sun. Behind her is Bob Whitman's Jeep.

"You're sunburned," Candler says.

"I'm supposed to say that I'm your care package. Bob Whitman insisted. He was at the house when Vi and I got back from the beach." She is embarrassed and looks at her feet. The accent is gone. "According to him, you want me up here. If he's not right about that, I'll leave right this second."

Candler feels a number of things, ranging from annoyance and indignation to something pleasant, an easing of pain, a small nodule of relief. In any case, Lolly has done nothing wrong, and he steps aside to let her enter.

"I'm making chili," he tells her.

"I have a bag in the Jeep," she says. "Should I get it?"

"Okay," he says. "If you want."

"Maybe I'll wait," she says. "Maybe I'll see how it goes."

It's Les Crews, of course, at the door again. No one else knows where Candler is. He says, "I got something for you. A present like. Something small. Don't thank me." He hands Candler a tiny shopping bag and says, "I'll leave you alone now."

Crews pulls the door shut on himself before Candler can look inside the bag. He carries it to the bed and dumps the contents onto the mattress. It's a silver key ring. It has the name of the place engraved on it: The Carlton Hotel. Candler sits on the bed to work his keys onto the ring, but what's the point of including his house key? He's never going back to that house. His car is sold and that key is gone. There are just the keys to the Hahn Building and his office, and he decides in this moment that he will not return to the job. He throws the keys into the plastic bin and slips the empty key ring into his pocket.

Pushing the room service tray to one side, he stretches out on the bed. He is still in his clothes, but he crawls beneath the sheet and bedcover. A television in the next room murmurs inconsolably. He has left the sliding door open, and there's the sound of traffic and the ocean.

Wind off the water, a wet and heavy wind, and cold now, sweeps up the side of the Carlton Hotel and chills the room.

How do people who have made terrible mistakes—mistakes that cannot be rectified—continue with their lives?

When he was a boy, in the weeks and months after Pook's suicide, Jimmy Candler made an effort every night to imagine his brother. He imagined him as Same Man, battling against the forces of evil, but also he imagined his brother in the yard, among the cats, with The Dog, with Jimmy and Billy, dipping his head in the cistern, painting, climbing a ladder but refusing to step onto the roof, riding the bicycle without a seat. To stop imagining his brother was to let him go, was to let him die all over again. But eventually there came a night when Jimmy fell asleep as soon as his head hit the pillow. And some time later still, a series of such nights.

Lying in the hotel bed beside the silver tray, Candler tries to conjure his brother. As might be expected—of course, naturally enough, it goes without saying—he pictures instead Mick Coury. This is the evening of the day that Mick was going to guide Lolly and Violet and the others to a secluded beach. Candler imagines who else would be on the trip. He imagines what each would wear. He puts them in vehicles and starts the wheels turning. He takes the Carlton Hotel stationery and the Carlton Hotel pen, and jots down some notes.

Mick Coury is dead and alive and driving on the freeway. In the world Candler creates, everyone is dead and alive and driving on the freeway.

They eat the chili on the porch. She tells him about Mick pulling her out of the ocean, but she does not mention the rest of it. (She will never tell him about the rest of it.) She reveals Violet's plan to move to Tucson. He listens. He brings up the book he's reading. He describes the strange encounter with the bear. They wash the dishes together. She puts herself in his arms. They make love on the double bed. There is no urgency in their lovemaking. They begin their real relationship, which is also imperfect but proves to be enough around which to build their lives. He resumes the PhD program, and she finds a job in the city. The wedding is small. Billy is his best man. Violet is maid of honor. Their firstborn is a boy, healthy and well formed and as loud in his cries as any baby the maternity nursing team has ever heard, to whom they give the name Paul. "What if Bob Whitman hadn't made me drive up the mountain?" Lolly asks from the hospital bed, from her perch in the conceivable future, baby Paul in her arms and her husband beside her, the permanence of this child granting her the permission to ask, to wonder about the alternate paths, the echo trajectories, the shadow lives that trail after all of us at every turn, and lend to the single life we lead the definition that gives it meaning.

In the car, on the way back from the beach, on the long stretch of freeway from San Diego to Onyx Springs, Mick feels that he is coming to—a feeling that often overcomes him when he hasn't taken his medication—and he does not know what has transpired in the past half hour, and he understands that he is not well, that he cannot make his mind quit racing, and that he is driving twenty miles over the speed limit. He lifts his foot from the gas.

"Did you like fucking her?" Maura asks.

Evidently, he told Maura about sex on the beach with Mr. James Candler's fiancée.

"I think I did," he says, while his brain piles on multiple answers about the sand and the twin rises, no curls, like wave curls, of her bottom, and that bathing suit off her, how she looked less naked without it, and her hand on his thigh—that was after—which he didn't like, but he felt a sweetened purity when he had the orgasm, the *o* in orgasm also like a wave, sort of, and—"What?"

"I'm glad you fucked her," Maura says. "I've been hoping to see a bump in your libido."

He nods, keeping his mouth shut. As long as he doesn't rag on like a, like a, like a . . .

"I mean I'd rather you direct your business toward me, of course," she says, turning shy before she can get the sentence out, swiveling from him to the highway. "Not that I've ever done it, but I'm ready to try it out. Whenever you're ready."

He offers that same nod, which she may have seen even though she's not looking at him. He is way up over the speed limit again, and he lets his foot off the accelerator.

"You need cruise control," Maura says. "This car is too old for it, which is kinda pathetic. I'd rather go too fast than too slow, though. Not that I drive worth a fuck."

If he doesn't say anything crazy, doesn't do the rag, then he isn't crazy, no matter how much it goes on in his head. That's what the fucking beach with Lollipop on his lollipop . . . He takes a big breath and checks behind him before pulling into the slow lane. He hates thoughts like that, like *lollipop*, but they're just thoughts, and what is it about Lolly? How on the beach he saw that she had her own inside problems, and everyone knows she's sane and not like him—*schizophrenic*. He makes himself pronounce the word in his head over and over.

"I know that's your diagnosis," Maura says.

So one of his thoughts slipped out.

He keeps nodding. Does nodding make you seem crazy? Lots of people nod yes, nod off, knot off, Knott's Berry Farm. *Cruise control:* that's what his medication is meant to be.

"You too long without meds right now?"

He continues to nod.

"I like you on or off 'em. It's like being hooked up with two different guys. I can cheat on you with him."

He laughs at that and the car changes lanes. Horns sound but nothing bad happens. He remembers the story that Karly told him about Mr. James Candler racing his car and wrecking, or maybe it was another car that wrecked. Karly is not great at telling and his receiving is mediocre at best, and it only matters that Mr. James Candler was racing—Mick takes his foot off the accelerator—and how everybody, it seems, has to live in this tumbledown world, not just him. He isn't alone, and following that thought comes another, sweeping in to join it. He understands that it is his former life that never existed, that is unreal, deluded, that is only a child's imagining. Believing in those days of seamless reality is the real madness. There is no going back, though maybe, if he's lucky, there's slowing down.

"You want to tonight?" Maura says. The question, he can see, makes her nervous. She reaches over and pulls on the steering wheel. "You're wandering," she says and laughs again.

"I'm not ever" *going to be who I was before I got* "schizophrenia. And if you" *want some guy who isn't*—he takes his foot from the accelerator and slows again to the speed limit. "Then . . ."

She doesn't respond, not with words. She knows she's not sexy like Lolly and not beautiful like Karly, and she can only hope to have this boy as long as he remains ill, which means that she is not ethical like

Barnstone, because Maura does not want him to get well. She wants him to belong to her. Without him, she is never going to be complete.

If this were a movie, she thinks, she would have a makeover and be suddenly gorgeous. He would get well and love her anyway. They would ride off in this terrible car into the sunset. But they have seen the sun set over the ocean, haven't they? And her time at the Center—hasn't that been something like a makeover? Not that she is gorgeous. That would take more than a makeover—a *do-over*. And nobody gets that. She unbuckles, leaning farther than necessary to let the wind have her hair. Then she slides over between the Firebird's bucket seats, putting herself in that unsafe, uncomfortable gap to be next to him.

The author wishes to thank
Antonya Nelson & Katie Dublinski
and
Noah Boswell, Rus Bradburd, Seth Cagin, Tony Hoagland,
James Kastely, Kathleen Lee, Todd Lieber, Jeff Lymburner,
David MacLean, Fiona McCrae, Bill Nelson, Julie Nelson, Susan Nelson,
Alexander Parsons, Lillie Robertson, Steven Schwartz, David Schweidel,
Peter Turchi, University of Houston Creative Writing Program,
Connie Voisine, Jade Webber, Stephen Webber, Warren Wilson MFA
Program for Writers, Wilkinson Library,
&
Kim Witherspoon.

The Pessoa fragment is translated by Chris Daniels.

ROBERT BOSWELL has published seven novels, three story collections, and two books of nonfiction. He has had one play produced. His work has earned him two National Endowment for the Arts Fellowships, a Guggenheim Fellowship, the Iowa School of Letters Award for Fiction, a Lila Wallace/Woodrow Wilson Fellowship, the PEN West Award for Fiction, the John Gassner Prize for Playwriting, and the Evil Companions Award. *The Heyday of the Insensitive Bastards* was a finalist for the 2010 PEN USA Award in Fiction. *What Men Call Treasure* was a finalist for the Western Writers of America Nonfiction Spur Award. Both the *Chicago Tribune* and *Publishers Weekly* named *Mystery Ride* as one of the best books of the year. The *Independent* (London) picked *The Geography of Desire* as one of the best books of the year. *Virtual Death* was a finalist for the Philip K. Dick Award and was named by the *Science Fiction Chronicle* as one of the best novels of the year. Boswell has published more than seventy stories and essays. They have appeared in the *New Yorker, Best American Short Stories, O. Henry Prize Stories, Pushcart Prize Stories, Esquire, Colorado Review, Epoch, Ploughshares,* and many other magazines and anthologies. He shares the Cullen Chair in Creative Writing with his wife, Antonya Nelson. They live in Houston, Texas, and Telluride, Colorado.

The text of *Tumbledown* is set in Clifford, first drawn by Japanese type designer Akira Kobayashi in 1994. Book design by Ann Sudmeier. Composition by BookMobile Design and Digital Publisher Services, Minneapolis, Minnesota. Manufactured by Edwards Brothers Malloy on acid-free, 50 percent postconsumer wastepaper.